BRAVING THOSE ANGRY SKIES

BRAVING THOSE ANGRY SKIES

An American Pilot in the Battle of Britain

F. Mackay Trapnell

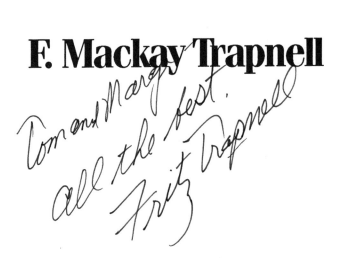

DELFIN PRESS

Los Altos, California

Grateful acknowledgement is made for permission to reprint lyrics from:

The White Cliffs of Dover Words by Nat Burton and Music by Walter Kent ©1941 Shapiro, Bernstein & Co., Inc. and Walter Kent Music. Renewed November 1968. Used by Permission.

Published by: Delfin Press
648 University Avenue
Los Altos, California 94022
USA
1-800-279-5163

ISBN 0-9639242-0-6

Cover design by: John Verducci of Studioem, Sunnyvale, California

Printed and bound in the USA by: Mountain View Printing, Mountain View, California

I'll never forget
The people I met
Braving those angry skies . . .

Introductory lyrics to *The White Cliffs of Dover* written by Americans
Nat Burton and Walter Kent to honor Britain's determination in
those desperate days.

PROLOG

This adventure is set in England from July to October 1940, during the Battle of Britain. It is not a history, and with obvious exceptions, all characters and units are fictitious. But it aims to be historically and technically accurate and to capture the mood of the times in Britain and the Royal Air Force (RAF).

This epic air campaign between the Luftwaffe and the RAF took place a full year before the U.S. entered World War II, while Russia and Germany were still allies. The Nazis, having conquered all of Western Europe, laid plans for the seaborne invasion of England. They calculated that if they could destroy British air power, they could defeat the Royal Navy, invade the island, and overrun the remnants of the British Army.

Had the Luftwaffe won the air battle and the German calculations proved correct, the Nazis would have occupied the British Isles, then taken North Africa and the Middle East without a fight. In a stroke, Germany would have secured its western and southern flanks and deprived the U.S. of a future base for its European operations. In these circumstances, the Germans probably would have defeated the Russians in the autumn of 1941, and the war in Europe would have been over by the end of the year, leaving Nazi Germany the unchallenged master of the continent.

Indeed, following World War II, German Field Marshall Von Rundstedt declared the Battle of Britain to have been *the* decisive battle of the war. Arguably, no other campaign in the twentieth century had such crucial impact on the western world.

And it was a near thing.

The Luftwaffe was larger, and its power and skill had been amply demonstrated in quick victories over other European air forces.

The RAF was largely unproven in battle and ill-trained in gunnery and tactics. More important, they were desperately short of pilots. Anticipating this, they earlier began to recruit volunteers not only from the United Kingdom but also from throughout the English-speaking world. These freshly trained aviators formed the bulk of Fighter Command. Though high in spirit, they were short on experience. And during the battle, there were never enough of them.

Chapter 1

July 1940

RAF Pilot Officer Keith Bayer stood on the parking ramp in front of a massive brick hangar, eyes wide and mouth agape, watching helplessly. A mile away, two Spitfire fighters came toward him, making a normal landing approach. But a third dropped from formation and descended rapidly, its wheels still up and trailing a fine plume of smoke.

Geezus, Bayer thought, that guy's going to crash!

Moments before, he'd watched the three returning planes wheel low over the field in tight formation and gazed in awe at the wicked beauty of their clean, sculpted lines. Their engines' roar had drowned out sound and thought when they rocketed low over the hangar, then it dropped to a soft growl as they departed. Bayer's chest had swelled with pride, and he'd blinked to keep his eyes dry. To fly one of these was why he'd come all the way to England.

Suddenly, he'd spotted the smoke, and his joy evaporated in cold fear.

Now, the crash siren wailed. People flooded out of the hangar onto the ramp, and Bayer found himself standing near a graying man with Squadron Leader's insignia on his uniform. All eyes were on the smoking plane.

Abruptly, its propeller stopped, and it settled toward the ground. The crowd gasped. The last glimpse Bayer had of the machine, it was below the treetops where its camouflage nearly hid it against the foliage. Then it dropped from sight behind a gray stone wall surrounding a farm field. For a moment, all was calm.

Then suddenly, like a angered rhinoceros, the wingless fuselage charged through the wall, hurling stones and debris aside as if it were a bursting bomb. For an instant, the impact lofted the structure into the air. It hit the ground and tumbled, rolling over and over, and came to rest at the edge of the airfield.

The scene had been quiet, like watching a silent movie. Then came the boom of exploding masonry and the screech of rending metal. Bayer winced.

Fire wagons raced across the grass, their bells clanging raucously. Without warning, the wreckage burst into flame, and a sharp groan arose from the crowd.

Bayer closed his eyes and shuddered; he suddenly felt ill.

He turned away, tearing his eyes from the fiery wreckage and forcing his mind to focus elsewhere. Birds wheeled in the air, and a few head of cattle loitered in a field. Across rolling farmland, he easily made out the hills of Kent, miles away beyond the Thames. The river itself was hidden by shrubbery and the gentle undulation of the surrounding countryside, but he knew it was there all right, not four miles away. To the east, the sun was a brilliant silver disc made fuzzy like a new tennis ball by the mists rising from the Estuary. Twenty miles upriver to his right was the hurly-burly of London, but here, everything seemed so natural, so peaceful. What a damned shame to fight a bloody war in a place like this!

He steeled himself and turned slowly back to the scene on the airfield. The other two Spitfires had touched down safely and were taxiing to the ramp where he stood.

Nearby, a car pulled to an abrupt stop, and the driver leaned out the window and shouted to the Squadron Leader. "Sir, I'm going out there to see what's up. Jump in if you want."

"Thanks, but I'll stay here and meet Lieutenant Duke. He'll be upset. Let me know what the score is."

"Right." The car pulled away and sped after the fire wagons.

The Spitfires pulled to a stop and cut their engines. The Squadron Leader moved toward the planes as mechanics, known as erks in the RAF, jumped onto the wings to help the pilots out.

The lead pilot, a big man wearing stripes of a Flight Lieutenant, vaulted from the cockpit. He shoved the erk aside and, leaping heavily to the ground, tore off his helmet and slammed it onto the concrete. His goggles shattered. He braced himself with both hands against the side of the plane and hung his head.

The erk cowered on the wing as the Squadron Leader approached the Lieutenant. From where he stood, Bayer could just hear the conversation.

The older man said, "I'm terribly sorry, Duke."

Duke choked out, "What bloody good does that do for Des?"

"He may still be all right."

"No fucking chance in that inferno. Besides he was already hurt bad. A twenty millimeter entered his cockpit from behind, came past the armor plate, and detonated on the inside of the windscreen. Poor devil was too badly injured to bail out, and he could hardly see. Manston was under attack, so we guided him here."

"You did your best."

Duke spun around, and glared at the Squadron Leader. His ears stood out prominently, and under other circumstances, he might have seemed comical. But there was nothing funny about him just now. His mouth curled savagely beneath his dark mustache, his slab-sided cheeks turned livid, and the muscles worked under them. "Christ, Chaplain, our best isn't good enough. First, I lose Charles and now Des. Two wingmen in a week."

"Peter, you're being too hard on yourself."

Duke's head slumped; he stared vacantly at the ground. "We're bloody losing, Chaplain. We're giving it everything we've got, and Jerry's having a field day with us."

"I'm sure you're giving better than you're getting."

Duke raised his eyes and glared. "There are too damned many of the bastards. They'll clean us out. One by one. Until nobody's left."

"Easy does it, Lieutenant," the Squadron Leader said soothingly. "We're starting to get replacements. I'll get you a new wingman today. He'll be young. Fresh out of OTU. But like all of them, I'm sure he's keen. He's --.

"Keen!" Duke shouted. "How's keen ever going to replace the year and a half Charles flew with Burt and me?" He waved at the Sergeant Pilot who had landed with him. "And how will keen make up for Des's four years as a fighter pilot?"

Suddenly, Bayer decided they might be discussing him. His throat tightened.

The Squadron Leader said, "Take it easy, Lieutenant."

"Easy, hell. I have to train the kid. Wipe snot from his nose. And show him which bloody way is up. I'd rather fight shorthanded."

"Peter, we'll have a lot of young replacements before this war's over. It's the best we can do."

"Well, it's not bloody good enough," Duke shouted. "I don't need some pink-cheeked youngster. Jerry'll just cut him to ribbons. Do we even know if he's flown a Spitfire?"

"I don't. I've not met the man. But I'm due to interview him shortly. I'll send him to you later in the day."

Dread of death still hung heavy on Bayer. Now, however, a new fear assaulted him, one that troubled him nearly as much: He might not make it in this outfit. Dear God, he thought, have I made a mistake coming all this way?

Chapter 2

The officers' mess was nearly empty. Freshly painted white plaster walls and polished concrete floors gave it the pristine feel of a hospital. Bayer walked from his room down the hallway, descended the stairs, and followed the lower hall to an office door, where he knocked.

A voice he recognized said, "Come in." It was the Squadron Leader he'd seen on the ramp. He entered and stood at attention. Behind the desk, the older man rose and peered over his half glasses. Then he glanced at the paper on his desk.

"Bayer? Pilot Officer Keith Robertson Bayer, is that right?"

"Yes, sir."

"Didn't I see you earlier on the ramp during all the excitement?"

"Yes, sir."

The Squadron Leader's eyes narrowed. "Bloody gripping, wasn't it?"

Bayer nodded silently.

"But grim, I'm afraid," the Squadron Leader said. "Anyway, life goes on. At ease, Mister Bayer." They shook hands. "Sit down." The man waved at a chair. "Good to meet you, son. My name's Parsons, Squadron Leader Parsons. I'm the intelligence officer. I also take care of things on the ground here when the skipper's gone."

Bayer nodded. "Glad to meet you, sir." It was a friendly face, Bayer thought, with studious, cheerful eyes.

"Welcome to RAF Hornchurch. Did you settle in all right?"

"Yes, sir. Moved in last night. By the way, I found a few photographs and things in a drawer in my room."

"Drop them off with me when you get a minute. They probably belonged to Truslove."

"He left?"

"Went missing over the channel a week ago."

Bayer suddenly felt cold. "Dead?"

The Squadron Leader nodded.

Bayer thought, I'm sleeping in a dead man's bed! "Seems you've lost a lot of people?"

Parsons eyed him obliquely. "Two or three a week now that Jerry's putting the heat on." Bayer thought it was odd that the British used the *term Jerry* for one German or many or even the whole German nation.

The man continued, "New lads get the worst of it. You want to be careful."

Bayer tried to look unconcerned. "I . . . don't suppose anyone thinks they'll be next?"

Parsons shook his head. Then he picked up a sheaf of papers from his desk and leaned back in his chair. "I read your file. You're from California, eh?"

Bayer nodded.

"That's a long way. We've had the most incredible hot, sunny summer here. A lot like California, I imagine. You must feel right at home."

"I didn't come for the weather, sir."

The older man looked up abruptly. "No. I don't suppose you did." He wondered how in the world the boy was old enough to be an RAF officer. "What brought you, anyway?"

"I came to be a fighter pilot."

"I see. Couldn't do that there?"

"I'd have to finish college first."

"And you didn't think that was a good idea?"

The image of his older brother, Brad, came to Bayer's mind, and resentment tightened his gut. He said, "I was fed up with college. I answered an ad for the RAF, and they accepted me."

"Finishing university might have qualified you better."

"But the war's here, and the RAF wanted me now."

Parsons thought he understood both Bayer's and the RAF's motives, but he wasn't sure that taking them this young was a good idea. The lad was handsome, though. Lean and trim with strong hands, thick black hair, and a firm chin. But did he shave those soft cheeks yet?

"How old are you, Bayer?"

"Twenty, sir."

Parsons eyed the papers skeptically. "You didn't lie about it on your application, did you, son?"

Bayer felt his anger rise, and he struggled to control it. "No."

The older man nodded. "Mind you, I wouldn't blame you. Anyway, twenty is par for the course for new pilots. Many are even younger. And the veterans around here are old farts of twenty-five."

Bayer gazed, puzzled, at the wings on the older man's chest. The Squadron Leader followed his eye, then tapped the emblem. "These came from the last war. I'm too old to fly now. Or so they tell me. And maybe they're right." He paused and examined the papers. "You studied engineering, I see."

"Yes, sir. Two years."

Parsons studied the papers again. "How much flying have you done?"

"Since I was sixteen."

"That's a pretty early start."

"I got interested in planes and worked at the airport to earn lessons and flying time. By the end of high school, I'd more or less decided that flying was the career I wanted. Then I learned about fighter planes. Seemed exciting. I wanted to fly them."

"You sound pretty keen."

Bayer liked this man. About the same age as his father, but how different. Dad had thought his flying a waste of time and a distraction, and that he should stick to his studies - like Brad did. Brad had always got top grades. Anyway, that was behind him now. He grinned at Parsons. "Yes, sir. I came here to fly Spitfires."

"How'd you know about Spitfires?"

"Popular Mechanics magazine. Said it was the best fighter in the world."

"Maybe we should send Jerry a copy. He has a different idea."

"Let's hope they're as screwed up about that as they are about politics."

The older man eyed him skeptically. "How much do you know about their politics?"

"I keep up with the news. My grandparents were from Germany. And I visited there a couple of years ago."

"What was that like?"

"Spooky. Kids my age running around in boy scout uniforms shouting about how wonderful Hitler was. Hitler making speeches about the great German nation and how it needed more living room and that war was unnecessary, but . . . . . You know the rest."

Parsons nodded. "Does it bother you to be fighting them?"

"Not a bit. My family don't like the Nazis. And I hate the bastards."

"Good. I see you speak German. Fluently?"

"Yes. I learned from my mother. We spoke it some at home. In Germany, I had no trouble unless they talked really fast."

"You read and write it?"

"Reading's okay. Writing's a little rough."

"I'll remember that. Could be useful. French too, I see."

"Only what I learned in school."

Parsons nodded and eyed the file. "How much RAF training did you get?"

"Five months in Canada and twelve weeks in an Operational Training Unit at Fairhaven."

The Squadron Leader frowned skeptically. "I thought OTU was a twenty-week course."

"They took some account of my experience. It was an accelerated program, sir."

More like, they cut it in half, the older man thought. What had they left out? "Ever flown a Spit?"

Bayer edged around in his chair nervously and said, "No, sir."

"You'll have to learn fast then."

"Oh, I've already studied the Pilot's Notes and memorized the cockpit."

"That's a promising start," Parsons said. He thought, What the hell were those stupid Ministry bastards thinking - sending us half-trained pilots, green as spring grass, and expecting us to fight a war with them? Peter Duke was right; Jerry'll cut them to pieces. But no point in discouraging the lad. He forced a smile. "Pay careful attention to what you're told around here, and I'm sure you'll do well."

Bayer grinned and shrugged. Yes, he liked this man.

Parsons scanned the rest of the file. Finally he closed it, leaned back in his chair, and lit his pipe.

"Son, you're coming into a tough situation."

"Oh?"

"This is an old line RAF squadron. A tight club. The older hands have been together since well before the war. It won't be easy to break in. You'll have to prove yourself."

Bayer nodded.

"Just don't get impatient."

"I won't, sir."

"Good." The older man eyed him somberly. "You're going to be assigned to Lieutenant Duke. He's one of our more experienced pilots, and I'm sure you'll learn a lot from him."

"Is he the one I saw you talking to after he landed?"

"Why . . . Yes."

Bayer swallowed hard. "He didn't want somebody new."

"You overheard our conversation?"

Bayer nodded.

"I wouldn't take that too seriously. We were all inexperienced once, and he knows perfectly well our replacements will be. He was just shaken by the loss of his friend."

Maybe, Bayer thought. But he wondered if he had a prayer of making it here. There was a long silence. "Is that all, sir?"

"Not quite." Parsons paused for a moment, drew on his pipe, and blew smoke leisurely toward the ceiling, while he eyed young man quizzically as if searching for the right words. "I presume you know that Mister Churchill calls this campaign we're fighting the Battle of Britain."

"Yes, sir."

"Well you need to know something of what's going on and understand the stakes." Parsons removed his glasses and looked at Bayer ominously. "Jerry's revving up for a full scale invasion of England. Troops and tanks are assembling along the French and Belgian coasts. They're bringing in ships to carry them across the Channel, lighters for tanks and trucks, and river barges for cargo and troops. They'll have to deal with the Royal Navy, of course, but under the right conditions, they could gain control of the Channel long enough to get across. And once Jerry's here, it's all over. We have nothing on the ground to stop them."

"But surely, the Army --."

"By the skin of our British teeth, we managed to pull a few hundred thousand of our troops off the beaches at Dunkirk. But the poor devils didn't even bring back their toothbrushes, never mind their weapons. And we don't have replenishments. They're in no position to withstand a Wehrmacht assault here."

"You mean if the Germans get ashore, there'll be no one to fight them?"

"If they get onto the beaches in Kent, they can have a bloody holiday parade up the A2 into London."

"But Churchill said we'd struggle on the beaches and landing grounds and fields and streets."

The Squadron Leader's eyes narrowed. "Certainly, we'd fight, even with our fists. But you haven't seen a modern army in action, have you? It would be simple slaughter."

Bayer digested this in silence.

Parsons continued, "If Jerry gets as far as the beach, Herr Hitler will dictate peace from a podium on Whitehall. Then the Nazis will own Europe from the North Cape to the Pyrenees and from Lands End to Istanbul. With their friends in Italy and Spain, they'll dominate the Mediterranean and Middle East to the tip of the Arabian peninsula. And with their pals in Russia, they'll control things all the way to the Pacific. They'll own the wealth and productive power of over half the world."

Bayer gazed at the floor, trying to visualize this vast geography.

Parsons went on, "Then you in America will face them all alone. Them and their Japanese pals. And sooner or later, you'll be fighting on your own beaches."

Bayer had joined the RAF to help in a war he felt sure they could win; the implications the man now spelled out had never crossed his mind. A knot grew in his stomach.

Parsons said, "But there is one fly in Jerry's ointment - the Royal Air Force, specifically, Fighter Command. He can't put his ships to sea and take on the Royal Navy while we're operational. He must destroy us first. And we can't let him do that." He hesitated while it sunk in, then pointed his finger at Bayer. "That means you. You and Lieutenant Duke and the other twenty surviving pilots in this squadron . . . and the few hundred other young flyers in Fighter Command. You have to defeat the Luftwaffe."

The knot in Bayer's stomach tightened. "How many planes have they got?"

"Thousands."

Bayer sat numbly turning the word over in his mind. How was it possible? Finally he said, "Thousands? Are you sure?"

Parsons nodded. "Three, maybe four thousand."

"Geezus!"

"It'll be no garden party."

Bayer had heard of Jerry's skill and cunning in the air, and now he was learning that they vastly outnumbered Fighter Command, as well. It sounded like suicide.

"I don't suppose it's what you expected to hear, son, but that's the story. Our backs are to the wall. And you . . . and the other pilots . . . have to get us out of this jam. Any questions?"

"Sir, is there no hope?

"Of course there's hope, son. But that doesn't change the odds."

He searched Parsons's face, looking for a hint of a cheerful slant on the problem, but the man's expression said Bayer had got all the answers the man had to give. Bayer dropped his gaze to the Pilot Officer's stripes on his own sleeves. My God, he thought, what have I done?

Then he said, "No. I don't suppose it does. I have no more questions."

"Then that's all."

Bayer stood up slowly.

Parsons rose and smiled grimly. They shook hands. "Come and see me if I can help with anything. Good luck."

Chapter 3

Bayer stood, rigid, on the concrete ramp in the shadow of the big hangar. A sign on it read ARROW SQUADRON. Even the building itself seemed menacing, and he felt a chill as he gazed dumbstruck into the glare of Flight Lieutenant Peter Duke's gray eyes.

"Geezus, boy! They send you to a fighter outfit with no bloody training? What the hell do you think this is, an aero-club picnic?"

Duke was six, maybe seven, years older, but it was painfully clear to Bayer that, in fighter-pilot time, that was a whole generation.

"And you never flew a Spit?" Even in anger, Duke's words rolled out with the lilt of the English midlands.

Bayer's left hand clamped tightly on his flight kit, while the other clenched repeatedly as the fingers tested the moisture in the palm. "No, sir. Ten hours in Hurricanes though."

Duke rolled his eyes to show what he thought of that. "You a Yank, lad?" He said the word *lad* as if he were talking to a misbehaved child.

"Yes, sir."

"Well we'll try not to hold that against you. Now listen to me. I consider you a liability. But we're desperate for pilots, and I'm stuck with you. You'll get one whole day to learn the airplane, and tomorrow you go into battle. I won't have time to wipe your nose or stop to explain what's going on. If you want to stay alive, you'll catch on fast."

For months, Bayer had itched to finish training and join an operational squadron, and the RAF had seemed to drag its feet. Now the tables were turned, and he was afraid. Would he survive? Could he measure up? But he strained not to look worried. "Yes, sir."

Duke eyed the young man's peach-skinned face and thought, that firm jaw makes him seem eager enough and those dark eyes look bright enough, but the Krauts will have him for breakfast.

Duke turned and strode off toward a pair of Spitfires parked on the ramp. He carried his helmet, leather gloves, and oxygen mask. A small clip board was clamped to his thigh. Over his blue uniform coat, he wore an orange Mae West life jacket, and a small revolver rode in a holster under his left arm.

"Come with me," he called over his shoulder. Bayer followed.

Approaching the plane briskly, he called up to an erk standing on the wing next to the cockpit, putting the final polishing touch on the Perspex. "She ready to go?"

"Right, sir. She's all yours."

The erk jumped off the wing, and Duke clambered up with Bayer following. He slid back the canopy, opened the access door on the side of the cockpit, and signaled for Bayer to climb in.

Bayer eased into the seat. The trapped air, heated by the sun, was thick with the mixed smells of oil and hydraulic fluid, and the plane's metal parts were hot to the touch. The gauges and controls in front of him were arranged for easy viewing and reach.

Duke closed the access door and said, "All right, lad, let's see what you know." Duke still spat the word *lad* as if it had a bad taste. "Talk me through the procedures I call for and finger the appropriate controls as you go. Now give me the engine starting sequence."

Bayer went through what he had learned from the book and remembered from starting a Hurricane.

"How do you shut her down?"

Bayer explained it.

And so it went; Duke quizzed and Bayer responded: takeoff, landing, combat settings, hydraulic failure, engine failure, everything in the Pilots Notes and a few cases Bayer had to work out for himself. When he didn't know an answer, Duke prodded him, then recited it from memory and explained why it was important. That made Bayer even more despondent.

At length, Duke said, "You study those Notes until you can quote them to me verbatim starting anywhere I choose. We'll go over it later." Duke pulled a fold of black cloth from his pocket. "Now put this blindfold on."

Bayer hadn't expected a blind test, and he sat stunned.

Duke waved a finger at him. "Over your eyes, lad."

Bayer took a deep breath and slipped it on.

"When I call out a control, you put one hand on it as if to operate it, always keeping the other on the stick." He began calling their names: "Throttle. Mixture. Elevator trim. Flaps. Fuel tank pressure control. Landing gear. . . .." Hand followed thought, sluggish at first. Then Bayer's confidence grew and the pace increased. The hot sun made perspiration run down his neck. Finally, Duke called them rapid-fire.

"Fuel cocks, ignition, windscreen deicer, cockpit lights . . . .." Bayer's fingers fluttered over the controls like an organist at a recital.

"Your gun sight's out, change the bulb, one handed."

It took a whole minute, but he stumbled through it.

"Right then, take off the blinders and listen."

Bayer thought he'd missed only one or two, and he felt pretty good.

Duke knelt on the wing and looked him in the eye. "You can get killed in one of these in lots of interesting ways, boy. One is to be tired and hurt at night with the lights shot away and not be able to drop your hand instantly on the right control without thinking. You got to know this cockpit like the inside of your bloody mouth. Understand?"

Bayer nodded and his gut tightened. Nothing was simple anymore; the stakes were life or death at every turn. Geezus, he wondered, will I ever get used to it?

"You can do better with practice, lad. Anyway, we fly now. Keep a loose two-plane echelon. I'll be pushing it, and you'll have to work to keep up. This is a combat zone, so we'll turn on the gun sights before takeoff. Keep your finger off the firing button, and leave your guns on safety unless I tell you or we run into Jerry. And if you shoot at me, I'll wrap this airplane around your ears. Do you hear me?"

"Yes, sir."

"If we find Jerry, stay on my wing and cover me. If you get a shot, get close enough to see his bloody rivets. And only shoot when your sight picture is dead on."

"Yes, sir."

"Right then, let's go."

Duke jumped off the wing and crossed to the other Spitfire.

Bayer blew a sigh. God, he was nervous. Flying a new airplane didn't bother him; he'd longed for months to get behind the controls of a Spitfire. But flying with Peter Duke was another matter. It seemed that Bayer's mere presence imposed on the man. He wondered if he'd ever be good enough to fly in this league.

Beside the hangar, he saw a man throwing a ball for a dog. His heart stopped. It was a big black Labrador like his own dog, Shadow, back home. Watching the animal frolic, he smiled and his tension eased. He recalled the feel of the shiny fur coat and the way Shadow stood in reverie, like a purring cat, whenever Bayer fingered the hollow behind his soft ears. There were things he missed about home, but none more than Shadow. He longed to go over and pet this dog, but that would have to wait. He pulled on his leather helmet.

The erk clambered back onto the wing and up beside the cockpit. He opened the access door and began to help Bayer adjust the chute, safety harness, radio, and oxygen system.

"First time up in one of these, sir?"

It irked Bayer that it showed. He nodded.

"It's not hard, sir. But be careful. And bring it back in one piece, please. It's the only one I've got."

Bayer smiled sheepishly and nodded. The erk latched the access door carefully, saluted, and jumped down.

With the door closed, the fuselage enveloped Bayer's body to the top of his shoulders, like a snug suit, and the closed canopy would give him only enough clearance to swivel his head. There was no headrest. This machine is built for speed, he decided, not comfort.

Atop the windshield crown, stood a wide-angle, rear-view mirror. It was no substitute for looking around, he'd been warned, but it allowed a quick glance for immediate danger from behind.

He laid his hand over the throttle. When pushed forward, it would stop at a detent, the normal full-throttle position, known as the gate. In desperation, you could push it through the gate and get extra power for a brief period before the Merlin engine destroyed itself.

He fingered the crowbar mounted inside the access door. Large letters printed on it read, EMERGENCY USE ONLY. A man trapped in this thing would find it handy, he thought. The bloody designers had considered everything.

Grasping the spade-handled control stick, he pulled it back and ran his thumb gingerly over the gun button on top. With the safety ring turned off, it fired the eight Brownings, which together delivered one hundred and sixty high-velocity rounds per second. And those guns, he reminded himself, were what this machine was all about.

He looked up at the sky and sighed again. Tomorrow he would take one of these into battle. Would he be ready?

The erk stood by a fire bottle spotted forward of the port wing and called, "Clear."

The throttle, pitch, and mixture controls were already set for starting the engine. The other plane's engine roared to life, and he reached forward to turn on the magnetos. As his hand approached the switches, it shook. For God's sake, do it right.

He snapped the magnetos on and pressed the starter. The whirr of the electric motor jolted him and the propeller began to turn; she was coming alive under him. He took a deep breath and advanced the mixture control. The exhaust stacks, just forward of the cockpit, erupted in a crack of thunder, and the whole plane wrenched from side to side. Bayer's mind went momentarily blank. Then he advanced the throttle and brought the mixture to auto-rich. The engine settled into a snappy, smooth idle. Thank God.

Ahead, partially hidden by the Spitfire's nose, lay the runway area, a grass field on which the planes landed and took off. The grass was encircled by a tarmac taxiway, known as the perimeter track, along which planes traveled from their parking spots to the takeoff point, at the downwind edge of the grass.

Duke taxied ahead, turned onto the perimeter track and pulled away. Bayer waved to have the wheel chocks removed, then sat nervously biting his lip while the erk ducked under the aircraft. Finally the man stood clear and signaled that the job was done.

Bayer released the brakes and, anxious to catch up, shoved the throttle forward. The engine roared, the plane lurched ahead, and he knew he'd overdone it. He idled the throttle and caught a glimpse of the erk. The man's face twisted into a grimace, as if he were preparing to witness certain disaster.

Bayer struggled to get the machine under control, but taxiing the beast was tricky. Unlike any other plane he'd flown, the big nose canted into the air, completely blocking the view forward, so on the ground the pilot couldn't see straight ahead. To taxi, he had to tack the plane from side to side to get a periodic view down the track.

In theory, tacking was simple, but in a new airplane with new controls, it seemed daunting. The machine jerked first one way then the other, and occasionally he had to bring it to a stop to keep from running off the taxiway. It proved a long, hot trip to the downwind side of the field. And as he turned into the wind, he felt sure his performance wasn't up to Duke's standards.

The idling engine made the Spitfire shimmy like a nervous racehorse waiting for the gate to open. At eye level in front of him, centered above the instrument panel behind the two-inch-thick bulletproof windscreen, sat the glass gun-sight reflector. He snapped a switch and watched it light up in an image of a bull's eye on the sky directly in front of the plane. A dot, or pipper, at the center marked the aim point of the guns.

He ran through the takeoff check twice, then signaled thumbs up. The other plane began to roll.

Now or never, Bayer said to himself. Stick back, throttle open all the way to the gate, release the brakes. What a surge! The butterflies went, replaced by a rush of terror.

She pulled to the right. Don't let the beast get away from you, he thought. Hold her straight. Rudder, man! Now, ease the stick forward to bring the tail up.

The machine bounded over the uneven grass, like a wild animal unchained, rocking from side to side.

Enough speed to fly. Back on the stick.

The bucking ride was over in a flash, and she lifted off. He brought the wheels and flaps up then trimmed the throttle.

Taking several deep breaths, he settled himself in the seat, and eyed the sky above and the green below. For the first time since he had started the engine, he wasn't desperately busy. She flew smooth as glass and responded to little control movements like a tuned racing car.

This was, indeed, why he'd come to England.

Duke was well ahead, and Bayer set about to catch up. Going through five thousand feet, he pulled into a tight echelon, just as he had learned in training.

The Lieutenant's voice sounded gravelly on the radio. "Those close formations are pretty to look at, and the skipper likes them. So when he's around, we fly that way. But they're no damned good for air fighting. Take too much attention away from looking around. And seeing's everything. Spread out and keep your eyes open."

Bayer maneuvered out to the side.

The pair wheeled northward, passing east of Cambridge as they climbed through twenty thousand feet. At twenty-five, they leveled off and eased the power.

Overhead, the sky was a deep blue. Northeast in the distance, toward King's Lynn and the Norfolk Coast, giant thunderheads rose higher than their Spitfires; and westward, the green and gold fields of Lincolnshire lay like a checkered quilt over the earth, extending to the horizon. The deep blue of the Wash was coming into sight ahead. For the thousandth time in his life, Bayer marveled at the exquisite beauty of the earth below.

He keyed the radio button and said, "What a pretty sight."

Duke's voice brought him up short. "No bloody chitchat on the radio, boy! Talk only when necessary. Use it to warn others. Otherwise shut up and keep it clear so they can warn you. And you may get orders over it. So listen up. Understand?"

Bayer wasn't sure he was supposed to answer.

Duke continued, "Now, confirm your guns are on safety."

"My guns are safe."

"Drop two hundred yards astern. And stay with me."

Bayer fell into position behind. His heart raced and his voice was weak when he said, "Okay."

In a flash, the other Spitfire half-rolled and the nose pitched down. Bayer strained to follow. When he did, the other plane flicked a roll, turned hard, and was gone.

Bayer rolled upright. Where did it go? He scanned the sky. High, low, all around. Nothing.

Strange! How could a plane simply disappear in a perfectly clear sky?

Bayer craned to search the air around him, and when he looked up toward the sun, it bothered his eyes.

Where the hell could Duke be?

Suddenly he was struck by a dark movement below. The other plane had rocketed out of the sun to come in from behind and flash by close underneath. Then, as in a nightmare, it nosed up vertically not thirty yards directly ahead.

What the hell's going on?

He drove the stick forward to avoid hitting the plane's tail. The quick plunge was unnecessary, but it added to the slipstream blast that hit Bayer's plane and slammed his body like a two-legged kick from a wild horse.

His plane seemed to be coming apart, and he gasped in panic as he struggled with the out-of-control machine. Then the violence passed, and he plummeted in smooth air. Slowly he brought the stick back, and the plane responded.

"I just rocked your cradle, laddie. Jerry would have sliced your balls off. That's no China Clipper you're flying. It's a fighter plane. And you can't always be gentle with it. You've got to make it do what *you* want."

Bayer's breath came in short gasps. Were you supposed to treat airplanes like this? Could he learn it all? In one afternoon?

He brought the plane around and climbed to join Duke, who flew straight and level above him. At last, he came alongside.

"All right," Duke said, "drop behind and we'll try once more."

They lined up and again the lead plane snapped into a roll and pulled down. Against all instincts, Bayer heaved the stick to the right, all the way to the stop. A firm push on the rudder bar kept the nose into the roll, and he held it for a moment as the earth whirled. Then he centered the stick and hauled back. G's drove him into the seat. But at the end of the first turn, the other plane was still out in front.

They rolled and turned, climbed and dived. Bayer heaved on the controls and twisted in the cockpit to keep the other plane in sight. His neck and shoulders complained, he breathed heavily, and perspiration dampened his neck.

Then the plane in front straightened out.

"Join up," Duke called.

They climbed smoothly together, and at just under thirty thousand feet, Duke leveled off and said, "You got any questions?"

"No, sir."

"Right then, back you go. This time, stay with me all the way down. I'm the enemy. Your job is to keep your gun sight on me all the time." Duke broke to the left and the chase was on.

Bayer followed, straining to keep the gun sight pipper on him. They twisted and curved. The other plane weaved to and fro across Bayer's windscreen as he struggled to follow. Whenever he brought the pipper to the kill point, Duke's plane turned and arced away.

Bayer moved constantly, like a dancing prizefighter, hauling on the control column, booting the rudder bar, modulating power, and adjusting propeller pitch. He fought the pull of G's and craned to keep his adversary in view.

His shirt stuck to his body, moisture blotched his gloves and sweat burned his eyes. Blink and live with the pain, or lose the bastard.

At first, he jerked on the controls, and the distance opened between the planes. But as he settled into it, his movements smoothed, and he was able to keep pace.

At one point, Duke was far out to the side, tightening his turn into an arc that threatened to bring him in behind Bayer's plane. His heart leapt. Geezus, he thought, Duke's turning the tables on me!

He rolled to follow, but it was sloppy, short of the bank needed for exact pursuit. He hauled the stick back, and the Spitfire nosed into a climbing turn. Before he could correct, he found himself nearly inverted above the other plane, which continued in a tight, flat circle. He knew this wasn't good enough and cursed himself for the mistake.

In a desperate bid to regain position, he held the stick back hard and let the G's press on him. His neck complained as he tilted his head back to keep his eyes on Duke, through the top of the canopy. With the plane inverted, the nose dropped quickly and he brought the pipper down to point directly at Duke's machine. Then he rolled to follow its turn and dropped neatly into firing position behind it.

It seemed a miracle, but there was no time to figure it out. Duke rolled in the opposite direction, and Bayer heaved on the controls to stay with him.

They spiraled downward until suddenly, two thousand feet off the ground, Duke turned due south and straightened out.

"Bogie!" he shouted. "Eleven o'clock, low. A Dornier. Arm your guns and cover my arse." His Spitfire racked into a right turn.

Bayer spotted the plane crossing their path, pushed the throttle to the gate, and rolled hard to follow. Christ, he thought, that's a real German, right here in front of me! He rotated the gun safety.

A stream of black exhaust from the German's engines gave notice that he had seen them, but they were between him and home and he was headed the wrong way. Bayer slid out to the left as they closed on the bomber, and when Bayer expected Duke to shoot, Duke moved even nearer. Then eight streams of tracers from the Spitfire converged into the Dornier's right engine. It spouted white vapor.

The bomber rolled to the left, throwing off Duke's aim, and he pulled up steeply. "Cut under me and shoot," he called.

Bayer turned to track the target. It startled him to see the big black crosses on the mottled gray-green wings, close up. The pilot's face peered upward at him through the bulbous canopy, like the pink eye of a cyclops. He pulled on the stick to tighten his turn and pushed the gun button hard with his thumb. But his concentration evaporated in the thunder and recoil of his own guns. Tracers streamed harmlessly into the green field beyond, and his finger leapt off the gun button. The target passed out of his windscreen.

Above, coming off the top of a loop, Duke nosed down to bore-sight the German, then rolled upright and let fly. The white vapor from the Dornier's engine turned into an orange blaze, and the plane rolled over slowly and curved downward, trailing smoke like thick brown molasses. It continued down in a drunken spiral until it plowed into the green earth of Hartfordshire and disappeared in a crimson ball of flame.

Bayer gazed in awe at the fire.

Duke said, "All right, let's beetle for the barn."

Bayer joined up loosely, and they climbed gently to the southeast. Sunlight drenched the cockpit, and overhead, a parade of puffy clouds stood out against the blue sky like white embossing on Wedgwood. Below, fields of green and soft gold bounded by dark hedges stretched away in neat rectangles. A farmer riding a flatbed wagon drawn by a brace of horses waved as they flashed by.

Bayer's heart pumped like a hammer and his fingers tingled. The heat and exertion made sweat roll down his neck and soak his collar. He pushed his goggles up and, unsnapping his oxygen mask, wiped his face with a gloved hand.

He was still recovering from the shock of his own guns firing, and he knew he'd missed. But he had managed to stay with Duke on the long ride down, and he was sure Duke had been pushing it. Maybe he could make it here after all. Then he wondered what Duke thought.

Chapter 4

Lieutenant Peter Duke relaxed in the lounge chair in his room in the officers' mess, drinking from a mug of tea. Bayer sat stiffly on a desk chair in front of him.

As he entered Duke's room, Bayer had noticed pictures of girls hanging on the wall, six of them! He would have been delighted with any one. They weren't pin-ups either; each had a note and a signature. How, he wondered, do you find girls like that?

Duke scowled. "You get any gunnery at OTU, lad?"

"Yes, sir."

"How much?"

"Maybe a week."

"Geezus!" Duke thrust up his hands in frustration. "Accelerated course, balls! They just left out unimportant subjects, like how to shoot."

Bayer was silent.

Duke continued, "You missed that bastard by a mile."

"Yes, sir. I couldn't roll fast enough to get on him."

"Christ, use rudder in a quick shot like that. Skid the kite. You don't have to look pretty. Just get the pipper on. Any old way counts. Do you know about deflection shooting? Leading the target?"

"Yes, sir. Used to hunt ducks back home. You have to lead them too. But in the rush, I forgot."

"I'll say! At two hundred yards range, a bomber travels one or two plane lengths before your bullets reach him. And a fighter goes two or three. Judging the angles comes with practice. But for Christ's sake, don't forget it."

"No, sir."

As he withstood Duke's tongue lashing, Bayer was wondering why those girls liked this man. He was handsome in an odd way, even with those big ears and a nose that looked as if it had been broken more than once. But how did they put up with his personality? Maybe he was different with them.

Duke continued, "And you're still too damned gentle with that machine. Not rolling fast enough or pulling hard enough in the turns. And you were late in maneuvering. Watch the other guy's ailerons and elevator. They deflect before the plane changes direction. When they move, you do too. Understand?"

"Yes, sir."

"And now don't go getting cocky, lad. You've got a long way to go to make it, around here."

Duke seems to hold out little hope, Bayer thought. I wonder if there is any. How will I remember it all?

"Any questions?" Duke asked.

"No, sir." Then Bayer remembered his one success. "Except that, there was once when I thought I'd lost you but I caught up. I don't know how I did it --."

Duke cut him off, "Beginners' luck. I must have fallen asleep. Let's talk about the enemy . . ."

Bayer's mind dropped out of the conversation for a moment. It hadn't been luck. He'd done something that worked. It had seemed like a miracle; now it was a challenge.

Duke continued, " . . . Luftwaffe are tough and well trained, and their planes are bloody good. They wiped out the Belgian and Dutch air forces in a day, destroyed French air power in a week, and kicked the RAF's backside over France. Now they aim to do it here, too. So this is not fun and games."

Bayer shook his head.

"Right then, tomorrow you fly against the bastards. Remember, always keep a sharp lookout. Jerry hangs out where he's hard to spot, up-sun and at your six o'clock. So pay special attention there. And remember the bastard that gets you is always the one you don't see."

"Yes, sir."

"Never fly straight and level in the combat area, for more than thirty seconds. It's an open invitation for Jerry to get low behind you, in your blind spot. You'll be dead before you know he's there."

Bayer nodded, but he was having trouble taking it all in.

"Always turn and face a fighter attack. Gun to gun evens the odds. And never break off until you're sure to ram him. Let the other bastard break off and kill him when he does. Got all that?"

"Think so, sir."

"All right, we're on the sheet tomorrow, and it'll be an early one. We'll probably go to Manston for the day, where we can get up quicker at Jerry over the Channel. You'll be Blue Three. Sergeant Burt Stark is

Blue Two. He's an old hand and a damned good pilot. And just because he's an NCO, don't think you can't learn something from him."

Bayer nodded.

"I wish you luck, boy. That's all."

Bayer stood up and started slowly for the door. He wanted to get another look at the pictures.

"By the way, Bayer," Duke said, "that name of yours sounds like the four-legged kind."

Bayer stopped and faced him.

A wry smile crossed Duke's face. "But you don't look mean enough for a bear, lad. Or old enough either. More like a cub." His smile spread into a leer. "That's what we'll call you: Cub. How do you like it?"

To Bayer, it seemed an insult. He knew he looked young, but why did people pick on him for it? "I don't know if I like it, sir."

Duke grinned, and they gazed at each other for a long moment. "Getting a running name is part of squadron initiation. We choose it. You may even grow to be proud of it one day. By the way, where are your records?"

"Squadron Leader Parsons has them."

"The Chaplain, eh?" Duke said with a wry chuckle. "All right, I'll get them from him. And by the way, if you have a problem with Cub, ask Parson's how he likes being Chaplain."

There was a flicker of humor in the man's eye, but Bayer didn't think it was funny. He turned for the door and forgot to look at the pictures.

"See you tomorrow, Cub."

*

Bayer's room in the officers' mess was spotless and almost Spartan. The floor was a dark linoleum, and the walls and ceiling were white enamel. He guessed it had been an ample single room in peacetime, but now it was tight with two metal beds against opposite walls, each with a bed table supporting a reading lamp and wooden bench at the foot. His bed was made up neatly; but a folded mattress, white sheets, and two dark gray blankets were stacked on the other. A small rug lay on the floor between them. Two open-fronted desks with wooden desk chairs, and two freestanding wardrobes with drawers were squeezed against the walls. There was an easy chair in one corner with a side table and lamp, and misaligned books lay on the shelves of a wooden bookcase. A white porcelain wash basin hung on the wall in a corner with a mirrored cabinet over it, and a towel warmer stood alongside.

As the red glow of sunset poured through the one large window, Bayer sat at his desk bewildered by the day's events. He dropped his head in his hands. So much to learn. So little time. Tomorrow! Could he remember it all? Cub, eh? Could he make a Spitfire perform? Suppose he ran into a German as good as Duke?

Yes, the sonofabitch was bloody good in the air. Talked sense too. But he sure didn't pull any punches. He spit *lad* and *boy* at him all day long, as if to put him down. What was behind that? And why did he have to call him Cub? Well, Lieutenant Duke was sure one tough nut to please.

It suddenly occurred to Bayer how often he had said the same thing of his father. Why was it so hard to please the ones that were most important to you? His dad, Brad, and now Duke. Why the hell did he care about pleasing Duke? Well, Duke was what Bayer wanted to become. At least up to now.

And how in the world did he get those beautiful girls? Just like Brad had done. Maybe it was the dark hair parted in the middle and the neatly cropped mustache.

Bayer rubbed his soft face and wondered if he could cultivate one. Cub, eh? Or maybe it was Duke's self-confidence. Also like Brad. How do you get so confident?

Then he began thinking about how he caught up to Duke in the air. Beginners' luck, my foot. In college, they hammered into you that there was always a reason for physical phenomena. There had to be a reason for this. He was too agitated to pursue it, but one day he'd work it out.

Cub? Maybe it wasn't so bad. Cub Bayer. At least it made sense. And if it was part of getting initiated into the squadron, to hell with the price; he'd pay it. Cub . . . okay. Cub it would be.

Chapter 5

Doreen Phillips sat alone in the back corner of the Lounge Bar at The Gannet. An English pub was as safe as a church, and she knew this one well. Yet she was haunted by a vague unease as she massaged her finger to erase the mark from her ring. Around town, it kept the oglers at bay. Here it would miss the point; so it was in her purse - out of sight, like Colin. And who knew when he'd come back.

Was it remorse that bothered her here? Not exactly, she decided. It was just that old habits were comfortable. And maybe she'd hung around too long with Peter Duke. He'd chided her overmuch, and now she had to find out for herself.

Sure, she'd put on a little weight, but mostly in the right places, and the blouse she wore left little to speculation. Her blonde hair was brushed to a luster, and the fingernails were manicured and finished in red. Her eyes were tinted with French eye shadow, and brows and lashes blackened. She had painted her lips with her best lipstick and shaded their edges with a darker color.

She'd noticed heads turn as she walked in, but she wasn't ready to draw more attention than she could help just yet. But for the occasional glance around, she kept her eyes on her hands or the dimpled glass mug on the table in front of her, as if she were waiting for someone.

The place had the feeling of well worn comfort. White ceiling tiles were tinged by age and smoke to the color of old ivory, and the much-used floor linoleum was dark red. A faded floral print decorated the upper walls, below which, the wainscoting was brown oak turned darker by the passage of time. The wooden furniture matched the wainscot, but the edges of the seats and tables and the arms of the chairs were worn to a patina the color of creamed coffee.

Behind the bar, wine glasses and beer mugs hung like baubles from an overhead rack, and bottles were shelved in military order. Cigarette smoke filtered through the light from table lamps in ever-changing swirls, and the air was laced with the smell of burning tobacco and the faint aroma of musty beer.

The sun had still shone when the blackout curtains were closed, but from the sounds of the airplanes orbiting for landing at Hornchurch, Doreen knew it was now dark outside. They never returned before the last light of the sun had faded away. It would be another thirty minutes before the pilots, in their smart blue uniforms, began to arrive.

Yes, there was something very special about those uniforms, for no matter how tired or worried they were, the pilots always looked wonderful. And however they felt, they were so bright eyed and enthusiastic. Just thinking about it gave her a warm, racy feeling.

Doreen decided that, alongside the pilots, the people in the room now looked stodgy and tired. Maybe it was just the end of the day, but perhaps the war was getting them down, too. They talked in low tones, sometimes smiled, and she heard an occasional chuckle but no outright laughter.

Here and there, men in dark suits with stiff collars and prim neckties pecked at sherry or half-pints of bitter beer. Others wore wool or tweed jackets and loose ties. They chatted and sipped at beer or rum or whiskey. And still others wore rough wool jackets and caps. They talked among themselves or scanned the evening tabloid or sat staring at the ceiling. Invariably they drank beer by the pint.

There were only a few couples, older ones at that. The women wore brimmed hats, high-necked dresses, formless wool coats, and wide shoes with short, heavy heels. Their arms were rounded and their ankles thick. A few couples talked with each other, but mostly, the women stared stony-faced while the men buried themselves in their newspapers.

The pilots began to arrive on schedule in twos and threes, their gestures garish and their voices loud as they worked off tension. Fifteen minutes later, most would settle down. Not many would get drunk; their morning came too soon, and carrying a hangover into battle could be deadly.

Doreen glanced furtively in the direction of the blue uniforms gathered at the bar. My, but they were good looking! There were two that she had briefly met before. She caught the eye of one and smiled broadly. The other looked at her too, and they both waved, but neither moved in her direction.

Dear God, had Peter Duke been right? Had she lost it?

Maybe they knew she was married. Nonsense. That was as closely guarded as a military secret. But Peter knew. Had he spread the word to ruin her? The bastard. Not likely though.

But they would know that she had gone with Duke. Too many of the Hornchurch boys knew it. That would stop them. Peter was an old hand; they wouldn't fool around with his girl. And just because she decided the affair was over, she couldn't put up a sign to advertise. Damn! It was a legacy she might have to bear for a while. The more she thought about it, the more troubled she became.

She sat brooding, when she sensed a familiar presence and glanced toward the bar. Her heart sank; Peter Duke had entered. He apparently didn't see her as he approached the group of pilots around the bar. They greeted him warmly, clapping him on the back and crowding around, and for some time, he was deep in conversation.

She wondered what to do. He'd been looking for her, she knew, and he was the last person she wanted to see. She could walk out, but why the bloody hell should she run from him?

Duke took a sip of his beer and, leaning on the bar, turned slowly to eye the place. Even with those ears, he was handsome, she thought, especially when he got that determined look. And she had nearly fallen in love with him. Too bad.

He tensed when he saw her; his jaw muscles bulged and eyes narrowed. He pulled himself upright, tossed off a sip of his beer, then separated himself from the crowd and marched toward her. She took a deep breath and resigned herself.

"Well, well," he said when he stood over her, "look who's here."

She eyed him with as little emotion as she could muster.

He said, "Aren't you going to ask me to sit down?"

"If you insist."

He slid into the seat opposite and leaned across the table. His eyes had the look of an alerted leopard, one that might strike at any moment. "Where the hell have you been?" he said.

"For half an hour, I've been here drinking my beer. Why?"

"Oh for God's sake. I've been trying to reach you for days."

"What for? A fourth at bridge?"

"Doreen, what the hell goes on with us?"

As if he bloody didn't remember. "Absolutely nothing. Have you forgotten?"

"But we were going together. And we had fun."

She chuckled. Fun for him began with their clothes off. "Did we?"

"You seemed to think so."

"That was before."

"Before what, for Christ's sake?"

"Before I let you down."

"Let me down?"

"Those were your words."

Duke licked his lips uneasily and inched around in his seat. "Well . . . maybe I was a bit disappointed, but --."

"And how do you think I felt?"

"I suppose you were disappointed too. But I don't think we should make too much of it."

Not make much, eh? Well, it was too much for her. Three times now, in bed, he'd made her desperate for him, then couldn't perform. She gazed coldly at him.

Duke leaned back and studied her, then smiled that devastating smile. "Surely, girl, we can fix this thing up again."

She looked at the crowd of pilots around the bar while she collected her thoughts. He still blamed her. Well, she wasn't going through it again. She looked at him and spoke softly. "There's something going on inside you that . . . I'm not even sure you understand. It eats at you. The best part of you. And it's still there. I see it in your eyes."

He considered firing back with: Rubbish! But Doreen would probably see through that too. He half expected her to suggest there was another woman. And the truth would hurt. How could Cecily have done this to him? Damn her! Why did he let her? From five thousand miles away, how could that bloody woman still haunt him?

But he wouldn't let Doreen get away with this, and he said, "That's one hell of an excuse if I ever heard it. You're all hot for those young studs." He chucked his head at the bar. "So you're going to kiss me off. Right?"

"I didn't come here looking for you, if that's what you mean."

Duke could think of no good retort; he slumped back and sipped his beer.

As the publican called for last orders, Cub walked in through the door, crossed to the bar, and ordered. Doreen's eye lingered on him, and Duke followed her gaze.

My, she thought, but he's a good-looking youngster. Not very tall, but strong and poised, with lovely thick hair and flashing eyes. And he looks like a cuddly cherub when he smiles.

"Just your type," Duke said. "A Yank. Joined the squadron yesterday. Fresh out of OTU."

She looked at Duke blankly and said, "He's cute."

"Cute, eh. For Christ's sake, he's a baby."

"Looks old enough to me."

Duke's face twisted into a snide grin. "If you unpin his nappies for him, he might get it up for you. But try making a fighter pilot of him."

Ever the he-man aviator, she thought. "Old enough to love but not to fight, is that it?"

"Jerry's old foxes'll cut him to pieces."

"You really think Jerry's foxes are older than ours?"

"Counting Spain, they've had four years of live practice." He tilted his head toward the bar. "And Christ, the Krauts must be more mature than this crowd."

"I think you're the old fox around here. Maybe you feel outclassed."

"Beg your bloody pardon?"

She angled her head toward Cub. "Why don't you invite him over?"

"Come on, he's barely able to drink milk from a glass."

"Seems to do well with beer. Ask him."

"We're having a private conversation."

"Didn't we finish?"

He leaned over the table and took her hand. "Doreen, I don't want to let you go." His eyes pleaded with her.

She withdrew her hand and reached into her purse for a cigarette. She couldn't let him get to her. "You're not letting go," she said. "We're just finished."

"Doreen, please."

God, he was exasperating. She put the cigarette in her mouth, lit it herself, and shook her head. "We've been over it all before. Now be a dear and bring your friend over."

Duke's face flushed. "Get him yourself. And if you want a go at him, you better do it quick. He's not likely to be around long."

"Give the lad a chance, Duke."

Chapter 6

Before first light, guided by dim blackout lights, a flatbed van carrying a cargo of sleepy pilots crawled along the Hornchurch perimeter track. Cub was troubled by many things as they bumped along, but mostly he worried about making errors. Tension gnawed at his stomach, and the vehicle's lurching aggravated it.

When the van stopped, he slid off onto the ground and glanced at his watch - three thirty. A gentle rain began to fall.

The evening before, Duke had briefly introduced him to the skipper, Squadron Leader "Woolly" Tweed. Now he heard the man's voice in the dark: "Gather round quickly, gentlemen, and listen. Going to Manston, keep your running lights on and stay in formation. I don't want anybody getting lost. Weather's rotten over the estuary. So we'll go south before turning east. Keep absolute radio silence. The landing direction is two four zero, and they should have a flare path out to mark it. Any questions?"

There were none.

"All right, we start engines in five minutes, on the first flare. We go on the second, three minutes later. Good luck, chaps."

Cub joined Duke and another man as they picked their way toward their planes. "Good morning, sir," he said.

"What's good about it?" Duke answered.

"Like going duck hunting."

"Some ducks."

They walked in silence, with each footstep sinking gently into the soft turf and the muddy earth underneath sucking at the heels of their boots.

"Saw you in the pub last night," Cub said.

"Did you now?"

"Yeah. I almost dropped over to say hello."

Duke grunted.

"That was a pretty girl you were with."

"What do you care?"

"I just thought she was pretty."

Duke grunted again. "Keep your mind on flying. And staying alive."

Lightning flashed to the east through the mist, but there was no thunder. Must have been a long way off. Cub felt a chill.

Duke and the man with him stopped at the tail of Duke's plane.

"Cub, this is Sergeant Burt Stark. You'll be flying together."

In the dark, Cub could hardly make out the man's shape, but they shook hands and said good morning. Then Stark walked toward his plane and Cub followed. They padded quietly across the soaked turf together, and Cub shrugged his Mae West up around his neck in a vain attempt to keep out the water.

Duke called after them, "Stick close together going out of here, chaps. The cloud layer'll be lumpy."

Blue section would fly on the squadron's left in echelon formation with Duke leading, followed by Stark then Cub, in trail to the left. Riding rough air was bad enough, but doing it in close formation was daunting, and real fighter pilots never got separated. A vague nausea came over Cub.

He looked across what he knew was the grass field; God, but it was black. How much visibility was there? He'd flown Miles Master training planes at night, but a Spitfire was no simple training machine. Could he handle it? "These night flights ever make you nervous, Sergeant?"

"Always a bit edgy, sir. This your first time at night in a Spit?"

"Yeah."

"Well sir, she's a lot cleaner and more powerful than the Miles you were used to in training. Just be smooth with her and go easy on the throttle. You'll be all right."

Stark drew up at his plane, and Cub hesitated. The encouragement made him feel better. "Thanks, Sergeant."

Cub sloshed on to his own plane. As he rounded the tail and turned forward, he didn't see the erk standing beside the wing, and his heart nearly stopped when the man's voice boomed out of the murk, close at hand, "Morning, sir!"

He heard the man scramble onto the wing and followed, clambering awkwardly and feeling embarrassed. The erk opened the canopy and Cub hauled himself into the nearly dry cockpit.

"She's already warm, sir, so careful with the mixture. I ran her up not fifteen minutes ago."

He helped Cub buckle in and together they checked the oxygen system and radio. Then he latched the access door. "Dark night, sir. Good luck."

"Thanks . . . See you tonight," Cub said. I hope, he thought.

"Yes, sir." And the erk jumped from the wing.

Cub closed the canopy and checked the controls, leaving them set for a quick start. Outside, he could just make out the silhouette of Stark's plane.

Bloody English rain, he thought. When the meteorologists said the weather was fine, they meant it wasn't pouring buckets, but he was ready to bet the birds would stay on the ground.

He looked past the nose of his plane - pitch black. One of those six-story hangars could be a hundred yards away and he wouldn't see it. Butterflies worked in his stomach. He squirmed and tried to relax. Rain splattered on the Perspex, and in spite of his heavy uniform, he felt cold. To pass the time, he ran through Duke's blindfold drill, lightly fingering each control: light switches, booster coil, starter, primer, fuel cocks, cutout --.

A flash of lightning in the clouds startled him, and he tried to stifle his fear. Breath came short, and his stomach grew queasy. The rubbery odor of the oxygen mask turned to a stench. He cracked the oxygen emergency valve to let the pure cool stuff flow, and breathed heavily. It helped. He shut it off and tried to settle again. More lightning. Rain eased a little. Acid rose in his throat.

To his right, a blinding flash jolted him as the first flare arced upward and entered the cloud, lighting the place like a misty day. It went out, and the world was black again.

He snapped the ignition switches up and brought his right thumb down on the starter button; as he gently advanced the mixture control, the Merlin coughed once and then roared. The plane shimmied as fire leapt from the exhaust stacks. Quick adjustments to the mixture and throttle, and the engine noise smoothed and the flame waned.

He turned up the instrument-light intensity. Temperature gauges were already in the green. He advanced the throttle and dropped the ignition switches one at a time to check the magnetos - both okay. Nausea was gone, replaced by an anxiety that made his breath come heavy. His clothes felt clammy. The time had come to perform. There was no going back.

Tweed taxied forward a little, and Duke and Stark moved ahead and waited. Cub gunned forward and stopped with Stark's red wing-tip light just beyond his own wing.

They waited. Had he forgotten anything? He ran through the cockpit check again. At his two o'clock, Stark's wing light bobbed up and down in rhythm with the idling engine. Further to the right, several others fluttered.

Suddenly, a row of brilliant lights came on: the flare path laid on the grass to mark the takeoff direction. The string stretched away to the front into the murky rain, each more-distant light appearing more diffuse, until they disappeared in a misty yellow glow. Cub counted eleven lights before they were swallowed up - just over a thousand feet visibility.

Another flare arced away into the mist. Tweed blinked his lights three times and began to roll. Duke and Stark followed.

Holding the stick aft, Cub opened the throttle to full boost and made a quick instrument check. In front, thundering blue flame leapt from the cherry-red exhaust stacks. He released the brakes and felt the surge at his back. The plane shuddered as it followed the undulating profile of the grass. He eased the stick forward to raise the tail. Left rudder, he remembered, then he focused on Stark's bouncing red wing light. The plane bored into the murk, on and on, picking up speed, bucking as the uneven turf hammered the wheels. He shot a look at the airspeed indicator. Still too slow to fly. How far was the end of the field?

Ahead he could only see the blue flame and bright red exhaust stacks against a curtain of blackness. They could plow into the hangar or a stand of parked airplanes and never know it. Takeoff seemed to go on forever.

Suddenly Stark's light lifted. Cub pulled the stick back. The ride smoothed. Thank God.

The only awkwardness in the Spitfire cockpit layout was the location of the undercarriage lever. It was on the right, so the pilot had to change hands on the stick just after liftoff to raise the wheels. The plane lurched clumsily as Cub raised the lever, and Stark's light was disappearing into the murk ahead. Get the flaps up! He reversed hands again and slapped the control into the up position as the landing wheels thumped into the wells beneath him.

Stark's light was riding above him, very faint now. He came back on the stick and nudged the throttle, but it was already at the stop. The light was drawing away. What the hell was wrong?

Propeller pitch! He pulled the control to reduce engine RPM and give the propeller a better bite on the air. Slowly, he began to gain on the light.

Suddenly it was abeam, then it slid past him. He hauled back on the throttle. The light popped ahead. Too much! She's slippery as a fresh-caught eel, he thought. Settle down now and handle her gently.

The air grew rougher. But slowly, forcing patience into every move, he struggled until he held Stark's light at his two o'clock and tucked in as close as he dared. Thus welded together, the fighters plunged through the cloud, where visibility was less than fifty feet. Breathing came heavy.

Turbulence began to toss the Spitfires like dinghies in a seaway. A small error and they'd separate.

He thought, Keep Stark's wing light in that one spot. When it lifts, you lift too. When it moves away, you turn. When it moves ahead, ease the climb and add power.

The plane heaved and pitched until it seemed the wings would come off. He began to perspire. They could easily collide. Should he break away and climb out on his own?

No! He wasn't going to face Duke and explain why he got lost. To hell with instinct, he had to hold on. And for ten more minutes, Stark's light was his lodestar.

Then suddenly, the formation popped through the cloud top, and the agony was over. The air smoothed. Ahead, a flame-yellow edge along the horizon proclaimed the dawn. The yellow washed upward into the sky, turning saffron-gold and, still higher, transforming to a red glow that darkened until it was black overhead. The scene struck him like a swelling chorus following a dirge.

By God, he'd done it! He'd stayed in there, holding formation in rougher weather than he'd ever imagined. A surge of pride ran through him.

Breathing deeply, he eased away from Stark, then saw Stark's plane pull away from Duke. He wondered if the Sergeant was sighing too?

Chapter 7

The sun crept over the horizon as they shut down their engines. They had parked at a downwind location on the perimeter of Manston's grass field, known as dispersal. From there, they could take off quickly, or scramble, without taxiing. Cub clambered from the cockpit and walked with the other pilots toward a small building, known as a dispersal hut.

It was a brick shack with a corrugated-roof. A dozen director's chairs were strewn on the grass around it, now heavy with morning dew. The outside of the building was drab camouflage, and the metal-framed windows panes were crisscrossed with black tape to curtail flying glass in a bomb blast. A big brass ship's bell, with a woven lanyard trailing from the clapper, hung on a wooden bracket by the main door. Beside it, a sign read: SCRAMBLE - Don't yell . . . Ring the bell.

The floor inside was concrete and the lime green enamel covering the brick interior bore the chips and scars of hard wear. Aircraft recognition posters, aeronautical charts, and faded racy pinups hung above command bulletins. Standing orders hung from clipboards on the walls. Well used chairs were scattered about the room. Playing cards and a chess board lay on tables.

A single telephone perched on a desk. It was the pilots' link to the world and the voice that would send them aloft.

Cub studied a local chart on the wall showing the Isle of Thanet, an area on the eastern tip of Kent terminating in a rounded point called the North Foreland, which jutted into the Channel. Manston was roughly in the center, about four miles from the shore, and around the coast lay the beach towns of Ramsgate, Broadstairs, and Margate.

The tea wagon drew up, manned by older women wearing Women's Auxiliary uniform caps and arm bands. They talked with motherly encouragement to the pilots as they offered cups of tea. The men helped themselves to rolls from a large basket.

Cub took his tea and roll and crossed to an empty spot near Duke. As he sat down, a Sergeant pilot stepped forward and held out his hand. Cub shook it.

"Hello, sir. I'm Burt Stark."

The man had a friendly grip. His squarish face was handsome, and his sandy hair parted in the middle. He grinned broadly, showing widely spaced teeth that seemed too big for the mouth, and his green eyes narrowed when he smiled. He stood slightly taller than Cub and looked seven or eight years older. Being called *sir* by him seemed strange.

"Pleased to see you, Burt. Thanks for the encouraging words. I needed them."

"You did well, sir. That was a bastard of a storm we came through."

Cub liked this man. "Thanks."

They sat on the grass.

Duke leaned toward Cub and said, "Now listen, boy. Keep your finger out up there and remember some things. When you go after bombers, one of their pea-shooters may get you, so don't give them a fixed target. But with a Messerschmitt, it's different. He can do you in quick and easy. At high altitude, you're faster than he is and can climb better. At all altitudes, you turn quicker. But he goes downhill faster than you. So whatever you do, don't try to dive away from him. Stay high and turn hard. Got that, lad?

"Yes, sir."

"Also, our top priority is to conserve pilots, so don't take any big risks. And stay close to our coast, so they can pick you up if you go down. Is that clear?"

Bayer nodded.

"When we take off this time, Burt, you fly my right wing. You take the left, Cub."

They nodded, and Duke resumed drinking his tea.

Cub scanned the sky. Clouds hung on the northern horizon, but to the west a high thin layer made a fine herringbone pattern. Eastward, the brilliant white sun rose toward the deep blue overhead.

The planes were parked on a rise near the downwind end of the main grass runway, and the roundel insignia and tail stripes showed brilliantly against their dull camouflage. People were quiet, struggling against fatigue and the early hour, but around them, bees and butterflies foraged busily, and swallows and house martins wheeled overhead. Blue uniforms and orange Mae Wests against the vast field of grass reminded Cub of springtime lupin and poppies blooming in the California hills. It might have been a picnic.

Cub said, "You reckon Jerry'll come today?"

"You must be joking," Duke said. "It's only a holiday for our side." Then Duke turned away and studied the sky.

Cub wondered if he were worried. Were real fighter pilots scared? Stark had been edgy, so at least some of them did. Cub studied Duke for a clue, but the man was deadpan.

He'll kill again today, Cub thought. It'll be some poor devil who didn't want to fly over England, but wanted to lie on the grass someplace pleasant and sunny like this. Yet they sent him anyway. And . . . poof.

It could happen to me too, he thought. Mom and Dad would get a nice letter from Tweed, or Duke, heaven forbid. It would say: he was a nice young man, we called him Cub, and given time, he might have made a good fighter pilot.

Cub looked around at the others. Some joked, others lay on the grass and mocked sleep. Were they afraid? He had taken a couple of bites from the roll, but his thoughts sapped his appetite. Fighter pilots sure did a lot of waiting.

A man with a bushy mustache and blond hair brushed back over his ears strode across the grass toward them. His carriage was erect, almost haughty. He was a head taller than Cub, and his steel-blue eyes danced as if in search of prey. His stilted posture reminded Cub of a photograph he'd once seen of the Cal rowing crew. The man wore the uniform of a Flight Lieutenant.

"Hello, chaps," the Lieutenant said.

"Hello, Tony," Duke answered with a grin.

"I came to meet the new lad."

Duke waved toward Cub. "This is Bayer."

The man looked at Cub with his head held high and a half grin, half sneer on his face, as if he smelled something distasteful. "I'm Lieutenant Hamilton-Price," he said. "Do you growl?"

"My name's B-A-Y-E-R, sir."

"We call him Cub," Duke said.

Hamilton-Price looked Cub up and down, then nodded. "Beah," he said, losing the final r with emphasis, "Cub Beah, eh? Rather appropriate. I gather you're a revolting colonial."

Cub sensed a challenge. "Pardon?"

"Just an expression. You blokes once fought a skirmish with us. You call it a revolution, I believe."

"That's right. And we won."

Hamilton-Price gave a wry chuckle and nodded. "So you do growl. Well, I suppose we must even make revolutionaries welcome. We need all the help we can get. First day out?"

"Yes, sir."

"Best of British luck. And remember the revolution is over."

"I hadn't forgotten, sir."

Tony turned to Duke. "Take care, friend." Then he clapped Duke on the back and said to Cub, "Stick with him, young man. He'll keep you out of trouble - at least in the air. See you later."

Cub watched him stride off toward dispersal. "What was that all about?"

"The old hands want to check you out," Duke said. "Tony leads Yellow Section and B Flight, and he's the squadron number-two, so you'll see a lot of him."

Too bad, Cub thought.

An orderly leaned out of the dispersal hut and shouted, "Arrow Squadron, alert status! Man your planes!"

Men scrambled to their feet and moved briskly.

As he clambered up the wing, Duke shouted at Cub, "Whatever happens, stick to me like a tick on a dog, lad."

They waited in their cockpits. The sun raised the temperature. Cub pulled at his wool jacket to ventilate it. Butterflies danced in his stomach.

"Arrow Leader, Shakespeare here," crackled over the radio. It was their ground controller. "We have mounting activity over the Pas de Calais. Come to readiness."

Woolly Tweed's voice: "Hello, Shakespeare. Arrow Squadron is ready."

The radio was quiet for several minutes. Cub studied the dampness in the palms of his gloves.

"Arrow Leader, start engines," Shakespeare called.

"Arrow Squadron, start 'em up."

Cub's Merlin backfired before it caught. His butterflies eased.

They idled in position, and radiator temperatures climbed. Sunlight streamed into the cockpit, and Cub leaned his arm and head out to catch the breeze off the propeller.

"Shakespeare, this is Arrow Leader. Engines are getting warm."

"Arrow Leader, stand by."

Cub pushed his goggles up and wiped away the sweat over his eyes. Why the wait?

A minute passed, and the radiator temperature was on the red line. Tweed again: "Shakespeare, our engines are hot. We're running out of time."

"Stand by, Arrow Leader."

Cub looked at Burt Stark, who responded with a wave. Cub raised his hand and mocked wiping his brow. Burt smiled and gave a little shrug.

The second hand on the cockpit clock had gone around twice more, and the temperature climbed above the danger line. Cub wiped his face again. He felt a twinge of nausea.

Tweed: "Shakespeare, we go now, shut down, or burn up. Take your choice."

Another silent minute. Then Tweed shouted: "Shakespeare, make up your bloody minds!"

"Arrow Leader, scramble."

Tweed's plane started to roll, and Cub's stomach illness disappeared. Red and Blue Sections roared down the grass runway side by side, and Yellow and Green followed close behind.

As they lifted off, the radio crackled. "Arrow leader, Shakespeare calling. Bogies, angels one five plus, over Le Touquet north-bound to Dungeness-Folkestone. Intercept heading is two one zero. Buster." Angels meant altitude in thousands of feet and buster, full speed.

They angled left and headed southwest above the hop fields. At full climb rate, it took all Cub's concentration to stay on Duke's wing. Now and then, Cub craned around nervously to check up-sun and at six o'clock.

Climbing through fifteen thousand feet, they crossed the Channel coastline west of Folkestone, and Tweed called: "Arrows, keep a sharp lookout now. Shakespeare, our feet are wet south of Hawkinge." Wet feet meant over the water.

"Tallyho! Ten o'clock, high." It was Tony Hamilton-Price's voice. "Twenty plus Heinkel bombers with as many Messerschmitts on top."

"Dammit, Shakespeare," Tweed said, "these bandits are higher than your fifteen thousand. We're at sixteen and they're still above us."

"Sorry," Shakespeare said. Cub had heard that ground controllers' height data was notorious; their equipment wasn't good enough to get it right.

The Spitfires turned parallel to the enemy and continued to climb.

Tweed called, "We'll attack the bombers before those fighters think we're ready. We'll get one clean pass, then they'll be on us. So make it count. Left turn, go."

Still below the Heinkels, they banked in steeply. Cub kept one eye on the fighters above. Geezus, he thought, are they going to let us get away with this?

But they must have been caught off guard by the Spitfire's quick turn, and now Arrow Squadron closed on the bombers from abeam. The Heinkels swept by in front and slightly above, holding formation as if on parade. Muzzles flashed from the gondolas in the Heinkels' bellies. They were shooting at him!

"Attack go!"

They pulled up into the gray-green beasts. Duke fired, and his bullets poured into a bomber's starboard engine. Burt Stark was shooting too. Cub picked out a target and turned to follow. The sight pipper wandered through the sky and the target was gone. "Steady," he said to himself. "Stop jerking the controls."

The closure rate took him by surprise; he was already on top of them. In desperation, he fired again and watched the tracers stream into emptiness.

The Spitfires entered the German formation, threading the ranks as if dodging cattle in a stampede, and Cub clawed to stay with Duke. Here and there, a bomb load tumbled toward the sea, an engine smoked, and a plane dropped out of formation. But there was no time to count their bag.

"ME's coming in overhead," Duke shouted.

"Right," Tweed called. "Pull up into them."

The Spitfires racked into the sky.

Acceleration drove Cub into the seat. His vision dimmed, and he shook his head. Climbing steeply, he neutralized the stick, and slowly his sight returned.

From nowhere, the Messerschmitts came out of the deep blue, down his throat. In less time than a breath needs, they grew from near-invisible flecks into repulsive beasts with great yellow spinners, ugly square cockpits, and winking guns. One German streamed a fine dust cloud; somebody was getting hits. Cub mashed the gun button, only to watch his tracers sail into the English stratosphere.

Then the Germans flashed by and were gone.

"Arrows," Tweed called, "hit the bombers again."

Duke's and Stark's planes were inverted, arcking through a loop. Desperate to stay with them, Cub pulled on the controls and staggered over the top.

Burt Stark shot a quick glance over his left shoulder and saw that Cub's plane was behind and a little wide in the loop, but Cub hadn't given up. Good for him.

With a series of quick, precise movements, Burt made his Spitfire track the path of Duke's plane as they rolled upright then plunged toward the Heinkels. Their first pass may have knocked out one or two of the bombers, but the rest cruised westward in formation as if nothing had happened.

The British fighters were five hundred yards astern of the enemy when Burt spotted tracers from Cub's plane streaming toward the bombers. Wasted ammo. You had to be in close before you fired. Lieutenant Duke would be unhappy.

Burt scanned the sky overhead. Where were the Messerschmitts? They hadn't given up and gone home, he knew.

Then, he spotted two off his right wing approaching in a turning dive and called, "Blue Two sees a pair of bandits, three o'clock high, a thousand yards. Closing."

"Right, Two," Duke called, "I see them. We'll give these fat ones a quick squirt, then break into them."

Burt forced his attention away from the fighters and onto the bombers. One filled his gun sight and he saw the winking dorsal gun. He pulled a small lead and pressed the firing button.

Cub realized there had been a quick exchange of radio calls between Burt and Duke, but he missed their significance. Burt's tracers converged into a bomber's engine, which began to generate a gray smoke trail, and the hits on Duke's target must have found an oil well. He cursed himself for having fired too soon, but judging distance was hard. Now his own target slipped off to the left and was disappearing under his nose, but the bastard wasn't going to get away.

He pushed forward, rolled left, and lunged on the left rudder pedal. For an instant, the gun sight picture seemed right, and he fired. Again his tracers went wide. He struggled to correct his aim, then released the firing button and hurtled past his target in a dive.

"Blue flight, break right, into those fighters," Duke called.

Right? What fighters? Cub rolled his plane, now pointed downward, until he could see Duke and Burt, far above, turn in formation, like an aerobatic team, to face the yellow-nosed Messerschmitts. To his horror, the two Germans steepened their dives to follow him.

His throttle was wide open, already at the gate, but he pushed at it anyway and lowered the nose to point at the blue sea fifteen thousand feet below. He had to get away. Behind, the Messerschmitts rocketed past the two Spitfires and closed on him. Over his shoulder, he saw their yellow propeller spinners grow. They would open fire at any moment.

Fear enfeebled him like a viscous mass that dragged on every thought and motion.

Was there no escape?

A flash appeared in the center of the lead plane's spinner, the first shot from the Mauser cannon, and Cub hunched himself in front of the armor plate for protection.

"Blue Three, pull out of that dive!"

It was Duke's voice from some distant place, calling somebody, and Cub's brain fought to comprehend it. Suddenly, it dawned that Duke was talking to him. "Pull out, for God's sake!"

He heaved on the stick, and the plane shuddered. Centrifugal force drove him into the seat, and his field of vision collapsed then his sight dissolved altogether into a gray haze that darkened as he continued to hold the control back.

His blindness terrified him, and he centered the stick, easing the pressure. He was still blind, and he swore never again to intentionally black out. Had the bastard followed him? Was he about to blow Cub's Spitfire out of the sky?

Slowly, his vision cleared, and he groped with his eyes, desperate to get his bearings. He was climbing vertically. Where was the goddammed Messerschmitt?

"Blue Three," came Duke's urgent voice, "that Jerry's on your belly side. Roll into him!"

Cub half-rolled and behind, over his head, saw the German. For an instant, the two planes climbed parallel to each other, cockpit to cockpit, two hundred yards apart, with the Messerschmitt astern and pulling hard to bring his guns to bear.

Duke's voice boomed: "Turn into the attack!"

Against all instincts, Cub hauled on the stick. His path carried him directly across the track of the enemy fighter, and for an instant, he found himself looking down Mauser gun barrels, not fifty yards away. Through the German's windscreen, he saw the pilot clearly - a man from another planet, helmet shiny like reptile skin, owl-eyed goggles, and a dark oxygen mask for a face - a man sent to kill him.

The German snapped off a shot as the Spitfire crossed in front, but Cub's quick move must have surprised him and the rounds passed harmlessly astern. Pulling over the top of the loop, Cub looked back to see the German following, and he hauled the nose down.

"Dammit, boy," Duke shouted, "don't dive away from that bugger."

In a heady rush, Cub realized he's already violated Duke's warning once. Instantly, he rolled wings vertical and turned left, pulling hard, on the edge of blackout.

Three hundred yards astern, the Messerschmitt rolled too. But being well behind, the German could track him with an easier turn, and Cub found himself looking over his shoulder down gun barrels again. The other plane tightened its turn to get the right deflection.

It became clear to Cub that the head-on image of the Messerschmitt, with its yellow nose and exposed white underbelly, might be the last thing he'd ever see. In the moment, it was a feeling of wonder rather than terror.

Time slowed and the scene became surreal, like a dream in which images swim as if seen through imperfect glass and the sluggish sequence of events follows no logic: On the side of the Messerschmitt, a plant sprouts, small at first, with willowy petals of bright yellow and scarlet that bend and twist in the wind, then spread and reach out to cast dark pollen into the breeze. Now the petals stand out around the yellow nose forming a sunflower, and through their brilliance Cub sees the shiny black head of a man with huge round eyes: the hooded image of death itself. Cub gapes in terror.

He blinked. The surreal evaporated. The Messerschmitt was on fire. It rolled onto its back, pulled down, and disappeared beneath him, trailing smoke.

From behind it, a Spitfire rocketed in, guns blazing, firing beneath Cub's plane. He rolled to see the German, below him now, enveloped in flames, pursued by the Spitfire, which snapped out repeated short bursts as the two arced downward.

Cub rolled wings level and gazed about, stupified. The sky seemed empty. He eased the throttle and held a gentle turn toward the English coast. As he began to breathe again, he started to pray silently.

Through the fear-mist in his head, he spotted another Spitfire climbing from behind. It pulled close alongside, and he saw it was Burt Stark. Burt signaled downward and behind, where a dark trail of distant smoke curved downward, growing ever steeper until it entered the sea vertically. Nearer, a Spitfire climbed toward them. They circled back and watched it approach.

It was Peter Duke. Cub owed him his life.

Duke joined up and called, "How's your ammo, Blue Two?"

"I'm out," Burt replied. "Good shooting, sir."

"Thanks, and lets beetle for it."

They turned toward Manston and reduced power to cruise. Duke led, weaving in shallow turns. It was still a combat area, and fighting against the fatigue that suddenly enveloped him, Cub kept his eyes moving.

They paralleled the coast less than a mile offshore. The cobalt sky stretched from horizon to horizon unblemished by cloud, and on their right, the sun's reflection dazzled from the sea in a shimmering path that stretched to the east and France. On their left, Kent lay slowly waking in the morning sun, the patchwork of fields looking like squares from a painter's palette - gold, emerald, sienna, chalk white, and the deep English green of copses and boundary hedges. Oast houses, where they dried the hops, dotted the countryside; the tops to their peaked roofs perched like white dunce caps. The scene was unbelievably tranquil, and it struck Cub that he had come within a hair of being a very tranquil part of it. He was shaking.

By twenty minutes to seven they were on the ground at Manston. As Cub cut the switches, the fuel bowser pulled alongside and hose handlers hustled to refuel his aircraft. Armorers scrambled under the wing to get at the ammunition trays.

Cub clambered down from the plane and staggered toward the dispersal hut. The owl-eyed image of death displaced other thoughts from his mind. He weaved as he walked, but he couldn't help it. Nausea tugged at him, and his legs began to collapse; he dropped his helmet and oxygen mask, and flopped onto the ground. The loamy smell of the sun-warmed grass nearly intoxicated him. His throat tightened; it was hard to breathe. Tears welled and ran down his cheeks onto the blades of green and down them into the soil below. He sobbed gently.

Slowly, his brain cleared, and images from the real world began to penetrate his senses. The sun felt warm. He raised his head and looked around to shake off his emotion. Birds warbled as they darted overhead, and butterflies danced around the uncut grass along the edges of the field. Excited laughter came from somewhere.

He felt a hand on the shoulder and turned to face Peter Duke, who squatted beside him. The man's eyes were steady, not angry, just cold. Like death.

"I suppose you know you nearly went for a burton up there?"

Cub nodded.

"What were you thinking of?"

"I don't know. It all happened so fast."

"You didn't remember a thing I told you, did you?"

Cub shook his head slowly. "Guess not. But I tried."

"You fired out of range. Didn't pay attention to the radio. You left me, and dove away from a Messerschmitt. And you didn't turn into the attack. You call that trying?

"I'm sorry, sir."

Duke glowered at him for a long silent moment. "You're a very lucky lad. Most people get only one chance to forget."

Chapter 8

Before sunset that day, Arrow Squadron scrambled four more times from Manston. Though he got several opportunities to break off and chase the enemy, Cub concentrated on staying close to Duke.

On the way back to Hornchurch in the evening, they were jumped by a lone Messerschmitt. One Spitfire was hit and had to limp home. From the radio chatter, Cub learned it was a man named Dennis Bolt.

Shortly afterward, they wheeled above Hornchurch Station in twilight and broke into landing sequence. The flare path was lighted to mark the landing direction, and the planes put down beside it. Some touched smoothly; others bounced like stones skipped on water, then rocked awkwardly from side to side before settling. Like those, Cub had trouble with his landing.

He taxied across the grass to the flight line and shut down the engine. The propeller clattered to a stop, and two erks jumped onto the wings to help him.

"Glad to see you back, sir," said the one who had sent him off that morning. "I don't see any holes in her. Looks pretty clean."

"Yeah, but it was a bloody near thing."

"Always is, sir."

Never that close again, he hoped.

He clambered out of the cockpit and dropped to the ground, then peeled off his helmet and gloves as he shuffled down the line of aircraft toward the briefing room.

From a distance, the fighters looked elegant and clean. But close up, the picture changed. Protective tape covering the gun ports was blown away and gun smoke streaked the wings. Dark traces of engine exhaust streamed along the fuselage. Rivulets of oil and hydraulic fluid ran down gleaming white bellies from seams in the engine cowlings. Paint around wing roots and cockpits was nicked by clambering feet. Some planes were holed in patterns like jagged lace and one had a piece blown away large enough for a man to put his head through.

A bell-ringing ambulance wheeled around the hangar, raced across the tarmac, and pulled alongside a plane ahead of him. People on the wing lifted a body from the cockpit. Accompanied by curt whispers and urgent gestures, they maneuvered it down. As they laid the man on a stretcher, Cub heard a sharp outcry. They carried the man to the van and closed the doors. Cub gaped at the vehicle as it disappeared the way it had come.

He walked again and watched pilots drop stiffly to the ground. They rolled their shoulders and peeled off equipment. Some collapsed on the grass, others slogged toward the hangar.

"Christ, I've had enough of that for one day," a voice said.

"How about a bloody lifetime?"

Cub saw Parsons waiting for Tweed, who landed last. The Skipper jumped off the wing and stepped more lively than the rest. But even in the half-light his face looked drawn.

"Only nine returned, sir?" Parsons asked.

Tweed nodded. "One's down mechanically at Manston. Should be ready by morning. Reid and Hardcastle are missing. Reid got out okay. Don't know about Hardcastle."

"Reid called in, sir, and should be here soon."

"That's something," Tweed said, rubbing his face. "How's Bolt?"

"Couldn't tell, sir. He was in pain. They took him straight to the station hospital."

The Skipper blew a deep sigh and they walked to the briefing room. Cub followed.

"Sounds like a rough day," Parsons said.

"Nothing unusual," Tweed replied. "Eight hours in the air, five scrambles, and four heavy engagements since three forty-five this morning. I only hope we can keep this up. The lads have nearly had it."

"How did we score?"

"Don't know." He waved toward the briefing room. "We'll find out in there."

Before entering the door, Tweed turned to the motionless ones on the grass. "Get a move on now, lads. Let's get this over with so we can get some sleep."

"How about a pint at The Scow, instead?" one announced, as he jumped to his feet.

"Or The Cricket Club," shouted another. "That crumpet with the big ones will be there looking for you again, Johnny."

"She's all yours, but I'll take the pint."

The Skipper rolled his eyes. "Ah, youth."

Cub took a seat at the back of the briefing room, and as he sat down, realized how tired he was. The others had been doing this for a month. How did they hold up?

He looked at the room. In the center, desk chairs were neatly arranged, theater fashion. Others were stowed upside down on the debriefing tables at the back. The men came in and pulled chairs from tables to sit on.

Aeronautical charts hung along the walls. Their colors showed terrain altitudes, ranging from deep blue in the ocean depths, through lighter shades of blue and green in most areas, to daubs of yellows and browns in high hills. One wall depicted all of southern England and the Midlands; another, the coast of Europe from the north of Brittany to the Elbe estuary. The charts showed towns and villages, roads and railways, ruling altitudes of the surrounding countryside, and compass variations. For England, they also gave locations and altitudes of RAF stations as well as their radio frequencies and Morse code beacon identifiers.

A Teletype machine in one corner of the room occasionally clattered away on its own. Next to it, hung sheets of yellow Teletype paper giving weather reports from other stations in the British Isles. Local area forecasts and barometric altimeter settings were chalked on a board. Nearby, another board showed the status of every pilot and the condition of each plane. In one corner, stood a large brass urn, and alongside sat a neat array of white mugs inverted on a tray.

More fliers filed in. Oxygen masks had pressed welts into their faces and their hair lay in matted tangles. Their eyes blinked slowly, and they worked at breathing. Most lit cigarettes, and smoke began to waft through the light of the hooded lamps that hung over the tables. Crisp uniform creases had evaporated in body heat, and the cloth sagged. The air became laced with the fetor of tobacco smoke and stale sweat.

The pilots gathered around the tables. Intelligence staff, known as spies, interviewed each, probing for information about enemy disposition, tactics, and damage. A half-dozen such conversations went on in the room at once. The aviators struggled to answer accurately, but now and then, tempers got the better of patience, and they erupted in curses.

In Cub's interview, he confirmed the sheet of flame that enveloped the Messerschmitt after it attacked him and the smoke trail into the sea, so Duke got credit for a kill.

Parsons answered the phone. He listened, then spoke in clipped tones, hung up, and turned to Tweed. "They picked Hardcastle out of the Channel. He's alive, but badly burned and not pretty. They took him to hospital."

The skipper winced.

"And unfortunately, sir, Bolt died in the ambulance."

"Bloody hell."

The spies made their estimates, and Parsons called the group to order. "Initial tally looks like four kills and three probables."

Pilots interrupted with groans; they imagined that everyone had gotten one or two apiece.

"We'll know more after we cross-check this," Parsons added.

The skipper took the floor, and the audience quieted. "Gents, even this would be a pretty good score if we hadn't lost three of ours. Two men are alive but they're bloody fortunate.

"And it was unnecessary. How often must I tell you to keep our formation discipline? Reid and Hardcastle broke off and hung around in that thicket of Messerschmitts after their first pass. No doubt they hoped for a second shot. Well they got it. Right up the arse. And others who stayed with them are bloody lucky. We cannot afford those mistakes."

He let it sink in.

"You'll be as sad as I am to know that Bolt didn't make it," he continued. "We were late spotting the Messerschmitt that jumped us on the last hop. And now we pay the price. I know we're tired, but so is Jerry. Questions? Comments?"

There was an uneasy silence.

Parsons handed Tweed a note. He glanced at it and said, "Takeoff will be at three forty-five again in the morning. We're back to Manston for the day."

Soft groans arose.

"Anything else? All right, stand down."

Weary bodies unlimbered and, slinging items of flight kit on their shoulders, shuffled out the door. Cub sagged with exhaustion as got to his feet. Then he heard Parsons's voice from across the room, "Mister Bayer."

Cub turned and walked over to him, where he stood with a young pilot officer in a crisp uniform.

"Hello, Cub," Parsons said. "How did you do today?"

"I managed to come out of it walking, sir."

Parsons frowned for a moment, then he said, "Let me introduce your new roommate, Ian Craigwell."

Ian's lanky frame stretched up over six feet to the wild shock of red hair at the top. Green eyes, danced under a Neanderthal brow, and his grin revealed teeth that seemed too many and too large for his mouth. He wasn't exactly handsome, but he was impressive. He wrapped his long-fingered palm around Cub's hand and said forcefully, "Pleased to meet you, Yank." The words came out in a slight Scottish brogue.

They chatted for a few minutes, then Cub led Craigwell across the room and out the door.

Outside, Duke was waiting for him. "Come to my room, lad. We need a private discussion."

Cub turned to Craigwell. "See you later."

*

Duke kicked the door shut and threw his gear on the bed. "After that fiasco this morning, you at least did one thing right. You managed to stay with me. God knows how."

"Tried my best, sir."

"Your bloody best is going to have to get one hell of a lot better. How in the world did you miss seeing the ME that got Bolt? That bastard came in out of your search sector."

"I . . . wasn't looking back there just then. Too busy trying to keep up."

"Keep up, my arse. You were trying to fly pretty formation. I told you to forget that. You haven't got time for it up there. Stay far enough away so you don't have to worry about colliding with me. You've got to know where I am by instinct and to keep that little round head of yours swivelling."

"But you said the skipper wanted us to stay together."

"Skipper be damned. You're in my section. You follow my rules. When we're not in the combat area, you can get in close and look pretty."

"Yes, sir."

"And you didn't hit a sodding thing today either, did you, lad?"

"I'm not sure. I tried."

"Balls. You hosed those guns the way my mother sprays her flowers."

"I couldn't line up anything."

"Remember our talk about deflection shooting and leading the ducks?"

"Yes, sir."

"Yet again today, you didn't lead any targets."

"My mind went blank going against those big formations."

"You've got to pick out one target and focus on it like it was the only thing in the sky. Both hands on the stick. Get in close. Get the lead right. Then shoot. You'll never hit a thing unless you focus and your aim is dead on. And even then you'll miss."

"I couldn't do it. No time."

"Jerry never gives you time. And I can't slow it down for you."

Cub shook his head in frustration. "I'll try, sir. But how do you cope with those head-on attacks? They're too fast to blink. I had no time to aim."

"Head to head, aiming is simple. No deflection. Just draw a bead in his middle and drill him."

"I . . . don't know if I can ever be that quick, sir"

"You'd better if you want to pull your weight in this outfit. We usually claw for altitude just to meet Jerry, and the only way to get at him is from the front. Head on."

"Yes, sir."

"Think about it. Especially what you did wrong. You get another try in the morning."

Duke dismissed him.

Cub started for the door and his eye was drawn to the girls' photographs. They were beautiful.

Then he had a sudden thought; he stopped and turned to Duke. "Thanks for saving my ass today."

Duke eyed him skeptically. "You're bloody lucky I was around to do it."

*

Though he wasn't there when Cub returned, Ian Craigwell had moved into their room. Cub dropped his gear on the floor, and sagged onto his bed. He wanted to sleep, but he struggled to relive the critical moments of the day. Why hadn't he pulled the right lead on that Heinkel? He knew the pipper was high and inside. Where was his brain? Why had he bothered to shoot? Use rudder, Duke had said, and a small push there would have done it. And a little control movement would have lined up that one-oh-nine coming head on. He could do it if only he reacted quicker . . . if only he had more time . . . time . . . time.

Then he fell asleep.

Chapter 9

Cub sat next to Ian at the bar in The Gannet and eyed his watch. "I was out of my mind to let you drag me down here."

"Oh come on," Ian said. "You had a nice nap. Forty minutes' sleep should be enough to last you the whole bloody night. The flower of American youth can't fade on us this early."

"After today, the hell I can't."

Ian shrugged. "You got out of it alive. That calls for celebration." He tossed off the remainder of his beer. "Come on, pal, drink up, and we'll have another. This place closes shortly."

Cub shook his head and grinned. "Bloody slave driver." He drank his down, and they ordered another.

Cub was stifling a yawn when he spotted Burt Stark across the room. "Hey, there's Burt, the NCO I told you about. Come on and meet him." They went over, and Cub introduced Ian.

Burt eyed Cub quizzically. "I saw Lieutenant Duke laying for you after debriefing. How did it go?"

"He tore off a strip. I know the bastard saved my ass, but why does he have to take it out on my hide?"

Burt winked. "There's not much shakedown time for you new blokes. He's probably doing you a favor."

Cub snickered. "He sure left welts. Tell me, Burt, did he really have all those good looking girl friends?"

Burt smiled mischievously. "Far as I know. He's said to be quite the ladies' man."

Cub shook his head in wonder.

Ian spotted two friends from his OTU who had also joined the Arrows that day, and he waved them over. Dickie Hudson was stocky with a ruddy round freckled face, reddish hair, and shocking-blue eyes. He'd gone to Exeter University, but left early to join the RAF. Reggie Wells was lean and almost as tall as Ian, with dark wavy hair and strong, handsome features. He smiled frequently. Like Ian, he trained at London University's Air Squadron.

Burt turned to Ian. "Who's your flight leader?"

"Lieutenant Hamilton-Price," Ian said. "Dickie's, too."

Reggie said, "I'm with the skipper."

"They aren't so easy either," Burt said.

Cub said, "What a madhouse that was out there today. Is it always that busy?"

"Since the first of the month," Burt said. "End of May and early June, we covered Dunkirk. That was worse."

"After one day, I'm pooped," Cub said. "How do you guys stand it?"

Burt winked and hoisted his mug. "It's the beer."

They laughed.

"Burt, how long you been in the RAF?" Cub asked.

"Eleven years. Started as an Airman rigger. Got into flight training five years ago. Joined Arrow Squadron right afterward."

Dickie said, "How is it being an NCO flying alongside officers?"

Burt shrugged. "It's all right. After all, I grew up on a farm in Hampshire and might still be there. Never thought of going to University. The Air Force has been good to me. Taught me a trade. Gave me a chance to fly. Allowed me to raise a family."

"You live around here?"

"I'm in the NCO mess. Sent the kids and wife off to her family's farm near Keswick."

"Beautiful country there, " Ian said.

Burt nodded. "But far away."

"You must miss them?" Cub said.

"Yes, but they're safer there. Jerry may bomb here any time."

"You think they'll hit London?" Reggie asked.

Burt said, "I don't know how we'd stop them. Neither do the Londoners. Look at this crowd. Quieter than they were a year ago. Most of their kids have gone to stay in the country. They're worried."

Cub eyed the civilian clientele. There was nothing happy-go-lucky about them. Some of that, he knew, was British reserve, but he saw fatigue in a lot of the eyes.

Ian said, "My father sent my mother and sister down to our place near Bath to live. Mother doesn't like being away, but father insists. He works in the City, same as usual, and won't leave."

"It'll take more than German bombs to drive these people out, too," Burt said. "They're your basic British - simple, honest, and stubborn as a stone dog. Tired now, perhaps, but determined."

Dickie said, "Think the Germans can land here?"

"Not while the RAF's around," Burt said.

Parsons's numbers went through Cub's mind, and he observed Burt carefully for any expression.

"You really think we can stop them?" Dickie asked.

"Either that or we'll all die trying."

For a moment, Cub took it as a figure of speech, but Burt's direct gaze and plucky smirk said it was no bluster. And Burt plainly assumed that the others had put their lives on the line too. Cub thought, Is that what I signed up for? But one thing for sure, he didn't want to let Burt down.

"I was afraid of that," Dickie said.

Cub asked, "Burt, how good is the Luftwaffe?"

"Jerry's got his tactics right. Makes all the right moves, elegantly."

Reggie said, "And they drubbed the RAF over France."

"But we learned a lot," Burt said. "This isn't France, and we've no place else to go. Jerry's never come across someone who'll really stand and face him. And when it comes to courage, nobody beats the British. We'll give him a fight he never expected."

Cub thought it sounded ominous, yet he hoped Burt was right and nodded along with the rest.

Burt drained the last of his beer and stood up. "I'm going to get some sleep," he said.

Reggie and Dickie left with him.

Cub watched them go then turned to Ian. "I only met Burt this morning. Sure like having him around. Seems so steady and reliable."

Ian nodded. "He's that basic British he talked about - the journeymen, the pikers, the yeomen - salt of the British earth. They defended this island for a thousand years and then built the Empire. They're courageous, dedicated, and smart. And given reasonable leadership, they'll follow anywhere. They demand only respect."

"And he has such an easy way of telling you what's what. Why can't bloody Duke be like that?"

Ian eyed Cub skeptically. "You've got the knife out for this bloke, Duke, haven't you?"

"Hell, I almost got myself killed today and nearly died of fright in the process. Encouragement and guidance would have helped. Instead I got a ration."

Ian looked down his nose at Cub. "You know what I think? I think you let this Duke humiliate you."

"Baloney. The bastard will just never be satisfied."

The two men eyed the room in silence. People hunched over tables and talked quietly, and here and there, couples huddled together. At the far end of the room two soldiers and two airmen worked intently at a game of darts. Tobacco smoke made the room hazy.

Finally Ian turned to Cub. "So what brings an American all the way to 'jolly old' to join the bloody RAF?"

Under the circumstances, Cub thought, that's a damned good question. "I came to fly."

"Surely you can fly in America?"

"Not Spitfires."

"Rubbish! You didn't come all the way over here and get tangled up in this mess just to fly some airplane."

Cub gazed at his glass and idly fingered it. "You're right." He looked Ian in the eye. "I came to get the hell away from home."

"No fooling?"

"Afraid not. I get along with my mother okay, but not Dad. My brother, Brad, is his favorite, and he always let me know it. I could never satisfy the man. I finally grew tired of it and got the hell out."

"Brad's older than you?"

"Yeah, and he has it all. I'm a fair athlete. He's outstanding. In school, he got top honors. Studying bored me, and I barely managed to make passing grades. And he always had the good looking girls. He's a boy wonder, and Dad would never let up about it.

"In high school, I got really interested in airplanes and worked at the local airport to earn flying time and lessons. Dad thought I should stick to my studies like Brad did. He kept after me about it from then on, but I wasn't going to give up flying. It was a waste of time, he'd say. That is, until Brad graduated from college and went to Navy Flight School. Wonder Boy was aiming to outdo me again, and Dad's tune changed. 'When are you ever going to be a real pilot like Brad?' he began to ask. That's when I decided I'd finally had it.

"I found an ad for the RAF in Flying magazine. I knew war in Europe was coming, and I said to myself: I'm going over where real fighter pilots are really going to fight. The RAF accepted me, and here I am."

"So," Ian said, "you came here to prove something to yourself, eh?"

Cub shook his head. "I'm as good as Brad. But maybe this way I can prove it to Dad."

"Your Dad sounds like your friend Duke. Never satisfied."

What an interesting idea! Cub thought. Over the years, with advice from his sympathetic mother, Cub had learned to tolerate his father's carping, learned how to avoid letting it get him down. It was a matter of listening respectfully, ignoring the venom, then pretending it never happened. Most of the time, it worked. Maybe it would work with Duke. Yet, Duke was a different challenge, because Cub wanted to learn from the man.

Well, he thought, I can do that too. I'll study old Duke. No matter what kind of a ration he hands out, I'll learn the man's every move, every trick, every nuance. Some day I'll be as good as he is. And some day he'll say so. But I'm not doing this just to please him, by God. This may be the key to my survival.

And that thought made him happy. "You may be right," he said. "And thanks."

"For what?"

Cub shrugged. "Something just fell into place."

Ian rolled his eyes in confusion, then gazed toward the dart game.

After a moment, he turned back to Cub. "You said you knew war was coming to Europe. As far as I can see, most Americans pretend nothing's going on over here. How did you figure it?"

"I have some distant relatives in Germany. I visited there for a month in nineteen thirty-eight. That convinced me."

"What happened?"

"Mostly I had a good time," Cub said. "But a couple of incidents drove the message home to me that we were going to war."

"No kidding? Tell me."

"The first happened one night when we went to an old beer hall outside Bremerhaven, where I stayed." And Cub related his story.

*

From the outside the place looked like any building on the back streets of the old city. But inside, polished wood floors, wood-paneled walls, and high wooden ceilings supported by massive timbers enclosed a huge single room. Indirect lighting augmented flaming torch baskets around the room. A matrix of massive gray rocks formed the wall and fireplace at one end of the room. The fireplace opening, where logs blazed, was big enough to stand in. A small band played lively German music, and a bar served beer in liter steins. Tables took up most of the floor. Cheerful, relaxed people thronged around and danced. The place echoed with laughter and music, and smelled of burning pine and fresh beer.

Cub's group picked their way to empty seats where a waitress served them. Cub was struggling to keep up with his friends' rapid-fire German, when a stunning woman with flashing dark eyes, and black hair approached. She wore an expensive dress that matched her hair. Gliding through the crowd, she went to the empty table next to Cub's.

Cub nudged the man next him and canted his head toward the girl. Conversation stopped.

Her escort was a slight man with equally dark hair and eyes. As he seated her, she turned briefly and gave Cub a faint smile. He was still looking at her, spellbound, when the man next to him prodded his ribs. The man screwed up his face like he smelled a bad odor and silently mouthed the word *Jew*.

Cub sat stunned. The best looking girl he'd seen in Germany was unattractive because she was a Jew? So this is what it had come to in that country.

He was wrong; it came to worse.

The proprietor arrived and spoke to the couple. Cub overheard only snatches of their conversation, but the man asked the couple to leave. Her escort protested. The proprietor was sorry, but local ordinances and all that.

Then a Nazi Brownshirt, in a uniform like a Boy Scout's, strode over and stood between Cub and the seated couple. He grabbed the escort by the arm and hauled him onto his feet.

Cub gut tightened, and he twisted his napkin as if he were wringing water out of it.

"Out. Now," the Brownshirt said. Then he hauled her to her feet, and she cried out.

Cub wasn't sure what came over him, but he was suddenly standing. His friend tried to stop him, but he shook him off and caught the Brownshirt by the biceps, squeezing hard. "Let her go," he said in German.

The Brownshirt spun to face him and jerked his arm from Cub's grip. His face was livid. "You, out too," he shouted.

"Fuck you," Cub said.

From behind, his friend shouted in English, "Bayer, have you lost your mind!"

The Brownshirt snorted angrily and signaled to a half-dozen others at the far end of the room, whom Cub hadn't seen. They came on the run, and the man turned back to face him.

Cub saw the Brownshirt's punch coming and ducked. The swing carried the man forward. Cub hit him in the solar plexus, and the man doubled over. Cub swung again, this time with his elbow, and the blow landed on man's nose. Cub felt it crumple. That was the last thing he remembered before something hit him from behind, and everything went blank.

When he came to, he was outside on the street in the dark, suspended between two Brownshirts, who held his arms tightly. There were much talk and commotion around. Someone held a flashlight. Apparently they were looking at his passport.

He shifted his weight and raised his head to see better, the two men tightened their grip, and he passed out again.

A few minutes later, he came to, safely wrapped in a blanket on the back seat of his friend's car, heading to the friend's home.

His friend, driving the car, looked back and said, "You are one lucky Yankee."

It was a week and a half before the bruises were gone.

Then, one day toward the end of Cub's stay in Germany, a big military review was held in Bremen. Hitler himself was to review the troops and make a speech, and Cub drove up to Bremen with a group to see it.

The ceremony took place in the Sports Platz on the edge of the city. Proceedings began with an endless parade of marching soldiers, then came motor cycles, trucks, tanks, artillery pieces - row upon row of them. Airplanes, by the hundred, flew over in neat formations - Messerschmitts, Heinkels, and Dorniers. Finally, some fifty Junkers came over and dropped paratroops. The numbers of people and vehicles and the precision with which they moved boggled Cub's mind.

Then, over a thousand uniformed men goose-stepped in and drew up in front of the reviewing stand. They stood at attention in close formation, blanketing the plaza. Brownshirts, in their Boy-Scout uniforms, were front and center. Looking at them sent a chill through Cub.

Hitler stepped to the podium and spoke of German successes under the Nazis. People had jobs. They had recovered their heritage in Sudetenland and restored their rightful authority in Rhineland. Now the time had come for Germany to gain the elbow room she needed. Living room, he called it. War was not necessary, he offered cautiously, but whatever it took, those assembled there were the means to success.

Then, a clear, sharp voice came from the plaza: "Seig heil!" And a thousand voices responded in unison: "Seig heil!" Again: "Seig heil!" And they repeated it over and over and over again.

*

Cub pulled a sip from his beer and looked at Ian. "The roar of voices from that plaza swept over me like the hot breath of a monster. And I knew then and there that war was coming. Nothing would stop those bastards but defeat."

Ian gazed at him round-eyed. "Geezus," he said. "They sound like such nice, friendly chaps. How'd you get away from them at the beer hall?"

"My friend explained that I was an American visitor with proper passport and visa. That I didn't understand German rules. That I had nothing to do with the two at the other table. And it would cause an international incident if they took me in. Fortunately, he convinced them."

"You were lucky."

Cub took a drink from his beer and nodded. "The couple disappeared. We never learned what happened. Prison probably. Maybe dead."

Ian shook his head in disgust.

The publican called for last orders. Cub looked at Ian's nearly empty beer glass. "Have another?"

Ian eyed his watch. "Reveille's in four hours. It'll seem like a bad idea then."

"What was it you said about forty minutes sleep being enough?"

"For Christ's sake, you're the one who bitched at me about dragging you down here. Drink up and let's get the hell out of here."

Cub chuckled and drained his glass.

He stood up and looked slowly around the room, and suddenly halted. The girl he'd seen with Duke sat at a table in the back with several fliers he didn't know. For a moment, their eyes connected, and she smiled weakly. Her look seemed an invitation. Then she turned away and talked to one of the men she sat with.

She was older than most of the girls he knew back home. He noted the exquisite curve of her bosom. Her glance darted his way again, she caught his eye, and time and place slipped away. He was sure he blushed. Then she returned to her discussion, and the spell was broken.

"We should get on our horse," Ian said.

"Yeah," Cub said, indicating her direction, "but have a look at that before you go."

Ian followed his eye and shrugged.

"She's really pretty," Cub said.

"Pretty big boobs, you mean."

"And a nice face."

"Christ, lets bail out of here. I can see I have to get you up to London soon, before you lose all perspective."

Ian led the way to the door, and Cub followed reluctantly. There, he turned and looked back at her. She was occupied in conversation. She might not be devastating, but what a figure!

"Come on, Pal," Ian said, "get the stars out of your eyes. We go to war in a few hours."

Chapter 10

Cub dug his heels into Manston's soft grass, leaned the director's chair back on two legs, and squinted toward the morning sun. "Ian, you lush, why did you have to wake me up last night and drag me off to that pub? I was sleeping like a baby."

Ian eyed a well thumbed, month-old copy of the London Illustrated News. Without looking up, he said, "Just so I could hear you scream in protest while I force-fed you the beer."

"And you kept me up too dammed late."

"How else could you fall in love with that popsie."

"A bit of all right, wasn't she?"

"Bit of a tart, if you ask me."

"Piss off. She was a looker."

"More like, looked well built."

"Come on, for all you know, she's a nice, sweet girl."

"Nice and sweet in bed, no doubt. Romeo, sweet girls don't hang out in pubs with a pie-eyed bunch of rutting RAF animals."

"Those are your brethren in arms."

"Which changes precisely nothing."

"Geezus, such loyalty! Still, she's attractive."

Ian pulled a sour face. "Stick with me."

"I'm stuck with you, all right. What difference will that make?"

Ian looked up from his magazine. "I'll tell you what. A friend of mine's been bragging about the big do his Air Ministry unit is throwing at the Savoy tonight. Let's crash it."

The telephone in the dispersal hut gave a soft click then rang. Conversation stopped, and there was a long moment of silence.

"Arrow Squadron scramble!"

*

South of Sandwich, the Arrows banked gently toward the Channel as they climbed through ten thousand feet. The sun was high to their left, and ahead the blue sea stretched away across the Straights of Dover toward where France was hidden in the coastal mists.

"Arrow Leader, Shakespeare here. We have many plots converging on Dover from the east. Come left to one-five-zero."

Cub struggled to hold his position on Duke. Occasionally he scanned the sky behind and strained into the sun. Where the hell were the Germans?

They crossed the coastline and Tweed called, "Feet are wet over Deal, Shakespeare. Where are the bastards?"

"Large plots are eight miles ahead --."

"Tally ho!" someone shouted. "Eleven o'clock high."

"And eleven o'clock low," came another voice.

Cub spotted the high formation, to the right of the sun, and the low group, tracking the edge of the shimmering swath of reflected sunlight on the sea.

Tweed led the squadron in a right turn to bring them across the path of the oncoming Germans. "Right, Shakespeare," he called. "We have Heinkels at five miles, very high and Stuka dive bombers below and closer. They're headed for Dover. We'll never reach the Heinkels before they get to the target. We'll go after the Stukas. Anybody see fighters?"

There was a brief silence.

"All right," Tweed continued, "Sections, line astern. Attack, go."

Tweed's Red Section peeled off toward the dive bombers, and Yellow and Green Sections followed.

Blue, the last in line, was about to join them when Burt Stark called over the radio, "Blue Two sees Messerschmitts overhead, diving on us. Look out everyone!"

Tweed's voice: "Arrows, press on the bombers. Break off only if you come under fire."

Duke must have decided the threat was direct enough. "Blue Section, follow me," he called. And he pulled up steeply.

Cub pushed the throttle the last half inch to the gate and, hauling back on the stick as hard as he dared, followed Duke into a vertical climb. He found himself gazing at yellow-nosed Messerschmitts again.

"Arrow squadron," Duke called. "Fingers out. You're under attack from above."

The Messerschmitts were coming right down Cub's throat. No deflection, he remembered. He maneuvered the pipper toward a yellow nose and struggled to hold it steady, but it crossed and recrossed the target in jerky motions. Each time it was on, he gave the gun button a quick push and cursed his incompetence.

Smoke streamed from the Messerschmitt beside the one he aimed at. Duke was shooting the hell out of it. Why couldn't he do that?

His target grew from a yellow spot with wings into full-fledged, oil-streaked airplane. Though now and then his tracers seemed to home on it and occasionally he saw an impact flash, he couldn't get the sight picture to settle down. Furious, he swore not to break off. He'd ram the bastard if necessary.

For an instant, the other pilot's head, with the big owl-eyed goggles, peered at him through the windshield. Then the Messerschmitt pulled up and rocketed overhead. The roar of the Daimler Benz startled him, and the Spitfire shook, as the enemy fighters passed close by.

The radio came alive as they got into the Spitfires below:

"Green Section, break. They're on us."

"Red Section, press on into the Stukas."

"Yellow Section, continue to attack the bombers."

"Yellows, they're on you too."

"Yellow Section break right."

"Green Two, there's an ME on your tail. Break."

"Green Three, get the bastard off me."

"Right, Green Two, break left. I'll get him."

"Yellow One, break left. Jerry's coming at you."

"Yellow Three, nail him."

"Green Two, break for Christ's sake, Johnny."

"Green Three, where are you? He's shooting me."

"Sorry, Johnny. I've got my own problems."

"Good show, Yellow Three. He's burning."

"Green Two's had it."

"Close up, Green Three."

Duke brought Blue Section to level flight, and Cub looked below at Messerschmitts and Spitfires whirling in space, like swarming bees. Plumes of oily smoke rose from the sea. On his right, columns of Heinkel bombers filed in over Dover harbor.

"Arrow Squadron," Duke called, "many Messerschmitts coming from above. Fingers out!"

Cub looked up to see more German fighters peeling off toward him. As they trimmed into their dives, it was clear that the first flight would bypass Blue Section and go directly for the Spitfires below.

"Blue Section," Duke called, "give the leaders a squirt, then pull up into the rest."

They had no time to track the targets that rocketed down in front of them; they simply fired a stream of bullets across their path, hoping to frighten them off.

Cub couldn't see results, for Duke then led them into another steep climb to face the enemy that followed. Again Cub fired ineffective bursts, and again he cursed himself. As the last Messerschmitt flashed by, he pushed over into level flight. His plane was stalling, and getting it under control took his attention for a moment. When he looked around, he was alone. Where was Duke?

On one side, two Spitfires streaked down toward the swarm below; on the other, two more arced away. Further down, machines wheeled and turned in all directions. He'd lost Duke, and finding him was hopeless.

How to get back into the fight? Jumping into the melee of fighters below seemed folly. Ahead on his right, he saw the flashes and shock waves of bomb bursts on Dover harbor. But the Heinkel bombers that dropped them were well ahead and too high for him to reach.

Suddenly on his left, he spotted a flight of Stukas. He looked around quickly for German fighters, and finding none, dropped the nose, nudged at the throttle which was already at the gate, and turned for the spot in the sky where he would intercept them.

They grew in his windscreen, looking like prehistoric flying beasts - boxy canopies, big square tails, and long spatted landing wheels that hung awkwardly. Their only pleasing aspect was the graceful curve of their gull wings.

As his Spitfire approached firing range, the German gunners pointed their weapons at him. To hell with those pop guns. Cub picked out a target on the near side of the formation, eased the throttle, and rolled to track it. He held the pipper on it and felt pleased for the way he'd set up the attack.

Out of nowhere the words popped into his head: "Six o'clock and up-sun." Should he check? Take his eyes off the target and look back? Hell, only a few more seconds and this bird would be dead meat. And the sky behind had been empty only a moment before. "The one you don't see is the one that gets you." Dammit! He didn't want to lose this one! He squinted at the perfect sight picture of the Stuka. Then smoldering in frustration, he jabbed the stick to level the wings and glanced over his shoulder. His heart stopped.

Not four hundred yards behind, two Messerschmitts dropped on him like a pair of hawks.

Terror gripped him as he heaved the stick into the right rear corner, stood on the rudder pedal, and pushed the throttle hard forward. The Spitfire lurched into barrel roll, driving him into the seat. As the wings came vertical, he eased the roll and held the steep, climbing turn; then he hunched himself, waiting for the impact of bullets.

The two Messerschmitts hurtled by on his left then pulled up into a vertical climb. He eased his turn to keep an eye on them. As they climbed, the leader flicked a little roll that, as they came down out of their loop, would place them directly over Cub. The wingman followed the leader; the two pulled over the top and started down toward him. Cub was suddenly struck by the recollection that this was exactly how he'd miraculously caught up to Duke on their training flight.

What to do? "Turn and face an attack," he remembered. That meant, pull up into them. But his airspeed was too low.

He rolled into level flight, let the Spitfire accelerate, and watched the Messerschmitts turn down toward him. Timing was everything now.

The angle of their fuselages grew narrower. Their guns were coming to bear on him, and they drew closer.

Now!

He hauled back on the stick and strained against the pressure, as the Spitfire's nose rose to meet the Germans. Vision dimmed and reluctantly he eased the controls.

From high in front, the two planes hurtled toward him. Cub couldn't bring his gun sight up to aim at them, but he'd given them a difficult shot. His plane shuddered under the shock of a brief impact, then the Messerschmitts flashed by.

Nearly in a stall, he nosed down into level flight and turned to follow them, expecting them to pull around and try again. But they continued downhill eastward, diminishing until they disappeared in the mist across the Channel.

Geezus, that was close! He took a couple of deep breaths and shook his head to relieve his tension, then looked around for the Stukas. They were gone!

Scanning the sky, he turned back toward Dover to watch the last of the Heinkels release their bombs. Each missile seemed so tiny, but the pall of smoke obscuring their target was huge. Poor devils down there, he thought. But the Heinkels were too far away.

He was considering his next move, when a glance at the fuel gauge told him to head for Manston. He turned northward and began to descend. Below on his left, lay the ever-peaceful fields of Kent, and he wondered if down there they knew there was a war going on.

He pushed up his goggles, wiped the perspiration from his brow, and took stock: He'd lost Duke, got his plane shot up, and had inflicted no significant damage on the enemy. Would he ever make a fighter pilot?

The town of Deal slipped beneath him and he called on the radio, "Manston, this is Arrow Blue Three, inbound for landing."

"Arrow Blue Three, Manston is under attack. Will advise when it's clear."

Cub sat up, alert now, and peered ahead. He could just make out the North Foreland, and at first things looked normal. Then he realized that what seemed to be low-lying cloud was actually smoke. He added power and began to climb again. Where were the Germans? Wary of friendly antiaircraft fire, he turned west to avoid the field and scanned the sky for planes.

Ahead and below, he spotted a fighter flying northeast, away from him. He pushed the nose over and dived to catch it. As he drew near enough to clearly see the German's afterbody and tail wheel, he felt the thumping of his heart. It would be a stern shot from close in - a piece of cake.

Cub closed in the target's blind spot, and at two hundred yards range, he decided to get even closer. Now clearly visible were the ribbed fabric covering the control surfaces, the stub of a tail light poking aft from the rudder, and tread on the tail wheel tire. He nosed up gently to center the pipper in the Messerschmitt's fuselage, and his thumb stroked the gun button. He imagined the fireball that would follow; it would make up for the rest of the morning.

Where were the tail struts? Messerschmitts had struts supporting the horizontal stabilizer. Where were they? What the hell goes on!

He took his thumb from the gun button and pushed the nose over for a clearer look. He nearly gagged. On the underside of the wings were RAF roundels! He blinked and looked again. Easing out to the side, he scanned around to make sure they were alone, then eyed the aircraft, now plainly a Hurricane, and shook his head in disbelief. How could he have been so stupid?

He added power to pull abeam. The aft section of the machine was shredded; ribbons of torn fabric fluttered in the airstream like a ragtag parade of flags. The Plexiglass canopy was perforated with bullet holes. A thousand tiny fractures radiated from each, rendering the glass nearly opaque. Through it, he made out the dark shadow of a man's head. There was a white and red discoloration where the neck would be.

Cub waggled his wings, but there was no response. He waved, but saw no motion in the cockpit. He thought, If I can get him back safely, it would at least be some contribution.

Using the fuselage designator letters, he called on the radio, "Hurricane Q-O-Y, can you hear me?"

No response.

"Manston," he called, "this is Arrow Blue Three. Is the field operational yet?"

"We still have damaged aircraft on the runway area."

Stupid bastards! Here's a guy dying, and Manston worried about finding someplace to land on all that grass. "But has the bombing stopped?"

"We are no longer under attack."

"I'm escorting a wounded Hurricane. He must get on the ground right away. Can you clear a path?"

"I'm afraid there are several wrecks. The clear paths are a bit doglegged."

To hell with that. We'll take our chances. "We're north of you about seven miles at fifteen hundred feet. Turning in now.

"Hurricane Q-O-Y, I'm a Spitfire alongside of you. We are northwest of Manston. If you hear me, start a gentle turn to the right and begin losing altitude."

For what seemed an age, they cruised straight and level. Then almost imperceptibly, the plane's left wing rose and it began an easy right turn and a slow descent.

The pilot had heard. Cub grinned.

"Manston, this is Arrow Blue Three, inbound for a two four zero landing and guiding the damaged Hurricane. Warn the antiaircraft units."

They were three miles offshore, over the Estuary. Their turn would bring them over Margate Bay, then across the town, where they would set up for final approach.

Cub examined the plane again and realized that the canopy was spattered with dark spots. Blood? Maybe dried blood! Was the man bleeding to death? Come on, chum, hang on a little longer.

They flew nine hundred feet above the bay, and ahead was the church on the hill in Margate. The field was three and a half miles away.

"Hurricane Q-O-Y, you're doing fine. Just hold that turn and we'll have you on the ground in a couple of minutes."

They crossed the town and were over farmland. Now they had to tighten their turn and set up final approach.

"Hurricane Q-O-Y, increase your turn and glide rate and put your undercarriage down. We're coming onto final."

The plane continued as before. Come on, pal, bring that thing around. "Hurricane Q-O-Y, tighten you're turn and --."

The plane's left wing lifted higher.

"That's good. Hold that. Now get your undercart down."

They passed a cemetery, and the Manston runway was only a mile away and nearly dead ahead.

"Hurricane Q-O-Y, straighten her up now and get your undercarriage down. We're one mile out on final."

Cub was peering ahead, trying to pick out the straightest landing path, when he realized that the other plane was still turning right, and the turn rate increasing.

"Hurricane Q-O-Y, come out of that turn. Straighten her up!"

The plane's left wing continued to rise and the nose dropped dangerously. "Q-O-Y, for God's sake, level your wings!"

Even as he said it, he knew it was hopeless. The machine was two hundred feet from the ground in a death-spiral turn, and not even an alert, skilled pilot could recover it. He watched in horror as the nose continued to drop and the plane augered into the field in a cloud of dirt.

Cub pulled the Spitfire up and circled the spot. There was only a dark hole in the ground. Had the pilot been already dead? Had Cub escorted a corpse the whole way? Or had the man died on final approach, knowing he was less than a minute from safety?

Cub took a deep pull on the emergency oxygen to clear his head, then straightened out onto final approach and lowered the wheels and flaps.

"Manston," he could hardly get the words out. "The Hurricane . . . crashed on your side of the cemetery. I don't think he survived. But better send somebody . . . to have a look."

Minute later, he negotiated the scatter of wrecks on the grass field and taxied to the perimeter. As he pulled up, he noticed that the big hangar was damaged. There was a large hole in the roof and the metal covering around it was twisted like rumpled paper. One of the huge main doors had been blown off and lay flat on the ground. Another hung askew from an overhead runner at one corner.

What a Godawful day.

As he cut the switches, an airman ran across the grass toward him waving his arms. Then he heard the air raid siren.

"They're bombing again," the airman yelled. "Get out of that thing. Shelter's there." He pointed to a dark, narrow hole in a pile of sand bags. "Hurry!" And the man ran for the hole.

Cub popped the safety harness, hit the quick release on the parachute, jerked the oxygen tube and radio cable free, and jumped from the cockpit.

As he landed on the ground, a pair of Dorniers crossed the eastern boundary of the field at treetop level - coming straight at him!

His muscles protested as, with each stride, he strained to plant his foot far out in front and to hurl himself toward the sandbags. But his legs seemed hardly to move, and the planes grew bigger.

They were nearly on top of him, and he heard the high-pitched roar of their engines when, in a desperate plunge, he heaved himself through the dark hole.

The earth shook violently. He lost his footing, and debris fell on him as he crashed to the hard ground. It was dark.

The low-pitched roar from the departing Dorniers' engines was replaced by the high-pitched scream of new arrivals. Cub lay without moving. Then the quaking ground made his head reel, and more debris tumbled.

What the hell was he doing in this rat hole? He should be up there killing those bastards. He thought of getting up and running to his plane. Then the ground erupted again, and thought ceased.

Seven formations raced one after another across the field, unloading their bombs. At last, the sound of engines died away and it was silent.

Cub's dreamlike thoughts were drawn to the little Hurricane fighter he had so gingerly guided to his final resting place. He could almost reach out and put his fingers through the bullet holes in the fabric fuselage, and he could still see the image of the pilot, vague through the crazed Plexiglass and dried blood. He felt sick. What was he doing in this god-forsaken place and this bloody war anyway?

Slowly, like struggling out of a coma, he lifted his head and raised himself. Sand and bits of wood fell off him. He sat up and gazed into the darkness and listened. The only sound was the people around him breathing the heavy breath of fear, but still breathing, still alive.

"I say," said a voice from deep in the darkness, "that was bloody close."

Cub was suddenly angry. Angry about the Hurricane pilot and Truslove and Bolt and Green Two and the bombs bursting on Dover. Frustrated by the men in the Dorniers and Messerschmitts, men who, like the Brownshirts, were out to kill him. He clenched his fists and gritted his teeth, then looked up into the blackness and shouted, "You fucking bastards, I hate every one of you!"

*

Cub dropped his gear on the floor of his room and sagged onto the bed.

"You look knackered," Ian said.

"Too right. How long you been here?"

"An hour. What happened?"

Cub told of his experience, then concluded, "The bastards wrote my airplane off too."

"How did you get back?"

"Rode a lorry to Croydon, took a bus into London, and caught the underground."

"Metropolitan Transport should give you a season ticket."

"At least they didn't charge me. Did you have a lovely day too?"

"When they closed Manston, Tony led Yellow Section into Biggin Hill. Others went into Lympne and Hawkinge. They got plastered, and we lost planes. We were up and down all day, but it didn't amount to much. Nothing like the fight off Dover this morning. We lost three pilots in that scrap." Then Ian's face turned somber. "Reggie Wells bought it."

"Geezus! On his first day out."

"First flight."

Cub gazed at the floor, shaking his head in silence. Finally, he sighed and looked at Ian. "Duke and Burt make it back?"

Ian nodded.

"Duke been looking for me?"

"No. Why?"

"I lost him in the Dover fight. I'll have to face the music with him."

"You weren't alone. Everybody got scattered today."

"Wonder what he thinks that's worth."

Ian shrugged. "Ready for that dance tonight?"

Cub's body ached everywhere, and the day's images continued to tumble through his mind. He'd forgotten about the dance. He shook his head. "I'm beat."

"Same line you fed me last night. Look where that got you."

Cub lay back on the bed and breathed heavily. "Tonight's different."

"I'll say. When the Air Ministry throws a do, there'll be nothing but the best. You can't bail out on me."

"Ian, goddammit, my brain went through the gate today, and it's still revving."

Ian leaned over Cub and clapped a hand on his shoulder. "Look, pal. You get into a clean uniform. I'll drive. You sit and relax. When we get there and you take one look at those girls, you'll forget about today. Just put on that innocent Yankee Doodle Dandy smile of yours, and the world will be your bloody oyster."

Cub grimaced in frustration, shook his head, and closed his eyes.

"Now, how will I explain to my mates," Ian said, "that this flower of young American manhood copped out on me tonight? Maybe I'll tell them that he just wasn't up to dealing with these smooth English girls."

Cub looked askance at Ian, then sat up and shook his head slowly. "You are one persistent bastard, Mister Craigwell. Let me pay my respects to Duke and get a bath, and we'll go."

Chapter 11

At ten that night, Ian Craigwell gingerly guided his MG roadster along Victoria Embankment in the blackout. "So what did Duke have to say?"

Cub said, "That getting lost in the air was no bloody way to win the war."

"That's all?"

"Then he threw me out of his room."

"Hard nut, isn't he?"

Cub shrugged, but the gesture was lost in the darkness. He was dog tired. The trip had taken longer than he expected, and he wished he'd stayed at Hornchurch and gone to bed.

They passed under Waterloo Bridge, and Ian squinted into the dark. "Ah, here it is." He swung the car onto a side street, then into the River Entrance of the Savoy Hotel, where he stepped out, leaving the engine running. "Park it for me, will you," he said to the doorman.

He and Cub entered a small foyer. Ahead, steps led to a pair of closed doors, through which music filtered. A concierge stood at a podium on the side.

"May I help you, sirs?" he said.

"We're here for the Ministry party," Ian said.

"It's a bit late, sir. Party'll be over soon."

"I know, but we came as soon as we could. Been up shooting down Jerries all day."

"I see. In that case, may I have your names, sir?"

"Craigwell and Bayer."

There was a long silence while the man scanned the guest list. "I'm sorry, sir, but I don't find either of you here."

"Look," Ian said, "I was invited by the Air Commodore, himself. He wanted some real fighter pilots to attend. Would you like me to go in there and bring him out to explain it to you?"

The man looked back and forth between the two, obviously struggling to make up his mind, then said, "No, sir. That won't be necessary." He led them up the steps and opened the door to let them in.

As it closed behind them, Cub said, "How do you know the Air Commodore?"

"I'm not even sure there is one here. But it worked."

Cub shook his head in admiration, then turned to look at the room.

A large bandstand was recessed into the wall at one end, and an ample dance floor stretched away from it down the length of the room. Around the floor were perhaps fifty circular dining tables. The room was enormous, but what struck Cub was the color and light that filled it.

The walls and ceiling were a soft blue, the hue of a summer sky. In the ceiling over the dance floor, a large crystal chandelier hung from each of five white recessed panels, and each recess was framed in elaborately carved moldings. The chandeliers were lighted from within by hundreds of tiny bulbs. Their light, refracted through a thousand cut-glass crystals, projected onto the walls and ceiling a dazzling display of spectral images which moved to the gentle sway of the chandeliers. Large mirrors hung on the walls, reflecting the moving light and images of people in the room. Between each mirror hung an elaborate crystal sconce that matched the chandeliers. It was like being inside an enormous Wedgwood vase decorated on the interior and lighted like a fairyland.

"Wow!" Cub said. "What is this place?"

"You have now arrived, pal. This is the Lancaster Room at the Savoy."

Couples filled the dance floor and swayed to Carol Gibbons's music. On the side, knots of people stood among tables chatting, while others sat drinking and talking. Waiters in tuxedo stood about attentively, and behind a bar at the back, white-coated bartenders mixed drinks.

Most party goers were in uniform. Men wore RAF blue. Uniformed women were from the services and volunteer organizations; the rest of the women wore dresses, most of which were dark, short in the skirt and high at the neck.

Ian and Cub got a drink, then stood watching the swirling crowd of dancers. The band was playing *Red Sails in the Sunset*, and the music was cool and smooth. Cub felt himself coming alive again in the vibrant atmosphere.

There were plenty of attractive women, but all paired up with men. They weren't young coeds either; some were really finished and lovely.

"All the girls seem to be taken," Cub said.

"What did you expect? You have to cut in."

"Isn't it a bit late for that?"

"You didn't come just to watch, did you?"

"I guess not."

"At dances in America, don't they cut in."

"Yeah, but back home, I knew everybody."

"You mean you never cut in on somebody you didn't know?"

Cub was embarrassed to admit that he had been shy around girls. "Not that I remember."

"Christ, that sure as hell limits your field."

Maybe so, Cub thought. Then it occurred to him that somehow here, far away from home, he just might feel different. "These girl's won't mind if we cut in?"

"Listen, man, right now, every skirt in England wants to hook up with a fighter boy. And how many righteous ones do you think are in this room? I guess, two."

Cub stood eyeing the dancers, trying to decide if any of the girls warranted the effort, when one, dancing with her back to him, caught his attention. Her blonde hair flowed, close to her head, back through a pair of combs, then tumbled to her shoulders like the mane of a wild horse. She carried herself with strength and assurance. Her Ambulance Corps uniform revealed wide shoulders and a slender figure, and her moves were easy and graceful.

This kind usually have a face like a truck, he thought, and they work to get everything else perfect to make up for it. He decided not to intrude and started to take another sip of his drink, when the couple turned so he could see her face, and his glass stopped halfway to his lip.

She had a firm jaw and chin, a slightly upturned nose, and a high forehead; her flawless skin revealed gentle hollows in her cheeks. For an instant, she looked at Cub directly, a lovely, intelligent look that utterly disoriented him. Then she turned away.

Slowly he recovered his senses, then nudged his friend. "Hey, Ian, look at that."

Ian gazed at the girl for a moment, then nodded approvingly. "There you go, sport."

The music paused between numbers. Deciding to dance with her had made Cub even more nervous. Would she want to dance with him? Could he possibly interest such a lovely girl? Was she enthralled with her partner?

Ian jabbed him with an elbow. "Hey, pal, what are you waiting for?"

It was now or never. Cub set his glass on a table, then began to pushed his way through the crowd until he tapped her partner on the shoulder. The man turned slowly. His scowl demanded: What in hell did this intruder want.

"May I cut in, please?"

The girl and her partner eyed each other for a moment, then he turned to Cub and shook his head in disgust. "Well, I guess the rules are the rules." And he walked away.

Cub stood facing her. Her blue-green eyes looked at him evenly, her steady gaze unsettling him for a moment. Then her face softened into a smile.

"Hi. I'm Keith Bayer," he stammered. "They call me Cub."

"Hello, Cub. I'm Victoria. Victoria Kendall."

"Did I interrupt something between you and him?"

"No. We just danced together a few times."

The music began again. Cub took her hand and slipped his arm around her back, and it dawned on him that she was nearly as tall as he. As they moved to the music, he looked at her, utterly enchanted. Then her delicious fragrance began to intoxicate him.

"I like your perfume," he said.

"Thank you. Have you been here all evening?"

"No. Just got here. And you?"

"I came at the beginning. Are you with the Ministry?"

"No. I'm in a fighter squadron."

"Oh! Where?"

"Hornchurch in Essex."

"Did you fly today?"

"Yeah. Had a full day and then some."

"You must be tired."

"A little. How about you?"

"I could do with a pause. It's been a long evening."

"Breath of air?"

"Sounds wonderful."

Cub couldn't believe his luck. He imagined that a dozen men stood waiting their moment to tap him on the shoulder. Now he would have her alone where no one could cut in.

They stopped at one of the bars to get drinks, then went out through the River Entrance into the blacked-out night. They crossed the

Embankment, and sat down on the stone bench next to the Obelisk. It was too dark to see her clearly. Still, he could hardly take his eyes off her silhouette.

"Lovely night," he said.

She tilted her head to look at the overcast sky. "Well at least it's not pouring."

He followed her gaze and suddenly felt chagrinned. "Guess you're right."

"You sound like a Yank."

"I am."

"What part of America are you from?"

"A little town you never heard of called Gilroy in California. Grew up on a ranch there."

"A ranch with horses?"

"Yeah."

"How marvelous. I love horses."

"I used to, but one day I discovered aviation, and since then, I've been in love with airplanes."

"But you can't be affectionate with a plane like you can a horse."

"You can with a Spitfire."

"Ah yes," she said knowingly. "You fly a Spitfire?"

"Yes, I do."

"And you love it?"

"When I'm not getting shot at."

"I envy you."

"Really? Why?"

"It's not easy for a girl to get a job doing something important and exciting that she's in love with."

This idea had never crossed his mind, and it set off a little bell in his head.

She continued, "And I envy you that California weather you left behind. What made you come here?"

"The adventure. I wanted to fly fighters and to fight Jerry. Saw an ad for the RAF, and I signed up."

"I thought Americans were neutral in the war."

"I'm not." And he told briefly of his trip to Germany.

When he finished, she assented with a nod. Then she said, "Weren't your parents upset about your coming?"

"Yes. And I didn't expect it. For several years, Dad and my grandfather warned that Hitler and the Nazis meant war, and everybody would get dragged into it. And Mom agreed. I was sure they'd understand, but when I told them I was leaving, Mom and Dad got really upset. It wasn't my war; I had no idea what I was getting into; besides I was too young. My choices came down to my way or theirs. I had to just walk away. Mom cried. And that hurt."

Victoria sized him up as he talked. He was nice looking, clean cut, with a kind of innocence about him. Yet he sounded more mature than she had guessed and more straightforward than men she was used to.

"Now tell me about you," he said. "Where are you from?"

"London, now."

"Have you been driving an ambulance long?"

"No. I started in May." Then she quickly said, "What do you do outside of work?"

He chuckled. "Lately not much. My days are all like today."

"I see. What did you do for fun before the war?"

"Played tennis."

"Are you good?"

"Some people thought so. I won a regional tournament before I left."

"In California? That can't be bad."

"Used to coach too."

"Tennis?"

"Lots of sports. Mostly for kids."

"Really? You like working with children?"

"Almost as much as flying."

"Fascinating."

Her interest excited him, and he told about teaching a young boy to spiral a football. The kid had struggled for days to master it; with Cub's help, he finally got it. One day the boy could hardly loft the ball; the next, he was drilling it like a bullet.

Victoria chuckled. "I'll never understand American football. But how unusual for a fighter boy to be interested in children."

Cub shrugged. "I even thought about being a teacher."

"You ever coach girls?"

"Oh sure," he said. And he spoke about teaching one little girl to play tennis. When they started, she could hardly hold up the racket. But he coached her three days a week, and she worked against the backboard every day for months. As she got stronger, she grew able to hit hard, so he taught her backhand. Then he showed her how to stroke her forehand so it rifled low across the net every time and how to place her backhand shots exactly where she wanted. It wasn't long before she was beating the boys.

"Good for her," Victoria said. "Women don't get many chances to do that."

The bell in his head rang again. This girl was either very interesting or very strange.

"Are you complaining about being a woman?" he said cautiously.

"Being a woman is just fine. But I don't like some of the roles we're stuck with."

"Sounds like there's a story there."

She eyed him silently for a moment then glanced at the luminous dial on her watch. "Oh my, but it's late. We'd better get back."

They stood up and walked toward the hotel. She still puzzled him, but it seemed best to talk about something else. "Where do you work?" he said.

"North London. Tufnel Park."

"Where's that?"

"About five miles that way." She pointed into the gloom. "By car, it takes half an hour with no traffic."

They approached the hotel entrance.

"Victoria, do you go out on dates?"

"Not often. I work the night shift, and it keeps me very busy. Tonight is special."

They pushed through the doors and entered the foyer.

"Well, I was just wondering --."

From ahead, a man's voice boomed, "So there you are, Victoria." It was her dance partner. "What in God's name happened to you."

"Cub and I have been outside talking. Didn't realize it was so late."

The man stood in the doorway to the Lancaster room, holding it open for her and glowering at Cub. "Come on, they're playing the last set."

She started to squeeze past the man, then stopped and turned back. "Thanks, Cub. Perhaps I'll see you later." With that, she gave a little wave and disappeared. Her partner followed and let the door close in Cub's face.

Cub was stunned. She was so lovely and nice and seemed genuinely interested. And she said that man was only a casual partner. What the hell was going on?

He stopped in the men's room, but his mind was elsewhere.

The band was playing Blueberry Hill as the door to the Lancaster Room closed behind them, and Victoria Kendall was furious: first with herself for letting this man intimidate her, then with the man. Cub had surely got the impression that there was something between them. She whirled on him and whispered viciously, "You had no right to do that."

"What?"

"Shout at me like that. As if I were a naughty child."

"I'm sorry. But you said we should dance together again, and it's getting toward the end."

"That's no excuse for being rude."

"Didn't mean to. I was hoping to escort you home afterward."

"Presumptuous, aren't you?"

"I was only hoping."

"Well, I have other plans. Perhaps you should find someone else to dance with."

She brushed past him and pushed through the door again, hoping that Cub was still in the anteroom. It was empty.

She walked slowly toward the outside doors, then saw the stairs on the left. Perhaps he'd gone up. She climbed to the main floor hall and walked down to the lounge. He wasn't there or in the dining room. Anxiously she strode into the main lobby. He was not to be found.

Five minutes later, she walked out the front door of the hotel with another woman ambulance driver. The doorman hailed a taxi, and they climbed in.

Victoria sat biting her lip and trying to decide why she found Cub interesting. She couldn't put her finger on it, yet there was something decidedly attractive about the man. As the cab pulled out of Savoy Court, she looked back at the hotel entrance and wondered if she'd ever see him again.

When Cub returned to the Lancaster Room, couples were dancing cheek to cheek. The orchestra played *Harbor Lights*, one of his favorites, and he was desperate to dance with Victoria. He searched the crowd warily, prowling the edge of the dance floor and growing more puzzled with every tick of the clock. Slowly a gloom came over him.

It must have shown, for Ian walked up and said, "Why so glum, pal? That was a real streamlined piece you picked out there."

Cub gaped at him. "She's gone."

"Gone? Christ, the dance isn't over yet."

"Well I can't find her. Do me a favor, Ian. Stay here and keep an eye out. I'll search the other side of the room. If you see her, tell her I must talk to her."

They searched until long after the music stopped and the crowd thinned.

"Come on," Ian said at last, "let's get out of this fire trap and find a drink."

Chapter 12

Cub and Ian sat at a table in the Trocadero restaurant studying the supper menu. Ian raised his glass said brightly, "Cheers."

"Cheers," Cub answered flatly. Ian's levity chafed.

"Still carrying the torch for that ambulance girl you met last night?"

Cub nodded.

Ian shook his head. "Some Romeo you are, forgetting to get her phone number."

"For Christ's sake, I didn't forget. When that guy showed up, she disappeared like a shot. How the hell was I to know she'd leave with him right then."

"How do you know she went with him?"

"Well, we didn't see either one of them afterwards. What's your theory?"

"Seems odd after she spent twenty happy minutes with you. No way to reach her?"

"None I can think of."

"Well, what the hell, Mom says girls are like trams. One along every ten minutes. So cheer up."

"Gee, thanks," Cub said. But he couldn't shake the thought. Why had she left so quickly?

Idly he surveyed the restaurant. The walls were paneled in dark walnut, nearly black in the dim light, and the floor was covered in deep-pile maroon. Crisp white table cloths were set with crystal and silver, and a shaded candle flickered from each. Waiters wore dinner clothes, with black bow ties and white cloths over their arms. Not many tables were occupied, and most of the waiters stood motionless, but here and there, some scurried about in service.

"Not much action here," Ian said.

"What did you have in mind?"

"A couple of girls without escorts would do for a start."

"Not for me, thanks. But what would you do about them?"

"Invite them for dinner, of course."

"Just like that?"

Ian frowned skeptically. "Why not?"

"I don't know. But walking up to a total stranger and inviting her over?"

"What would you do, get on your knees and sing to her?"

"Fugoff."

"I forgot. You're the bloke who never even cut in on somebody he didn't know. How the hell did you meet girls?"

"Mixer dances or got introduced."

"You mean you never just picked out a good looker you didn't know and introduced yourself?"

"Not that I remember." Cub suddenly felt on the defensive, and he began to eye the table.

"Did you know lots of good-looking girls?"

None like at the dance last night, Cub thought. He said, "There were some around, all right."

"Around?"

"Yeah. In classes, and afterwards they mostly hung out at the football field."

Ian broke into a knowing grin. "Where your brother, Brad, was, I'll wager."

Cub looked up, startled. "Yeah. They all went for the football players."

"Look," Ian said earnestly. "Girls today are more interested in fighter boys than they ever were in any football player. You stick with me, and I'll show you how to meet women."

A few minutes later, Cub was looking over Ian's shoulder toward the front entrance, when two well dressed young women appeared and began talking to the headwaiter. "Okay, Casanova," he said, "look what just walked in."

Ian turned to follow Cub's eye. He nodded slowly. "Wow! Look at the brunette."

She was finished and racy," Cub thought. "Perhaps she wore too much makeup, but she was pretty. "Not bad."

"Let's ask them over."

"Think they'd come?"

"One way to find out, pal," Ian said. "Go ask them."

"I'm not interested. Besides, what the hell would I say?"

"Ask them to join us for supper."

"Go ask them yourself."

"Look, friend, I told you to stick with me and learn something. Here's a chance for a new experience. Go and invite them."

"Suppose they say no?"

"Insist. Tell them a couple of red-hot aces would like to share their company."

Cub gawked around the room. "Which red-hot aces?"

"Lad, you're hopeless, sitting here blowing your big chance."

Cub faked a grin. "They'd probably laugh at me."

"Well, you're sort of funny looking, but we'll chance it. Now go ask them."

"Go yourself."

"You risk your arse against those Messerschmitts every day, pal, but you haven't got the balls to go over and ask those girls to dinner?"

"That's different. Besides I'm not interested."

Ian leered at Cub and spoke deliberately. "No balls."

Cub glared at him.

"No balls at all." He pronounced each word with emphasis.

Cub slid back his chair and stood up. "All right, my sweet, ever encouraging roommate. This is for you. In the meantime, get fucking stuffed."

He turned and looked at the two women. This was scary, he thought. Different somehow than tangling with Messerschmitts, yet still frightening. But he had to do it.

The women followed the headwaiter to an empty table, and Cub crossed to intercept. He spoke to them for a few moments, and they looked toward Ian. At length, they smiled and nodded, and the headwaiter led them across the room. Ian stood up as they approached, his eyes fixed on the brunette. The headwaiter seated her next to him, and Cub pushed in the chair for the other girl.

"This is Martha," Cub said, indicating the blonde, then he gestured toward the brunette. "And this is Joyce. Meet Ian."

She turned to Ian and held out her hand. For an awkward moment, he stood like a carved stone image and gaped. Then he grasped it.

"Hello," he managed.

"Hello, Ian." Her words came out breathy, as if she were sighing.

Cub smiled to himself as he watched Ian struggle. He caught Joyce's pungent gardenia fragrance, and his eye wandered to her cleavage, plainly revealed by her low cut dress. Her face opened into a broad smile and she gripped Ian's hand warmly. She wasn't Cub's type, but he understood why Ian was interested.

The men sat down. The waiter hovered close at hand.

"What brings you here?" Ian stammered.

Joyce chuckled. "The same thing, I suppose, that brought you. We were hungry."

Cub saw Ian's eye waver between her face and her bosom.

"You come often?" Ian said.

"Now and then."

"You must like it here?"

"Would I come if I didn't?"

"Ian," Cub said, "the waiter is standing by for you to order that young lady a drink?"

"Oh! Of course. What would you like?"

"Gin and tonic."

He repeated it to the waiter as if the man hadn't heard, then turned and looked at her again. An awkward silence followed.

Joyce flicked an eye toward Ian's wings. "I gather you're one of our heroes. What do you fly?"

"Spitfires."

"Sounds exciting. I couldn't wait to meet you. Cub says you're an ace."

Ian grinned. "Yes. Well, it's no big thing."

Cub said, "Pay no attention, Joyce. He's just shy."

"I can see that." Then she said to Ian, "Actually, when I told Cub I'd once met another ace, he said you were a double ace. Ten victories! That's amazing."

Ian swallowed hard. "Yes. Well, I . . . I'm working on it. What'll you have to eat?"

Martha was pleasant, but Cub was poor company. He tried to be polite, but when he looked at her, his mind drifted to Victoria, and the comparison was no contest. He wanted to get away.

They finished dinner, and in a moment of awkward silence Joyce said to Ian, "What do you do for fun?"

"Well . . . flying's fun."

"I mean diversion."

"It is diversion. Really exciting. Take yesterday. We got to Manston before dawn and waited for Jerry to show up. Sure enough, a half-hour after sunup, the controllers scrambled us."

Ian's words came easily, but it occurred to Cub that Joyce wasn't listening.

"Up we went," Ian continued, "flying south, hanging on our screws. And there they were, over the water, fifty Stukas headed for Dover. We tore into them. Then today, twelve of us jumped another big formation and --." He stopped as if interrupted and said, "Something wrong?"

"No. I'm still wondering what you do for fun."

"Fun?" he said. "That is fun. You're up there in the open sky, just you and a Messerschmitt in a duel. And only one of you is coming back. You see those guns winking at you, and you know --.

"Hello, chaps," rang out across the room. Tony Hamilton-Price approached the table. Ian eyed him soberly, and Cub felt suddenly cold.

"Well, surprise, surprise," Tony said. "Ladies. Good evening." Then he looked at Joyce. "Learning all about the air war?"

"I'm afraid I don't understand a word of it," she said.

"Dull stuff anyway. So what are you up to?"

"Just finishing dinner," Ian said soberly. "Won't you, er . . . join us for coffee?"

"Afraid not, old chap, I was just on my way to the Palladium for the Glen Miller concert."

Joyce's eyes rounded and her mouth dropped opened. "Glen Miller? The American band leader?"

"The same."

"My God," she said, "that's been sold out for weeks. I'd kill to go."

"Really?"

"Oh yes," she gasped. "His *String of Pearls* just sets me aglow. I offered five quid for a ticket, but found no takers."

Tony turned to Ian. "If you had a ticket, you'd sell it to her for five quid, wouldn't you?"

Cub knew Tony was driving at no good.

Ian gave a flustered chuckle. "If she wanted it."

"And if she had it, you wouldn't deprive her of the chance to use it, would you?"

"I, uh . . . suppose not."

A grin spread slowly across Tony's face. He reached into the inside pocket of his tunic, pulled out two slips of paper, and held them for Joyce to see. "It happens that I have an extra ticket."

The silence was stunning.

"It's yours if you'll join me," Tony said.

Joyce said, "Oh my god --."

Cub glared at Tony. "Now just a damned minute --."

Tony pointed at Ian. "Didn't the man say he'd be happy to have her go if she had a ticket? Now she has one. What do you say, Joyce?"

"Oh my God, I'd love to, but --."

Tony said, "He's only playing in London tonight."

She looked plaintively at Ian. "Would you mind terribly? I really am desperate to go."

Ian clenched his jaw and sat silent. Finally, he tilted head toward the entrance and said, "Go on."

She eased herself gingerly to her feet. "Thanks, Ian. I enjoyed dinner. You're very understanding."

Tony took her arm and they crossed the room and left.

*

Cub and Ian headed up Shaftsbury Avenue toward where Ian had left his car. The street was dark, and they walked gingerly along the pavement, staying to the left to avoid oncoming pedestrians. Occasional vehicles passed by in the street, their blackout lights glowing blue and casting muted orange flickers on the roadway ahead.

Cub brooded about how to avenge Ian's pride, but nothing effective came to mind. Finally he said, "I hate that sonofabitch."

"Forget it. He's not worth it. The bastard. But thanks for the sentiments."

They passed a hotel where, through the entrance door, they saw a waiter serving in the lounge.

Ian said, "Let's see if we can get a drink in here."

They entered, sat down, and ordered. Cub was still troubled. But when they were served, Ian took a long pull on his drink and gave Cub a wry grin. "She was a corker, wasn't she?"

Cub felt suddenly better, and he looked at Ian and winked. "A bit of a tart if you ask me. A good looking lad like you could do better."

"Get stuffed," Ian said. "She'd make a man out of you in bed."

"And you forgot to get her address."

"Piss off."

"By the way, I had a thought while we were sitting in the restaurant. You ever heard of a place called Tufnel Park?"

"Sure. It's a tube station in north London, not far from where I live. Why?"

"Just wondered. I think that's where Victoria said she worked."

Chapter 13

The hot sun shone on the North Foreland out of a cerulean blue sky, marred only by the occasional wisp of high cloud. Cub lay on the Manston grass watching swallows corkscrew through the air in search of flying insects. Peter Duke sat nearby reading a book.

With each heartbeat, Cub felt his head pulse. He hated himself when he drank too much. But that sonofabitch, Tony, made him so mad. He had to get his mind off the man, think about something else. A knot hung heavy in his stomach, the one that was always there when he waited to go. He tried to ignore it.

His mind wandered back to the image of the Messerschmitt fighter hard on his tail with its nose cannon winking. What would he have done if Duke hadn't rescued him? He turned the question over in his mind.

Finally, he said to Duke, "Can I interrupt you for a moment?"

Duke looked up. "You just did. What is it?"

"Is there anything you can do if a Jerry fighter really locks onto your tail?"

"Bend over and kiss your arse goodbye."

"Seriously. Is there no hope?"

Duke looked at him in frustration, as if he were a bothersome child. "Lad, try anything. Violent and risky as you like. Don't worry about breaking the airplane, because short of a miracle, you're history."

Duke calmly returned to his book.

Cub wondered, Did this waiting bother Duke? Was he afraid? He said, "God, I wish we didn't have to wait around like this."

Duke kept his eyes on the book. "Not a hell of a lot you can do about it, is there?"

"I suppose not. Do you get scared?"

Duke eyed him skeptically. "Do I look like a zombie?"

"I mean right now. You have butterflies in your gut?"

"We all do."

"What do you do about it?"

"Think of something else."

"Just like that?"

"Yes, lad, just like that."

Cub idly plucked blades of grass as he mulled Duke's response.

"By the way," Duke said, "I hear Tony Hamilton-Price ran into you chaps last night up in town."

Cub glared at him. "Yeah. What about it?"

Duke grinned. "I hear he managed to win one off you."

"Win, bullshit! The bastard stole."

Duke leaned across and, grabbing Cub's arm painfully.

"What do you mean, stole?"

"The sonofabitch stole Ian's girl. He had no fucking right --."

Duke jerked him upright, pushed his face close to Cub's, and growled, "Don't call him a sonofabitch, lad. Tony Hamilton-Price is a friend. A bloody good pilot. An old timer around here. And you two are just new kids."

Cub continued to glare as Duke eased his grip.

"He wasn't fair," Cub said.

"All's fair in love and war, lad, and you've got a hell of lot to learn about both."

The dispersal bell clanged. "Arrow Squadron, scramble!"

*

They vectored north from Manston to intercept a raid coming toward the Thames Estuary. The altimeter read twenty-two thousand feet, and over Cub's right shoulder, the sun blazed. Ahead, Spitfires stretched upward in a line as if on parade. Already the oxygen was clearing his head.

Cub adjusted throttle to match the speed of Stark's plane, ahead of him. Blue Flight was the last in the formation, and Cub brought up the rear. He rolled his shoulders to ease the stiffness and the pain where Duke had grabbed him. But it hurt less than his pride.

He held his distance from Stark and forced himself to study the sky, especially up-sun. Scanning around the blinding orb made him squint and he had to blink away tears.

"Arrow leader," Shakespeare control called, "enemy aircraft ahead, nine miles."

"No contact yet, Shakespeare," Tweed said. "Keep a sharp lookout, everybody."

"Tallyho," came Tony's voice. "Bombers at eight miles, two thousand feet below."

Tweed: "I see them. Arrows, full throttle now. Prepare to attack!" Then his voice turned angry. "Blue Three, what the hell are you up to back there?"

Cub was still studying the sky above. He jerked his head around to look forward and found himself well above Stark and the line of Spitfires. He pushed the nose over to catch up. But something had caught his eye as Tweed spoke, a tiny flash that came and went in an instant up near the sun.

"Close it up now, Blue Three!"

Smoke poured from Tweed's exhaust stacks, and he began to descend, causing the formation to arc downward.

Cub pulled closer to Stark, then tore his eyes away to look again into the painful glare. Nothing. He blinked and struggled to focus. Then a glint sparkled, all but obscured in the brilliance. He pinched his eyelids to squeeze away tears and looked again. It was gone. Was it a trick of his imagination? A leftover flicker of last night's booze? For an instant he caught it again. Was he certain? Had to be sure. He'd make no fool of himself. But there it was again.

"Duke, I think I see something in the sun," he called in a wavering voice. Then he lost it. Gone. Duke would skin him alive for a false alarm. He blinked again and gazed into the glare. Nothing.

There was a long silence, then Duke's voice blared, "Bandits, six o'clock, closing!"

Cub snapped his head around to look aft. A pair of dots dropped out of the sky behind him and descended until they were nearly hidden behind his tail. As he gaped, the dots grew, maturing into Messerschmitts coming like death itself.

"Hold formation, Arrows," Tweed said. "We'll attack in strength first, then break into the fighters."

"Blue Leader breaking," Duke called. "We're under attack."

Cub looked around to see Duke's and Stark's ships reef into a climb. He hauled back on the stick, shoved the throttle to the gate and, struggling against G forces, followed the two planes upward.

"Damn you, Blue Leader," Tweed shouted.

With Cub bringing up the rear, the three planes nosed into the sun. The Messerschmitts pulled up to track them, but were going too fast to follow, and the opponents passed each other head-on, cockpit to cockpit, as the Spitfires staggered through the top of their loop. There Duke rolled out and led the three into a sweeping up-sun turn over the rest of the squadron. Cub scanned the sky; the German fighters had vanished.

"Must have been only those two," Duke said. "Lucky."

Cub's breathing returned to normal, and he replayed Duke's maneuver in his mind. It had posed the Germans a dilemma: they could press the attack on the main formation and risk the three Spitfires coming down on the their tails, or pull up and pursue the trio. The latter was safer, but offered a trickier shot. And they'd missed it. Duke knew his business, and as difficult as the man was, Cub was glad to be flying his wing.

Below, the remainder of Arrow Squadron shredded the ranks of the bomber formation.

"Blue Flight Leader," Tweed called, "are you taking the day off up there? Get back down here where the fighting is."

"Right, Arrow Leader," Duke snapped.

Blue Flight joined the squadron to chase the remnants of the bomber formation, but the Germans turned east toward thick clouds and, before the Spitfires could catch them, disappeared. Low on fuel, the Arrows turned back for England.

When they landed, Blue Section's were the only guns that hadn't been fired.

*

Peter Duke stood at ease in Woolly Tweed's office; Tweed sat behind his desk and spoke angrily.

"Mister Duke, you set a fine example. I have lectured and cajoled this outfit to keep together in the air, but you, a senior Flight Lieutenant who knows the doctrine as well as I do, can't seem to remember. And when I ordered the attack, you led your section swanning off and took twenty-four guns out of our formation."

Anger worked behind Duke's eyes as Tweed talked. Now he took a pace forward and leaned over the desk. "For Christ's sake, Woolly, Bayer was arse-end-Charlie when those bastards jumped us. No way I was going to leave him."

"So you broke formation and blunted our attack."

"Damned right. And I'd do it again to cover a wingman."

"See here, Duke, you're an old hand. You know that concentration of firepower carries the day. How often have we practiced it?"

"I don't care what we practiced. It might work against bombers, but you can't keep twelve planes in formation with fighters around. Jerry'll cut us to pieces."

"So because of a few losses, you'd abandon years of planning and training?"

"The bloody plan didn't work. By the time you blokes in front started shooting, the ME's were on us at the back. We had to defend ourselves."

"That's what battle discipline is all about. Not gawking around. Sticking to business. Going in together to punch with everything we've got. Without discipline, we're cooked."

"Woolly, much of Fighter Command has given up close formations in combat. They're good practice and lovely to look at. But the blokes in the rear are sitting ducks. And there's too much to worry about besides keeping together."

"The heart of our fighting doctrine is attack, attack, attack!" Tweed hammered his fist on the desk in time with his words. "We get in trouble when people's minds are on anything else, and that's what happened today. You three ended up parading around in the sunshine leaving the rest of us below to finish off your assignment."

"Some of us should have been up there in the first place to protect the rest. It's damned lucky there was only one pair of not-very-aggressive Krauts."

"Lieutenant, firepower at the point of attack wins the day. Every gun counts. And if there's some risk in keeping all the guns together and focused on the target, so be it. It's a risky business at best."

"For God's sake, Wooly, Jerry has learned to operate in pairs. He cruises with two pair in a loose four, but in a fight, the pairs split. He doesn't go for this parade drill stuff. He's smarter than we are."

Tweed got to his feet. "Now you listen, Lieutenant. Jerry has very experienced pilots. He can make it up as he goes. But our lads are fresh-caught. They need direction. A method to follow. Strict formations. So everyone knows what to do. And by God that's what we'll give them."

Duke drew his six-foot frame to attention. "You'll kill a lot of young Bayers."

"Lieutenant Duke, we are going to fight this war with thousands of young pilots like him. And they'll all be as wet behind the ears. You're an experienced officer, and it's your duty to mold these young men into disciplined fighter pilots. Understood?"

"Yes, sir."

"We can't just throw these kids off the deep end."

Duke blew a heavy sigh. "Is that all, sir?"

Tweed gave a quick nod, and Duke left.

*

Duke sat in a chair in his room and looked up at Cub, who fidgeted.

"Where the hell did your radio discipline go, lad? Duke, I think I see something . . .," he mimicked. "For Christ's sake, the call is, 'Bandits or Bogies, six o'clock high.' Have you forgotten bandits and bogies and the clock system already?"

"No, sir. I was just nervous."

"By God, you get those nerves under control, boy, or you'll get us all killed."

"Yes, sir."

"How long had you been staring at those buggers before you said something?"

"Don't know. Saw a glint maybe ten or fifteen seconds before."

"So we sat there fat, dumb, and happy for a quarter of a minute with those bastards boring in on us while you tried to make up your weak mind. Is that it?"

"I guess so, sir. But I wasn't sure."

"Glints don't go flying around at twenty-five thousand feet all by themselves. When you first see one, you call it. You hear me, lad?"

"Yes, sir."

"Then get your indecisive arse out of here."

Chapter 14

Air raids on the coastal cities of Portsmouth and Southampton had been heavy the two previous days. Victoria Kendall had worked back-to-back fourteen-hour grinds, driving down at night to bring wounded from overworked hospitals there to less crowded facilities in London. Today, she had slept only four hours.

It was barely dark. The dispatcher had assigned her to pick up patients at the Royal South Hampshire Hospital in Winchester, and he wanted her to hurry. She might have to do it twice before dawn.

God, she was tired, but tonight they were short handed. She could have protested, but what was the use? She heaved her bag onto her shoulder and slogged across the main hall of the ARP Center toward the front door.

"Miss Kendall," a telephone operator called across the room. "Telephone call for you."

Victoria stopped and slowly turned around. "Who?"

"Didn't say. It's a man."

She gaped at the operator for a long moment, while she tried to cut through the fatigue in her mind. She had to hurry, besides she didn't feel like talking to anyone. "I've got an urgent run to make. Do you suppose you could take a message?"

"He says it's important."

She sighed and shook her head in disgust, then reluctantly crossed to the phone.

The operator said, "Sounds like a Yank."

Victoria vaguely remembered that it had been three nights since the dance; it seemed like three months.

"Hello," she said. "Of course I remember you. How are you? . . . Oh Cub, I can't. I work nights and I'm so busy . . . I'm sorry, but there's too much going on. I explained this to you . . . Don't know. When will the German's stop bombing? . . . You're not being fair . . . "

The pressure seemed too much, and her mind was muddling.

"That's not it at all . . . For heaven's sake, I never met the man before. Had a row with him and left with a girl friend . . . Even went looking for you . . . Cub, I *am* telling you the truth . . . Look, I have an emergency run to make right now. Can't talk any longer . . . Cub? . . . Cub?"

Slowly she put the phone down and stood for a moment with her eyes closed, digesting what had happened. He would write her off. But what difference could that possibly make, anyway!

Suddenly she felt overwhelmed by the bombing, the destruction, the wounded, the incessant demands on her time, and now Cub. She turned and shuffled toward the door striving to hold back the tears until she got to the privacy of the ambulance cab.

*

Cub hung up the phone and dragged himself up the stairs. Why hadn't he left well enough alone? As he entered his room, Ian looked up from a magazine and said, "Did you talk to her?"

"Yeah."

"Geez, you sound cheerful."

"Piss off."

"What the hell's the matter?"

"She won't go out with me."

"Oh? Did she say you were ugly and smelled bad?"

"Get stuffed."

"What did she say?"

Cub filled him in on the conversation, then said, "All that crap about having an argument with that jerk and leaving with a girlfriend sounds fishy. She's not interested in me - Too many other irons in the fire."

"Faint heart never won fair maid."

"Christ, she could hardly wait to get me off the phone. She and her goddammed emergencies! I'm obviously not one of them. To hell with her."

Cub dropped his head into his hands. What in the world was he doing here? Fighting a goddammed foreign war. Messing around with girls that were no part of his background. What the hell for?

Ian said softly, "Why don't we go drown ourselves at The Gannet?"

Cub lifted his head and blew a sigh. "Why, indeed."

*

Cub and Ian sat on high stools in the Lounge Bar and ordered beer. Cub recognized many of the clientele, quietly drinking and talking.

Some airmen played darts. Tobacco smoke hung thick, and by the smell, someone was smoking a pipe. For Cub, the place was taking on a familiar, homey aura.

He and Ian chatted, and they had started on a second beer when he spotted the woman he'd seen there with Duke. She sat at a table with three pilots, apparently telling a joke, for all at once the others at the table laughed loud enough to turn heads in the room.

"Well, well," Ian said. "That skirt of yours is here again."

"Yeah. And under heavy escort."

"That never bothers a real fighter pilot."

Cub pulled a wry look at Ian then turned to study the girl. She had a wild look about her, and her silk blouse fell along her body like a layer of skin. "Who said I was bothered?"

"I only noticed sweat breaking out on your forehead."

"Get out of here! Maybe I'm not interested."

"Then why the heavy panting?"

"She's not unattractive."

"Not unsexy either."

"Oh, I forgot. Sexy doesn't appeal to you."

"Not without a semblance of a brain to go with it."

"Sure. That's why you couldn't take your eyes off Joyce the other night."

"Leave Joyce the hell out of this."

"It's your eyes I'm talking about."

Ian studied the woman at the table. "Well, I'll give you this much. If you got lost in her cleavage, it'd take you a week to find your way out. But otherwise, she's not half that Kendall girl."

"But she's here, and Victoria isn't."

Cub debated. Should he go over and introduce himself? Would that be too forward? Would she laugh and send him away? Maybe he should just sit tight and look.

He had nearly finished his beer, when suddenly her eyes locked with his. She smiled, and he smiled back. He sat, still unsure.

Doreen Phillips liked the look of this young man, a clean-cut American look she'd seen in the movies, fresh and enthusiastic. A little rush stirred inside her, and she wanted to meet him. She beamed.

Her smile made Cub catch his breath. Tonight, by God, he was going to meet her. He stood up and said over his shoulder to Ian, "I may or may not be back."

"Where the hell are you going."

"To introduce myself."

"That crowd'll give you a big welcome."

"Faint heart never won fair maid."

Carrying his beer, he crossed to her table. As he approached, a man there was gesturing to simulate one plane chasing another, but the woman had her eyes on Cub.

"Good evening," he said and offered his hand. "I'm Keith Bayer. They call me Cub."

The man paused in mid-flight.

She took Cub's hand. "Cub bear, I get it. Nice to meet you Cub. I'm Doreen Phillips. I've seen you here before." She made introductions, then said to them, "Move over and make a place for Cub to sit."

The men's faces showed they weren't happy about it, but they inched around, and Cub sat down.

The man returned to his dogfight: "I had the old Spit racked into a blinding turn, with this ME on my tail, and pulled out all the stops. If he was any good at all, he'd have had me. I tell you, that new Messerschmitt is one dangerous machine."

"Too right," said another, "I got behind one, and he rolled before I could even put the stick over. He was on his back and headed downhill - gone, mother goose. The old ones could never do that."

"Come on, chaps," the third man said, "Cut out the hangar flying. We've had enough for one day. Doreen, tell us another joke."

She smirked and edged around in her chair. "Have you heard the one about the American, English, and Dutch girls?"

They shook their heads.

"The question is, what does each say to her partner after having it off in bed?"

Blank looks. Cub felt his face flush.

She leaned forward conspiratorially. "Well," she said, imitating accents, "the American says, 'Gee, honey, that was a gas. Let's do it again.' The English girl says, 'Really, Geoffrey, that was marvelous. We must have a go more often.' The Dutch girl says, 'I see a cobweb on the ceiling.'"

Laughter burst like shattering glass and she smiled proudly.

"I should warn you," the third man said, looking at Cub. "Doreen is Queen of off-color jokes."

They drank and the conversation turned back to flying.

The publican called for last orders, and Cub realized how quickly time had passed. He looked over and smiled at Ian, still at the bar, and got a sneer in return.

Doreen stood and said, "Must be off." She looked at Cub and thought, what a nice young man, but he's certainly shy. Hardly said a word.

The third man said to her, "I'll run you home."

She said goodnight, smiled warmly at Cub, and turned for the door. The third man followed.

As she moved away, Cub grew desperate. "Try anything," he recalled Duke saying, "as violent and risky as you like."

He stood up. "Doreen!"

She stopped and turned around, wide-eyed.

"Can I speak to you alone for a second?"

"Why . . . yes . . . of course." She shot a glance at her escort, who frowned. "We'll only be a moment."

Cub led her to a quiet corner. "Doreen I wondered . . . if you'd go out with me. On a date. I mean I'd . . . like to get to know you better."

This was more like it, she thought. What a gorgeous smile he has. "Oh Cub, that would be nice. When?"

"Well, it's hard to plan. Our flying schedule is awful and I never know. But --."

"I'll tell you what. The next time we're both here, we'll sit together and talk.

"But if you're with others and I arrive late --."

"Not to worry. I'll break off and say we had an engagement. We can find a table by ourselves. How's that?"

"Wonderful."

She reached for his hand and squeezed it. "Good night."

She left. And though the scent of her perfume lingered, Cub's sense of time and space departed with her.

A clap on his back brought him back to reality. "Romeo, Romeo," Ian said, "wherefore art thou? Somewhere in space?"

"I got a date with her," Cub said breathlessly.

"Like climbing Mount Everest, was it?"

"Piss off, Ian."

"Piss off home, you mean. Let's go."

Chapter 15

As the calendar turned to September, German air raids struck at RAF bases deep in southern England. Manston, Hawkinge, Tangmere, and Biggin Hill, were pounded. Hornchurch had suffered, and even the main London airport, at Croydon, was hit. RAF facilities in the south were being reduced to rubble. But the worst problem was the desperate shortage of pilots and the debilitating fatigue of those still flying.

The RAF was losing a battle of attrition, and the Luftwaffe needed only to keep the pressure on.

* * *

The sun was well down in the western sky, and at a remote point on the Hornchurch perimeter, pilots lounged, exhausted, in chairs inside the dispersal hut or outside on the grass. They had flown four hours and made three interceptions since dawn. Their faces sagged and there was little chatter. Some sipped tea; others pretended to sleep.

Cub stretched on the grass, eyes closed. His clothes were clammy, and he chilled. The last thing he wanted was to move again. He'd had too much craning around in the cockpit, fighting G forces, and struggling to breathe through the mask at high altitude. He craved rest, sleep, a cool beer, and most of all, freedom from the goddammed waiting.

Ian lay in the grass alongside him. "Jesus, I've had enough of this."

"Me too. And those bastards just keep plastering us."

"I heard they hit Duxford."

"Duxford? Bullshit! That's way the hell up in Twelve Group country."

"You think we built some sort of wall between here and there? For Christ's sake, they've been operating as far west as Wales and Lancashire. Why not Duxford? I also heard they shut down Manston. That's why we haven't been back. People are holed up in air raid shelters there and won't even come out between air raids."

"Not so dumb."

Ian blew a heavy sigh. "Right now, I just want to sleep. Think we'll have to go up again?"

Cub turned his face westward and opened an eye to gauge the height of the sun. It proved disappointing. "Jerry's probably not ready for bed yet. Damned if I know how the bastards do it? They must get a new air force every day."

"Well, they'd better find new pilots to take some places here. A lot of us may not to be around that long."

"Cut that shit out, Ian."

"I'm serious. I forgot to put my undercart down on that last landing, until somebody shot off a flare in my face. Mistakes are going to get us."

"Yeah? Well, maybe Jerry's getting tired too. Maybe he won't show up again today --.

He was interrupted by the dreaded soft click from the dispersal phone. Pilots heard it even out on the grass, and everyone froze in mid-breath. A cold chill ran down Cub's back, and a knot tightened in his stomach. Then, came the ring.

"Arrow Squadron, scramble!"

Lethargic bodies contorted as they struggled to their feet, then moved stiffly across the grass. Inside the hut, cups crashed to the floor and tables overturned as pilots scurried for the door. The bell clanged.

Adrenaline began to pump as Cub picked up speed in the dash for his plane. Fatigue was gone, displaced by urgency. And as he ran, he scanned the horizon for Germans. For God's sake, don't get caught here on the ground.

He scrambled onto the wing where an erk, Cub's rigger, waited to help him. Grabbing the crown of the windscreen with both hands, he swung himself in one motion into the cockpit seat. Like one being with four hands, he and the rigger rapidly made Cub part of the airplane: strapping on the parachute, snapping the safety harness, connecting the earphones and the oxygen tube, and snapping the mask into the helmet. Twenty seconds after entering the cockpit, Cub's right thumb jabbed the starter button and his left hand brought the mixture control forward. The rigger slammed the access door shut and leapt off the wing as the Merlin caught, with a smoky blast from the exhaust stacks. Duke's plane was already rolling when Cub released the brakes.

*

At full power in an easy circle to the left, the Arrows spiraled upward for eight minutes over the field to twenty thousand feet. Then they headed east still climbing.

The radio crackled: "Arrow leader, Shakespeare here. Many bogies, angels two zero plus, bearing one zero zero, ten miles ahead of you and closing."

Tweed's voice: "Arrows, keep a lookout."

Cub looked all around, then strained his eyes through the windscreen. Nothing. Nervously he scanned the sky again. Ahead, he saw a distortion on the horizon, like a hazy cumulus cloud. Where the hell was Jerry? How could that many airplanes hide up here? But the haze was still there. Funny place for it, so high. Suddenly it came to him: It was a cloud of airplanes!

"Tallyho!" Tweed called. "Dead ahead, twelve miles. One hundred plus Heinkels at angels twenty-two, and as many Messerschmitts at twenty-five. We'll take the bombers head on, then pull up into the fighters. Line abreast, go. Everyone shoot on the first pass. Make it count. And stay out of dogfights!"

Cub glanced quickly around at the eleven other Spitfires. He couldn't believe it. Given the odds, he'd be lucky to even survive this one. But the odds were always in Jerry's favor, usually three or four to one in fighters; ten to one was only a matter of degree. And the Spitfires had one advantage - they were coming at the Germans right out of the afternoon sun.

The cloud ahead was decomposing into individual machines, sprouting wings and engines, and taking on the familiar identity of Heinkels and Dorniers and Messerschmitts.

"Attack go!" Tweed urged.

Cub maneuvered away from Stark and made a quick scan of the sky all around. Then he chose a Heinkel near the end of the oncoming gaggle. He could see the engines with big air scoops, the gun pod in the belly, another in the dorsal position, and the bulbous nose of Perspex panels. The machine looked like an ugly giant insect. He took a deep breath and focused his entire self on the thing.

With both hands on the control column, he held the gun sight pipper on the top of the tail. It was a thousand yards away now, still out of range, but they would close fast and he would shoot all the way in. He thumbed the button, and the Brownings hammered.

Fine particles, looking like smoke, flew off the big insect as it grew in his windscreen, and Cub dropped the pipper into the cabin area. Perspex shattered and debris churned into the air stream. Still he held the button. The insect grew until it filled his windscreen, and he was sure they would collide. Only then did he jam the control column forward with both hands and release the button. Acceleration drove him against the harness. He groaned and his vision blurred. The Heinkel roared overhead.

He eased his machine into a climbing turn. His vision slowly cleared, and he searched the sky. The armada had carried on past him into the sun, and he could no longer see it. Some Spitfires turned away to his left. Where were the German fighters? If they attacked him now, they would be coming out of the sun and hard to see. He S-turned and rolled to look all around.

As he leveled out still flying east, over his right shoulder, he saw a lone Heinkel with a smoking left engine headed away from him, turning slowly toward France. He wheeled to intercept, and opened the throttle. Approaching gun range, he rolled left to close from inside the bomber's turn. The Heinkel's dorsal gun began to wink at him. To hell with it. He drew closer, until the target filled his gun sight. He felt in absolute control. This bird was his.

Smoothly, he maneuvered the Spitfire to put the pipper in front of the machine. Now! And he pressed the button. The Brownings roared in unison, and a long burst poured into the right engine. Much smoke but no fire. Man, they were hard to kill.

He was on the verge of ramming the target, when he pulled up and rolled hard to the right to carry him across the bomber's line of flight and give the dorsal gunner a difficult shot. Turbulence shook the Spitfire as it passed above the big plane. He imagined the gunner firing blindly into the Spitfire's underbelly as it flashed by a few feet overhead, and he hunched involuntarily, anticipating the impact of a lucky shot.

To get out of gun range, he let the Spit run for a few seconds at full power perpendicular to the course of the Heinkel, then he pulled up and rolled left into a climbing turn. The turn became a loop, carrying him high over the target, and he dived to attack again. His burst hit the already smoking left engine, and it erupted in flame. With a few quick moves of the controls, he had a good sight picture on the right engine. One short burst, and it caught fire too. Slowly the Heinkel nosed over toward the sea.

This Jerry was a goner. He'd done it! His first kill. Elation swept over him.

Easing the throttle, he circled in a steep left turn and gazed down the wing to watch the Heinkel plummet in an uncontrolled rolling dive, dark plumes trailing from both engines, extending downward like black velvet ribbons intertwined in an ever-tightening spiral silhouetted against the azure blue of the sea. She would make a big splash when she hit. He gazed intently to catch it and smiled to himself as he watched.

Suddenly, a thunderous explosion under his seat shattered his reverie, and the Spitfire shuddered. Stupefied, he eyed the instrument panel. Nothing. Another sharp crack behind his head. What the hell! He blinked to clear his vision, and flicked his eyes up to the mirror.

A Messerschmitt fighter was neatly framed in the center of the reflector, its guns winking and the big Mauser cannon in the nose spitting high explosives like a fire-breathing dragon.

He was gripped by the terror of a cornered animal. His reactions lost pace with events, and time changed to slow motion. He seemed unable to advance the throttle or more than toy with the stick. Duke's blindfolded cockpit drill drifted through his mind . . . booster coil, undercarriage, mixture, radio selector . . . .. Hand followed thought in crippled half-gestures.

So this is how it ends, with winking guns for a pyrotechnic sendoff. The one you don't see is the one that gets you.

Then a distant voice echoed up from his memory and dragged his panic-sodden mind back to reality. "Lad, try anything! Because short of a miracle . . . .."

He clenched his teeth and, in a single unbridled motion, heaved the stick into the right rear corner, lunged on the right rudder, and jammed the throttle through the gate.

The Spitfire reefed up abruptly into a spine-crushing turn and juddered on the edge of stall; but ever a lady, she continued to fly, pirouetting into a barrel roll that no fast-moving Messerschmitt could hope to follow.

Cub sensed rather than saw the German flash by his port wing. He rolled level, nearly stalling again, and watched, impotent, as the Messerschmitt rocketed downhill away from him toward the French coast.

His hands shook and his mind tumbled. Frantically, he searched the sky. Not a plane to be seen. He was over the water. Home, he thought. Westward. He shoved at the controls like a drunk. As in a dream, the nose came around toward the sun and dropped. The plane vibrated. Easing the throttle, he tried to read the instruments. Hopeless; they were shattered. He reached out and touched the dials; their glass covers were intact. It was his mind.

He pressed the radio call button. "Shakespeare, Shakespeare. Help!" His voice quavered.

No answer.

"Shakespeare, for Christ's sake, give me a bearing. I've got a sick airplane."

Nothing.

"For the love of God, Shakespeare, speak to me."

He unsnapped the mask and wiped the sweat from his face. Get hold of yourself, he thought. Your radio is back behind the armor plate, and it probably bought it. But you lucky devil, you didn't even pick up a nick. And your plane's still flying. Worst case, you bail out and hope somebody'll pick you out of the drink. Now use your eyes and figure out where the hell you are.

To the right, he saw only water. But on the left was a coastline, a large, rounded point of land sticking out to the northeast. He blinked and tried to focus on where he was.

Slowly, through the fog of the afterclap, he recalled the map on the wall of the Manston dispersal hut. That was it! The North Foreland with Margate, Broadstairs, and Ramsgate wrapped around the point. As day follows night, just beyond lay the Manston aerodrome. Maybe it was operationally wiped out, but they must have someplace to land.

He turned toward it and lowered the nose as much as he dared. With the airframe vibrating and the engine coughing, the plane crept across the sea, toward the coastline, like a lackadaisical ant on a giant map.

He spotted the lighthouse as he crossed Margate bay. Maybe his transmitter still worked. "Hello, Manston, Arrow Blue Three. I'm unable to hear you, but I'm four miles out." He had to blink several times to read the compass. "Coming straight in on two four zero with a dying Spitfire."

Ahead was the church on the hill. He was less than a mile out. Then the cemetery. He shot a glance at the spot where the Hurricane had gone down and felt a twinge of awe. "Dear God," he said to himself, "keep this thing flying just a little longer."

He slid the canopy back and locked it, then tugged on the safety harness. His hand moved to the undercarriage lever and pushed it down. Nothing happened. Too low to bail out. Had to be wheels up. He released the parachute harness.

The plane glided toward the grass, and he retarded the throttle and closed the fuel cocks. As the machine settled, he held the nose up to keep her just off the grass until, too slow to fly, she bellied onto the green and plowed to a stop.

Utterly drained, he laid his head back on the armor plate and heaved a sigh. He closed his eyes and said a silent prayer.

Then suddenly, he thought, Get out! She could still blow up! He slipped the buckle on the safety harness, slammed the access door open, scrambled across the wing to the grass, and ran. Forty yards away, he drew up and turned to look back at the dead machine, bathed in the setting sun. He heard the creaking of the cooling engine and thought, What a lovely bird.

*

Hours later, at Hornchurch, Cub struggled to his room, flopped onto the bed still in flight gear, and drifted off into anguished dreams. The Mauser was spitting at him and nothing he could do would stop it. A knock at the door jarred him awake, and Duke poked his head in.

"Heard the spies gave you credit for a Heinkel, lad. About time you were earning your keep. Congratulations."

Cub nodded somberly. "Thanks. But I damn near bought it." And he told Duke the story. "I'll remember that One-Oh-Nine long after I forget the Heinkel."

"Lucky. Don't suppose I'll need to give you another lecture about keeping your eyes open?"

Cub shook his head.

"So you got one and they got one. We're not going to win the war this way, are we, lad?"

*   *   *

Squadron Leader Parsons looked over his half glasses at Cub and said, "Come in. Sit down. You look troubled."

Cub closed the door to the man's office and sat in a chair. Now that he was there, coming didn't seem such a great idea. He fidgeted with his hands, and Parsons sat gazing, waiting for him to start the conversation. He had to say something. "Sir, I don't know if I'm making it here."

"I haven't had any bad reports. What's up?"

"I can't seem to get anything right. Especially for Lieutenant Duke. Nothing is good enough."

Parsons eased back in his chair, drew a match, and lit his pipe. Through a long moment of silence, the smoke billowed and drifted toward the ceiling.

"Son, I warned you it wouldn't be easy."

Cub nodded.

Parsons continued, "Some old hands around here are set in their ways. They've proved themselves. They've survived. And you're still new. An outsider. Not proven yet. They're not going to make it easy on you. Actually Duke is more creative than most. And though I am sure he can be a stickler, he doesn't strike me as a martinet. Is he fair?"

"Strictly speaking, maybe so. But his tone never changes. Whatever the words, it always says, 'You don't measure up.'"

Cub hesitated. That wasn't the whole story. And he had to tell somebody. "Also, I nearly got killed flying today. Never been so scared in my life. Lost all self-control. Couldn't see straight, much less think. Don't know if I'm up to this."

"Scary business, isn't it? Everyone who's had a close call feels the same. You've wanted to be a fighter pilot for some time, as I recall?"

Cub nodded.

"Then you can't let this break you. It's like falling off a horse. You have to get back on and ride. Follow me?"

"Yes, sir." But Cub wasn't convinced.

"And as far a Duke's concerned, I'm sure he thinks flying's an unforgiving business and Jerry will never do you a favor. Do you really want Duke to be more tolerant than they are?"

Cub hadn't thought about it that way. Logically, the answer was obvious. But just then, he wasn't feeling logical.

"How long have you been here now?" Parsons asked.

"A little over a month."

"Hardly long enough to shake down, wouldn't you say? Lots don't survive this long. Maybe Duke taught you something."

Bloody Parsons sure had a way of presenting his case. How could Cub argue? Maybe he wasn't taking this thing right.

"Look, son. Something tells me you're a pretty good pilot and student. And tough teachers can be hardest on their best pupils. They can't stand to see good people not come up to their potential. Maybe that's why Duke's hard on you."

Not coming up to potential. That sure fit. "Think so?"

"It's a possibility. And if I were you, that's the way I'd look at it."

Cub gazed at the floor, and Parsons could see he was mulling over the sell job. He'd seen youngsters fall apart in situations like this. It was tough to grow all the way up at age twenty, but that's what these kids had to do, or it was all over. He mentally crossed his fingers.

Cub had never been in a situation so scary and frustrating. Though, thinking about it, he had to admit that Duke reminded him of a tough coach. And he'd had those before.

Maybe it was like learning anything worthwhile - always a bloody, frustrating struggle with yourself. Yourself, idiot! Your own worst enemy, remember? You've got to get hold of yourself.

Parsons leaned back in the chair and let the smoke spiral upward. It was a long, uncomfortable silence, but he wasn't about to break it.

Finally Cub looked up. "Guess I feel better, sir. Thanks."

Parsons drew deeply on his pipe and smiled to himself. "Any time, son. Good luck."

Chapter 16

Cub and Doreen sat together at a table in the back of The Gannet as closing time approached. They were on their second round of drinks. Lounging in the scent of her perfume, he felt sublimely isolated from the crowd around them.

"What a good idea," he said. "Sorry I kept you waiting."

"Nonsense. I'm grateful that you're defending what's left of our country. Too bad your hours are so long. And the battle's not going too well, I take it?"

He wasn't sure, and that, itself, was troubling. "Everyone's fagged. Make mistakes. Jerry's relentless. Just keeps coming. In unbelievable numbers. And we continue to lose pilots. Given the stakes, it seems pointless to keep score."

He looked even younger than she remembered. So bright and fresh. Nothing like Pud, with his leathery face and hard jaw. Too bad, in a way, that Pud was off playing soldier in Egypt. But this young man was gorgeous.

She put her hand over Cub's and said, "Let's not talk about the war."

Her touch sent a rush through him. He could hardly believe he was alone with her. And so close. She was in her late twenties, he guessed, and not shy and playful in the silly way lots of younger girlfriends back home were.

And she was sexy. Maybe too sexy - the kind that generates plenty of excitement, then won't even kiss goodnight.

"Okay," he said, "let's talk about you."

"I'm not very interesting."

"Where are you from?"

"Originally, the north. Newcastle."

"Long way from home. What brings you to The Gannet?"

"I live nearby in Elm Park now. This is a comfortable pub and always full of nice young men."

He knew he was blushing. "You don't have a boyfriend?"

"Not now."

"And not married?"

"If I don't even have a boyfriend, how could I be married?" Over time, she'd grown comfortable with that lie, especially when she avoided a flat denial, but she was uncomfortable with this line of conversation. "Don't you have a girlfriend?"

It irritated him that the question brought Victoria to mind. "No."

"I expected you to say, lots. What do you think of English girls?"

"They're . . . nice."

"How do you know?"

The challenge made him nervous. "Well, I mean they look nice. Some of them."

"Do I take that as a compliment?"

"Why . . . yes. You're --."

A male voice interrupted, "Hello, Doreen!" A Flight Lieutenant walked up to their table grinning with enthusiasm. It was like a douse of cold water.

"Hello, Charlie," she said. And she withdrew her hand from Cub's.

"It's been a long time," Charlie said and turned to Cub. "May I join you?"

Why now? We were just getting started, and she seemed to be . . . . . But then she was always with other men. Would she want to sit alone with him when an old friend showed up? Cub's mind labored to a halt. "Well . . . I suppose --."

Doreen interrupted evenly. "Charlie, this is a private party."

"Oh. I didn't know." His face sagged in disappointment. "I'm sorry. I'll . . . see you later." And he left.

Cub heaved a sigh. "Thanks. I . . . wasn't sure what to say."

"You're tired, aren't you?"

"A little."

She squeezed his hand gently, and that electric sensation ran through him again.

"Do you like Americans?" he asked.

"You're the first I've met in the flesh. But I see them at the cinema. Gary Cooper and Clark Gable can put their slippers under my bed any time."

"Men's slippers under your bed?"

"If they're nice woolly ones."

"I don't have any like that."

"Clark Gable probably doesn't either. But he knows how to take care of a woman."

Where was this going? His heart pounded. "How do you know?"

"Remember in *Gone with the Wind* when he kissed Vivian Leigh?"

He nodded.

"Every girl in the cinema was ready to jump in bed with him, then and there."

"Just like that, eh?"

"Just like that. You mean to say that Vivian Leigh didn't give you the same idea?"

What kind of a game was she playing? "Well I . . . hadn't thought about it," he lied.

"Oh come on. What were you thinking about?"

"That Gable was lucky."

"And you'd like to be doing what he did?"

"Well . . . yes."

"I'm sure Vivian would like that."

"Really?"

"Well, you look like you could take care of her."

If this was a game, it was moving too fast and still going nowhere. He struggled for words. "I wonder if she'd agree?"

"Does it matter?"

"Well, if I were going to do something with her, it would."

"Yes, but you're here and she's there."

"You're right. If I were to do something . . . it wouldn't be with her, would it?" Geezus, did he mean to say that?

She eyed him coyly. "No, it wouldn't."

"Last orders, gentlemen, please," broke the spell like a gun shot.

Cub heaved a sigh of relief and quaffed deeply on his beer. Time to get the hell out of there, away from this dame before he . . . . . "How are you getting home?" he said, trying to sound casual.

"Well, I don't like walking it alone. I was hoping you'd give me a ride."

*

Cub followed Doreen into her cottage and closed the front door behind them. His palms were damp. It was like entering an opium den. Should he be doing this?

"Take your coat off," she said. "I'll be back straightaway." She stepped through a door at the side, leaving him alone.

He stood in her living room and gazed warily at the tidy, simple surroundings: A small fireplace with a few vaguely glowing coals, a well-used stuffed sofa and matching chairs shrouded in comfortably worn slipcovers, a wooden coffee table covered with a white crocheted lace cloth, and a pair of wooden lamps with yellowing shades. Flocked Victorian wallpaper had been enameled over to make a sculpted white surface. And on the floor, lay a well worn oriental rug with backing threads exposed here and there. The air smelled vaguely of perfume and coal smoke. Cub sensed danger lurking everywhere.

Doreen stood in front of her dressing table mirror and fluffed her hair with her fingers, then quickly daubed on eau de cologne. She looked at the picture of Pud. Why did it always come to this? How many times had she promised herself not to do it? She could still. Just walk out there and send that young man on his way. It would be easy. Stay away from those blue uniforms. Away from that pub. Stay home. And wait.

She folded the picture and slipped it into a drawer.

Cub knelt in front of the small fireplace and stoked the embers.

"Oh, thanks," she said.

She startled him, and he looked around without getting up. She stood in the doorway, her raised arm resting on the doorjamb and showing her form to advantage. The Angora sweater clung like a loving animal as her bosom stretched it. Her waist was surprisingly small, and strong thighs tapered to firm calves and slim ankles.

"Whiskey?" she said, crossing to a small cabinet in the corner. "I've been saving some."

"Why sure. We're just having a nightcap, right?"

"What else did you have in mind?"

Oh God, here we go again! "Nothing, really."

He sat down on the couch. Her oblique glance caught him staring at her, and he was sure he blushed.

"Like what you see?"

"Oh yes."

She approached with a drink in each hand.

"So what are you going to do about it?"

"I was just looking."

"That's all?"

"Well . . . . ."

"Well what?" she said.

He'd been in clinches with girls before, but never with a voluptuous woman like this one. He felt the awkward growth of his hardness. What was he doing here anyway? His eye fell on her breasts. God, what he wouldn't give to . . . .. Suppose they were false?

"Say something," she said.

His thoughts tumbled out: "I can't help wondering if they're real." His own words shocked him.

She set the drinks down, straightened up, and put her hands on her hips. Her face twisted into a sly smile. "Why don't you find out for yourself?"

My God, he thought, did I hear her right? Her gardenia fragrance addled him, as if he'd downed a double shot. But she had said it.

He stood up and put his hands on her shoulders, then gingerly drew her in. He felt the firm press of her body. Her lips on his. Her mouth working gently. The racy shock of her tongue. She, pressing herself against him. Without thought, his hand went to her breast. The downy wool and pliancy came as an exquisite shock.

"You can't tell if they're real through clothing," she whispered.

He struggled again to digest her words. Then his hand slipped down to probe under the wool, trembling, slowly moving upward over her belly, pulling at the angora as it went.

"Don't tear the goods, young man. The pullover's worth a lot. Just take it off carefully."

He smiled sheepishly, then quavering, grasped the edge of the wool and lifted it over her head.

She gestured to the brassiere. "Know what to do with this?"

He hadn't a clue and gazed blankly.

"It hooks in back," she said.

He knew he blushed as he moved behind her, and his fingers trembled while he groped to decode the clasp. At last he succeeded, and while she held her arms aloft in an uninhibited stretch, he lifted off the brassiere.

Smiling proudly, she pirouetted to face him. "Well?" she said.

For a long moment, Cub simply gaped. He raised his trembling fingers to run them across a nipple, then gingerly traced the full curve of her breast, struggling to comprehend its scope.

"They won't break, you know."

He'd never touched a naked breast before. Was he really here, really doing this? His fingers pressed gently into supple flesh.

"Now what do you think?"

Electricity seemed to dance between her flesh and his fingers.

"I'm wondering if this is really me," he said.

"I take it then, you've decided this really is me?"

He laughed nervously and nodded, then took a breast in each hand and massaged her deeply, continuing on and on in oblivious fascination as if time had lost meaning.

A surge of excitement had gone through Doreen when she decided Cub was a virgin. Spice on what already promised to be a delight. What a lovely boy! For him, she would work all the sensual tricks in her repertoire, teach him the ways she knew to pleasure a woman, and show him every position she'd heard of.

They began with a warm bath together. And four hours disappeared in a beat.

Cub lay on her bed, half in slumber, breathing deeply. Along the way, she had complimented him, saying that only a young man could keep up with her. Pigs could fly too, he thought; he was finished. But he guessed she could go on forever.

Next to him, propped on her elbows with her nipples grazing the sheet, Doreen gave him a bright smile. "So, how was that?"

"Unbelievable!"

"First time, eh?"

"Well . . . . ."

"Not with yourself, silly. I mean with a girl, naked, in bed."

There was a long silence.

She said, "That's what I thought. Now you know what it's all about. You were good, for a first timer. Another whiskey? Tea?"

Chapter 17

Ian Craigwell sat sucking on a blade of grass and grinning. "I say, Romeo, you get any sleep last night?"

In his uniform and Mae West, Cub sweltered under the late morning sun as he lay prone on the ground, head resting on his hands and eyes closed. He could feel the throb in his head. Visions of Doreen tumbled through the languorous mists of his mind like a fantasy. A fantasy he didn't want to share. "Shut up and leave me alone."

They were on the grass near the perimeter track at Hornchurch recovering from a long patrol earlier that morning. The squadron was down to twelve pilots, less than half its normal complement. All of them were at Readiness.

Ian grinned and said, "Hell's bells will ring any moment now, and you'll get off your arse and run for it. But you don't even have to open your eyes for me. Just answer a simple question."

"Get off your ass yourself and take your bloody questions where I can't hear them."

"My, but we're friendly this morning."

"Stuff friendship," Cub said. God, she was lovely. And she was his. How could he have been so lucky? He wanted to hold her and care for her and --.

"Unfriendly, hell," Ian said. "You're downright testy. That popsie must have disappointed you?"

Dammit, she was no popsie! Cub raised his head, making the ache worse, and opened his eyes to look at Ian. "She's a nice girl. And wouldn't you like to know?"

"Nice, eh? And was she nice in bed?"

"Who says I slept with her?"

"By the look of you, I don't suppose you slept at all. But how was bed?"

Bed was all these studs could think about. Didn't love enter their heads? "How the hell would I know?"

"Now, now, little brother, it's no good lying to me. What did you do? Play Parcheesi all night?"

Was this what love felt like? Did she feel the same? "Ian, get stuffed."

"And I keep asking if you did that to her."

Cub sat bolt upright and glared. "Shut the fuck up! Can't you see I'm trying to sleep?"

The scramble bell clanged, and they struggled to their feet.

"See, old boy," Ian said with a chuckle. "I warned you."

*

Still climbing at eighteen thousand feet, the squadron hurried eastward down the Estuary along the Kent coast north of Whitstable.

"Arrow leader, this is Shakespeare. Your targets have turned away, south down the Channel. We're calling this show off for you. But we have another."

"Right, Shakespeare," Tweed said. "What instead?"

"A target to investigate. Vector zero two zero." They swung to the left.

In spite of the throb, Cub's head turned constantly, and his eyes swept the sky. When he craned behind, he rolled the plane gently to get a look below. The sky was clear, and he was nervous.

"Arrow Leader, Shakespeare here. Bogies ten miles ahead."

"Right, Shakespeare," Tweed said. "Arrow Squadron, line abreast, go."

Duke's Blue section was on the right-hand end of the line. Cub adjusted his throttle to keep position below and clear of Duke on the outboard side, while Stark flew inboard.

"Enemy is ahead of you five miles, Arrow Leader," Shakespeare said.

Cub's eyes scanned all around, probing near the sun then looking ahead nervously. Surely they should see them by now.

Shakespeare called, "You are very close to the target, Arrow Leader." Then a few moments later, his anxious voice said, "You should be on top of them now."

What the hell goes on here? Cub thought.

"Tallyho," Hamilton-Price called. "A flock of twin-engine ships orbiting two miles ahead and below.

"Prepare to attack," Tweed said.

Cub saw the orbiting planes, but something was fishy. Shakespeare's radar was worthless at telling a target's altitude, and it might be vague about azimuth, but in gauging range, it was usually on the money. Was the radar picking up the same target that they saw in front? He chewed his lip nervously and looked over his right shoulder toward the sun. A minute flicker caught his eye, and his heart jumped into his throat. "Bandits, four o'clock high," he shouted.

"Hold formation, Arrow Squadron," Tweed called. "Press the attack on the bombers ahead!"

"But they're rolling in on us, Arrow Leader," Duke called. "Blue Section breaking."

"No!" Tweed yelled.

Duke's plane pitched up and the ailerons deflected, signaling a hard right roll. Cub jammed the throttle to the stop and followed Duke, whose plane disappeared into the orb of the sun. The first Messerschmitt flicked by. Duke reappeared outside the sun's disc spewing cartridges and belt links from under wing as he fired at the second German.

A third Messerschmitt came head-on out of the sun, and not being able to see his own gun-sight pipper, Cub pointed the Spitfire's nose blindly at the German and fired. The enemy's gun flashes and his own tracers were lost in the glare. Then the silhouette of the oncoming Messerschmitt elongated upward and he shoved the stick forward. As the two machines passed, his plane shook, and he heard the thunder of the Daimler-Benz.

The three Spitfires continued to climb, and other Messerschmitts hurtled past them like a rain of meteors.

"Arrow Squadron, break," Duke shouted. "It's a trap! There's a whole squadron of the bastards coming down on you."

Rolling out of the climb on Duke's wing, Cub scanned the sky overhead. It was empty.

"Blue Leader, this is Blue Two," Burt Stark called. "I'm hit. Permission to return to base."

Cub looked across at Burt's machine. It was dropping behind and leaving a thin trail of smoke.

"Beetle for the barn, Blue Two," Duke said. "Good luck."

Now, calls came rapid-fire over the radio channel.

"Green Section, break."

"Yellow Section, break."

Green Two, get this bastard off me!"

"Green One, break right."

Tweed's voice: "Press the attack!" Then: "Oh my God . . . Break off, Arrows, and defend yourselves!"

"I'm hit! I'm hit!"

"For God's sake, break right, Green One."

"Red Three, watch it. On your tail."

"Arrow Leader, break left."

"Yellow Two, they're bracketing you. Pull up. Pull up!"

"Red Three's had it."

"Yellow Two's had it."

Below, four Spitfires augered toward the sea trailing smoke. The Messerschmitts had threaded through the squadron and climbed out on the far side, too far away for Duke and Cub to reach quickly. In a loose formation of six pairs, the Germans arced over the top of their loop, as if in an air display, and started down.

"Watch it, Arrows," Duke called, "here they come again." Duke rolled inverted. "All right, Blue Three, let's help our friends."

Cub followed.

More urgent calls.

"Red Section, break left."

"Arrow Leader, look out, five o'clock high."

"Yellow One, break right, I'll nail that bastard."

"Arrow Leader, break, for God's sake!"

"Got him. I got him, Yellow One. You're clear."

Then Tweed's quavering voice: "This is Arrow Leader. I'm hit. Going Down. Take over Yellow One."

As Duke and Cub dived back toward the fight, most of the Germans disappeared to the east, but a few still hung around. Cub was well astern as Duke closed on one, when another swung in front of Cub onto Duke's tail, but out of Cub's gun range.

Cub called, "Break left, Blue One."

Duke's Spitfire rolled hard into a turn, and the Messerschmitt tightened his arc to follow. Cub called, "That Jerry's inside of you, Blue one. Watch it."

In desperation, Cub decided to ignore the distance. He angled his machine toward the Messerschmitt, pulled a big lead, and fired. Like magic, the German broke off and flicked to the right.

Cub turned with him and closed rapidly. He snapped another burst and watched the tracers home on the target and erupt in impact flashes.

The German wavered but held his steep bank. Cub hauled around to follow, but the speed of his dive wouldn't let him match the Messerschmitt's turn, and he hurtled past its tail. The German, turning well inside the Spitfire's arc, was coming around at a frightening rate and would soon edge into his stern quarter.

Remembering his first flight with Duke, Cub hauled the Spitfire into a climb, and as he reached vertical, he rolled to aim the machine behind the Messerschmitt and continued to arc into a loop. From the top, he pulled down hard toward the German, who continued his flat turn. Dropping vertically, Cub rolled again to slant in behind his prey like a stooping hawk.

With both hands on the stick, he pressed himself back into the seat and brought the gun sight pipper onto the target less than two hundred yards ahead. For an instant, he tracked the cockpit area then pulled a short lead and pressed the firing button. The Brownings thundered, the Spitfire shuddered from the recoil, and his tracers poured into the German's wing root. The plane erupted in black smoke, and its wings leveled. Cub pulled up hard to avoid overshooting. Check your six, flashed in his mind, and he craned to look behind. A Spitfire followed a few hundred yards astern.

Duke called, "Keep after him, lad. I've got you covered."

Cub hauled around toward the Messerschmitt, but before he could fire again, its canopy came off and the pilot tumbled out.

"Not bad for a beginner, lad. But now we have a couple of Krauts coming in, eleven o'clock high. Break into them."

Cub rolled left and pulled the nose up. But while still out of gun range, the two Germans broke off and slanted away to the east.

Duke and Cub leveled out and made several circuits looking for friend or foe. The sky was vacant.

Under Shakespeare's direction, they went down to search the water for survivors, but the effort was in vain.

*

When Cub and Duke landed at Hornchurch, Burt Stark greeted them, but there were no smiles. Arrow Squadron had lost six pilots in the engagement, including Tweed and Dickie Hudson.

By order of the Group Captain, the squadron stood down. The next day, they were relieved of combat duties and ordered north, out of the battle zone, to Kirton-in-Lindsey.

Chapter 18

Peter Duke and Tony Hamilton-Price sat in Duke's white-painted room in the Transient Officers Mess at Kirton. It was furnished simply: a desk, two wooden chairs, a metal bed, and a small wardrobe. Blackout curtains were drawn tightly over the window.

The mood at supper had been somber, and now the two men sat holding glasses as they talked. A half-empty bottle of Vat 69 stood on the desk.

"So," Tony said, "we get a new squadron leader. You think they'll promote from inside or bring in someone else."

Tony was fishing, Duke thought. "Outside. Especially after a fiasco like we had."

Tony tamped his pipe. "It was a shaky do, all right,"

"Shaky do, my arse. It was a fucking disaster. The bastards set us up, and it worked like a charm."

Tony nodded wistfully. "We all fell for it."

Duke thought, Almost all. "Bayer called it for us, but not all of us listened."

Tony snapped, "Listened to what? Are we supposed give up the attack any time some green kid cries wolf?"

"I don't care who spots the enemy first, we've got to pay attention. It happens this kid has pretty good eyes."

"A regular fucking eagle eye, eh? Since when are you defending him?"

Duke squinted at Hamilton-Price. "If we'd listened to Cub, we wouldn't be counting all those empty places in the mess, would we? And yes, I've changed my mind about the newcomers. I don't care if they're Yanks or Poles or polecats. If they can help us win this war, we need them."

"I still say, we have to press our attacks."

"Of course. But pressing them when their fighters are ready to pounce is plain stupid."

"So what do you propose?"

"Listen to every radio call, and give up those bloody dress-parade formations."

"And scrap all our training?"

"You can't keep big formations together when you're mixing it up with fighters. You're too busy keeping track of what's going on."

"Look, we've practiced formation attacks until we're blue in the face. That's how you deliver maximum firepower, and they're our stock in trade. We can't just abandon them."

"I don't care what we practiced, Tony. They may be fine against unescorted bombers, but when fighters are after you, they don't work. We've got to be more flexible. And when we attack, we should leave a section behind, up high, to discourage the Jerry fighters from coming after the attackers."

"But that dilutes our firepower."

"Tony, stop reciting from that manual. Close-formations are good practice, good for sticking together in bad weather, and lovely on air parades. But they're no damned good for real air fighting"

"Rubbish! New tactics will get us in trouble. We should stick to what we know."

"And what we know is that our way costs us casualties. Have you been watching how Jerry works his loose two and four plane formations?"

"Maybe he never practiced large formation attacks?"

"Oh balls! He's been flying for four years in live combat. He knows what works and what doesn't."

"Given a couple of months off, maybe we could train everybody. But we don't have that luxury. Jumping pell-mell into new tactics will be disaster."

"Hornet Squadron operates with three four-plane flights. The fours fly in loose line astern. In battle, they stay in pairs for mutual protection. And they changed to it overnight."

"What makes you think that will work better?"

"Spritt, their squadron leader has been at this longer than any of us. He invented it. And my friend, Gunnar Christian, who's one of their Flight Leaders, swears by it. Besides, how the hell could it be worse?"

Tony tossed back the last of his Scotch and set the tumbler on the desk. "Well, friend," he said, standing up, "I say we can't afford to screw up what we have right now." Tony eyed Duke skeptically for a long moment. "I suppose you and I'll never agree. Anyway, I'm going to sleep." And he left.

Duke refilled his glass and lay back on the bed against his pillow. Bloody Tony did everything by the book. Too many people went by the book. Just couldn't adapt. God, he hoped they didn't make Tony skipper.

In France, where Duke had been assigned during the battle there, the Germans had cut the British and French to shreds in piecemeal air combats. When he returned to Hornchurch, he had patiently explained the German tactics and how to counter them. But Tweed and Tony and some of the others didn't want to know, and the disaster that finally befell the squadron seemed so predictable. Mister Churchill might talk of winning against all odds, but the facts were that Fighter Command was losing. And part of the problem was tactics.

And the fuddy-duddies worried that the youngsters couldn't learn new ways. For Christ's sake, the youngsters, untainted by outdated training, might be the only hope! But they had to learn fast. This was no time to coddle. They had to be pushed hard. Would it hurt them? Hell, the alternative was too grim think about.

Besides, it hurt Duke more to push them than his pushing ever hurt them. However hard he'd worked at it, however much he'd wanted to command, however they'd harangued about leadership at Cranwell, pushing people came unnaturally to Duke. He had to gird himself for it. Upper-class lads, like Tony, carried it off with aplomb - never unsure in their opinions, always ready to give orders. But command came harder to those from simpler beginnings.

Peter Duke's father was a miner who was proud to work at the coal face, but his mother made it her business to keep Peter from becoming a miner too. She insisted he go to school and study and learn about the world beyond the tailings. He was not a good student, but hard work paid off and got him into RAF college. He still called Cannock home, but he had been back only once for a visit in several years. And fortunately, his life was now a long way from the coal face.

And despite his inclinations, he had learned to take command. However he felt inside, he could instantly transform himself, put on that dour glare, speak with authority, pick at details, and demand perfection. It was a pretty good act, he knew.

* * *

Cub and Ian shared a room in the Kirton officers' mess. Cub lay on his bed, wide awake, with his eyes closed. He welcomed the rest, but why did he have to be so far away? Down south, when he flew all the hours of the day, it kept his brain occupied, but now he couldn't get his mind off Doreen. If he couldn't be with her, he wanted to be alone.

The door opened and Ian entered.

Cub raised his head slowly from the pillow and opened his eyes.

"Sorry. Did I wake you?"

"No. I was just . . . thinking."

"The war?"

"Sort of."

"You've been kind of distant lately. What gives?"

The last thing Cub wanted to discuss was Doreen; Ian would have it spread all over the squadron. They had to talk about something else. "I'm trying to figure out Duke." It was the first thing that had come to him, but it had the advantage of getting his mind off the woman.

"He's a hard nut."

"But that's the military way."

"Why is the military different?"

Parsons had called it, Cub thought. Duke was about as tolerant as the enemy, and that wasn't all bad. "Lives are at stake."

"So what?" Ian said. "People still have to do their best."

"I mean lives are at stake here and now. If doing your best means learning by mistakes, forget it. We've got no time for that."

"Geezus, are you standing up for Duke now?"

Well, the man was bloody competent, Cub thought. In air fighting, not Tony, not Tweed, not any of those senior guys could match up to Duke. Cub had joined the RAF to learn to be a fighter pilot, and much as he hated to admit it, the man was probably the right person to learn from. "Maybe so, " he said.

"Best of British luck. By the way, the Group Captain's coming up from Hornchurch tomorrow. He's called a pilots' meeting right after lunch."

"What's up?"

"Damned if I know.   But he's got to do something with Arrow Squadron.   Maybe he'll transfer us to a new outfit.   I might get rid of Hamilton-Price and maybe you'll get out from under Duke."

"Not bloody likely."

"Nice thought, though, isn't it?"

"I'm not sure."

"Geez, you're decisive today.   Listen, some of us are headed into town to find out what goes on there.   Interested?"

"Don't think so."

"Have you lost interest in girls and beer?"

"No. Just don't feel like it."

"You sure as hell felt like it down south."

"Yeah, well, we're not down south now."

"What the hell's the matter with you?"

"Nothing. Just want to stay here."

"You feel all right?"

Cub hesitated. "So, so."

"Well, come into town and maybe you'll get over it."

"Go on. I'll see you later."

"Geezus, I've never seen you like this before. Not even after flying all fucking day long."

Ian gazed at Cub in silence for a long moment.   Then his eyes narrowed and he said, "I've got it! You're in love, aren't you?"

Cub tried desperately to hide a reaction, but he knew he controlled his eye motion poorly.

"I'll be a sonofabitch," Ian said.   "You fell for that skirt at The Gannet, didn't you?"

Cub closed his eyes, hoping the subject would evaporate.

"Come on, for Christ's sake," Ian said, "I'm your roommate. You can tell me."

"Tell you what?"

"The truth. I'll keep it quiet."

Oh sure you will, Cub thought.

"Come on, man, " Ian said, "tell me all about it."

"Get stuffed."

Ian smiled and shook his head. "So Big Boobs got you, did she?"

"Goddammit, I really like her."

"I'll bet she's some number in bed."

"Who the hell said anything about bed?"

Ian threw his arms up in exasperation. "Not this routine again!"

"Piss off, will you."

"She got under your fingernails as well as into your knickers, didn't she?"

Cub sat up and glared. "Will you shut up, dammit?"

Ian was silent for a moment. Then he said solemnly, "Okay, so you like her. That doesn't mean you have to lay here and make yourself sick over her. Life goes on, pal, even when they're not around."

"Christ, didn't you ever fall for a girl? So you didn't want to mess around?"

"Who said anything about messing around? Besides, she's not your type. That Kendall dame's more like it."

"So you already told me."

"Look, why don't you come with us and have a beer? You'll feel better."

Cub lay back down. "I'll pass."

Ian stood up and shrugged. "Okay. I'll see you later." He slipped into his uniform jacket and opened the door.

Cub said, "I'll count on you to make sure everyone else knows about this."

"Not me, friend. I'm going to tell them you're sick."

"I'll bet."

Chapter 19

The morning dawned cloudless and warm; even the incessant Humberside wind was calm. Cub and Duke, dressed in tennis clothes and carrying rackets, ambled onto a court nestled in the trees. The dirt surface was rolled to a smooth finish; the net was new and the fencing recently painted. Roses bloomed along the edges, and the air smelled of fresh-cut grass.

"You ready to lose, lad?"

"I'm out of practice."

"Tell me about it. Did you play a lot at home?"

"Yeah. In school. And a few tournaments. Even won one. How about you?"

"I played a little as a kid, but worked hard on it at RAF College. Got into the Air Force finals in thirty-eight."

"Hope I can make it worth your while."

They entered the court, and Cub crossed to the far side. Duke walked to the near base line and glanced up at the sun. "Going to be hot before we're through."

Duke led off with a gentle forehand, which Cub returned neatly. The ball arced back and forth over the net as the players settled into their moves. Slowly, they warmed to it; the ball shuttled briskly, and they scrambled to make returns. Duke began to put his whole body into his shots, sending them flat and dropping them just at the baseline. Cub stepped to them and, in sweeping strokes, fired them back. Feeling for each other's limits, they discarded any pretense of caution.

With a determined grimace, Duke drove a low forehand deep into the corner and sprinted to the net. In a running plunge, Cub ticked it off the tip of his racket into a lob that passed out of reach over Duke's head and dropped short of the baseline. Watching helplessly, Duke scowled as it bounced again.

He turned slowly, and his face stretched in a wry grin. "You held out on me, you bloody ringer."

"Just lucky."

"You ready to play for real, lad?"

Cub nodded.

"Then serve."

Duke hunched, weaving slightly, behind the serve court. Standing at the center of the baseline, Cub arched and tossed the ball high. His racket head accelerated, arcking over his head to full stretch where it connected with the ball and drove it, dead straight, into the inside corner of the opposite serve court. Duke barely flinched before it passed him and spent itself against the fence. He turned to eye the ball, rolling slowly back toward him. "Would you like to try that serve over, lad?"

"Not a chance. Change courts."

So the rallies began. Duke played a charging, driving game with strokes that sent the ball whistling over the net. Cub moved economically to deliver precise, modulated shots - easy dinks when they paid off, smashing drives when it counted. As time passed, a few squadron members gathered to watch.

Cub and Duke split the first two sets, and after thirteen games in the third, it was set-point to Cub as Duke stepped to the baseline to serve. Sweat ran freely down his face and his shirt was wet. He glowered across the net.

Cub hunched down at the opposite baseline, dancing from side to side. He worked his mouth against the dryness and toyed with the racket nervously. His face and arms glistened.

Duke wiped his brow with his forearm, then arched and tossed the ball high. Unlimbering with the full power of body and shoulder, he smashed it into the outside back corner of the serve court, a sure ace in most competition. But, like so many Duke thought were killers, Cub returned it, and the rally was on.

The ball crossed the net four times with the players drilling their shots. Then, Cub drove the ball into the corner and started forward. Duke dove awkwardly for it and sent it into a high lob, then stumbled sideways to catch himself at the side fence. But Cub turned and raced for the baseline, and when the ball bounced, he delivered a clean shot into the opposite corner. Duke watched helplessly.

Spectators cheered.

Cub went over to Duke and offered his hand. Duke squeezed it sharply and glared at him. "Out of practice, eh? We'll try it again when you're better prepared, lad."

"Tomorrow, if you like."

"Maybe I'll remember how to play by then."

Together they walked back toward the quarters in silence. Duke's jaw worked, and he thumped his racket into his hand repeatedly, as if to punish it.

Cub should have felt good; he'd finally bested Duke at something. But he wanted Duke's respect, and now all he could feel was the strain between them. Maybe he should have let Duke win.

Suddenly, Duke stopped and faced him. "Lad, do you know a girl named Doreen Phillips?"

Cub froze. "Why do you ask?"

"Somebody said they saw you with her several times at The Gannet."

"Who said it?"

"Don't remember."

"Craigwell?"

Duke shook his head. "Wasn't Craigwell. Said you were there the other night and you left with her."

"So what?"

Duke gave a sly grin. "You seeing much of her?"

"What if I am?"

"Well, she's nearly old enough to be your mother. And did she tell you she's married?"

It was as if Duke had hit him in the solar plexus. Married? His eyes rounded. "I don't believe you!"

Duke put his hands on his hips and chuckled. "You got the hots for her, eh? Well let me tell you, she's been in bed with every blue suit around, and she's hitched to an Army bloke."

Cub shook his head slowly.

"I'm not surprised she didn't tell you. Her old man's away in North Africa, and while he's gone, she has it off with whoever'll have her. Keeping the marriage quiet helps."

Cub glowered. "How the hell do you know?"

"Christ, everybody knows."

"Well I didn't. And I don't believe you."

Duke broke into a broad leer. "Well tell me lad, did she give you a good roll?"

"Fuck you, Duke."

Duke chortled. "No longer a sweet young thing, eh? Well, you've still got a long way to go, boy."

*

Cub took a bath then sat alone in his room, his mind free-running. What the hell am I doing here? Fighting for the bloody English. Messed up with English girls. I ought to be back in California, in the good old USA, where there's no war, no Duke, no Victoria, and no . . . Doreen.

But maybe Duke was wrong. Maybe it was all lies. Maybe she hadn't really slept around? And perhaps she wasn't married.

But maybe she was. Had Duke had her too? How could she hold out on me? Would Duke make up a story like that? Why? Because he got beaten at tennis?

Nothing made sense.

Ian Craigwell entered. "You ready for lunch?" Then he looked at Cub obliquely. "Hey, pal, you look awful. Duke beat you?"

Cub shook his head slowly.

"Oh shit," Ian said. "It's that dame again. What happened?"

Cub told of his conversation with Duke. When he was finished, Ian said, "Geezus, I swear I didn't say anything to anybody."

"Somebody said something. And I think Duke's lying."

Ian gazed at the floor in silence for a moment, then said softly, "Duke went to town with a bunch of us last night. I didn't say a word. But Doreen's name came up, and before I even realized who she was, someone said they saw you with her. There was a lot of talk about it. From what was said, I don't think Duke lied."

"What do you mean?"

"This lady has a reputation. And it's not just with Duke."

There was a long silence. Cub wanted to grieve all alone, to ponder how he got into this mess, how anything could be worth the anguish he felt. At length, he said, "Leave me alone, will you?"

"Sure." Ian turned and opened the door. "But this, too, will pass, you know." Then he left.

* * *

Arrow squadron pilots gathered in the Kirton briefing room for the Group Captain's meeting. They lounged in chairs and chatted. Duke and Tony Hamilton-Price sat to one side. Cub took a seat in the back next to Burt Stark. He'd had a nap and felt better.

At the podium, the Group Captain eyed his watch, then called the meeting to order, and the chatter died out. "I hope everyone's been getting some rest, here."

The audience let out a relaxed chorus of affirmation.

"Well, my pitch today is short. First, you're getting new Spitfires, Mark Twos. They have more power and speed, especially at altitude. Should give you more advantage over the One-Oh-Nines."

The audience cheered.

He continued, "I just returned from a briefing at Fighter Command Headquarters, so let me pass on a few things. As I'm sure you know, Jerry has started bombing London in daylight. That's bad news for Londoners, who we're supposed to defend, but it's bloody good news for us.

"The Luftwaffe had nearly wiped out our airfields in the south. Manston, of course, has been out of business for some time, and they just about finished off Biggin Hill and plastered Hawkinge, Lympne, Detling, Kenley, Eastchurch, Rochford, and the list goes on. They destroyed facilities and aircraft. Eleven group was all but out of commission. And it showed in our kill ratios. Last week we barely kept even with Jerry.

"But those bastards can't hold that pace and go after London, too. So we're getting a reprieve. And we're coming back fast, rebuilding and reequipping.

"And there's more good news. The extra distance to London is just enough so the One-Oh-Nines have only enough fuel to stick around for five or ten minutes. Their bombers don't get the protection they need, and the fighters are always on the defensive. Furthermore, we in Eleven Group don't have to carry the whole load anymore. Twelve Group's fighters from the north can get in on the act over London. If he keeps this up, Jerry may find his invasion plans getting a bit sticky. So cross your fingers."

Excited comments raced through the audience.

"Now the big news. It is my pleasure to introduce your new commanding officer, Squadron Leader Gunnar Christian, just promoted from Hornet Squadron."

Except for Hamilton-Price, who gave a perfunctory clap, the audience applauded enthusiastically.

Christian mounted the podium. "Thank you, gents. I'll be brief. Some new people have joined us." He pointed into the audience. "You may know Roger Bodington and Stan Warwick who came across with me from Hornet Squadron. Stand up gents." A flying Officer and a Sergeant Pilot rose briefly. "And we have number of fresh replacements." Christian waved at a clutch of young men at the side. "Be sure to welcome them. Flight leaders and I will assign them after we discuss it.

"Effective immediately, we will organize differently in the air. The basic flying unit will be a pair of fighters - a section - a leader and a wingman. They fly together, fight together, and stick together, with the wingman responsible to cover his leader. Two sections make up a flight. We'll have three flights, Red, Yellow and Blue. I'll head Red, Duke will lead Blue, and Hamilton-Price Yellow. We tried it in Hornet Squadron, and it works well. Jerry has flown a similar organization for a long time. Now we're going to turn the tables."

A murmur went through the audience, and Cub saw Duke nodding in approval.

"Tomorrow morning at seven thirty," Christian continued, "we'll take a bus to Castle Bromwich, where our new planes are ready. We'll pick them up and fly back here by early afternoon. Then we have three days before returning to Hornchurch. We'll use that time for flying drill to work out new formations and tactics. I want everybody to pitch into this. We haven't much time. Then we go back and give 'em hell!"

The audience gave a rousing cheer.

When the meeting was over, Burt introduced Cub to Bodington and Warwick, then they went over to meet the new replacement pilots. They were fresh from OTU and hungered to learn about combat flying. The youngsters asked a battery of questions and hung on every word, fixated, as the two veterans spun out the answers.

These fellows looked so young, Cub thought, with red cheeks and dancing eyes. He could scarcely imagine that it was just over a month since he'd arrived. Had he looked so eager and nervous as these lads? So naive? How many of them would survive?

Burt struck up a conversation a bright-eyed youngster named Colin Darrow, who came from Alton, near where Burt grew up. There was obvious warmth and common ground between them.

When the group began to disperse, Burt went over to briefly buttonhole Duke. Then he and Cub went outside and walked down the flight line. The squadron's remaining six Spitfires were parked in a neat row.

"Good to get new ones," Cub said.

"Yes, but I feel a bit nostalgic for mine. She brought me a long way."

"You had her since the beginning?"

"Yes, and I might be the only one. We sure lost a lot of planes."

"And pilots."

They walked in silence. Finally Cub said, "Seeing those new kids makes me think. I've been in the squadron a matter of weeks, but it seems like years."

"It ages a man."

"Yeah, and changes you. When I arrived, I worried about saving my skin, and that hasn't changed. I also wondered if I'd make it here, and that still niggles a bit. But the other day, after I shot down that Messerschmitt, I found myself with a new problem. I realized I'd become a killer. A cold-blooded professional, no less. I'd never given it a thought before. That poor bastard never had a chance once I started on him.

"I wonder what he was like. Probably a nice guy. The sort you'd buy a drink for if he showed up in a pub. And I killed him. On purpose. I know that's what I'm supposed to do, but it bothers me. Does that ever concern you?"

"Bothers all of us some. Anyone who's ever fought in a war, I imagine. It's one of those things you ponder. Like, What's our purpose in the universe? Or, Why did God arrange to have wars at all?"

Cub nodded thoughtfully, but was still troubled.

They walked on, eyeing the planes wistfully. Their paintwork was nicked and scratched, even gouged in places. The sandpaper treads on top of the wing roots had been worn away by the scuff of boots. Some of them dripped oil, and most had patches here and there covering skin damage.

Cub stopped by the wing of his machine and fingered one of the gun ports.

"By the way," Burt said, "congratulations on nailing that Jerry."

"Thanks."

Cub suddenly turned to Burt. "Say, that reminds me. Let me show you something."

"Sure."

"I want to explain how I got that bird."

Cub led the way back inside. The briefing room was empty now, and he found a piece of paper. They sat down at a table.

"It's a maneuver I came across accidentally the first time I flew with Duke. And I had a Kraut try it on me once. I call it the short-cut loop." And he began to sketch as he explained.

"Suppose you attack a slow moving adversary from behind, and he breaks into a hard turn. With your excess speed, if you try to follow, his turn rate will be quicker than yours. So he may get around onto the your tail and turn the tables.

"However, instead of following his turn, suppose you pull up into a loop. You lose speed, as you climb, and gain the aid of gravity in pulling over the top. So for the same G force, your arc can be tighter than the other guy's. Moreover, traveling vertically, on both the up and down sides of the loop, you can change compass headings easily, by simply rolling the plane. Thus, you break the loop into three segments - the pull-up, going over the top, and the pullout. Each can be on a different heading, and by picking the last two skillfully, you can arrange to come down behind your target.

Cub looked up at Burt. "What do you think?"

"I don't follow the theory, but I get the idea. Why don't we fly it and see?"

"Now?"

"Why not? In the old ships, for old time's sake."

Cub jumped up. "I'll get my gear. See you on the flight line."

*

At seven o'clock that evening Cub and Burt tripped up the front steps of The King's Arms, just outside the entrance to the air station.

"You sure Duke's here?" Burt said.

"Somebody in the mess said so."

They pushed through the door. Inside, the place was filled with men in blue uniforms. All the seats were taken, and many people were standing. Smoke hung thick in the air.

They got drinks, then picked their way through the raucous crowd until they found Duke sitting at a table with Tony Hamilton-Price and others. As Cub and Burt approached, Duke and Tony were in a vigorous conversation; the others listened.

Duke said, "But head-on is a terrible way to attack fighters."

"Why?" Tony said. "Puts the fear of God in them to see a rank of Spitfires coming line-abreast down their throats." His tongue sounded thick.

"Balls. Jerry never runs away just because we rush him en masse. And we have no advantage going head to head. We shoot, they shoot, and who get's hurt depends only on who's the luckiest shot. Lousy odds. We have to find ways to shoot him when he can't bring his guns to bear."

"Can't always do that. Sometimes the fight develops with us facing each other."

"Even then," Duke said, "we don't need to fly straight at him."

"Losing your pluck, are you?"

Everyone tensed, and Duke eyed Tony skeptically. "Come on, friend. You don't mean that."

"Then tell me what you mean."

Duke nodded slowly and pulled a pencil from his breast pocket. "Okay." And he began to explain while he sketched on the back of a beer coaster.

"The two sections in a flight going head to head against Jerry fighters split the moment they first sight the enemy and hopefully before they see us. The sections turn forty-five degrees away from each other, so they depart at a right angle, while the Germans approach down the center, between them."

Duke drew the Y-shaped path of the Spitfires. "Our sections, which are now separated on the limbs of the Y with the Germans closing down the middle, turn back toward each other and approach the enemy from abeam. And by turning hard, they can swing onto the enemies' tails.

"Now, the Germans may react in any of three ways. They might see our move and split too, turning into both sections. Or, they might spot only one section and turn toward it. But with luck and if we start the maneuver early enough, they might not see us until they're attacked from behind.

"So some of our planes may still face Jerry head to head, but they are no worse off than before. But if we can carry the maneuver to the point where we turn into Jerry before he reacts, then the Germans that turn toward one section necessarily expose their stern quarter to the other. And at least one section will to get a tail shot out of it." Duke eyed Tony directly. "And that, my friend, gives us better odds than a simple head-on attack."

Ingenious, Cub thought.

Tony shook his head. "Duke, you're drinking strong stuff. It's hard enough for us to coordinate our moves in the air when we're all together in formation. But if we're spread all over the sky, it's impossible."

"Why?" Cub said. "What's the radio for?"

Tony scowled at him. "The radio, laddie, is for the ground controllers to pass directions and squadron leaders to give orders. When you've been around longer, you'll get the idea."

Cub glowered. "Look, we're talking about new tactics."

"When you've had experience," Tony snapped, "you can tell us how it should be done. Meanwhile, young lads should be seen and not heard."

"Piss off, Tony," Cub said. "Bet you haven't entertained a new idea since you discovered sex."

Tony reeled slightly as he got to his feet and his eyes fixed Cub unsteadily. "You little Yankee shit."

Cub clenched his fists.

Duke got to his feet and thrust himself between them. "Enough, both of you." He held Tony by the shoulder and grabbed Cub firmly by the arm.

Cub glared at Tony and said to Duke, "Don't worry. I'm not going after him. But keep him away from me or I'll deck him."

Minutes later, Tony lurched through the crowd and left the pub, escorted by a fellow officer.

Duke sat down and Cub and Burt took the vacated seats.

"Sorry about that," Duke said. "I guess we're all a little edgy, and he started here earlier than the rest of us."

Cub was looking at the door through which Tony left. "What kind of a chip is he carrying, anyway?"

"Let's just say that Tony Hamilton-Price has a strong sense of tradition. He likes everything in its place. Including junior officers." Then he hesitated. "He'll be better when he's sober."

They chatted and the tension eased.

Cub relaxed and took a good look at Duke, and it struck him that the man looked wan. It troubled him, but Tony grated on him even more. "I don't give a damn what Tony thinks, that split attack's good idea."

"Don't like going down Messerschmitts' throats, eh? Well, one of these day, we'll fly it and see how it works."

"Speaking of experiments, Burt and I flew this afternoon and tried something new. Something you should know about." Cub explained the short-cut loop and how he'd discovered it.

"And it works?" Duke said.

"Works good," Burt said. "We also figured out how to counter it, but you have to understand exactly what's happening and make your move quickly. Against someone who's unaware, it's a killer."

"By God, they taught you something in school, didn't they, lad? You and I'll check it out tomorrow."

"Right, sir."

They chatted a while, then Burt announced he was ready for bed. Cub agreed and the two stood up to go.

"I've got something else to talk about, " Duke said, looking at Cub. "Can you stick around for a minute?"

Burt gave them a knowing smile and left.

Cub sat down, and they ordered another beer. Again, Cub noted the pallor in Duke's face.

When the waitress brought the drinks, Duke pulled out his wallet, to get money, and laid it open on the table. A woman in a photograph smiled up from it. Like the pictures on Duke's wall, she was stunning.

"Boy," Cub said, "you sure pick good-lookers."

Duke followed his eye. "Thanks." And he snapped up the wallet.

"May I have look at the picture?"

Duke frowned, then flopped the wallet open again.

Cub gazed at the photograph. The signature at the bottom read: All my love, C.

"She's beautiful."

Duke took a pull on his drink and nodded slowly, then he closed the wallet and pushed it into his pocket. "She's pretty, all right. But she's not here."

"What's her name?"

"Cecily. Cecily Sheldon."

"Girlfriend?"

Duke was silent for a long moment. "Used to be." There was a catch in Duke's voice, and he suddenly seemed distant. An awkward silence followed.

Cub guessed there was more to the Cecily Sheldon story, and he hesitated, wondering if Duke had any more say.

Finally Cub said, "You wanted to talk to me?"

Duke did a double take as if to free his mind from other thoughts. "Oh. Yes. Look, in the new formation, each two-plane section is going to have a leader and a wingman."

Cub nodded.

"I want you for my wingman."

For a moment Cub wasn't sure he'd heard right. Was this the Duke he could never satisfy? The man who called him lad as if he were a bad boy? The man who couldn't resist needling him? "I . . . I thought you'd want somebody with more experience, like Burt."

"You'll do, lad. He'll lead the second section, and he's picked out a new pilot, named Darrow, for a wingman."

"I never expected --."

"Never mind what you expected, lad. You just stick to my wing and keep Jerry off my arse."

"Yes, sir. Is that all?"

Duke nodded. "And you can skip the *sir* from now on."

How long had Cub waited to win Duke over? Was it only this morning that this man had cut him down with the story about Doreen? And that thought stopped him cold.

He looked at Duke and said solemnly, "I need to get something straight. Did you tell me the truth about Doreen?"

Duke's was stone-faced. He nodded slowly.

"She's really married?"

"Yes."

"Why did you tell me?"

"A bolt out of the blue, eh?"

Cub didn't answer.

Finally Duke said, "You in pretty deep with her?" There was another awkward silence. Then Duke continued, "For better or worse, you and I have to fly and fight together. We can't harbor big secrets from each other, and it does me no good for you to be in pain. You might get distracted at the wrong moment. I figured the sooner you knew the truth, the less it would hurt."

Cub turned that over in his mind and concluded it sounded like the truth. "Okay," Cub said. He stood up and bid Duke goodnight.

After Cub left, Duke pressed his hand to his upper abdomen. The gnawing in his gut was back. Stress, the Doc had told him. Too much booze and flying, and not enough sleep. A lot of people had it. After all, the Doc said, he'd been in combat continuously since the invasion of France. What did he expect?

And he had to be careful not to get too close to Cub. The lad was a likeable kid. Lots of courage and sincere confidence. But close squadron friends were a liability. Not worth the friendships. To survive, you had to keep your distance.

Chapter 20

The brief respite at Kirton ended, and Arrow Squadron returned to Hornchurch.

Two days later, they scrambled in midmorning and encountered a large enemy formation over eastern Essex, headed for London. The battle opened with an assault on German fighter escorts.

Cub's plane was hit several times on the first pass, and he was losing coolant, so he dropped out of the fight and returned alone to Hornchurch with the engine coughing.

He was descending through a scattered layer of small clouds at five thousand feet, when the airfield came in sight to the south, six miles ahead. He made out the grass field and a dark surround that would be the perimeter track. He keyed the radio and tried to call the field, but got no response. My radio must be out, he thought.

The radiator temperature gauge was creeping toward the upper peg. The engine might give out soon, and he'd have to glide. He leveled off to preserve altitude and give himself maximum glide range. Come on, baby, he thought, keep ticking over a little longer. With that, the engine died.

Frantically, he worked the throttle and mixture control in an attempt to restart it. But the effort was vain, and he slammed the engine RPM control forward to put the propeller in full fine pitch. Airspeed dropped until he lowered the nose to hold it at just over on hundred miles per hour, the speed that he guessed would give the flattest glide with the engine out. He cranked the rudder trim dead center and brought the elevator tabs up until he had to hold a slight back pressure on the stick.

She was as clean as he could make her. Now it was a matter of keeping her headed for home and working the stick to hold optimum glide speed. He flicked an eye to the airspeed indicator - right on one hundred.

Leaning against the side of the canopy, he sighted past the nose trying to estimate the touchdown point - the spot on the ground that, relative to his plane, wasn't shifting up or down as he approached.

Careful, he recalled, not to stretch the glide by raising the nose. It'll only make her sink faster. And if she stalls, you're dead. He satisfied himself with another glance at airspeed.

The landing could be rough. He heaved on the buckles of the security harness, tightening it as hard as he could around his hips and shoulders. He'd leave the canopy closed for now, to get maximum streamlining, but he pulled his goggles over his eyes.

The field was still far away, and making it was going to be nip and tuck. Studying the ground ahead, he suddenly realized, that if he landed short, he would go down on the farm where he'd watched the ill-fated Spitfire crash on his first day at Hornchurch. He could just pick out the stone fence at the far end, and he vividly recalled the wingless fuselage exploding through it. God, don't hit that, he thought. Land to the side.

But on either side were woods.

Then if you can't make the field, go in short and hope she stops before you hit the wall. But make that decision later, closer to the ground. For now, keep her going as flat as possible.

He shot another look at the airspeed - a little below a hundred. He dropped the nose slightly. Come on, baby, all the way!

Now he was near enough to make out the concrete band on the top of the stone barrier. Would he clear it? He squinted past the exhaust stacks and tried to estimate whether the wall was rising or slipping by underneath him. It held position, growing in size. He was flying right at it!

He glanced at the airspeed - nearly down to eighty-five. Too slow, dammit! Against all instincts, he let the stick inch forward. The nose dropped and the wall rose. The airspeed climbed back to a hundred, and it stopped climbing again. But it was getting close now.

Open the canopy: After a belly landing distorted the fuselage, it might not budge. He hauled it back, and the airstream blasted into the cockpit.

Decision time: Do you dump the flaps, slip her hard, and hope to stop short of the wall? Or do you hold on and try to clear that thing? He could now see that the field short of the wall was rough and uneven. Beyond, the ground leading to the perimeter track was smooth. Beyond beckoned. He wavered. Come on, decide. Now or never!

With a pang of terror, he realized he'd waited too long, passed the point of no return. If he tried to drop her quick, the stone barrier would have him.

Airspeed! Still slow. Get the nose down.

He'd hoped to lower the flaps, and possibly even the wheels, for the actual touchdown, yet the only hope of clearing the wall lay in keeping her clean. Screw it, it would have to be a fast belly landing.

Looking at the stone fence, he spotted the darker area where it had been patched after the other plane plowed through it, and now he could even pick out its individual stones. Hell, he was going to hit the damned thing!

He eyed the airspeed: ninety-five. Keep her moving. He dropped the nose ever so little. No doubt about it, the farmer'd have to patch the bloody thing again. Fuck!

It was a hundred yards away, approaching rapidly.

There was one chance. Wait for the moment.

Now!

Cub pulled firmly back on the stick, the nose pitched up, and the Spitfire climbed, briefly, just enough to clear the wall.

But in pulling the plane up, Cub had sacrificed speed and she would stall. Desperate to keep her flying, he dropped the nose again, but no matter, it was going to be a hard one. He hunched himself for the impact.

The Spitfire fell the last fifteen feet from the sky, and the impact slammed Cub into the seat, jarring his senses. He vaguely caught the sickening vibration of longerons buckling beneath him and the sound of aluminum skin and frames rending all around. In front, the plane's nose dropped out of sight; her back had broken. Even through his tightened helmet, he heard the grinding wail of metal against stone punctuated by thumps as the machine's vitals were ripped away and transformed to flying debris. She seemed to skid endlessly.

Then suddenly everything was quiet.

Cub blinked. He felt okay. But his lower pant legs were wet, and his feet and the rudder pedals were submerged in fluid! What the hell? Then it dawned: The main fuel tank must have ruptured. Get out!

He threw off the safety harness, hit the quick release on the parachute, and grabbed the access door catch to wrench it open. It wouldn't budge. To hell with it. He wormed his way up through the cramped opening between the canopy rails. Thank God he'd remembered to open the damned thing. Then he was out, onto the wing, then the ground, and running his fastest.

When the fire engines arrived at the wreck, Cub stood a hundred yards away, breathing hard and watching them. There had been no fire, but they played it safe. He had stripped off his boots, socks, and trousers to avoid fuel burns and stood in his shorts and bare feet, watching the firemen check the wreckage. A stiff breeze from the southwest stirred the trees and ruffled his hair. The sky was dotted with a parade of small white clouds, like popcorn, sailing before the wind. The evaporating fuel felt cool on his legs.

The Squadron Maintenance Sergeant pulled up nearby in a car, stepped out, and saluted. "I see you're dressed for the occasion, sir."

Cub looked down at his bare legs and then at the sergeant. "Yes, I thought it was a picnic."

The man grinned. "Well, it was a bloody good landing, sir."

Puzzled, Cub looked first at the wreckage then at the Sergeant.

The Sergeant said, "That's anything you can walk away from, isn't it?"

Cub chuckled and nodded.

"Seriously, sir, we worried you'd have a go at that wall."

"You weren't alone." Cub chucked his head toward the wreck. "Think you can fix that thing?"

"Be lucky even to scavenge useful parts. Anyway, sir, can I give you a lift back to the Officers Mess?"

"Thank you, Sergeant." Cub climbed in, and the vehicle sped back toward the base complex.

Twenty minutes later, dressed in a fresh uniform, Cub stood with Squadron Leader Parsons near the dispersal hut at the downwind end of the field watching the squadron return and land.

Flights of Spitfires passed low overhead, with wheels and flaps lowered, and touched down on the turf in front of them.

Cub felt a twinge of pride. They looked bloody good. Like an air parade.

The planes taxied onto the perimeter track and around the field to the dispersal area where, guided by the signalmen's ballet, they wheeled upwind onto the grass and cut their engines.

As propellers clattered to a stop, riggers clambered up to assist the pilots out of their cockpits. Armorers dodged under the wings to unlatch the ammunition bay hatches, which then hung, waving in the breeze, making the planes look half-dressed. Fuel bowsers braked in front of them, and fuel-men dragged black hoses up and shoved nozzles into the fill points in front of the cockpits. It all took place like a choreographed dance without a word spoken.

Gunnar Christian and Duke pulled off their helmets as they approached. The Squadron Leader's face broke into a grin as he spotted Cub. "Well good-oh," he said, "you made it." He pointed down the field at Cub's plane, laying on the ground with a mobile crane backed up to it. "That your kite?"

"Yes, sir. The Maintenance Sergeant says it's a write-off."

Christian frowned. "Parsons, do we have another serviceable aircraft?"

"No, sir. But headquarters have arranged for Bayer to pick up a new one at Castle Bromwich this afternoon. Ferry Command will take him up there at two o'clock."

Christian's grunt showed his dissatisfaction. "Well, looks like you get the rest the day off, Cub. Be back tonight. We'll need you tomorrow."

"Yes, sir." Cub felt embarrassed to be left out.

Pilots clustered around the tea wagon, then returned to the grass around the dispersal hut, drinking tea and wolfing rolls. Their eyes were hollow, and some seemed to shake. They had been back from Kirton two days and looked as if they'd never left.

Ian came over and the two of them sat down. His face was drawn, and he was quiet.

"What's up?" Cub asked.

"Hamilton-Price's gone round the bend. He resents the new formations and tactics, I think. And he's taking it out on us. Become a regular little martinet. Pulled a sodding personal inspection on us in flight gear this morning. Can you believe it? Nobody passed. Maybe we're getting a little sloppy, and I don't mind our having to straighten up and look like proper fly-boys. But it's his attitude."

Cub gave a wry chuckle. "That's the military way."

"But he treats us like bloody school kids. Hell, we're fighting a war. 'Do this, do that,' he says. And all he does is get everybody browned off. A leader has to make people want what he wants. Believe in what he believes. Follow his example."

"You mean you're not ready to follow him into hell?"

"Shit! It wouldn't surprise me if one of us shot the bastard down one day."

"You serious?"

"Half."

Cub shook his head. "As if we didn't have enough trouble fighting the bloody Krauts."

Duke had wandered aimlessly among the pilots, and now Cub spotted him approaching. He looked wan. Cub said to him, "You feeling all right?"

Duke scowled. "What difference does it make how I feel."

"I was just asking. Look, I'm sorry to leave you in the lurch today."

Duke looked askance at the remains of Cub's Spitfire, now being hoisted by the crane. "Not a hell of a lot you could do about it, was there?" He sounded sarcastic.

"How will Blue Section operate, one person short?"

"We'll go back to the old three-plane vic. You just get your arse up there and beetle back tonight so you can fly tomorrow. Blue Section survived before you got here."

It was as if Duke had punched him.

Duke gazed at him for a long moment, then said, "Talked to Doreen since you got back?"

What the hell did Duke care about him and Doreen? Cub wasn't sure if he ever wanted to see her again. And it was none of Duke's business. But he said, "No. I went to The Gannet last night. She wasn't there. And she has no phone."

Duke gazed off toward the grass field. "She can be hard to reach when she wants to be."

"You ought to know."

By the way that Duke's head snapped around, he knew he'd struck a chord.

"You bet your arse I know. Now, have a good fucking day off." Duke turned and walked away.

Cub stood watching him. What was eating at the man now?

Armorers replenished the ammunition and closed the hatches under the wings, and the fuel bowsers completed their refills and withdrew. Fitters checked oil and eyed the engine compartments. Riggers inspected the airframes for damage and cleaned away the gun smoke and exhaust marks. Now they polished the windscreens and Perspex canopies, while the pilots lounged, some reading, a few talking, and many laying on the grass, eyes closed, feigning sleep.

The call came to scramble, and men dashed for their planes.

Whipped by propeller blast, Cub stood watching. A wave of helplessness swept over him. In the nearly two months since he'd arrived, he'd never missed a scramble.

The planes lifted off, and as soon as their wheels and flaps retracted, they banked to the left and climbed hard. As they disappeared to the southeast, Cub's frustration was joined by pangs of guilt.

Parsons nudged him. "Let's get over to the Operations Room and watch this show. Hurry!"

Cub nodded. At least he'd know what was going on.

They grabbed bicycles and raced toward the main station complex, then pedaled hard through the streets to a building not far from the Officers Mess. It was the Sector Operations Room from which the battle was directed: Shakespeare's workplace. They jogged up the front steps, and slipped through the door, then turned up a flight of stairs, and at the top, stepped onto a balcony that overlooked a large room.

Cub had once seen an idle Operations Room, but this was his first time in an active one. He knew little about how they worked.

From the ceiling overhead, bright lights illuminated an octagonal table fifteen feet wide and twenty long, which nearly filled the room below. On it was painted a map of southern England from the Isle of Wight to Great Yarmouth, the Continental coastline from Le Havre to The Hague, and the North Sea and English Channel in between. This was the Hornchurch squadrons' operational area.

On the back wall of the room, hung a lighted display that showed the status of every sector squadron. Around the table, half a dozen women in blue WAAF uniforms stood solemnly, earphones on their heads, holding long sticks like billiard cues.

Parsons gave a brief explanation. Moveable counters on the table represented the current position, or plot, of aircraft formations. Their color, black or red, designated them as friend or foe, and numbers on each gave track identification, the size of the formation, and altitude. Moveable arrows alongside each counter showed the location and time of earlier plots, and thus, the prior flight path.

Plot information came to the WAAFs, via the earphones, from the radar system and ground observers. Like croupiers in a gambling casino, the WAAFs nudged the counters with the cues to reflect newly reported aircraft positions. Occasionally, they updated information on the counters with a heavy pen. From the balcony above, the scene gave a continuous picture of the changing air situation.

A succession of enemy flights, shown by three red counters, was on a bee-line for London. One was over Deal on the Kent coast, another over Canterbury, and the third over Faversham. Other red counters were further to the south.

"Arrow Leader, Shakespeare here. Present position?"

The words made Cub start. He'd only heard Shakespeare's voice on the radio; now the man sat on the balcony beside him peering intently over the railing at the map below. He wore the uniform of a Wing Commander, but his silver hair and slight paunch marked him as older than his counterparts.

The radio loudspeaker crackled, and Cub recognized Christian's voice. "Hello, Shakespeare. Arrows are crossing the coast east of Tilbury. Angels twelve. Heading one two zero."

Shakespeare leaned down to the desk microphone, depressed the transmitter button, and spoke with the voice of a BBC announcer. "Right, Arrow Leader. Your target is twenty miles ahead bearing one two zero. Sixty plus at angels eighteen. I'm going to vector you onto their beam. Come left to one zero zero. And continue to climb. Buster."

"Right, Shakespeare. Understand one zero zero and buster."

At least sixty German airplanes, and Cub could only sit and watch.

He looked over the railing at the three red counters spread across the north of Kent. They were all marked sixty plus, but from Shakespeare's description, the lead one was the Arrows' target. It's track number was H-12.

A short blonde WAAF nudged a black counter down the south shore of the Estuary toward Sheerness, and Cub decided that was the Arrows.

God, he felt useless.

Shakespeare spoke over the balcony rail: "Officer Carley, is that a radar plot on the Arrows?"

A dark haired woman standing behind the blonde looked up at Shakespeare. She looked like a supervisor. "No, sir," she said. "It's from an observer in the marshes near Cliffe."

Shakespeare made quick notes on a sheet of paper. The H-12 counter was moved west to Sittingbourne.

"And the H twelve plot?"

"That's radar, sir."

Shakespeare nodded, then worked a slide rule deftly and jotted results.

Cub's puzzlement must have shown. Parsons said, "He's estimating the time-lags on those plots. They come via telephone from all over the country. Radar relay is automatic to Bently Priory and is repeated here quickly so the information may be only thirty seconds old. But observers have to place phone calls, so their data can be minutes late. The Controller has to correct for all that."

Occasionally Shakespeare spoke to a younger officer on his left, who seemed to be his assistant. The younger man made notes, consulted manuals or placed phone calls, then passed notes back to Shakespeare. Further down the gallery, another controller and assistant sat directing other units to their targets. In between whispers, the occasional sounds of controllers voices, and the crackle of the radio loudspeaker, the silence was metered only by the cadence of the clock on the wall.

Cub marveled at the difference between the atmosphere around him in the room and the noise, cold, and tense excitement the pilots felt in their cockpits. Here were quiet efficiency and anxiety. People nibbled on their lips and rubbed their hands; their eyes were focused and their faces tense.

The blonde WAAF moved the Arrows' counter east opposite Canvey Island.

"Shakespeare calling Arrow Leader. Come right to two zero zero. Out of the turn, your target will be eight miles at your ten o'clock. You should merge with them over Chatham. What is your present altitude?"

"Shakespeare, Arrows turning to two zero zero. Climbing through seventeen."

Eight miles? They should spot them any moment.

A WAAF leaned across the table and moved the H-12 counter westward to Rainham. The blonde woman and her supervisor stood motionless. Why doesn't she move the Arrows' counter? They must have turned by now. Cub's foot tapped the floor, and he rubbed his hands together, feeling the moisture in his palms.

The blonde woman said something to the supervisor, who nodded, and the Arrows' counter moved southward. The supervisor looked at the gallery and said to Shakespeare, "That's a radar update on the Arrows' position, sir."

Four miles to Chatham, Cub said to himself. Christ, couldn't they see them yet?

"Tally ho." It was Duke's voice! "A flock of Heinkels ten o'clock, level. Many Messerschmitts on top."

God, but Cub wished he were up there.

As he watched the blonde WAAF push the Arrows' counter beside H-12, it dawned on him that there was no way the pilots by themselves could have found their target. Yet such rendezvous were completed many times each day. It was astounding.

He had always considered the planes and pilots as the prime battle weapons. But in the vast space where the battle was fought, bringing the Arrows and H-12 together was a miracle. A miracle wrought by these thoughtful, anxious people in quiet surroundings using an enormous battery of electrical paraphernalia. The planes and pilots might be the cutting edge, but these people wielded the haft.

He turned to Parsons. "Some operation, isn't it, sir?"

Parsons gazed down at the map and nodded. "As far as we know, there's nothing like it anywhere else in the world."

So this was how they could be superior to the enemy at the point of contact, how Fighter Command's small band might match the mighty Luftwaffe. Cub felt a sudden burst of pride.

"If we beat Jerry, this'll be why," Parsons said.

Now the radio calls came in rapid succession, the tense, cryptic words of men going into battle.

Shakespeare pulled out a pack of du Maurier, lit one, and drew deeply. His job was over for the moment. He sat back and, gazing at the ceiling, listened raptly.

Below, the blonde WAAF and her supervisor stood attentive, biting their lips. Other plotters continued their work, but their eyes, too, drifted occasionally upward to the loudspeaker as they listened.

"Right, Arrows," Christian called, "Red and Yellow, follow me to attack the bombers. Blue, stay up and divert the fighters. In we go!"

Duke's voice: "Blue Flight, line abreast. Some are turning toward us. Take them head on, then dive on the ones that go after Red and Yellow."

Cub felt his heart pound. Don't take them head on, Duke. Split!

"Arrow Leader," Duke called, "watch it. Some are coming down after you."

"Right. We see them. Press your attack, Red and Yellow, then pull up into them."

There was a long silence.

"Blue Leader . . . I'm hit . . . . ."

Cub heard the agony in the voice, but didn't recognize it. Then suddenly he knew it was Burt Stark, and a shiver ran through him. Would this have happened if he had been there?

Darrow, Burt's new wingman, called: "Blue Three's hit, sir. He's going down."

"See a chute?"

"Not yet, sir."

Cub chewed painfully on his lip. Get out, Burt. For God's sake, bail out.

In full cry, Christian's called: "Let 'em have it now! Let 'em have it."

"Blue Four," Duke called, "break left, lad."

In spite of the tension, Cub chuckled to himself. His highness had bestowed the title *lad* on someone else.

"Bloody good, gents," Christian called, "I count five burning. Now let's have a go at those Messerschmitts."

Duke's voice: "Blue Four's going down."

A long silence followed. Cub breathed heavily.

"Blue Leader," Christian said, "where are you?"

"Just north of Maidstone at twelve thousand. I have three or four of the bastards cornered here. Could use some help."

"Right, Blue Leader. Hang on. The cavalry's on its way."

"Get over there, dammit," Cub said to himself. "Get over there and help him."

The radio speaker was silent. Cub stared at it in dumb agony.

Christian made a rapid succession of calls: "Blue Leader, have you in sight . . . Watch out for an ME closing at your seven o'clock! . . . Blue Leader, break left . . . Those bastards! . . . Blue Leader's hit . . . Duke, get out of that machine, now or never!"

In blind frustration, Cub slammed his hands onto his knees. Every ear in the room heard it, and every eye turned on him as he shouted, "Goddammit, that never would have happened if I'd been there!"

*

Two hours later, the rest of the Squadron had returned. Someone said they had seen a chute from Duke's plane, but there was still no word. As Cub took off for Castle Bromwich in the back seat of a Miles Master, his eyes brimmed. He hoped the young woman flying the plane from the front cockpit didn't notice.

Chapter 21

Peter Duke struggled up the stairs to his room. Tossing his blackened Mae West on the bed, he slipped out of his tunic, examined the charred cuff on the right sleeve, and dropped the coat over the back of a chair. He gently fingered the bandage on his right forearm; the touch triggered a searing pain underneath. Then he crossed to look at himself in the mirror and winced. The movement sent a pang through the burned area on his face.

The raging fire in the cockpit had frightened him more than anything in his life. Flames had reached his skin where it was exposed. Thank god he'd been wearing gloves, goggles and an oxygen mask, and that his helmet was buckled tight.

The struggle to escape from the spinning plane, the wrenching jolt when the parachute opened, and the hard landing in the hop field had also taken their toll. Every muscle rebelled as he peeled off his clothes.

Today of all days, why the hell hadn't bloody Cub been around? He couldn't exactly accuse him of evading duty, but it came to the same result.

Despite today's trauma, he still felt that familiar, sickening ache deep in his gut. He eyed the pain pills the Doc had given him for the burns and considered taking a couple. But if he did, he'd never get through the letter.

The warm bath soothed his muscles, and he wanted desperately to sleep, but the agony of the burns jolted him with every move. He dried off, shuffled back to his room, and slipped into his underclothes.

The letter from Cecily lay on his dresser; maybe it would get his mind off his injuries. But even as he contemplated opening it, he hesitated.

Women! Trouble! One and the same. It started with the girl he'd fallen for long ago in Cannock. Some called it puppy love, but after she dropped him, his agony was real. And it seemed to last forever. He had sworn it wouldn't happen again.

He liked beautiful women, though. Finding them took time and effort, but it was always worth it. They were exciting in their own right. Also, everyone noticed a stunning woman, and her escort. Men looked on him with admiration; women, with piqued interest; he relished both.

And in bed? Well, some might say all cats look gray in the dark, but not Peter Duke. Besides, he liked it better with a little light on the subject.

And one woman wasn't enough. A man needed his freedom. Especially a fighter pilot. Freedom to come and go. To choose whom to be with. To change his mind. Life was too short to be tied down, and not getting entangled had come easy. That is, until Cecily.

At first, she was just another date, then he began to miss her when she wasn't around. It hurt to know she was out with someone else. She hadn't been easy either. Wanted a lot - attention, companionship, sympathy - behaviors that came unnaturally to Peter Duke. Yet he was drawn in by her, dragged into the affair and ensnared. And even as he disliked himself for it, he couldn't stop.

At one point, he had wondered aloud to her what she saw in other men, and to his utter surprise, she suggested they go steady. Just like that, she wanted him to give up his freedom!

He told her he'd think about it and toyed with the idea for weeks. And weeks stretched into months. Then one day, she said goodbye and left for California with an American who'd been in England making motion pictures.

Duke couldn't admit it hurt, either then or now. He didn't care, dammit! Yet he hadn't been able to get her out of his mind, as he had the others, and since she left, he'd been unable perform in bed, with Doreen or any others. He'd blamed them. Yet, deep down, where wit and logic vanish and instinct begins, he knew the cause was Cecily. She haunted him like a ghost that rode on his shoulder.

So why not open the letter?

He pondered the matter and decided there was no reason. No logic at all. Still, he sat without moving for a long time.

Finally he got up gingerly, took the letter and his wallet and sat down at the desk. Enfolding the wallet between his hands, as if to hide it from prying eyes, he opened it to Cecily's photograph, laid it down delicately, and gazed at the picture. No doubt about it, she was lovely. Then he took the letter from the envelope and began to read.

> . . . It was kind of you to worry about my welfare.
> Your letter was so cryptic I had to read between
> the lines, but it gave me the strangest impression

that you wanted me back, though you never said so.

Funnily enough, I miss you, though I don't miss the way you treated me. I am nobody's plaything, not even yours. I need a friend, someone who cares, who truly loves me. Roger has fulfilled that. It's just that, well, there's no electricity between us. And though he begs me, I haven't been ready to tie the knot.

With you, there was high voltage, and maybe there still is. But I will not accept what you put me through. I suppose you can have any girl you want, and I know you value your freedom to live your way. I won't ask you to change.

I wish you all the luck in the world. And don't worry about me. Things will work out. The weather is nice here even in winter, and who knows whom I'll meet as time goes by.

All the best, Cecily

PS. We read the newspapers avidly and hear Ed Murrow on the radio, so we know something of what goes over there. The RAF seems to do a terrific job. We cheer for you every time we hear you score against Jerry.

Duke caught himself reaching for his handkerchief and stopped midway. A man had no business crying.

How could he let her do this to him? She was no lovelier than the others, and being smart and self-assured didn't make her unique either. Why couldn't he shake her?

Well, he wouldn't give in, by God. He'd neither beg nor plead. Wouldn't give her the pleasure. He was still in control. Free to do as he pleased. Free to choose whom he wanted. Eventually, she wouldn't haunt him. He just had to hang on.

*

Cub trotted, panting, down the upstairs hall of the officers' mess, past his room, to Duke's door and pounded on it forcefully.

"Come in."

He threw the door open and gaped.

Lines of pain were evident on Duke's face. On one side, under the eye, the skin looked raw and inflamed. His eyes were red. A huge angry welt rose on one thigh, and the bandage on his arm was the kind they used on burns. Cub winced. But at least, Duke was alive. "You made it."

"Of course I bloody made it. And you don't have to break the door down."

"I'm sorry, I . . . didn't know. How's Burt?"

"In hospital for a week or so."

"And Darrow?"

"He's had it. Never got out."

"I'm sorry."

"What for?"

"Not being there to help."

"Had a nice day down here, did you? We sure as hell could have used you."

"I know. Listened to it all."

"Bully for you."

Cub pointed to the Mae West and tunic. "What the hell happened to you?"

"Took a short ride in a burning Spit. Canopy was a bit sticky. I was slow getting away. That's all."

"It must hurt."

"It doesn't. Now, quit worrying about me. Worry about tomorrow. It'll be another full day. Did you bring back an airplane?"

"Yeah."

"You're better off than I am. Until they deliver me one, you'll fly Christian's wing. You better get some sleep."

Cub had seen Duke's wallet laying on the desk and the handwritten letter beside it, but he didn't make anything of it until he turned and saw the envelope on the dresser. It was addressed to Duke in a rounded, feminine hand. The stamps were American. He eyed the return address: C. Sheldon at a location in Hollywood.

Cecily Sheldon! Maybe there was more to Duke's depression than just his injuries. What had she said? He turned slowly to face Duke. "Letter from California, I see."

"Put your beady eyes back in your head."

"That girl means a lot to you, doesn't she?"

"What fucking business is it of yours."

"Remember me. I'm your wingman. For better or worse, you and I have to fly and fight together. We shouldn't harbor secrets. I'm only trying to help."

Indecision worked behind Duke's glare.

Cub said, "So why not tell me?"

"My business is my fucking business. Now get out!"

*

To the accompaniment of Ian's soft snore, Cub lay in the dark, thinking. For a brief spell at Kirton, he and Duke got along well. Yet the vicious side of the man lurked beneath the surface, ready to cut when you weren't looking. But the poor bastard was battered and burned. Wasn't that reason enough to be testy? Yet he'd been that way this morning, even before he was injured. There had to be another problem.

Could it be Cecily? Was she the reason Duke was always irritable? What had she done to him? Suppose he were in love with her, and she walked out on him. And he won't admit it's a problem. Not even to himself, maybe. Does that make sense? Hell, he wouldn't even concede that his injuries hurt him. By God, that would be exactly like Duke.

Chapter 22

At the end of an exhausting day, Cub stepped through the door to the Hornchurch officers' mess. His shoulders drooped, and his hair lay matted by his helmet. He pulled off the Mae West as he ambled toward the stairs.

"Beg pardon, sir," the desk orderly said sharply, "Squadron Leader Parsons would like you to meet him at the guard room right away."

"Can I clean up?"

"He said, as soon as you came in, sir."

"Any idea what's up."

"They've got a prisoner. I think he wants you to talk to him."

The guard admitted Cub to the closed room. A young man wearing a tan Luftwaffe flying suit, sat in the center with his back to the wall. The light raised shadows behind his angular facial bones and the rhythmic working of his jaw played them across his cheeks and neck. His grey eyes gazed straight ahead and he gripped the side of the chair, white knuckles straining, as if to break the wood. Occasionally his hand swiped at the brown hair that fell over his face.

An armed airmen stood at the door, and Squadron Leader Parsons leaned on a chair at the back. Cub moved beside him.

Tony Hamilton-Price sat close in front of the prisoner smoking a cigarette. He leaned forward with his elbows on his knees and exhaled smoke into the man's face.

"All right," he said in awkward German, "tell me again about your fighter formations."

The man responded in German. "My name is Walter Mueller. I am a Lieutenant. My number is four zero three --."

"I don't care about your bloody number! Tell me about the Messerschmitts."

"My name is . . . .."

Cub nudged Parsons. "What goes on?"

"This man's a Heinkel bombardier. The POW blokes will be over to pick him up in a bit. Meanwhile, we thought we'd try to learn something. I let Hamilton-Price talk to him. His German's better than mine."

"That's not saying much." Cub turned back to study the prisoner.

Tony shouted, "I do not want to hear your name again."

Mueller began in deliberate German, "My name is --."

Hamilton-Price's arm shot forward and his open hand struck the man across the face, with a crack like a gunshot, and made his head snap to the side. Mueller's jaw dropped open and his eyes rounded in alarm. There was a long moment of silence. Then his eyes and mouth closed slowly. "My name is --."

Tony coiled to strike again.

Holy Christ, Cub thought, we're not allowed to --.

"That's enough," Parsons said firmly.

Tony spun in his chair. "This bastard --."

"You know the rules. Keep your hands off him."

"But dammit, Chaplain."

The Intelligence Officer waved firmly toward the door. "Let's talk about it outside."

Tony followed Parsons through the door, and Cub brought up the rear.

"Look, sir," Tony said. "I'll break that bastard."

"You've been at it over half an hour and got nowhere. And there'll be no physical contact."

"What do you want out of him?" Cub said.

Tony glared. "I want to know why they changed to those close-in escort formations."

Parsons added, "We'd also like to learn how badly they are really hurting."

Tony said, "I can make him talk. He just needs the fear of God put in him"

"He's already scared," Cub said.

Parsons said, "And it's not doing any good. We need to change tactics."

Tony drove a fist into his hand with a crack. "I'll beat it out of him."

"You know the regulations as well as I do," Parsons said.

"Dammit, I tell you he's close to breaking."

"I doubt it," Cub said.

Tony turned slowly. "Who asked you?"

"Who cares? I don't think you'll get him to talk."

"Well now, lad, how the hell do you know?"

"He's scared, but he's sticking to the authorized line. I think you're at a dead end. Unless of course, you propose to get out the whips and needles."

"Have you a better idea?"

"Yeah. Let me talk to him."

"You! What makes you think --."

"Mister Hamilton-Price," Parsons interrupted, "That may be a good idea. At least his German is fluent."

"So what? I know enough to understand the answers to my questions."

Parsons said, "Nevertheless, we're going to try something different. Let's get him out of this place. Take him somewhere pleasant. How about the tennis hut? Cub, you talk to him."

"Right, sir. Let me make a quick change of clothes." And he left at a run.

Cub, dressed in a fresh uniform, met Parsons at the side door of the mess, leading out to the tennis court. Through the window, they could see Mueller reclining in a white lounge chair with his eyes closed. An armed guard stood nearby.

Parsons turned to Cub. "Be nice to him. Get him talking about anything. The weather. His family. Anything at all. Something he's comfortable with. Understand?"

Cub nodded.

"You have to win his trust," Parsons continued. "He's got to believe that in some important way, you're on his side. Once you've got him talking and have his trust, lead him to the subject of interest by showing your humanity, exposing your own weaknesses. You tell him how difficult things are for you, and he may reveal how bad things are for him. Get it?"

"Think so, sir."

Parsons smiled and clasped Cub on the shoulder. "Good luck then. And remember, you'll probably have to take some risk to make it work. Just do it. Also, the man has refused food since we picked him up this morning. I'm having some sandwiches and beer sent out. Let's see if the food will soften him up a little."

Cub saluted, turned on his heel, and started for the door. As he reached it, he stopped and turned back.

"Sir. In addition to the sandwiches and beer, could we have a bottle of Scotch and a couple of glasses? Some good stuff."

Parsons winked at him and nodded. Cub went out through the door.

The tennis hut stood on the lawn beyond the court next to the mess. Along the foundations of the building, flowers danced in the wind, and the hazy sky glowed pink as the sun settled. Larks darted overhead and, far above, sea gulls wheeled.

As he approached the resting prisoner, Cub waved back the guard, out of the prisoner's view. Then he said in flawless north German, "Good afternoon, Lieutenant."

The prisoner jerked to his feet and came to attention. "I'm sorry, sir. It was a bad dream. I --." He halted in mid-speech. His eyes rounded as he gazed at Cub, then blinked as recognition dawned. "My name is --."

"Oh for heaven's sake, Herr Mueller, I'm not interested in that nonsense. I apologize for what went on back there and came to make sure you were all right. Sit down."

Cub pulled up a chair and sat beside him facing the lawn. The Mess Sergeant arrived carrying sandwiches and two mugs of beer on a tray, and an orderly followed with a bottle of Glen Fiddich and glasses. Cub directed them to a wooden garden table just out of reach. Then he and Mueller were left alone.

Cub gazed at the afternoon sky for a long time. Finally, he said, "We used to play a lot of tennis here. War ended that. You play tennis?"

"My name is --."

"Herr Mueller, you're a broken record. I'm not your interrogator."

Another long silence followed while Cub studied the surroundings. Then he said, "You know, this is a really nice place, a little flat maybe, but good farmland. We're not six kilometers from the Thames here. Get a lot of sea birds."

Mueller's eyes looked aloft and then back at the plate of sandwiches.

"In the spring, the flowers are every color you can imagine. And they keep the gardens looking nice."

And so it went, as Cub described the scenery and the seasons and the beauties of the Essex countryside. Mueller's eyes occasionally followed the directions Cub indicated; always they returned to the sandwiches.

Finally Cub said, "I forgot to ask, are you comfortable?"

Mueller nodded warily.

"Anything you want?"

"No."

Cub got up and crossed to the sandwiches, took one and picked up a beer. He sat down and munched voraciously and drank. Get him talking, he said to himself. He finished one sandwich and stood up to get another. The German's eyes followed every move. Cub took a bite, chewed loudly, then swallowed and looked intently at Mueller. Gaunt eyes stared back.

"Are you sure you're all right?"

"Yes."

"Would you like anything?"

"No."

Cub went back to his monologue: the scenery, wildlife, and climate. Mueller mouth worked involuntarily. In mid-sentence, Cub stopped and followed Mueller's eye, to the sandwiches. Take the risk now, he thought.

"Would you like a sandwich?"

Mueller shook his head. Cub picked up the tray and pushed it at him. "Have one. There's plenty."

"No. I don't think --."

"Oh come on. I'm eating them. And a sandwich isn't going to make you talk. Have one." And he pushed the plate at the man.

"Well . . . thank you."

Mueller bit into it ravenously. Cub restarted his soliloquy. Mueller had taken three bites when Cub stopped again.

"How about something to drink?"

"Well, I don't --."

"Heavens, it's going to waste. Here." He handed Mueller the beer. The man hesitated a moment, a quizzical look on his face, then he pulled at it deeply.

"You must have places like this in Germany?"

Mueller eyed the evening sky and began to nod. "Yes. When the weather's good."

"I suppose your weather is as bad as ours here."

Mueller bobbed his head to indicate, maybe yes, maybe no. "Perhaps not so wet."

Cub chuckled.

So they began their discussion of Germany and England, comparing notes on weather and flowers and trees and the countryside.

The German ate until he was satisfied. At length he asked, "Where did you learn to speak German?"

"At home, in America."

Mueller's eyes rounded in surprise. "You're American?"

"Yes."

"Amazing!" Mueller said with a grin. "I learn about America from the movies and records." He hummed a few bars of *Begin the Beguine.* "Cole Porter, yes?"

Cub smiled and nodded.

So they launched into cowboys and New York and Hollywood and jazz and Mickey Mouse.

Mueller finished his drink.

"How do you like the beer?" Cub asked.

"Not bad."

"Not as good as German beer though, is it?"

Mueller smiled sheepishly. "Well, it's not the same. Do you know German beer?"

"I was in Germany before the war. I have a distant relative in Bremerhaven."

"Really? My aunt lives near there. I used to go in the summers."

"Is that right? Listen, you may not like English beer, but try Scotch."

Mueller looked at Cub suspiciously for a moment. Then his face softened. "Why not?"

Cub poured two glasses of Glen Fiddich, handed one to Mueller, and raised his glass. "Prost."

Mueller responded and they drank together.

"Now that's good stuff," Mueller said. "When were you in Bremerhaven?"

"Summer of thirty-eight."

"I was there then, too. Where did you stay?"

"My friend lives on the Behringstrasse just off the Burgerpark."

"Ah yes. That's close to the main railway station. My aunt lives in Langen."

"I know that place. We went to a pub there. Near the Speckenbuttel station. Owned by a man named Boethe."

"Oh, Boethe's place is famous. He's a sailboat fanatic. Has sailing pictures all over the walls."

"That's the one," Cub said. "My friend knows him. He's a boat man too. I sailed with him from the Wesser River Yacht Club."

"On the Neuer Hafen?"

"Right. By the old lighthouse."

"Why, I've spent many afternoons watching the boats go in and out through the lock there."

"Small world," Cub said. "I don't suppose there's much sailing there these days. But some day I'd like to go back."

Mueller frowned. "You'd go back to Germany?"

"Sure. Mostly, I had a good time there. And someday the shooting will be over. Here's to a short war."

Mueller smiled, and they drank together.

Here goes nothing, Cub thought. He looked at Mueller obliquely and said, "I don't see how it can go on much longer. It's been grim here. Lots of casualties. Civilians too."

"Not many of us like bombing cities. But they tell us it has to be done."

"Bombing and air fighting have taken their toll. Our reserves are thin."

"No thinner than ours, I'll wager."

"Really? Has it been bad?"

"Our bomber losses are dreadful. On every mission, maybe ten percent don't make it back. Not only are planes downed, but so many come home shot to pieces. Blood spattered all over the inside of the cabin and sloshing in the bilges. It's awful. I doubt if we can keep it up long."

"Sounds like our fighter losses."

"So our intelligence tells us. Every day for weeks, they said we'd shot down the last Spitfire. Then the next day, we'd arrive here and run into another hornet's nest of them."

"It cost us heavily," Cub said. "Half our squadron are out of action. Now your fighters seem to have given up hunting too. They stick to the bombers like frightened chicks."

"Frightened, hell. Our bomber leaders complained because the fighters were never around. Always off somewhere else chasing the enemy. So Goering himself stepped in and ordered them to fly close escort."

"Does that make sense?"

"Our fighter boys don't think so. But orders are orders. It's supposed to give the bombers better protection."

"Does it work?"

"Can't prove it by me. I'm here as evidence."

Cub chuckled and reached for the bottle. "Have another Scotch."

*

Parsons lounged behind his desk. Cub sat comfortably relaxed in a chair, enjoying the pleasant haze from the alcohol. Tony Hamilton-Price paced at the side; his jaw and mouth worked angrily.

Cub related his conversation with Mueller and closed by saying, "So that's the story on your fighter escort formations, Tony. It was Goering's orders."

"What the hell did you do to drag that out of him?" Tony said.

Cub shrugged. "Nothing. We were chitchatting about life in Germany and England and what we might do after the war, when he dumped it on me."

Tony glared, first at Cub then at Parsons, who responded with a grin of feigned amazement, then raised his hands, palms up, and shrugged.

Tony slammed the door as he left.

Chapter 23

Cub stood at the Lounge Bar of The Gannet and studied the room, sipping his beer amid the din of voices. Smoke wafted through the lamplight, and the perennial game of darts carried on.

His mind drifted to Mueller. Lucky bastard, he thought, he's out of this war. But I'm still here, mucking around in this bloody mess with Duke and Tony and . . . .. There was no damned justice. He took a deep draft on his beer and continued brooding as he looked at the faces of the clientele. When he spotted Doreen, it brought him up short.

She was in the back with several pilots. She saw him too and gave a vague smile of recognition then returned to her conversation. It was hardly an invitation, and his first inclination was to ignore her. But as he stood there playing with his glass and mulling it over, he knew he couldn't. He had to face her and get the truth, first hand.

He approached her table, and she said, "Hello, stranger."

"Good evening." He gestured toward the men around her. "I see you're under heavy escort."

She smiled broadly and waved at a half-empty space at the table. "Yes, but you're welcome to join us."

Cub said solemnly, "I need to talk to you alone."

"Oh?" She glanced at the men then back at Cub.

He held his eyes steady on her, but angled his head toward an empty table. "How about over there?"

"Well," she said to the others, "if you'll excuse me for a moment."

She rose and led the way to the other table. "Nice to see you again, luv," she said, as they sat down. "Where have you been?"

"Had a few day's rest up north. Since then I've been flying every day. All day."

"With the blighters bombing London, it's been heavy going, hasn't it?"

He nodded, groping for a way to avoid confronting her.

"You don't look very happy," she said. "What's the matter?"

He looked at her for a long, silent moment. She was still an attractive woman, but older than he remembered. God, she might even be thirty. "I don't know exactly how to say this, but . . . Are you married?"

She visibly started. "Well . . . yes."

Even though he expected that answer, it hurt. How could she have set him up like this? Why had he been so stupid?

She said, "Are you surprised?"

"You never told me."

"You didn't ask. Would it have made a difference?"

"Of course."

"Why? Worried about my husband turning up?"

Cub struggled for how to make his next point. How to be subtle, not sound like a fool, how to seem unconcerned. He failed. "Doreen, I fell in love with you."

Her eyes rounded, and she hesitated. "You? Fell in love with me?"

He nodded. "When we went north, I even felt sick being away from you."

"I didn't know that."

"And it devastated me to learn you were married."

"Who told you?"

"What difference does it make?"

"Well, I never asked you to fall in love."

"It wasn't what you said. It was what you did. I couldn't help it."

"But we just had a little play together. It was all in fun."

After that incredible night, how could she sit there and say it meant nothing to her? Cub recalled a song about one fooling and the other falling in love. Maybe nights like that weren't incredible when you weren't in love. What a bloody fool he'd been. "You led me on," he said.

"Then you're easily led, young man."

"Only because you kept him a secret."

"Not to worry. He's far away."

"So what? You're somebody's wife. I slept with you under false pretenses."

"Pretenses?" She gave a wry chuckle. "You mean you only pretended to enjoy yourself?"

"No. But that doesn't make it right."

"It felt all right to me."

Geezus, did this woman think only of her own pleasure? "Doesn't it upset you to go behind his back?"

Doreen disliked this turn in the conversation. How could he know anything of her discomfort? Know that after fifteen years of fighting her own sexual desires, and not always winning, she'd finally married Pud, who made wonderful, ferocious love to her, night after night. She couldn't get enough of him. Know that, suddenly, two months after their wedding, he was gone - sent to North Africa. And she was left alone, hundreds of miles from her home. God only knows, she was lonely. What was she supposed to do? Sit home at night and mope?

She had done exactly that for three months, until she'd gone crazy. That's when she found The Gannet and began to come, and the fly-boys found her. They were friendly and fun, and some were terribly good looking. And one thing led to another.

No, Cub couldn't possibly know all that.

"How bloody chivalrous of you," she said. "Look, he's gone a long time, and he's not returning soon. I'm a woman. A normal healthy woman. He understands that."

"He understands you slept with me?

"Well, not exactly, but he wants me to be happy."

"I wonder if he believes it takes sleeping with other men to make you happy. How many have there been?"

"What kind of a question is that?"

"I heard there were a lot. Every blue suit around, was how it was put."

She glanced angrily at the men sitting at the other table, then looked back at Cub. "That's a lie."

"I'll bet you slept with Peter Duke."

That gave her a start, but she hoped he didn't notice. "Peter's an old friend. But that's over now."

"An old friend hanging around while your old man's away, eh?"

"Now you're getting personal."

"Don't you think what we did was personal?"

"Yes, and I'm not discussing it with anyone."

"I don't suppose you will. You'll just go merrily on changing partners like it was a ballroom dance."

"Poor little Cub, you haven't seen much of life yet, have you?"

"Enough to know what I don't like."

"And you don't like me?"

"I don't like people hiding the truth from me."

"But you liked what we did, didn't you?"

"Maybe. But I dislike you selling yourself cheap to whoever comes along."

She glared at him. "I'm never for sale."

"What's the difference? You're like Duke. Here and now is all that counts, isn't it?"

"To a point, Peter Duke and I understand each other pretty well. How is old Peter, anyway?"

"Like the rest of us, surviving." But Cub wasn't going to let her deflect the conversation. "He goes after girls like some people collect stamps."

"And you don't approve?"

"Approve, hell. I don't understand. Don't you value trust and faith?"

"I trust what I like."

"And how about your husband? Do you trust him?"

"He's probably playing the Sheik of Araby in a tent with half-naked little brown girls scurrying about like nervous fawns." Even as she said it, she hoped to God it was nowhere near the truth.

"And that doesn't bother you?"

"Why should a fact of life bother me?"

"You don't care about what he does there, so you're shacking up with the world here. Is that it?"

"How quaintly put," she snapped.

"And you can't imagine that he's not doing the same."

"If I concerned myself about him, I'd worry to death."

"And deep inside, that's exactly what's happening."

Dear God, this bloody little man read her mind.

He continued, "How do you think he feels?"

"What he doesn't know won't hurt him."

"Like it doesn't hurt you not to know what he's doing, eh? Rubbish! It upsets the hell out of you to imagine him sleeping with those dark haired, sloe-eyed beauties. Doesn't it?"

"It doesn't worry me in the least."

"A different one every night."

Now he'd made her tell bald lies. Well, to hell with him. She knew how to fight back. "Little man, I fucked with you like you'd never dreamed of. And now remorse has got you. You're afraid to live. To enjoy life without inspecting and moralizing over it. You'll scurry back to the mess and hide your face. Then no doubt, in a month, you'll be bragging about it."

"I'd be afraid to brag for fear I'd learn the rest of the squadron has been there too."

Her eyes began to well. Damn! But she couldn't help it. "You bastard."

The tears started down her cheeks, and he handed her his handkerchief. "I didn't mean to make you cry."

"Well, you did a bloody good job of it!"

"Look, I'm sorry."

For a long while, she buried her face in the handkerchief. He hadn't meant to hurt her; he just wanted the truth. Maybe he'd pushed too hard. He considered apologizing.

Finally, she blew her nose and looked up at him. "You don't like anything about me, do you?"

"Look," he said, "you showed me something wonderful. I can never forget that."

She breathed a deep sigh and looked warily into those flashing brown eyes of his. Could they really see through her? Never mind, they still elicited desire. "We could go again," she said.

There was a long silence.

"I'm not interested."

"Because I'm not attractive anymore?

"Look, you're married to a guy who's risking his neck to defend this country too. Maybe I haven't seen much of life, but under those circumstances, I don't want to be involved with you."

Oh God! She had lost it, after all. "You want somebody younger, don't you?"

"Not necessarily."

"Oh no? You youngsters all want sweet, young things. Someone you can dominate. But a woman gets older, and she loses it, and where does that leave her?"

"Doreen, you're very pretty. If you were single, I'd be interested."

She buried her face in her hands.

He struggled for a way to stop her crying. "How long have you been married?"

"A year."

"Do you like your husband?"

"When he's around, he takes good care of me."

"But do you like him?"

"Well, sure."

"Do you want to hurt him?"

"No."

"But don't you see that's what you're doing?"

"But what does he know? He's thousands of miles from here."

"And what happens when he comes back. Don't you think he'll find out?"

"Why should he?"

"Word gets around, you know. But even more important, your playing around makes you believe the worst about him, and that hurts him a lot."

Her tears flowed freely again. How did Cub know exactly where to put in the needle? "It's not like that," she stammered.

"Oh, isn't it? Then why are you crying?"

"Cub, you make it so complicated."

"No. It's simple. You don't respect yourself, and that makes you not respect him. In the end, you both lose."

Tears ran down her cheeks. "Why can't you just live a little?"

"Doreen, wouldn't it be better to quit playing around? When he comes back, you can look him in the eye and feel proud of yourself."

"Proud of what? Growing old? Proud because I still have the urge? Proud because a gorgeous young man turned me down flat?"

"How about proud because you stuck by him?"

It sounded like a jail sentence to her. She lay her head on her hands and sobbed.

Cub wasn't sure what to do. Everything he'd said only made things worse, and he'd got the truth he sought. Maybe the best was to say no more and just leave matters as they were. "I think I'd better go now."

He stood up slowly. She kept her head lowered and continued to sob silently.

"See you around," he said. He crossed to the door and left.

Chapter 24

Burt Stark was released from the hospital, and the following day Cub and Ian got thirty-six-hours off. Burt could only get an overnight leave, so they invited him to join them for the evening in London. They would celebrate Burt's release and let Ian show them the town. At three o'clock in the afternoon, the two officers arrived at the Sergeants' mess in Ian's MG Roadster. Burt was waiting for them.

"Well Burt," Ian said, "risen from the dead, eh? Jump in and we're off."

"Not dead yet, sir," Burt said as he clambered into the jump seat, "but on occasion, it seemed preferable."

The car roared off through the air station streets and out through the main gate to the A125, leading to the A13, where they turned west for London.

"So when do you fly again, Burt?" Cub said.

"They say a few days, sir."

Cub, in the front seat, turned around and pushed his face close to Burt's. "For Christ's sake, cut out that *sir* stuff when we're off the base, will you?"

"Why, yes, s--." Burt chuckled. "Gets ingrained, I guess."

Cub turned back and said to no one in particular, "Having two classes of pilots, officers and enlisted, makes me uncomfortable. We're all in this together, and guys like Burt are even section leaders. We should all be officers."

"The theory is," Ian said, "that lots of men who are capable of flying couldn't qualify as officers."

"Nonsense," Cub said. "They offered me a commission because they wanted to attract foreigners. But I don't have a university degree. And in training, who made officer seemed arbitrary. What do you think, Burt?"

"I would never have got here if I had to qualify as an officer. But now, we all get the same responsibilities and we're held to the same standards. It does seem a bit awkward."

Cub said, "Well, for tonight, Burt, you're an honorary Pilot Officer."

"Right," Ian said. "And if you hold your liquor well, we'll make you a Flying Officer before the night's out. And if you get blind, stinking drunk, you're a Flight Lieutenant."

Burt said, "I don't suppose Mister Duke or Mister Hamilton-Price would like that much."

"Serves them right," Ian said.

The MG hurtled along the A13 by East Ham and Canning Town, and down East India Docks Road into Stepney, where they began to see bomb damage. Ian slowed to take in the scene. Cub had heard about it, but he had not been through the area in daylight.

At first, the damage was limited to the occasional shattered building amidst others that seemed untouched except for broken or missing windows. But as they went on, the scene transformed into a picture of destruction everywhere.

The above-ground floors of many buildings were gone, leaving low webs of scalloped brick parapet, looking like the ruined foundations of ancient Troy. Brick faces of buildings were blown away to reveal shattered wooden structures and fractured interior walls of white plaster. Here and there a brick edifice was gone, leaving behind the supporting iron frame, looking like a Meccano toy gone wrong.

Glass seemed to have disappeared from the face of the earth. In some structures that seemed otherwise undamaged, every window was a vacant black maw, making the building look like a haunted castle presiding over the rubble.

All that remained of one terraced house was the back wall, a three-story facade of brick. An interior stairway to the missing upper floor was attached to it, and at the top of the stairs, clothes still hung in an open closet, intact and twisting slowly in the breeze.

Here and there steam rose out of the devastation as if from the fires of hell.

Ian had the car at a crawl, and the men eyed the scene in wide-eyed disbelief. "Christ," Cub said, "I had no idea it was anything like this. Newspapers must have held back to keep Jerry in the dark about his success."

The others shook their heads in bewildered wonder.

Random arrangements of old bricks and dark wooden beams, lay piled in the streets, and people climbed to pick them over, looking for valuables and keepsakes. Crews of men used wooden poles to batter down shaky walls that might fall and injure people. Workmen dug in the streets to repair telephones, electrical cables, and pipes for water and gas. The occasional street was blocked off where fire fighters poured water into still-smoking ruins.

At one point, the car was stopped by police for almost half an hour while a bomb removal team deactivated a warhead that lay next to the road in front of them. Then, once the traffic could move, the police hurried them along.

One pretty, young woman carrying a baby shambled down the pavement. Her dark eyes were round and vacant, and her gaze wandered unfocused. She seemed utterly disoriented by the horror. Cub stared at her in stunned fascination. Yet she was just one of hundreds who shuffled aimlessly along in shock, their gaunt eyes gaping blankly ahead.

The three of them rode in stunned silence. Nothing could have prepared them for this. And it went on for mile after mile.

Their journey ended an hour later at Claridge's in Mayfair which, with the occasional exception, still seemed intact. The hotel offered pilots a special leave rate for a one night stay.

After an early dinner there, they sat in the inner lounge, under the oval ceiling centerpiece, having coffee. In spite of the excellent meal, they were somber.

They contrasted their lives as volunteer flyers with those of ordinary citizens. Aviators had clean quarters and prepared meals, and they fought alone high in the clear sky and faced fear and death occasionally. But they were not witness to wholesale destruction and loss of life all around them, day after day. That was left to civilians who had volunteered for no part of war.

Finally, Ian shook his head to get rid of the thought and said, "Let's find out what goes on around here."

They filed out through reception into the blacked-out night. Ian suggested they start on Oxford Street, so they turned toward it, up Duke Street. They had gone about halfway when the air raid siren began to wail.

"Damn," Cub said. "Guess we better find a shelter."

Ian said, "Bond Street tube station is just ahead. People use them for shelters."

They set off briskly.

Cars inched along the streets guided by dim blue blackout lights. Hearing the air raid signal, they pulled to the curb, and their lights went out.

The men passed a policeman encouraging people in a theatrical voice, "Step lively, now. Straight on to the tube." They found themselves in a growing crowd, hurrying along the pavement in the dark.

Approaching a corner, they turned with the throng into a dimly lit entry and started down the stairs. A jostling press of people filled the staircase, working its way downward, deep into the earth, like a snaking reptile headed for the bright lights that marked the Central Line platform. People dressed warmly in coats and hats, and carried blankets and other necessities for the night.

A guard stood at the entrance waving people in. "Move right along now, please," he said. The three pilots picked their way down the edge of the platform.

At the back of the platform, next to the wall, people had set up camp. Some sat leaning against the rounded wall of the chamber reading or playing cards. Others chatted. Still others lay on blankets or sleeping bags. Some sleepers rested their heads on purses or rolled clothing; others brought proper pillows. At the end of the platform, women volunteers had set up a canteen where they served tea and sandwiches.

The aviators felt uneasy taking up platform space, so they stood near the canteen, next to a group playing cards. An older man in working clothes was dealing. He looked at their uniforms, then pointed at the ceiling and said with a grin, "What you lads doing here? You're supposed to be up after those buggers."

"It's our night off," Ian said.

The group laughed, and one spoke up. "I wish those bastards would take a night off."

Cub felt embarrassed, as if he were shirking duty. The three pilots gazed at the ground and shuffled their feet.

The dealer leaned over and touched Cub on the trouser cuff. "No offense meant, lads. We know you're doing your part. But it's a funny place to have to spend your night off."

During the next half hour, they neither heard bomb explosions nor felt any tremors.

"Bastards must be hitting the East End," one of the card players said.

That's where they had driven that afternoon, Cub thought.

The tube station was quiet except for a whisper here and there. He examined the people around him. These poor devils went out every day amid the devastation, to work, to keep the country together, and to rebuild their homes and lives. Then they came here for the night. Even with all the destruction above, there was no whining, no crying, no complaints. Tough people. Cub wondered if Jerry knew what he was up against.

After forty-five minutes, the guard at the platform entrance announced quietly, "The All Clear has sounded."

"Buggers'll be back," said one of the card players. A few heads raised, then dropped back onto pillows, otherwise hardly anyone moved.

"Let's get out of here," Ian said.

The other two nodded and followed him toward the entrance. Cub turned and waved goodbye to the card players.

"Come back again, chaps," the dealer said with a grin. "We're here every night."

Out on the pavement, they walked down Oxford street.

"This place is dead," Burt said. "Everybody must have packed it in."

Cub said, "What do you think, Ian?"

"Seems awfully quiet, all right." Then he drew up short and said with enthusiasm, "I've got an idea. Let's get out of here. We'll get my car. I know a pub up near my house. I'll wager they're open. Come on."

The MG made the last of the climb up Highgate West Hill and wheeled into the parking lot of The Flask, alongside several other cars.

"See," Ian said, "they're open."

They jumped out and pushed through the front door into the Lounge Bar. The room was smaller than Cub expected and the ceilings were low. It was softly lighted by candles and low-power electric bulbs; blackout curtains covered the windows. The rough-wood beams in the walls and ceiling were a dark chocolate brown; they contrasted with the glistening plaster, which had gone tawny with age. At the bar and in wooden booths along the walls, people conversed in friendly voices. Occasionally, Cub heard a laugh. Shadows on the walls danced to the flicker of the candles. Over the bar, hung a rack of glasses, sparkling like a gaudy chandelier in the wavering light. The mixed aroma of hops and Turkish tobacco hung in the air.

"Cozy place," Cub said.

Ian said, "Makes The Gannet look like Waterloo Station at rush hour, eh what?"

Burt nodded. "Very nice."

"It's one of the oldest in town," Ian said. "And my favorite."

They started on their second beer, when Ian said to Cub, "You know, we're not far from where that Kendall girl told you she worked."

"Victoria? Really?"

"Tufnel Park, wasn't it?"

"I think so."

Ian looked at Cub obliquely. "You still got something cooking with Doreen?"

Cub shook his head.

Ian grinned and turned to the man behind the bar. "You know an ambulance station at Tufnel Park?"

"There's an ARP Center there. Across Junction Road from the Boston Arms, near the tube station."

Ian said to Cub. "Hell, that's just down the hill." He nudged Burt, "This is a great-looking blonde that Cub fell for once. She plays hard to get."

"All the good ones do," Burt said.

"How about it, Cub? Let's go down there and see what's up."

"Why don't we stay up here and see what goes down."

Ian laughed. "Faint heart never won fair maid."

"To hell with maidens. Beer's friendlier."

Ian waved him off with his hand.

The publican called for last orders.

Twenty minutes later they paid their bill and stepped through the blackout vestibule into the night air. Stars showed clearly around the clouds blowing like shadows across the sky.

"Beautiful night for bombing," Burt said.

As if to punctuate the sentence, antiaircraft fire far to the east lit the sky with soundless flashes, and the Air Raid warning howled.

"Makes you feel helpless," Cub said.

"But I'll bet it's worth watching," Ian said. "Come on. Hampstead Heath must be safe as a church, and we can see most of London from Parliament Hill."

They trotted down Highgate West Hill then turned off and picked their way along an uneven path leading into the park. There, they walked briskly up a long slope to the top of a hill. In plain view six miles away, bombs were falling in the East End.

Amid the crump and crack of antiaircraft fire, searchlight beams crisscrossed, and airbursts lit the sky. Flame-pink flashes reflected off the clouds to mark bomb explosions on the ground below. It might have been a circus celebration.

As the minutes passed, the reflection from the clouds became a shimmering pink glow that gradually intensified until it lighted the sky like the coming of dawn. The fires were spreading.

Occasionally a searchlight beam impaled a bomber, and it twisted and turned like an insect caught in a flame. Other beams fixed it, and the tempo of crump and crack increased. Then the plane disappeared from the beam, usually without trace, but sometimes aflame, arcking downward like an ember returning to the conflagration.

A rapid-fire string of bomb bursts was followed by an enormous flash, and a massive fireball rose into the blackness. Thirty seconds later, they heard its thunder and the earth trembled under their feet.

"Geezus," Cub said, "it's hard to believe even those bastards would do that."

"I bet we'll do it too, before this war is over," Burt said.

Then the bombers wheeled away to the south. Searchlights ceased their scissor-dance in the sky, and the crump and crack of antiaircraft ceased. The All Clear wailed. The three men worked their way back toward the street.

In the dark, they got lost and ended up at the Gospel Oak station, where they crossed to Highgate Road and turned up the hill to retrieve Ian's car. Trees lined the road on their left, while on their right, Cub barely made out a block of town houses.

They walked in silence, and Cub was brooding about what he'd seen when a distant sound from behind brought them up short. It was a hiss in the sky, like a whip cleaving air. Then it stopped and they heard only the far off bell-clang of ambulances and fire engines.

Cub's eyes searched the night and he angled his head to catch the sound again. It was gone. "What was that?"

"Don't know," Burt said. "Weird noise."

Cub shrugged and they walked on. A hundred yards ahead on the right, from the front steps of the Victorian house on the corner, two cigarettes glowed, and Cub heard children playing nearby. He guessed it was a couple and their young, out for a breath of air, winding down. No one slept during an air raid, except in a tube station.

The sound again! They halted and faced it. It was stronger, like the whistle of a stooping falcon somewhere in the murk. Then it faded.

"What the hell is that?" Ian said.

They waited and listened and studied the pink sky to the south. Finally, they gave up and began to walk again.

Suddenly, out of nowhere, the stooping falcon hissed, loud now. They spun around, and Cub felt a rush of air. As in a nightmare, a mass loomed - the head and shoulders of a black behemoth rising to darken the pink cloud. For a stupefied moment, he gaped.

"What in God's name?" Ian shouted.

Then the fear-mist in Cub's brain parted, and the head and shoulders of the monster transformed into the bulbous fuselage and engines of a Heinkel bomber. It approached in a flat glide, engines dead, as if to land where they stood. Perhaps it was controlled by a man in death's throes or maybe guided only by spirits. Cub threw himself to the ground.

A roar drowned the hiss as the machine clipped off roadside trees, as if breaking match sticks. A squall whipped Cub's clothes and blew his hat away. The dead airplane skimmed over him and settled onto the road, skidding along the pavement, taking out garden walls and entry ways, until it careened into the corner home, where the smokers had been, and came to rest.

Cub lay stunned for a moment, then struggled to his feet.

"Ian? Burt? You all right?"

"Yeah."

"Yes, sir."

"Geezus, that was close."

Cub peered in the direction of the wreckage. Blackness. The smokers had been there somewhere. Could he help?

He stumbled toward the building, hearing the creaking of cooling metal and the thump of falling masonry. Breaking into a run, he tripped and fell on an unseen curb, then pulled himself to his feet.

Ian shouted, "Where the hell are you going?"

"To help those people."

Cub set off again, stepping cautiously, groping through the debris. He approached the house warily, trying to pick out the steps where they sat, but he could barely discern shapes in the gloom. Then it dawned on him that the whole front of the house was gone - the wall peeled away to reveal fixtures, appliances and furniture inside, as if it were a child's doll house.

That smell? Fuel! The plane's tanks had ruptured. In his mind's eye, the lethal stuff cascaded over the debris, oozing into the pores of the masonry, spreading through the dried wood fibers, and soaking into torn wallpaper.

"Where are you?" Ian said.

"Here. Can you follow the sound?"

"Yeah. But I smell petrol."

"I know."

Cub heard a tiny sound, like the mewling of an animal, close by, to his right. He crept softly toward it, listening.

"Cub, come out of there," Ian called.

"Shhh! I heard something."

He heard it again. It came from down low next to where the missing steps had been. He crept toward it.

"Anybody there?" he said softly.

"Daddy?" a small voice answered from below.

"I'm not Daddy. But are you all right?"

"I'm stuck. I'm scared."

"I'll get you out in just a minute."

Ian called out, "Who the hell are you talking to?"

"There's a kid trapped here."

Cub still wasn't sure where the boy was. He had to keep the youngster talking in order to find him. "What's your name, son?"

"Nigel."

"Nigel, are you alone?"

"My baby sister's here."

"Is she all right?"

"Think so."

Cub followed the sound until he arrived at a ragged stack of twisted wood cabinets, loose timbers, and fractured sheets of plaster. The sound came from below it. He puzzled a moment, then decided the boy was in the well of the stairway leading to a below-ground-floor entrance, and the well was covered by the debris. If the building went up, the children were finished.

"Nigel, take it easy while we try to clear this stuff away." He turned and shouted, "Burt, Ian, I need help. Two kids are trapped here."

As they joined him, Ian said, "This whole bloody thing could blow in a flash."

"But what do we do? We can't leave them."

"Then, let's get them out, quick."

"They're down underneath this stuff," Cub said. "We've got to move it to get at them."

Burt said, "Be careful not to knock loose bits down onto them."

For some minutes, they carefully heaved masonry and splintered wood. The smell of fuel thickened Cub's throat and sweat ran down his collar. They nudged aside pieces that were too heavy to lift. Finally they had made a hole through which Cub could barely put his head. It was small, but maybe enough. He lay down and put his face to it. Inside it was pitch black; he dared not light a match.

"Nigel, can you climb the stairs, up toward me?" he panted. "And bring your sister with you."

From below, came the sounds of little voices and feet scraping on concrete.

Finally Nigel said, "I can't get any higher." It was a frightened voice from below and off to Cub's right.

"Take it easy, now," he said. "Put your arm up high over your head."

He removed his face from the opening and, slipping his left arm through it as far as it could reach, trolled his hand around in the darkness. Suddenly he brushed the warmth of small fingers, and quickly, like a bass taking a lure, the little hand clamped onto his.

"Is that as far as you can reach, Nigel?"

"Yes. I'm on tiptoes"

"Well, be patient and let my hand go. I'll get you out, I promise."

The clamp held.

"Come on, let go. We've got to get your sister out first."

Slowly the little hand relented. Cub put his face back to the hole.

"Can she reach my hand?"

"No. She's little."

"Well can you lift her high enough so she can?"

"Think so."

"Okay. Lift her up, right where you're standing, and tell her to put her hand over head like you did. When I tell you, let go of her and I'll pull her out. Understand?"

"Yes."

He heard Nigel talking to her, then there was silence. The fuel odor made him queasy.

"God, that stuff smells awful," Ian said.

"Just pray the place doesn't go up."

"Not to worry. Our Father hasn't heard from me in a while, but he's hearing now."

"Nigel, Are you ready?"

"Yes."

"Be sure she puts her hand up. Lift her now."

Again Cub slipped his left arm through the hole and began to fish around. He stretched and groped and found nothing. The stench was making him ill.

"No luck?" Burt said.

"No. Can't feel a thing."

He heard a small cry from below and withdrew his arm and leaned into the hole. "What's the matter?"

The boy sobbed. "Couldn't hold her any longer. She's too heavy."

"Then, rest for a minute, Nigel. We'll try again." Cub lay breathing heavily and trying to ignore the stench of the fuel. Below, there was an unintelligible exchange in baby talk.

"Geezus, mates," Ian said, "isn't there any way we can speed this up?"

"Can't think of any. I'm sure the kid's doing his best." Cub put his face back to the hole. "Ready to try again, Nigel?"

"Yes." It was an uncertain voice.

"Make sure she puts her hand up as high as she can reach."

There was more baby talk.

"Nigel, what's her name?"

"Yona."

"Yona, honey, put your hand up high when Nigel lifts you, please. Do you understand?" Cub heard the desperation in his own voice. Get hold of yourself, he thought. It was no good scaring them.

"Ready, Nigel?"

"Yes."

"Okay, let's try it. Now lift her."

Cub's hand trolled in the dark. No contact. In desperation, he shoved his shoulder into the hole, until the sharp edges bit into him painfully, and stretched his hand and arm as far as his fingers could reach.

He was ready to give up when his middle finger felt something warm and soft. He'd forgotten a hand could be so small, but just then, it was the loveliest hand he'd ever felt. He slid his fingers around her wrist. "Okay, Nigel, I've got her. Let her go."

Cub lifted her easily, scarcely believing there was a child attached, and rose to his knees as he swung her up to the opening. Fumbling to reach her other hand, he lifted her clear and set her on the ground. Thank God.

Then he said, "You guys take this girl and get the hell out of here."

"And run out on you?" Ian said.

"Yes, both of you, go. Take her out of here. I'll get the boy."

"But, sir," Burt said, "we can't leave you here alone."

"Cut that sir stuff and go. I can pull the boy out by myself. There's no point in all of us risking it here. You take the girl, Burt, and get her out of here. And, Ian, fetch your car. We'll need it."

Burt lifted the girl. The two men turned toward the street and picked their way through the debris, grumbling about leaving Cub behind.

"For Christ's sake, Cub," Ian called over his shoulder, "hurry up."

Cub turned back to the hole. He heard the boy sobbing softly below.

"You ready now, Nigel?"

"Yes." The word came out like a cry of despair.

"Give me your hand then."

The grip was firm and the load heavy. Cub struggled to his knees as he pulled the boy's arm through the hole.

"Now let me have your other hand."

Grasping both, Cub lifted until the boy would budge no further. The insides of his upper arms were wedged in the opening. He lowered and rotated the youngster, but the boy wouldn't fit.

Panic clutched at Cub. He twisted the body around again, and Nigel cried out as the sharp edges nicked his soft underarm. It was no good, the hole was too narrow.

Cub gagged on the fuel smell. He couldn't drop the boy; he'd fall and hurt himself and maybe never get out. And he was heavy; Cub would tire holding him.

To his left, the wreckage suddenly hissed, like an old locomotive venting steam. God, they couldn't wait.

"Nigel, I hate to do this but . . . . ."

With his full strength, he wrenched, twisted, and heaved the boy through the hole. Through his soft nightshirt, ragged edges of debris flayed the youngster from the underside of his upper arms to the bottom of his ribs. Then he came free, and Cub swung him clear onto the ground. A long moment of eerie silence followed as the boy labored, gasping for breath, then he erupted in a scream like the howl of a bear-trapped wolf.

Gritting his teeth, Cub scooped him up and fled across the wreckage. In the process he tripped and nearly dropped him. Reluctantly, he slowed and picked his way more carefully. The wreckage behind them hissed again.

He was ready to panic when he stepped off the curb and began to run down the street. As he rounded the corner, the shock wave hit him, and the house and surrounding trees blazed.

Burt was leaning against a brick wall and rocking the girl in his arms when Cub came up, breathing heavily.

"Is Ian getting the car?"

"Yes, he'll meet us here. By Jove, that was one close call."

"I'll say." Cub leaned against the wall, clutching the crying boy and gasping for breath. Slowly his tension eased, and the boy's crying turned to a whimper. Finally, Cub looked at Burt and smiled weakly. "But like gunnery, close doesn't count."

Chapter 25

Ian Craigwell guided the MG, laden with Cub, Burt, and the two children, through the blacked-out streets of the Kentish Town. Cub held Nigel, who whimpered softly. They turned down Dartmouth Park Hill toward the Tufnel Park Underground Station, then at The Boston Arms, swung left up Junction Road. A bell-clanging ambulance pulled out of a gateway in front of them.

"Must be it," Ian said. "I knew we'd get here tonight, one way or another."

They entered where the ambulance emerged and found themselves in the forecourt of a building, where they parked and got out.

The stucco-over-brick structure might once have been a fine home. Cub carried Nigel toward the front door; a makeshift sign over it read: Air Raid Protection Center. He entered the building and stepped past the blackout curtains then stopped and squinted in the unaccustomed brightness. The others joined him.

Bulletins, notices, first aid procedures, and aircraft identification silhouettes papered the yellowed walls. Floors of once-polished wood were grooved and pitted by the incessant tread of heavy shoes. Thick black curtains hung over windows.

The place throbbed with scurrying people and staccato voices. Uniformed ambulance drivers bustled in and out, and nurses' aids hurried intently here and there. On one side, wardens spoke gravely into telephones and occasionally called out casualty reports. At the back, women plotted them on a large table-map of the area. Eyeing the map, the dispatcher scratched addresses on slips of paper and handed them to ambulance drivers.

Workers, carrying stained mugs, stopped at a small stove in one corner and poured tea. In another, lay piles of dark blankets, and next to them, people dozed, fully clothed, on the hard floor.

The three pilots stood gaping at the scene. Their chalk-streaked uniforms were frayed where the cloth had caught on debris, and Cub's jacket was spotted with Nigel's blood. He held the whimpering boy in one arm, and the little girl stood between him and Ian, holding their hands. Nobody paid them the slightest attention.

"Well, what do we do now?" Ian said.

"Beats me."

From behind, a low, even female voice said, "May I help you?"

They turned to face Victoria Kendall.

For Cub, time halted. Her blue-green eyes gazed directly at him with that same steady look that had unnerved him before. Her dark blonde hair swept neatly off her forehead, and her strong jaw curved under gently hollowed cheeks to a firm chin. She looked strong and vigorous, yet slender and elegant at the same time, and she filled out her uniform as if it were a tailored evening suit.

He had forgotten precisely what she looked like, and he stood eyeing her, entranced, not even breathing, and finding her at once intelligent, dignified and utterly stunning.

She glanced at the other two men, then back at Cub. "Why, Cub, it's you! What on earth are you doing here?"

"Well," he said, pulling himself together, "the boy's hurt. We came to get him fixed up."

"Yes, of course," she said and lifted him gently out of Cub's arms.

Cub said, "It was pretty nasty." He explained what happened, and concluded, "I have no idea where the parents are."

She winced. "Follow me." And she led them to a room in the back.

Nigel's wounds proved to be superficial; they dressed them and gave him a sedative. Then, Victoria had to leave on an ambulance call. The children were put down to rest in a back room, but they lay awake calling for their mother, so Cub sat with them until they cried themselves to sleep. Then he went out and joined Ian and Burt in the dark forecourt.

"Good thing we knew about this place," Ian said. "We'd never have found it otherwise. Shall we get on our horse?"

"Somebody's got to stay and look after these kids," Cub said. "And try to find their parents."

"Look's like they're in good hands. Don't you think we could just leave them?"

"We can't do that. Nobody's taken responsibility for them. The supervisor's due back; he should know what to do."

Ian rubbed his chin and nodded.

An ambulance rounded into the parking area with its bell clanging, and it brought them upright. Two orderlies trotted out of the ARP Center and gingerly hauled a form covered with a sheet out of the vehicle and onto a stretcher, then they hurried it back into the building. In the darkness, the driver dropped from the cab and, holding the front fender, bent double and retched. Cub gazed anxiously at the person before he recognized her, then he leaped to his feet and shouted as he ran, "Victoria, are you all right?"

Her voice quavered. "I suppose. But that poor woman's a goner. She's the mother of the children you rescued. The crash killed her husband outright, and she won't last the night. Before I arrived, it took them an hour to untangle her from the wreckage. The whole time she cried about her children, Fiona and Nigel. She pleaded with the rescuers to stop working on her and find the little ones. They looked all over, but of course, no kids. I got there, and when they were loading her into my wagon, she called for them again. I told her they were here and safe. That was the last thing before she passed out. She just gave a faint little smile and went off. What a godawful business."

"So the girl's name is actually Fiona," Cub mused.

Victoria nodded.

"And they're orphans now," Ian said.

"As good as."

"Have you seen the supervisor?" Cub asked.

"He's at the site," she said. "Others are trapped there and the fire's spreading. I don't think we'll see him here tonight."

In the dim light, she looked pale. "Are you sure you're okay?" Cub said.

"I'm all right, thanks."

Her vague smile made him swallow hard.

"Can you stay . . . and have some tea?" he asked.

She hesitated. "I'd like to, but I have to get back there. I'm terribly sorry."

Cub followed her as she walked toward the ARP Center.

"Victoria, will we see you again?"

She stopped and turned. "Perhaps. Come back another night when we're not so busy."

They looked at each other for a long moment, then she turned slowly and continued on her way. He watched her until she disappeared into the building. Dear Lord, but she was attractive.

"Now that is one streamlined piece," Ian said, "eh what, Burt?"

Burt nodded. "Very nice."

Cub shrugged. "Anyway, we've got these youngsters to worry about."

Ian said, "But surely these ARP blokes are used to taking care of displaced people."

Ian's comment went almost unnoticed, because Cub was brooding about Victoria's departure. He'd made a mistake in not pursuing her the first time; he wouldn't repeat it. Maybe she'd even be back that night. And suddenly he had an idea.

He pondered a moment, then said, "Look," I don't feel comfortable leaving them alone here. I'll make you a deal. I'll stay with them tonight. You go to the hotel and come back to get me in the morning."

After some debate, it was agreed, and Ian and Burt left.

Cub poured himself a cup of tea and sat on a bench to wait. Were Ian and Burt laughing at him for staying behind? Would she laugh when she found him here? She must have boy friends standing in line. What would she see in him? It was probably a waste of time, though he did have to think of the kids. What a great excuse!

He had dozed over an hour, when an ambulance pulled up in front. Orderlies hustled two stretchers into a back room, and Victoria stepped through the door with her trench coat shrugged up around her neck. She moved slowly and gazed at the floor as she went.

"Hi," he said from the bench.

"Oh, hello," she said, as if interrupted. "Are you still here?" She looked ashen.

"You don't sound happy to see me."

"I'm sorry. I didn't mean it that way. It's just that this was a rough trip."

"Apology accepted." He slid off the bench and moved to the stove. "How about a cup of tea?"

"That would be nice. Thanks."

He poured a mug and handed it to her. Her eyes raised to rest steadily on his, and her mouth widened into a smile that took his breath away.

"Thank you," she said. "I needed this." She blew the steam off her cup. "Shall we find a quiet place to sit?"

They went outside and settled onto the stone bench in the forecourt.

She said, "So, you stayed behind."

"Yeah. Had to look after the children."

"That's thoughtful of you. Though I remember now, you like children."

He nodded. "Are you sorry I'm here?"

"Not at all."

"After our phone conversation, I didn't think you wanted to see me again."

"What gave you that idea?"

"You sounded . . . cool."

She shook her head gently and smiled. "I'm sorry for how I spoke, but I was absolutely shattered that night."

"When you said that work kept you from going out, I guessed that was your way of saying you weren't interested."

Her face clouded. "Not at all. I told you the truth. I take my job as seriously as you take yours. And with the blitz on, I work every night."

He turned this over in his mind and decided that if she were lying, he didn't want the truth. "I . . . didn't know. I apologize."

His turning up earlier had caught her off guard. He had looked so heroic carrying the boy and leading the girl by the hand, but he'd acted cool. Now his words warmed her.

"Apology accepted," she said, "and we're even. You do take your job seriously, don't you?"

He chuckled. "You bet. There are too many ways to come a cropper."

"We hear a lot about you fighter-boys. How does it feel to be one of our heroes?"

"To be honest, I haven't given it a thought."

She sensed this was neither deference nor a hollow dismissal to mask arrogance, just a simple truth. "No," she said slowly, "I don't suppose you have."

"Nor has any one else I know. The papers call us heroes, but we wonder where all those heroic fellows are. This battle is our mission, and we're only doing our best."

"Do you get frightened up there?"

"Not often. But I nearly bought it a couple of times. Then I was scared."

This man had no need to pretend. How different from so many others.

He said, "You like driving ambulances?"

"Not really."

"Kind of grim, eh?"

It would have been easy to answer that she wanted to be home acting domestic, but she preferred the truth. "Yes, but that's not the reason. There are just other things I'd rather do."

"Like what?"

How to make her point without putting him off? "You see, when I was growing up, I liked to play with my brother and his friends - climb trees, walk fences, throw stones, and all the things that boys like. Dolls and tea parties were no fun."

"You wanted to be a boy?"

"Not at all. But I like doing some things that only men are allowed."

"Such as?"

The plain truth had sent many men on their way. Often she had wanted that; tonight it would be a shame. "For example, flying a Spitfire."

"Wow. For that, you have to learn mechanics, navigation, aerodynamics and so on. Most girls aren't interested."

At least he hadn't laughed at her. "I know it's hard to believe a woman can have a good mind. That she likes to think about things other than men and cooking and babies. But that's the way I am."

"Especially hard," he said, "when she lacks redeeming features, like being fat or ugly. But I take your point. What makes you that way?"

She wondered if he were just being polite and tried to dismiss the question: "It's a long story. And not very interesting."

"I'm interested."

Was he serious?

"Tell me about it," he said.

She eyed him skeptically for a moment, then decided it was pointless to hold out. "All right, but I warned you. My father was an Army officer. As a little girl, I reveled in his stories of fighting bandits in the Punjabi hills, putting down an uprising in Kenya, and chasing thieves across the Persian desert.

"My earliest memory of him is in cavalry uniform with red flashes and glistening brass buttons, sitting astride a fussy bay gelding on a parade green in Devon. The leather strap of his hat passed under his nose and hid his blond mustache. His boots glistened like polished walnut carvings, and the sun reflected like a beacon off the hilt-guard of his saber. He checked the restlessness of the huge animal with tiny wrist movements that held it nearly motionless, under his complete control. I thought he was God.

"When the bugle sounded and the band struck up the Colonel Bogey March, the men and horses moved out in formation, and a lump came to my throat. One day, I too would be a soldier."

Cub sat squinting at her skeptically.

"It never occurred to me," she continued, "that there were no women on the parade field then or any other day. That dawned slowly over the years, until finally, at age eleven, I put the question to Daddy point blank.

"He smiled his wonderful, warm smile and took me in his arms and explained that they had no girls in the army; it was only for boys. Obviously that didn't mean me, and I told him so.

"I don't think he could bring himself to discourage me then, so he said if I wanted to be a soldier, I had to learn to march and ride and shoot. We started close-order drill that afternoon. By the time I was fifteen, I was clearing five foot fences on horseback and could hit a walnut at thirty yards with a twenty-two-caliber rifle.

"I began going bird shooting with Daddy and my brother, Giles. At first, I didn't carry a gun, but it was wonderful to get out in the open, with pheasants rocketing overhead and pigeons careening by. Daddy would track a bird with a smooth swing of his gun, then fire, and invariably drop it like a stone. He showed me how, and at sixteen, I got my first pheasant.

"We lived in a tiny house in the village of Norton Bavant in Devon. It never occurred to me there was trouble between Daddy and Mother until one day I heard them fighting. And it was over me.

"She accused him of ruining me with all that guns and horses business. I would never be a lady. Daddy argued that I obviously enjoyed it and was jolly good at it. Mother said that was precisely the problem. Women weren't supposed to enjoy that sort of thing, and I had to learn to behave like a lady, not a lance corporal.

"The upshot was that Mother left him and Giles, and brought me with her to London. We moved into a lovely home in Hampstead. It was utterly depressing.

"In my head, I knew, by then, that I couldn't be a soldier, but somehow that didn't settle the feeling in my heart. Daddy and what he taught me and our time together were the happiest memories of my life.

Being away from him was like being separated from my soul. And I envied lucky Giles, but I missed him too.

"Mother sent me to a proper girls' school. I didn't like it, but to please Daddy, I worked hard at it. I graduated with a distinction in French and won a scholarship to Oxford. But Mother would have none of that, and instead, sent me to finishing school. It was a crashing bore. I hated it."

Cub said, "I'd say the school did a pretty good job. Go on."

She smiled weakly and hesitated. She would skip part of this story, the part that really hurt.

"Well, to shorten a long saga, I was out of the country for several months until May of this year. And when I got back, I was determined to do something important for the war effort. Driving an ambulance was the first thing I found, but it's not exactly carrying the war to the enemy."

"And that's what you want to do?"

She nodded. "I'm giving up ambulance driving. Have another job. Not in a cockpit like you, but it's not exactly what you'd call woman's work either."

"Doing what?"

"I can't say."

"A secret?"

"Yes." Her cards were on the table, she thought, as much as she was allowed. Would this be the end of him?

He hesitated, a funny quizzical look on his face. "Victoria, will you go out with me?"

She felt a delightful little heady rush, and her instincts prodded her to say, of course. But Mother's training held her in check, and the job did come first. "I don't date much."

"You aren't married, are you?"

The wistful look on his face made her chuckle. "No."

"Then why won't you go out?"

"I've explained before, I'm so busy at night."

"Too busy for just a date? Can't we find one evening, even a few hours?"

"Look, I work a ten-hour night shift here, and sometimes twelve or fifteen. And my new job is already part-time during the day. Doesn't leave time for much else."

Even as she said it, she decided it wasn't convincing.

"How about just a drink?" he said.

"Look I might. But . . . .."

"But what?"

"Well . . . I've never been out with a Yank before, and they don't stand very high among my friends."

"Why is that?"

"They're thought to move a bit fast for a girl's comfort."

"I'll bet your friends think they hate dogs and children, too."

She laughed at her own chagrin. Why was she fighting him? "You're probably right."

From a pocket, he drew a pencil in one hand and a blank card in the other. "You got a phone?"

She gave a smile of defeat and dictated while he wrote. Then he looked up and gave her a wonderful, warm smile.

Suddenly, as if an apparition had descended onto the scene, it dawned on her. Cub's smile reminded her of her father. And so did his unpretentious manner.

She hesitated, pulling herself together, then said, "But you'll probably find it easier to get a message to me here in the evening."

"I've got their number too."

Suddenly, a man's voice called from the door of the ARP Center, "Miss Kendall."

"Yes."

"You're wanted right away. We have an emergency near Liverpool Street." The words hit like a gust of frigid air. The man jogged across the forecourt and handed her a piece of paper. "It's urgent, ma'am." Then he returned to the building.

They stood up. She said, "Oh, I am sorry."

He shrugged. "That's the way it goes."

He took her hands in his, and they gazed at each other silently for a moment. For an instant, she wondered if he'd try to kiss her, and the warm rush came over her again.

"It's been lovely," she said. "Thank you. I must go now." She slowly disengaged her hands. "Please call me."

"I will."

She turned and walked to the ambulance.

Cub watched her in the cab examine the paper with a flashlight. Then the light went out, the van started, and the blackout lights came on.

The van idled for a moment, and the lights blinked. He was certain it was for him, and even though it was dark, he waved.

The ambulance wheeled around and passed through the exit with the bell clanging raucously. To Cub, it sounded like the lilting notes of a symphony.

Chapter 26

After putting Burt Stark on the tube back to Hornchurch, Ian returned to the ARP Center early the next morning. He parked his car in the forecourt and came inside. The blackout curtains were open to let in the sun. Morning-after lethargy replaced the urgent hubbub of the night before, and displaced people slumped on benches or lay on the floor. Wardens and nurses' aids were mostly gone, supplanted by officials in civil clothes. As Ian entered, Cub waved him over to where he stood talking to an older woman behind a desk.

"Two or three days in this joint?" Cub barked. "This is no place for kids!"

The woman scowled at him. "Look here, Mister Bayer, we're doing our best." She gestured to the room full of people. "We don't have ready answers for all these problems. I have no idea where they'll send the children, but it surely won't take longer than a few days to do it."

He glared at Ian. "Geez, we can't just leave them here." His eyes riveted the woman again and he waved at the room. "These people are at least adults. They understand what's going on and can fend for themselves. But those little kids are helpless, and scared. There must be something you can do."

"Not today, Mister Bayer. All these things take time. Now I'm sorry, but I'm busy."

Cub turned to Ian, threw his arms in the air and cursed softly. "Their mother died last night, and today nobody gives a damn. Now what the hell do we do?"

"You've done your duty. What more can anyone ask?"

"Dammit, I am not leaving them until I know they're in the hands of someone who cares."

Ian rolled his eyes then turned to the woman. "Look, ma'am, don't you know some place where they might send these young ones."

"Not a clue. Talk to the Day Supervisor. She'll be along in a while."

It took an hour to find the supervisor, but she was more helpful. She knew several orphanages where the children might go; and the Central Office, who were responsible for assigning them, had listings of many more. And perhaps, if Cub were willing to furnish transport, something could be arranged quickly.

After a number of phone calls and the hard-won approval of a senior official, Cub, Ian, and the children piled into Ian's MG in the late morning. They drove west through Maidenhead to Henley, then headed northward through the Chiltern Hills until, short of Watlington, they turned off and climbed up a private road.

Grass covered the rolling slopes around them. Dark groves ran along the hilltops and meandered through the vales, groves of big oaks and elms that stood proud and cast deep shadows in the sunlight. To the west, hedge-bound farms stretched, like quilt work, across the flat valley into the haze toward Oxford.

The house at the top of the hill stood three levels high and stretched across the green hilltop looking comfortably indigenous, as if a receding glacier had deposited it. Ivy clambered up the gray stone walls, and moss and lichen squeezed between the shingles in the slate roof. Leaded windows opened onto the hillside.

Ian pulled the MG up in front and shut off the engine.

"Will Mummy be here?" Nigel said.

It wasn't the first time he had asked, and each time, Cub felt a pang of despair. He smiled weakly at the boy. "I don't think so."

The boy whimpered softly and his tears flowed. Cub clenched his jaw.

The front entrance was a massive dark oak door that swung on black iron hinges a foot high. It had an arched top, and chiseled deeply into the stone lintel above it were the words, Croton Abbey. Cub raised the lion-headed knocker and rapped it on the striking plate.

A woman in nuns' habit let them in and asked them to wait in the entry hall. Shortly, a tiny older lady in black robes hurried in. A tightly drawn white cowl squeezed her cheeks making them look puffy, and her skin glowed pink against the whiteness. Behind gold-rimmed glasses, her blue eyes darted about with curiosity. She smiled. "How do you do?" she said with enthusiasm. "My name is Mother Louisa. I'm in charge here."

They introduced themselves. Then she spoke to the children, kneeling, taking their hands in hers, and saying to each, "We're so happy to have you here with us."

Fiona returned it with a blank gaze. Nigel pouted and looked at her with round red eyes. "Is my mummy here?"

"No, not now," she said, "but she wants you to come and stay with me."

"I want Mummy."

"She'd like to be here, but she can't. Now let's go and have a sweet biscuit and meet the other children." She turned to the men. "Wait here a moment. You'll see these children later." And she led the young ones away, down the hall, chatting ardently with them.

Cub studied the place. The floors were pocked gray stone, and whitewashed walls rose to high vaulted ceilings. Sconces and chandeliers looked as if they were handmade ironwork. Maybe the place was a little austere, but it seemed comfortable enough. Through a lead-paned window, he looked out onto the back garden. It was simple and well kept, and a lawn opened into a broad grass field that extended across a valley. Lots of room to play.

Measured voices of children carried through the house, and sisters scurried about attending to chores.

Ian said, "Sure was a tough ride with those little ones."

"Yeah. Poor kids. Looks like we found the right place, though. It's a long way from town. Nobody's going to bomb here."

Mother Louisa hustled back wearing a big smile. "There now, they're having tea and biscuits and meeting some others. Won't you come and have some in my study?"

They followed, as she sailed down the hall, her white wimple riding on her head as if it were a perched bird and the loose black habit trailing like streamers in a fresh breeze. She led them to a small room and gestured toward chairs. They sat, and she poured tea and offered a biscuit. "Now," she said, "how was your trip?"

"Fine, except for coping with the children," Cub said. "Poor things want mom and dad. We had no idea what to tell them."

"That can be difficult," she said. "We try to distract them long enough so they learn they can survive without parents, then we gradually let them in on the truth. Usually they can handle it. But the first days after they're alone are the worst."

She explained enthusiastically that Croton Abbey was an orphanage run by the Church and that Nigel and Fiona were welcomed. They would be as comfortable as she and her people could possibly make them, and her staff would track down relatives and friends. Visitors were always welcome.

She asked about the children's rescue and sat engrossed as Cub and Ian described it. Then she wanted a firsthand account of the air war, and she urged the two men on as they talked.

When they finished, she said, "That was marvelous. We have radio and newspapers, but it's not the same as hearing you tell it. Now, what do you lads do in your time off?"

Ian said, "Our free time is between eight thirty at night and two forty-five in the morning, ma'am. We try to sleep but it cuts into our drinking time. This is the first day we've had off in weeks. And it'll be the last for a while."

"Oh dear. Would you like to lie down? We have plenty of beds."

The two men shook their heads.

"Don't ask me how, ma'am," Ian said, "but we get used it. Too much sleep would break the pattern, and we'd discover we were exhausted."

She looked askance at them and chuckled.

Cub said, "I want to meet the other children. Back home I used to coach youngsters."

Her eyes brightened. "Coach them in sports?"

Cub nodded.

"What sort?"

"Mostly gridiron football and tennis. A little basketball."

An impish look crossed her face. "You wouldn't like to do that here, would you?"

"Teach sports?"

"Yes. Spend a little time with them today. They are always around women, and they see so few men. Mother Nancy has tried to teach them cricket, but I'm not sure she knows all the rules. They'd love to have you show them and be so thrilled to meet two real pilots. Game time is after lunch. Won't you stay for an hour or so?"

"How about it?" Cub said to Ian.

"Why not?" He angled his head at Cub. "After living with this crazy American for so long, I might as well learn about their crazy games."

Her eyes widened and she snapped her fingers. "You just reminded me of something. The Church sends us where we're needed, and I spent some years at an orphanage in Germany. There was an American priest there who taught the children the most wonderful game. Baseball, I think you call it."

Cub nodded. "Baseball's an American game, all right."

"The children there loved it, and I know they'd like it here. Can you teach them?"

"I can try." Then he frowned. "But we need a ball and bat. I have no idea where to get equipment."

A grin spread across her face and she jumped to her feet. "Wait here," she said, and she hurtled out the door. A few minutes later, she was back carrying an old Babe Ruth Slugger and a serviceable softball. "I brought these from Germany after the American Father left, and I've had them stored away all these years."

Cub squeezed the ball and inspected the bat. "Okay, they'll do. But I've never tried to teach baseball in an hour."

At game time, most of the children gathered around the two pilots as they walked onto the cricket pitch. To Cub, they looked leaner and ruddier than the kids back home, but they pushed and shouted and tormented and teased like children anywhere.

A few of them seemed shy and removed, with gaunt, vacant looks in their eyes. They hung back as if afraid to join in. Nigel and Fiona were among them.

Cub spoke to as many as he could and struggled to remember their names.

They began practice by throwing and catching cricket balls, and Cub showed them how to hit. Soon, they wanted to play. Cub stood on a makeshift marker in the center of the pitch tossing the softball in his right hand. "All right, who's the first batter."

Peter, the biggest in the group, was given the honor. He walked out to the wicket and stood holding the bat with its head on the ground.

Cub went over to him. "Remember this isn't cricket. Put the bat on your shoulder like I showed you."

Peter gave an embarrassed frown and heaved it up. Cub adjusted it.

"Stand sideways a little more." The boy moved around. "That a boy! Now I'm going to toss the ball so it comes by you like this." Cub showed him. "When it's right here, you swing the bat and hit it. Okay?"

Peter nodded, and Cub walked to the center of the pitch.

"Ready?"

Ian stood on the grass beyond the opposite wicket. He looked idly relaxed with his arms folded. Mother Louisa came over to him. "You out here catching the sun?"

"No. Cub's got me playing long stop. Center field, I think they call it in this game."

"It's a bit like rounders. Wonderful for kids, and Cub is good with them, isn't he."

"Yes, ma'am. Like a kid himself."

"I take your point. Are all our fliers as young as you two?"

Ian gave an embarrassed grin. "Most."

She frowned and turned to watch the practice.

On Cub's third pitch to Peter, the youngster took a roundhouse swing, and the bat connected squarely. The ball rocketed over Cub's head, arced high beyond the opposite wicket, and bounced on the grass beyond Ian and Mother Louisa.

Cub yelled at Ian, "I warned you not to play so close." Then he turned to the boy. "Good hit, Peter. We'll call that a ground-rule homer."

"What's a ground-rule homer, Mister Cub?" Peter said.

"You scored."

The boy smiled uncertainly for a moment then, turning to the other children, raised his hands over his head and grinned broadly.

Mother Louisa had been right; the kids loved having a man for a coach. They didn't learn much baseball, but they tried hard. And they lionized the pilots.

When Mother Louisa finally called the end of game time and the beginning of rest period, they raised a chorus of disappointment.

"Can't we play longer?"

"Can't Mister Cub and Mister Ian stay for dinner?"

"When will they come back?"

"When will we play baseball again?"

After the children were at last quiet in their rooms, she ushered the two men to the front door. Her face glowed as she said goodbye. "Thank you so much. You were wonderful, and the children loved it. Please come back any time. You're welcome to stay overnight, too."

The men promised to return, bid her goodbye, and drove off in the MG.

Cub liked the woman; the children were lucky to be looked after by someone so cheerfully down-to-earth. He felt good about the day's work.

In the waning sun, Ian guided the car eastward through St. Albans and Harlow, and around the north end of London.

"You really get on with children, don't you?" he said.

Cub nodded. "Always have. Even thought of being a teacher or coach. Might do it yet."

"Staying with those two last night was a real sacrifice. I felt sorry for you."

"It wasn't so bad," he said casually. Then on impulse he added, "Victoria returned later and we talked."

Ian shot him a quizzical glare. "Oh hell! Now I get it. You sneaky bugger, you figured she'd come back, didn't you? Here I had you picked for sainthood, and the whole time, you had your mind on that dame."

"Even saints need diversion."

"Oh sure. The last time you got diverted, you lost your virginity."

"But this isn't the same."

"Of course not. You can't lose it twice, right?"

"I mean Victoria's different. She's the real McCoy."

Ian grinned and looked over at Cub. "What did I tell you? And it's good you decided to go for her, because otherwise I would. Now, aren't you glad I dragged you to that ARP Center?"

Cub smiled and nodded. Indeed, Ian was a good man.

Chapter 27

Early one afternoon, Duke and Cub stood together near their planes, which were parked on the downwind perimeter at RAF Biggin Hill. They had landed there after a fight above the Sussex Downs when they became separated from the others and ran short of fuel. Now they waited near a dispersal hut for the order to scramble. Inside the hut, and orderly sat by the phone, and several airmen lounged nearby on the grass. Otherwise, they were alone.

From the north came distant detonations and the high pitched whine of aircraft engines. Their gazes darted around the sky in the direction of the sounds, and Cub poked the ground nervously with the toe of his boot.

"Why the hell do they keep us standing around here?" he said.

"Don't know, lad. The grand strategists must figure they don't need us."

The sounds subsided.

Duke looked pale, and his eyes seemed unsteady.

"You feel okay?" Cub said.

"A little tender."

"Getting out of that Spit was a rough one."

Duke rubbed his solar plexus. "Hell, it's my gut that bothers me. Too much of this. Up and down four, five, six times a day."

"The rest at Kirton didn't help?"

Duke snickered. "Shit, I needed a month off."

Duke had always been demanding and sarcastic, but never discouraged. Something was clearly wrong. Cub knew there had been another letter from Cecily. Maybe that was it. He considered asking, but thought better of it. Instead he said, "Jerry's really got the heat on. Hasn't he?"

"Don't know how he does it. Bastards just keep coming, no matter how many we knock down."

"They've got to quit sometime."

"I'm not holding my breath, lad."

Overhead, the sun had nearly burned through a gunmetal-gray ceiling. They leaned on the wood fence railing and gazed eastward over a grass field that spread across several hundred yards to the edge of a wood. Cattle grazed there, and birds darted about.

Duke rubbed his chest again. His skin seemed white, and his eyes darted about in agitation. If he got distracted in the air, it could spell trouble for both of them. Cub would have to watch for that. If only the man would open up and say what was bothering him. The more Cub thought about it, the more worried he got.

Duke gripped the fence rail as if to steady himself and his eyes seemed to glaze over. Cub had to do something.

"Look," he said, "are you sure there isn't more to your feeling bad than just a heavy dose of flying?"

Duke glared at him. "Like what?"

Cub thought, In for a penny, in for a pound. "Like you got another letter from California."

"What the hell do you care?"

"She's . . . pretty important to you, isn't she?"

Duke looked at Cub for a long silent moment, uncertainty working in his eyes. Then he turned away and grunted disgustedly.

"Bad news?" Cub said.

Duke seemed to study the distant horizon. Finally, he said softly, "She wants to come back."

"Christ, that must be wonderful news?"

"I don't want her."

"Are you serious?"

"Too right! The bitch ran out on me. Why should I get on my knees to have her back? I don't need her."

"Got someone else instead?"

"I've got my freedom."

"Freedom for what?"

"Whatever I like." The pitch and volume of Duke's voice went up. "To come and go as I wish. To take out whoever I please. To make out when and where it suits me. That's what." The last words were delivered in a shout.

"Okay, okay. No need to raise your voice."

"Except that you keep sticking your nose in my bloody business. And while we're on this subject, lad, have you seen Doreen lately?"

"Yeah. You were right."

Duke shook his head in disgust. "Bloody slut."

"She asked after you."

"I'll bet she did. Joking about me while you were having it off with her, no doubt."

"For Christ's sake, we were sitting in a pub."

"Did she have her knickers on?"

"I wouldn't know."

"Of course not. You don't touch that stuff, do you?

"Come off it. She has a problem and I was trying to help."

"Bully for you."

Cub was pretty sure he'd been right about Cecily. There was more of her in Duke's ills than he let on.

The two men stood in awkward silence for several minutes eyeing the sky. Suddenly, in the distance, Cub picked out an approaching airplane and, as it drew closer, saw it was a Spitfire. It turned onto base leg trailing a fine plume. Cub pointed at it. "He's leaking oil."

Duke gazed at it. "That's a pretty heavy oil leak. He may be on fire."

The two men stared as the wounded craft staggered onto final approach.

Cub squinted again. "It's one of ours. By God, it's Ian! I can read his designator."

The plane struggled toward them low over the trees. The left main landing wheel dropped to the down position. Cub's eyes rounded. "Right undercart's locked up solid."

"Rotten luck for young Ian," Duke said through his teeth.

They stood spellbound as the sound and aspect of the plane grew. Suddenly, the right wing dipped.

"Power! Sod it, power!" Duke cried. "She's stalling!"

The uneven engine roar hit them, the wing came level, and the nose began to rise. Then, without warning, it dropped, and the plane settled toward the trees.

"Geezus, he's going into the woods."

Duke broke into a dash, leapt the fence, and ran for where the plane was falling. Cub followed.

With a thunderous death-rattle, the Spitfire plunged into the trees, heavy wood rending fine aluminum as if it were tissue paper.

Gasping for breath, Duke and Cub crashed through brush, struggled through undergrowth, scurried around tree trunks and over dead limbs until they broke into the area where the wreckage lay under a pall of black smoke. Heat brought them up short, and the stench of burning rubber and fuel made them grimace.

Wings and tail assembly were gone and the spinner and cowling stoved in. The fuselage canted drunkenly to one side. The one remaining propeller blade lay back against the engine. Flame raged from the exposed wing root, and the noise of the fire was so loud they had to shout to be heard.

"Looks like the cockpit's still intact," Duke said. "You don't suppose he's alive in there?"

With heat keeping them at bay, they picked their way around the wreckage to where they could see past the smoke into the cockpit. There, they gaped. Inside, Ian lay still.

"Shit!" Duke shouted. "They'll never get the fire wagons in here."

"We've got to do something," Cub said, "I'm going to try to help him."

He turned and, raising his hands to shield his face, started toward the blazing plane.

Duke grabbed him by the collar. "Don't be stupid. You'll fry before you get near him."

They turned and looked again at the cockpit. Ian's eyes flickered as he came conscious. He appeared dazed, then horror came over his face as he seemed to grasp his predicament. He grimaced and his mouth contorted in a scream swamped by the fire's roar. Then he struggled to free himself, heaving, straining at the still-sealed canopy, pounding on it with his fists.

"The crowbar, Ian!" Duke shouted. "Use the crowbar." His voice was lost in the din.

Ian's young face contorted in agony.

Cub looked at Duke then at the struggling Ian. "But we can't just let him roast in there!"

Duke held Cub firmly by the shoulders. "Stay here, lad. That's an order."

Cub shot a glance at Ian. Then he turned and flung his right arm around Duke's upper body, slammed his buttocks into Duke's hip, and with a primordial grunt, hurled the man over his back, onto the ground.

"Sorry, Duke. Had to. Can't just leave him there." And Cub plunged toward the blaze.

"Come back, fool."

Ian twisted and strained to break out of the furnace.

The heat flayed Cub's hands and face, seared his throat, and scorched his lungs. His vision blurred as the fluid in his eyes vaporized. Still, he stumbled on, until he lost his way in a tumbling kaleidoscope of raw determination, blinding heat, smoke, and unwilling flesh. Then he tripped and lost his balance.

A powerful hand hauled him backwards, out of the heat and smoke, until he lay on the cool forest floor.

"You crazy bastard. We can't afford to lose two pilots in this."

Cub sat up. Smoke curled from his smoldering cuffs and tears flowed down his cheeks. "But we got to do something!"

Duke's face was gaunt and his eyes wide. Through the canopy, he saw Ian writhing in agony and mouthing screams lost in the din. Cub was right, Duke thought. They couldn't just stand immobile, witnessing this ghastly scene. They had to take action. But what?

Suddenly, he knew. "We'll do something, all right," he said.

With his left hand, he grasped the bottom of his holster, and his right hand fumbled for the pistol grip. He tried to pull the gun free, but it stuck. His movements seemed to him so awkward and slow.

Ian struggled, his contorted face made more horrible in the dancing light of flames that apparently burned low down in the cockpit.

Duke heaved on the pistol, and it came free. He stepped closer to the wreck, until the heat stopped him.

But, Duke thought, this is nothing to what that boy feels, and I can't afford to miss. He moved even closer, until he knew that any further and he'd be unable to hold the gun steady. He cocked the hammer, raised the pistol, and leveled it at the tortured figure in the cockpit.

Cub scrambled to his feet. "What the fuck are you doing?"

Ignore Cub, Duke said to himself. Both of Duke's hands gripped the gun, and he gritted his teeth against the scorching heat. He sighted down the gun barrel at the bobbing head, now partly obscured by smoke in the cockpit. Then he fired.

He saw the bullet hole in the Perspex, but through the smoke, he couldn't tell if he'd hit his mark. The searing heat flayed his hands. To hell with it. Finish the job.

Again Duke fired. And again. Six times in all, until the gun was empty.

He lowered his hands and staggered backwards. His head hung as if in prayer.

A thousand fine crazes splayed from the neat pattern of holes in the Perspex bubble, and Ian lay quiet in his crematorium.

Duke weaved and his knees buckled. He dropped the gun and sagged into Cub's arms. "Sorry. I lost my . . . God, what did I do?"

Images of his dead friend tumbled through Cub's mind. Happy Ian behind the wheel of his MG. Ian teasing him about Doreen. Ian's soft snore in the bed beside him at night. An astonished Ian learning that Cub stayed with the kids to see Victoria. Ian encouraging him to go after her. Now he was gone. Ian . . . ..

Cub looked blindly down at Duke and shouted, "You killed him. He never had a chance."

His grip on Duke loosened, and the man sagged to the ground.

A group of airmen led by a sergeant stumbled through the underbrush into the clearing and ran toward the two. "What happened?"

Tears streamed down Cub's face as he turned to the sergeant and choked out, "Ian was stuck in there, and he shot him." He pointed at the wreck. "Killed him in cold blood."

Through the flames that nearly filled the cockpit, they could barely make out the body. But the Perspex canopy was still intact, and the bullet holes were evident.

"My God, sir," the sergeant said, "he would never have got out of there."

"How do you know?" Cub shouted mindlessly. "With you here, we could have done something."

"But sir, we only brought our bare hands. Killing him might have been the kindest thing the Lieutenant, here, could have done."

"Christ, there must have been something we could do!"

The men gaped at him.

Cub could see they didn't believe him. Damn them! They just wrote Ian off!

He dropped his face into his hands and sobbed.

* * *

Squadron Leader Parsons sat in one of the chairs across from Gunnar Christian's desk, and Peter Duke hunched down in the other. Added to the pain in Duke's upper abdomen was a persistent nausea and occasional dizziness when he stood up. It was only yesterday, but he could barely recall firing the pistol.

Once he understood the law and the charges against him, his mind had gone numb. Killing in cold blood, for whatever reason, was murder. And the penalty for murder was death.

Parsons spoke: "The Group Captain says we have no choice. We must hold a court-martial."

Duke said, "And for this I'll die?"

"Most unlikely," Parsons said. "In the worst case, surely the Air Marshall will grant a reprieve. After all, you had reason with which we all sympathize, and you're a serving officer with a fine record."

"But it's not impossible, is it?"

Parsons edged around nervously in his chair. "Nothing's impossible in a court of law."

Death might be better than feeling this way, Duke thought. But his real problem was that sonofabitch, and he said it out loud. "It's Cub's fault."

Christian frowned. "What do you mean?" he snapped.

"Had it in for me."

"I don't bloody well believe that. Why the hell would he?"

"He thinks I ride him too hard."

Parsons said, "He thinks you ride him, all right, but he isn't bitter about it. And he respects you."

Christian said, "I don't believe it, either, Duke. Even you admit you shot the man. That wasn't Cub's fault."

"But if the sonofabitch hadn't made such a bloody fuss, nobody would have noticed."

"For God's sake," Christian said, "he was distraught over losing his friend. Lost his head. Of course, we'd like to have hushed up the whole thing. But five witnesses are too damned many. And now the word's spread all over the station. Well, I want this thing over quickly. Put behind us, and every man-jack back on the job."

Parsons said, "The Group Captain says he can convene the court next week."

"Next week!" Christian shouted. "Geezus, has he forgotten there's a war on? That we're fighting for our lives? We can't wait that long!"

Parsons shrugged. "Said it was the best he could do, sir."

Christian fumed silently for a moment. "All right, then. Duke, are you able to fly?"

Duke nodded.

"Then you're on regular flying duty until the court convenes."

"Yes, sir."

There was long silence. Then Christian shot a look at Parsons and said, "What should Duke do, plead guilty and throw himself on the mercy of the court?"

"It's possible," Parsons said, "but I don't recommend it."

"Why not?"

"It would be better all around if Peter were found innocent."

Duke had listened as if it were a radio program playing in another room. Now he slowly turned and said to Parsons, "But I did shoot him."

"I hear you, but you can still plead, Not guilty."

Christian said, "But for God's sake, man, the witnesses all say --."

"I know what the witnesses say, sir, but we should try. I have an idea."

"What is it?"

"I have a barrister friend, and I took the liberty of discussing this case with him last evening. He had several suggestions."

"What were they?

"Sir, it's possible that I can recall them for you, but I have a different recommendation."

"What is it?"

"We should have him defend Peter Duke in court."

"Bloody unusual to bring a civilian into a court-martial."

"Sir, he's better than anyone we could possibly find."

"Really? What's this man's name?"

"Nigel Denniston."

The skipper's eyes rounded in awe. "Nigel Denniston? The Nigel Denniston that gets all those rapists and murderers off?"

"Precisely."

"Bloody hell!" Then Christian leaned back in his chair and stroked his chin. "But I take your point. What makes you think he'd accept the case"? How much would he want?"

"He understands what justice we all want here, and he's agreed to take it for nothing. Says it's his way to help the war effort and thank the RAF."

"And he can be here for the trial?"

"He'll start his investigation tomorrow if I call him."

Christian turned to Duke. "What do you think, Peter?"

Duke's thoughts were distant. "I don't know if it's worth it. I feel so . . .." And he just shook his head.

"Of course, you feel awful. But dammit, man, you're an officer in His Majesty's Service. You can't just give up."

"No, sir. Whatever you say, sir."

Christian eyed Duke and grimaced. Then he turned to Parsons. "You better get on that phone."

Chapter 28

In the dark, Cub followed Duke down the walkway and through the door into the Briefing Room. They wore heavy flight jackets, sheepskin with the wool inside, to shield the cold of the altitudes where the German fighters now operated. They didn't speak to each other. Cub felt sick with guilt.

"Morning gents," said Squadron Leader Parsons, as the door slammed behind them.

"Oh fugoff, Parsons," Duke growled. "No bloody Jerry's up this early in the morning. They've got better sense. Why in hell can't you grand strategists let us simple aviators get some sleep?"

"You know the rules," Parsons said. "Readiness at dawn, come rain, snow, sleet, or hail. And the bombing crescendo over the last few days has everyone on edge."

They set their watches. Dawn in fifteen minutes. Others filtered into the room to make a milling crowd of sleepy aviators.

Duke thumbed at an urn on a side table. "Is that tea?"

"It's old, but it's hot," Parsons said. "Have some and we'll get started."

Duke filled his cup, sipped it, and grimaced. "Geezus, this stuff's turned to horse piss. Haven't you got some fresh?"

"It'll be along in a minute," Parsons snapped, then he raised his voice to the crowd. "Now listen everybody and we'll get this over with. It should be another lovely day for Jerry's bombing, and we expect him right on schedule. If he follows the usual pattern, it'll be big bomber formations with plenty of fighter escorts, making straight for London an hour after sunup. As usual, Shakespeare is your controller. And here comes fresh tea."

The men milled around the trolley for several minutes.

Then Gunnar Christian stepped to the podium. "Today will be a little different. Fighter Command has designated Spitfire squadrons to go after the fighters, while the Hurricanes tackle the bombers. They should send us up early and high. If we have the time, Red and Yellow flights will climb to twenty-eight thousand, and Blue will go in as high cover at thirty-one."

There were a few soft whistles from the crowd.

Parsons said, "Any questions? All right, gents, your transport is waiting."

First light broke as they bounced along the perimeter track in the back of the open lorry. Cub was nagged by tension in his upper stomach, and he had a mild headache. He was slowly turning over in his sleep-bogged mind what the skipper had said. They would go in high with Blue Flight as top cover. That meant they were likely to encounter the Jerry fighters head on, exactly the setup Duke had envisioned for the split attack. Shouldn't they try it now? Dare he suggest it?

On the downwind side of the field next to the dispersal hut, their planes were run up and checked by the erks. The engines' din died away as the flatbed truck drew up. Pilots dropped off and moved to stake out a place at a table, a chair outside, or just a plot of grass. They settled quickly. Most slumped, eyes closed. Wan faces sagged and nobody chattered.

Fatigue, Cub thought. Fatigue as he'd never seen it before. Fatigue that could spell the end of caution, and life.

For Cub, waiting at dispersal had become a ritual. Pacing the grass, finding an overstuffed chair, dozing but unable to sleep, getting up for tea, watching a labored chess game for a few moves, riffling a well-thumbed copy of the Illustrated News for the twentieth time, tossing it away. Then doing it all over again.

But this time, Cub couldn't sit still or concentrate on anything. Ian had haunted him for the three days since he was killed. Cub had got away from the scene of the crash, calmed himself, and then begun to piece together what had happened. As he considered all the angles, he realized that there had never been any hope of rescuing Ian. Whatever Cub had felt in the heat of the moment, the Sergeant had been right: Duke had done the kindest possible thing. And Ian had died in action just as surely as if he had augered in.

Now, because of Cub, Duke faced a murder charge, and Cub felt hounded by a terrible guilt. Why, in God's name, hadn't he kept his mouth shut? How could he ever make it up to Duke?

Cub walked out of the dispersal hut and gazed toward the sun as it climbed off the horizon. Duke sat slumped in a chair, eyes closed, appearing to sleep. He'd been as cold as a clam; hadn't even said, good morning. Cub walked over to where he sat.

"You asleep?" Cub asked quietly.

Duke opened one eye. "If I was, you woke me."

"I'm sorry. I mean . . . .."

"What are you mumbling about, lad?" Duke's eyes quivered.

"I came, in the first place, just to say I was sorry. For the way I behaved. I didn't mean for anything like this to happen to you."

"Sure you didn't. It was just a big mistake, wasn't it? Here I taught you nearly everything you know. Then you thought I was pushing you too hard, so you decided to get rid of old Peter Duke. He's a has-been anyway."

"For Christ's sake, Duke, it's nothing like that."

"It isn't, eh? All that gloating over my problems with Cecily was just casual conversation, is that it? And now you think you can apologize your way out of this murder rap."

"Honest to God, Duke, I didn't want this. I realize you did Ian a favor. I'm sorry for the way I behaved."

Duke grunted, then lay back and closed his eyes.

Cub said, "Can I ask you something else?"

"Nothing's ever stopped you before."

Oh God, Cub thought, this meant trouble. But they still flew together and fought together. They had to try to work together. And he had to raise the issue. Just keep it low key.

"We practiced your split attack last week," he said. "Seems like this morning, going in high and head-on, might be the perfect setup to try it. What do you think?"

Duke slowly opened his eyes and glared. "Bloody hell! You can't keep your nose out of my business at all, can you? Well, I'll show you. You're going to lead the sodding flight today. The skipper's been after me to give you a crack at it. Says we need to build leaders. Well, today's your chance. I'll fly your wing. You call the split. You take responsibility. And if you look around and I'm gone, don't weep."

"Duke, for Christ's sake --."

The phone in the dispersal hut gave a soft click.

"For Christ's sake, yourself," Duke said, and angled his head toward the phone. "That's not the Queen asking us to tea. You're Arrow Blue One. Go to it, Commander."

"Arrow Squadron scramble!"

*

As promised, Shakespeare Control got them off early, and while the German formations assembled over the Pas de Calais, the Arrow Spitfires climbed to twenty-eight thousand feet over the Thames Estuary. Cub led Blue Flight even higher, until the altimeter read thirty-one. There he leveled off, but kept the throttle at high boost to catch up with the flights below. His thighs felt cold through his trousers, and he sucked heavily to get oxygen.

They were crossing the eastern tip of the Isle of Sheppy, near Whitstable, when he spotted the German formations miles ahead. For once, the Arrows had height on the bastards.

"Tallyho!" Gunnar Christian called. "A gaggle of two hundred plus bombers at angels two two, westbound over Canterbury. A hundred fighters at angels two five. Fifty more in top cover at angels two seven. And a few more still higher.

"Red and Yellow, we'll take the main top cover. Blue, go after those high birds. Remember, our job here is to shoot down what we can on the first go, make them burn fuel, and avoid damage. Hit hard, disengage quickly, and reassemble over Rochester. After that, we'll attack again in strength. All right, lads, in we go."

Cub called, "Blue Flight, split go," and opened the throttle. The two sections turned away from each other in the thin air, with Cub and Duke rolling gingerly to the left and Burt leading the other section to the right, toward the sun. The Messerschmitts closed down the middle between them.

They had learned that timing the turn-in was critical, and Cub studied the eight Messerschmitts, now only vague specks to his right and below, striving to choose the moment. The Germans kept coming until they were at his two o'clock.

"Blue Flight, turn go," he called. Duke followed Cub as both sections turned in toward the Germans.

Suddenly all eight of the enemy fighters broke toward him and Duke. They must have missed seeing the other pair, and Burt would get a clean tail-on shot. Just as Duke predicted!

"Coming at you, One," Burt called.

"I see them. We'll take them head on. You nail them from behind."

The distant specks quickly fleshed out into Messerschmitts. Cub forced himself back into the seat, put both hands on the stick, and maneuvered the pipper onto the cockpit of an oncoming German. From five hundred yards, he looked down the Messerschmitt's gun barrels through the Spitfire's bulletproof windscreen. Idly he wondered, would it stop a Mauser? He pressed the firing button and felt the Brownings hammer, and his opponent's cannon began to wink. Smoke came off his target.

The head-on encounter was over in an instant, and the Germans passed, close aboard. Then Burt and his wingman flashed by on Cub's right, turning hard on the heels of the Germans.

"Watch out, One," Burt called. "There's another flock on your port beam."

Cub snapped around to look left and spotted four Messerschmitts closing. He turned hard into them, but couldn't bring his guns to bear before they passed by.

"Heads up, Three. They may follow you."

"Right, One. We nailed a pair out of that first bunch, and we're turning to cover the second."

Great! Two down for no losses.

Below, Red and Yellow sections had already attacked the leading Messerschmitts, and by the sound of it, had scattered them. Now, the rearmost formation of German fighters was passing abeam and below. Cub turned hard to follow.

He called, "Join up, Blue Three. We're going after the last of the top cover."

"Right, One. Have you in sight."

Burt closed from Cub's left.

Cub called, "Blue Flight, down we go."

He lowered the nose and rolled into a right turn. The sun was behind them as they dropped on the clipped-wing fighters nearly a mile below. Apparently the Germans hadn't seen them.

Cub singled out a target near the back of the formation. A thousand yards out, he gave a quick look around and took a deep breath. Pressing himself back into the seat, he put both hands on the stick and focused his whole being on the gun sight. He held the pipper on the target, and his Spitfire tracked in behind its prey.

The Messerschmitt's drab upper surface evolved into dark blue-gray on the wings and spine of the fuselage and mottled green and graphite-gray on the sides. The image spread until the wings filled the sight's inner ring. He made out the ailerons, elevators, fabric-covered rudder, the flat glass panels of the canopy, barrels of the wing guns, the radio mast atop the fuselage. The wings grew to fill the outer ring.

With minute motions to stick and rudder, he edged the sight pipper out in front of the target. He could see the pilot's tan leather helmet and black earphones, the antenna wire, paint scratches where men had scrambled up the wing roots, smudges of soot behind the exhaust stacks.

He pressed the gun button, and the Spitfire shuddered from the hammering recoil. Using small control corrections, he held the sight picture, and tracers arced across the distance to the target. On arrival, each bullet erupted in a flash and made a small dark hole. In two tenths of a second, thirty of them passed into the engine compartment making a pattern of holes that looked like a dark disease on the skin of the Messerschmitt. Half a second later, the disease had spread back along the fuselage to the wing root and up to the cockpit. Perspex shattered and smoke streamed. Slowly the German rolled to the left until he was upside down, and the remains of the canopy came off and sailed by. A figure followed.

Duke and Burt drew blood as well, and the German formation scattered like a surprised covey of quail. Blue Flight climbed to disengage and turned to join Red and Yellow. No Arrows were damaged. Below, vertical smoke trails rose from the hop fields. It had been a perfect bounce.

Gunnar's voice: "Good work, lads. Their top cover's spread all over hell. Assemble over Rochester quickly now. We'll hit the main fighter escorts this time."

Minutes later, Arrow Squadron joined up and maneuvered into attack position over the Luftwaffe juggernaut droning up the Thames toward Greenwich.

"Arrow Squadron, Shakespeare here, keep your eyes peeled for a formation of Hurricanes joining the battle in your area from the north."

Cub scanned the sky to his right and picked them out on the horizon. Hallelujah! Reinforcements! Must be Twelve Group. At this rate, we might even have numbers on our side. "Arrow Leader," he called, "Blue One sees a flock of Hurricanes, three o'clock, ten miles."

"I see them too," Christian said. "That'll make Jerry nervous. Stick together now. In we go. Let 'em have it!"

Cub pushed the throttle to the gate and turned toward the Messerschmitts. G's pushed him into the seat as he reversed the roll to track his target. But this German was not fooled; he pulled into a climbing turn to meet the attack head-on, while others broke to the right. Cub would shoot it out with this one, down the throat, then worry about the rest.

But as the German brought his guns to bear, he must have decided not to play, for he broke off the engagement, exposing his white underbelly. Holding the gun button down, Cub eased the stick back to keep the needed deflection and watched his bullets stitch the engine compartment and along the belly to the wing roots. A wisp of flame appeared at the rear of the engine cowling. When the German filled his windscreen, he shoved the stick forward and hurtled underneath.

Check six o'clock, he thought, and he looked over his right shoulder to spot another Messerschmitt diving on him. He hauled the Spitfire into a hard right turn; his neck muscles protested as he craned, but the turn spoiled the German's aim.

Suddenly, his plane shuddered under the impact of a cannon shell in the engine, and heavy machine gun bullets cracked into the armor plate behind his head. He wrenched the controls in the opposite direction. Another bastard, coming out of a blind spot!

Black oil sprayed over the windscreen and smoke swept into the cockpit. Then the engine seized, wrenching the airframe. Smoke thickened, and he could no longer see the instruments. The controls froze.

Get out now!

With both hands, he reached overhead and pulled on the canopy. For an instant, he thought of Ian trapped. Dear God, don't let that happen. But the canopy opened. He pushed the stick to one side, the plane rolled lethargically, and slipping the catch on the shoulder harness, he tumbled out.

For nearly a minute, he fell free, and when he guessed he was low enough to breathe, he pulled the ripcord. The chute billowed and jerked him upright. Hanging in space under a warm sun fifteen thousand feet over the Tower of London, Cub drifted slowly westward in the breeze.

A half-mile further west, over the City district of London, sunlight glinted off the canopies of Heinkels and Dorniers disgorging their loads. Bombs landed with heavy thumps, and the City lay wreathed in smoke that obscured all but the dome of Saint Paul's.

Anti-aircraft guns boomed, and their shells detonated among the bombers with a flash and a sharp crack, then blossomed into black smoke like poisonous flowers. A dozen smoke trails rose from the pall to mark the final plunge of planes that lost their way in the garden. Now and then, a new lost soul trailing smoke dived to join them.

Suddenly, several hundred yards away, a four-plane parade rocketed by: Messerschmitt leading Spitfire leading Messerschmitt leading Spitfire, each prey to the one behind. Except for the last, they all trailed smoke as they disappeared downward.

To the east, neat ranks of bombers stretched as far as he could see, droning in to follow the others to the target. Darting among them like sparrows, Hurricanes rattled out their death message. The light guns of the Heinkels and Dorniers were no match for their eight Brownings, and an ongoing shower of German wreckage tumbled onto the Essex countryside.

Only an occasional Messerschmitt came to their aid, for they were occupied high above in battle with Spitfires, no quarter given or asked. There, hundreds of fighters twisted and curved, trailing condensation like chalk scrawled in curlicues across the cobalt blue. Engine noises tuned between scream and growl. Mausers jackhammered, and Brownings rattled like sticks dragged across a picket fence. White trails of the losers turned dirty black and curved earthward.

For ten minutes, Cub gaped, stunned at the enormity of the cataclysm. Then the parachute dropped him gently into the Thames by London Bridge.

He was pulled from the river by a fire boat, and after spending three quarters of an hour in a bomb shelter, he carried his parachute down the steps at Monument Underground Station. People waved and cheered as he passed. He had no money, but the platform guard grinned at the parachute and let him through without paying. Within minutes, he sat on the District Line train, as it rumbled eastward out of the station toward Hornchurch.

Children in school uniforms began to gather around and ask questions. Then they wanted autographs. He signed them all the same way and felt an incredible glow of happiness watching the delight on their faces as each read what he'd written: Cub Bayer - Spitfire Pilot. And underneath he'd drawn a cartoon face of a bear cub.

Chapter 29

Peter Duke's court-martial convened in a room in the RAF Hornchurch headquarters building. The head of the court was a Group Captain, reportedly from the staff at Bently Priory; he was flanked by the other two judges, Wing Commanders whom Cub did not recognize. Peter Duke sat in the front facing the court, flanked by Squadron Leader Parsons and the barrister, Nigel Denniston. The audience was made up of the Station Group Captain, four officers who were strangers, and Gunnar Christian. Doors to the room were protected by armed guards.

Cub sat in the witness box; it was his third time on the stand. The hearing was all but over, and he felt drained, barely able to keep his surroundings in focus. All other witnesses had been heard; and the Prosecutor, a Squadron Leader, had finished questioning Cub and was summing up the evidence and testimony for the court.

He related that all six rounds in the gun had been fired, and all by Peter Duke. The body and the Perspex canopy were so consumed by the fire that there was no forensic evidence; however, all witnesses saw six well-placed bullet holes in the canopy opposite Craigwell's head. Testimony showed that the deceased, who had been struggling to escape before, lay motionless after the shooting. Here the Prosecutor pointed at the witness box and reminded the Court that they not only had Cub's firsthand testimony, but also corroborating evidence from the airmen who had previously testified. Whatever the motive and whatever the sympathies of the Court, it was clear-cut murder. And the Court should find it so.

As the man droned on, Cub's mind tuned in and out. Everything had gone wrong, and he felt utterly depressed.

When the Prosecutor sat down, Denniston was allowed to cross-examine. He approached the box. The profusion of somber black folds that billowed around him was at odds with the comic white wig that perched on top of his head, seemingly shrunken by too many washings. The man's hair was fair and his skin pale, nearly white. His narrow face tapered to a pointed chin, his eyelids drooped, and he carried his head high so that his sleepy gray-eyed gaze came down his nose in a look of uninterested contempt. But close up, Cub could see his eyes darting about, snatching up every detail.

Denniston filled the image Cub had of the men who had, in centuries past, sent the guilty and innocent alike to be burned at the stake. His blood ran cold. Could this sort of man possibly get Peter Duke off?

"Mister Bayer, you said that you made two attempts to approach the burning aircraft?"

"Yes, sir."

"What was your purpose in doing this?"

"To rescue Ian Craigwell."

"Both times you were stopped by the defendant, is that right?"

"Yes."

"If you hadn't been stopped, could you have saved Mister Craigwell?"

Cub hesitated. "Realistically, I doubt it."

Denniston eyed Cub with the look of a Hawk. "Then why did you try?"

"I guess I wasn't being realistic."

"Have you any idea what would have happened if you hadn't been stopped?"

"I fell the second time. If Duke hadn't pulled me out then, I'd have been badly burned. Maybe died."

"So now you think the idea of rescuing Craigwell was not feasible, is that right?"

"Yes."

"Would you say that you weren't rational, at the time?"

"Not completely."

"By Mister Duke's testimony, you ran straight into an inferno without apparent thought for yourself, and he had to drag you out. You, yourself, testified that you were desperate over the plight of your friend. And when the airmen arrived, they found you sobbing uncontrollably, raving that Mister Duke had shot Craigwell, and suggesting that they might have helped rescue him. Yet, in their opinion, there was never any hope saving Craigwell. Do you agree with this testimony now?"

"Yes, sir." Cub glanced at the tribunal. They seemed to study him skeptically.

"Then explain to the court in what way you were rational at the time."

Cub hesitated. What the hell was this guy up to? "I guess I wasn't rational at all."

Denniston leaned on the side of the box and said conspiratorially, "How well do you remember seeing things at the time of the shooting?

Cub thought for a moment. "Not too well. I was pretty stressed."

"And you might have missed details?"

"I might have."

"Well, let's go back to the moment when Mister Duke leveled the pistol at the cockpit. Did you see that?"

"Yes."

"Did you see him fire the gun?"

Cub nodded. "That too."

"Could you see the aircraft at the time?"

Cub thought, What goes on here? We've been over this ground before. "I could."

"The cockpit?"

"Yes."

"How about inside the cockpit?"

"I could see that too."

"At the moment the gun was fired, what was going on in there?"

"I remember there was smoke inside. It now seems bizarre, but it occurred to me then that we had to be quick or Ian might die from breathing smoke."

"Now, why is that so bizarre?"

"Well, with the raging fire and heat, it just seems that smoke would be the least of his problems."

"Yet it is a fact, is it not, that the greatest proportion of deaths resulting from fires are caused by smoke inhalation?"

"Objection!" rang out from the Prosecution. "This witness is no expert on the causes of death in fires."

"Sustained."

Denniston hesitated for only an instant. "Mister Bayer, during your RAF flying training, did you receive instruction in fire safety around aircraft?"

"Objection! Irrelevant."

"Overruled," the Group Captain said. Cub could see that the man was annoyed with the prosecutor.

Denniston smiled at Cub for the first time. "You may answer the question."

"Yes, sir. I did."

"And what are the RAF's instructions about the effects of smoke inhalation and what to do about it?"

"It's to be avoided at all costs. Even with aircraft fires where there's lots of volatile fuel, it's one of the major causes of death."

"So, the RAF believes and teaches that smoke inhalation is a deadly problem?"

"Yes, sir."

"Then, do you still think your on-the-spot concern about Craigwell dying from smoke was so bizarre?"

"No, sir. I guess not."

"So at the time the first shot was fired, there was smoke but no visible fire in the cockpit?"

"I don't remember any visible flame, but reflected from Ian's face, we could see light from a fire low down in the cockpit."

"But you did see smoke inside?"

"Yes, sir."

"Could you see through the smoke?"

"I don't remember."

"At that moment, could you see Craigwell?"

"Yes."

"What was he doing?"

"Well, he'd been writhing around in there."

"I mean at the precise moment when Duke leveled the gun and fired, what was Craigwell doing?"

"I don't remember."

"Was he moving?"

"I'm not sure. I . . . just don't recall."

"So you saw him, but you're not sure he was moving."

"No. I'm not."

"Mister Bayer, is it possible that he wasn't moving when the gun was fired?"

"Yes, sir. It's possible."

"If he weren't moving, is it possible that he was already dead?"

Cub was silent for a long time. Duke was looking at him with that hard, baleful look of his. "Yes," Cub said in a near whisper.

"Is there any reason to believe he wasn't already dead?"

"Well, sir, I . . . It never occurred to me that . . . . ."

"For example, from breathing smoke?"

"But he'd been alive moments before."

"Yet he had been moving then, and you're not sure he was moving when the shot was fired."

"That's right."

"You know that the airmen testified that in their opinion nobody could be alive in that cockpit as they found it?"

"Yes, sir."

Denniston fixed his eyes on Cub and leaned toward him. "Mister Bayer, can you be certain that Craigwell was alive when the first bullet hit?"

It was a long moment before he answered. "No. He could have been dead."

"And if he were already dead, then Mister Duke can't have murdered him, can he?"

The implications were staggering, and a strange heady sensation welled up in Cub's chest. He dropped his head into his hands and let tears flow and a flood of emotions rack his body. Every eye in the room was on him. He didn't care.

It was a full minute before he shook his head and choked out, "No, sir."

"Thank you. That will be all Mister Bayer."

*

Peter Duke was acquitted.

Cub felt utterly exhausted, and Christian gave him the next day off. He went to bed early. Stress from the trial had been worse than any flying, and though he wanted to sleep, he couldn't.

Thoughts somersaulted through his mind. Would Duke ever forgive him? Could he ever be Duke's friend? Was Duke willing to teach him any more? Where was Victoria? He had tried to reach her so often, to no avail. Had she abandoned him too? Did anybody care?

A few of Duke's friends were celebrating at The Gannet, but Cub had earlier decided not to go. Now, being unable to sleep, he changed his mind, got up, and put his uniform on.

*

Burt Stark and several others were there, but Duke wasn't. Tony Hamilton-Price had been killed that day.

"Anybody see it happen?" Cub asked.

A flying officer from Yellow Flight said, "I did. Tony was leading the squadron. Took us line-abreast into a flock of Messerschmitts. He was hit about the time we opened fire. Must have been a cannon round in the nose. Blew the airscrew clean off, spinner and all. The plane pitched up and disintegrated immediately under withering fire."

"No chute?" Cub said.

The man shook his head slowly.

Geezus! Tony had been no friend, but Cub didn't wish that on him.

"And Duke never showed up tonight?" Cub said.

Burt shook his head. "Sent a message saying he wasn't feeling well. We heard you got him off, though."

Cub nodded somberly. Poor Duke. If it wasn't one thing, it was another.

Nobody said much. They sat around with drawn faces languidly sipping their beer. Then someone said that the BBC reported one hundred and sixty enemy planes destroyed the day that Cub went down over London and that Fighter Command was winning.

"Rubbish," another said. "Jerry fights as hard as ever as far as I can see."

"Me too," said another.

"Fucking reporters are counting their chickens too soon."

Several nodded, and Cub agreed silently. He finished his beer, wondering why it tasted awful, and decided to leave. He bid them goodnight.

Outside, he climbed into the MG and sat. His eyes welled as he thought of Ian making out the will that left him the car. He felt out of place; Ian belonged there in the driver's seat.

Driving slowly back to the mess, he brooded. Everything seemed to drag him down, like an illness getting worse and changing the colors of his life to ever deeper shades of gray. He had never felt so tired.

He parked the car, entered the building, and shuffled across to the stairway. Even the steps looked daunting, and his thighs ached as he gripped the bannister and hauled himself up.

"Sir," the desk orderly called out sharply.

Cub was struggling to get to the top of the stairs, the same way he struggled against the odds to prove himself, and this grating voice was dragging him back down again.

He turned, glared at the man, and shouted, "What!"

The orderly visibly started, then frowned and hesitated. "Sir, you have a message."

Cub was about to tell him where to stuff the message, when the orderly continued, "She said it was important, sir."

She!

Dear God, he was losing control, exactly as he had at Ian's death. This poor man was only being helpful.

He stumbled back down the steps and crossed to the desk, where he mumbled an apology. The man handed him a slip of paper with a London phone number on it.

The operator took a minute to put him through, and a sleepy female voice answered.

His heart pounded, and he nearly shouted, "Victoria, is that you? I'm sorry to wake you."

"I'm so glad you did."

"Where have you been?"

"The new job sent me away for a while. But I'm back, and I have tomorrow off."

"So do I! Let's go someplace for the day."

"Sounds lovely."

They agreed to meet at her flat in the morning.

Cub hung up the phone and grinned at the orderly. "Thanks much. Sorry I snapped at you."

The man smiled. "Not to worry about it, sir."

Cub turned and bounded up the stairs.

Chapter 30

In bright sunlight the MG wheeled west along the A40 past High Wycombe and into the Chiltern Hills. While Cub drove, Victoria Kendall sat in the passenger's seat enjoying views of the rolling green countryside. She leaned back and reveled in the feel of her hair streaming in the breeze. Soon she'd have to cut it short.

"This was Ian's car?"

"Yeah." His voice was solemn. "He left it to me."

She placed her hand on his. "I only met him that once when you brought the children to the ARP Center. He seemed like a nice chap."

"He was." Cub nibbled pensively at his lower lip.

"The three of you caused quite a stir around there that night. You were everybody's heroes, and they all wanted a look at you."

"Guess we never noticed."

"And I still can't get over how gentle and devoted you were to those children. Most men would have dumped them and gone on their way."

"I couldn't just leave them, could I?" Then he glanced furtively at her and added, "Besides, if I'd left, we wouldn't be here now, would we?"

She looked at him coyly. "So there was method in your heroics?"

He winked at her.

She felt a warm stirring inside and smiled, then turned to look at the scenery.

He said, "How did you manage to get a day off?"

She didn't like answering the question. "They gave it to me because I . . . have to go away again.

"Where?" he snapped. "For how long? How soon?"

"The day after tomorrow. I'll be gone for several weeks. After that, I may come back for a few days, then I'm gone for a long time."

"How long?"

"Months."

"And you can't tell me where or why?"

She shook her head. "Let's just enjoy today and talk about something else?"

They turned off the A40 onto the road to Watlington. Shortly the car climbed the hill to Croton Abbey and parked near the front entrance. For a moment, they sat admiring the old house, then they gazed over the rolling grass slopes, past the dark groves of trees, toward the mosaic of farms that spread across the broad plain to the west.

"You're right," Victoria said. "It's beautiful here. So peaceful after London."

"Come on. Mother Louisa expects us for lunch."

Cub rapped the lion-faced knocker on the striking plate. In a moment, the heavy oak door opened, and a Sister let them in. She went to get Mother Louisa and left them standing in the entry hall.

Two children exploded into the room and raced to grab Cub's legs.

"Nigel! Fiona!" he said, hoisting one in each arm. "How have you been?"

"Okay," the boy said, "but you didn't come and see me for a long time."

"It's only been a few weeks. And I've been busy. Boy, are you getting heavy!" He turned to the girl. "How are you, Fiona?"

She looked at him, smiled, and put her thumb in her mouth.

"And where's Mister Ian," Nigel said.

"He's uh . . . I brought Miss Kendall instead. Remember her?"

The boy looked at her obliquely, then plunged his face over Cub's shoulder. Fiona shook her head.

"That's no way to say hello, Nigel. You can do better than that."

The boy eyed Victoria again, then looked at Cub dolefully and shook his head.

"Cat got your tongue?"

Nigel shook it again.

"Well, say something."

"Where's my mummy and daddy?"

Victoria was stunned. Had nobody told them after all this time?

Cub gaped. "What did you say?"

"Mummy and Daddy, where are they?"

Cub looked shaken. He set the two down, then knelt and took the boy's hands. "Has nobody talked to you about it?"

The boy's troubled eyes fixed Cub, and he shook his head. Victoria looked on, bewildered.

Cub said, "Have you talked about this to other boys or girls?"

"Yes."

"What do they say?"

"They don't know where their mummies and daddies are either."

"Have you no idea, Nigel?" Cub said urgently.

"Maybe somewhere very high, like the top of the tallest mountain in the world."

"You mean nobody here knows what's happened to their parents?"

The boy looked at him quizzically for a long moment. "They're dead."

Cub gasped, "And what happened to your mummy and daddy?"

"They're dead, too."

"And what does that mean?"

"It means I won't see them until I die."

"But I thought you asked me --.

"I know what's happened, but I don't know where they are."

Victoria felt a rush of relief, and Cub broke into a chuckle.

Suspicion crossed Nigel's face. "Why am I funny?"

"You're not. I'm the one who's funny. I didn't understand your question." Cub hugged the children tightly. "Your mommy and daddy are surely in heaven."

"I know, but where is it?"

"I don't know either. But like you, I guess it's somewhere up high. Higher than the top of any mountain."

"Above the stars and the sky?"

"Yeah."

"Oh," the boy said, looking at Cub blankly. "Well, when do we play baseball?"

Mother Louisa rounded the corner. "How nice to see you, Cub." She took his hands in hers. "Congratulations. The news reports say you're beating the Germans. We're all so proud of all of you."

"Thanks, but Jerry hasn't given up yet. Those reporters are getting ahead of themselves."

"Well, never mind. We're proud of you anyway. And the children are so excited you're here."

Cub introduced her to Victoria. Then Mother Louisa said, "Well now, come to lunch." And she turned and led the way.

When game time came, the children demanded baseball. The same teasing, shouting, jostling group of youngsters were anxious to play; they crowded around Cub on the pitch. Others, like Nigel, held back and watched somberly.

Cub signalled for them to join in, but nobody moved. He beckoned to Nigel. "Come over here, young man. I want you to try this."

The crowd around Cub became silent, and they all turned to look at the boy.

Nigel hesitated.

Cub called out, "Come on, Nigel." But the boy didn't move.

Peter, who stood in the crowd next to Cub, said, "Yes, Nigel, come on. You can play with us."

Reluctantly, Nigel came slowly forward, and the crowd parted as he pushed his way through, until he stood next to Peter in front of Cub. He looked nervously at the faces around him as if surprised that they accepted him.

"That a boy," said Cub. "Now let's practice a little before we play."

Cub handed out cricket balls and started one group practicing throwing and catching. Then he took aside the ones who had not had a chance to hit before. He demonstrated how to hold the bat and hit the ball, then had them line up for practice.

Nigel was the first one up. Cub began pitching to him and coaching him on how to swing, but the boy had trouble connecting with the ball. The others grew restless, yelling that it was someone else's turn. But Cub persisted and pitched several more, unsuccessfully. Finally, the others rebelled.

"All right. All right," Cub said. "We'll give him one more chance, then someone else can have a go. Now, Nigel, concentrate real hard."

Nigel assumed a determined look, gritting his teeth and pressing his lips together tightly. Cub pitched carefully. Swinging with great effort, Nigel connected cleanly and sent the ball flying high into the outfield.

Peter shouted, "That's a groundrule homer, isn't it, Mister Cub?"

Cub smiled and nodded.

"See, Nigel," Peter said, "you scored, just like I did last time."

Nigel's eyes widened and a smile came to his face. Then he beamed. It was the first time Cub had seen him happy.

Victoria found the game hard to understand, but was intrigued by the way Cub handled the kids. He remembered some of their names and quickly learned most of the rest. He always offered gentle encouragement. When a youngster had trouble catching or hitting or remembering what to do, he took the time to show them; his patience seemed endless. The children tried so hard, and by the look in their eyes, they adored him.

She turned to Mother Louisa, sitting on the bench beside her. "I've never seen this diabolical Yankee game, but the kids seem to enjoy it."

"They do. And Cub is so good with them."

"Yes. And he seems completely absorbed."

"Who would have guessed a veteran pilot would get so much joy out of little ones?"

Veteran? It was hard to see him as one, Victoria thought, especially here, today. He was so gentle, and somehow she hadn't expected that of an American. Happiness and enthusiasm were written all over his face, and he looked so handsome, so full of life.

Game time passed quickly, and Mother Louisa's voice rang out, "All right, children, that's enough for one day. Everyone in for quiet time."

While the children rested, Cub and Victoria took a walk across the grass hillside above the abbey, where the sun warmed them and the smell of moist turf filled the air.

"You certainly have a way with children. It seems so unusual for a fighter-boy."

"Well," he said with a shrug, "I don't know if I ever told you that I have an older brother. Name's Brad. At one point, Brad wanted to be a coach. He even studied physical education in college. But he's no teacher. Never taught anybody anything in his life, that I know of. I was better at that sort of thing, and I figured I could do it better than he could. So I decided to try coaching while I was still in high school.

"When I wasn't at the airport, I started going down to the YMCA and showing kids how to play. I was good at it, and the sports director there said I should consider being a coach when I grew up.

"I especially like young people. If you get them motivated, they're so full of enthusiasm and they want to learn so bad. I understand them, what they like and what they don't, when to push and when to leave them alone. Little ones, like those here, are so straightforward. They only need encouragement."

"Have you thought about being a teacher?"

He nodded. "And may think about it again when the war's over."

"Won't you want to continue flying?"

"Don't know. Flying can be thrilling, but when you teach somebody something, it's rewarding in a completely different way. Working with kids and watching them develop is very satisfying."

She nodded understandingly, and they walked on in silence. What an unusual man, she thought, young looking, yet mature underneath, and without any ugly veneer of ego. Like Daddy.

When she looked at him, he seemed preoccupied. "Penny for your thoughts," she said.

"I'm thinking about you. And where you're going."

"We weren't going to talk about that."

"You're in some kind of intelligence work, aren't you?"

She was stunned. "You said that. I didn't."

"And you're going someplace scary, aren't you? And doing something dangerous?"

She stopped and gaped at him. Could he see right through her? "What makes you say that?"

"I don't know. Intuition, maybe. Plus your going away in secret for long periods. It's all very spooky. I'm right, aren't I?"

"Cub, please. Don't."

"Answer me, Victoria. So I can quit guessing."

For a long moment, she stood glaring at him, frustrated, not knowing what to say. She wanted to answer him, but that was not allowed. And yet . . . . .

"Victoria, how did you manage to get so caught up in this war?"

"Oh Lord, Cub." She turned and started walking again, silent and pensive, looking at the ground. He followed.

Suddenly, she wanted to tell him the whole story. Wanted him to know everything about her. Nothing hidden. No secrets. But . . . that was absolutely forbidden. She gave a deep sigh, and tried to shake off her frustration. "I guess I owe you that much."

He nodded.

"I already told you part of the story," she said, "but there's more. My mother was from France, down in the southwest, near Bayonne. When Giles and I were growing up, we spent many vacations there. It was a sort of getaway place for us, and we loved it.

"In nineteen thirty-eight, when he finished school here, Giles went back there for a visit. He met a French girl who had recently come back from Spain, where she'd fought for the Loyalists. She was a wonderful, strong person named Josephine. We call her Jo. They fell in love. He decided to stay and settle in Saint-Jean-de-Luz, and they were married. Then when Germany invaded Poland, he took a commission in the French Army.

"Meanwhile, early this year, Daddy was posted to the BEF in France, near Lille. In March, two months before the Germans invaded, Daddy was killed. He was a passenger in a plane, on some sort of reconnaissance flight close to the German border. They were shot down by antiaircraft fire.

"I was utterly devastated. Couldn't concentrate on anything. Suddenly, Giles became the most important person in my life, I had to see him. I left school and went to Saint-Jean-de-Luz."

Cub looked incredulous. "You went to France when the war was on?"

"Had to, don't you see. Had to have someone to share my grief. It was the sitzkrieg, the phony war, and absolutely nothing was happening. Besides, if the Germans invaded, I was sure the Allies would hold them along the Belgian border, like they had in the last war.

"Giles was in an infantry unit stationed far up north on the Meuse near Sedan, so as it turned out, Jo got the brunt of my emotions. She was sweet, and we became very close. Giles visited when he could get away, but it wasn't often.

"On the Wednesday before the German offensive began, he got the week off and came down to see us. Then on Friday morning, the Germans attacked Holland, and he was recalled. We put him on the northbound train about the time the panzers started south through Belgium. Apparently he got back on Sunday, just when Guderian's tanks arrived on the opposite bank of the Meuse and German troops started their river crossing."

She felt her eyes welling and hesitated, trying to squelch it. "My brother's unit fought to the last man."

Her tears flowed, and there was a long silence.

Finally Cub said softly, "I'm sorry." And he handed her his handkerchief. "So in two month's time, you lost the two most important men in your life?"

She nodded. "Most important people," she corrected. "The German's killed them both."

"And you want vengeance?"

She nodded.

Cub said, "I guess I understand that."

There was another long silence while she got control of herself.

He said somberly, "My guess is, you're going back to France again."

Suddenly she was livid. "Why can't you stop guessing?" she shouted.

"Because I care."

Obviously, he meant it. She felt foolish. "I'm sorry. I didn't mean to snap. I'm supposed to say I'm going to Scotland if I must say something. And it's very dangerous for you to guess, dangerous to me. Please don't."

Cub frowned sympathetically and nodded. "Yes, of course it is. I'm sorry." He gazed at her and swallowed hard. "I missed you the last couple of weeks."

He took her by the shoulders, and his dark eyes riveted her.

A warmth rose in her and her breath quickened. "I missed you too."

He drew her toward him. She slipped her arms around his neck and eased into the circle of his arms until she felt the touch of her bosom on his chest and the press of his body on hers. The wind blew her hair and wafted it across his face. His clean, warm smell intoxicated her. Then the soft working of his mouth carried her away.

When the embrace ended, she turned and looked to the west into the breeze that made the wildflowers dance and riffled the grass.

She said, "On a lovely day like this, I could walk all the way to Land's End."

"I don't care what the weather is, I'd gladly go with you."

Chapter 31

Victoria had been gone for a week. Cub lay in bed, gripped by a desperate longing like a sickness, a constriction in his chest that shortened his breath, a diffuse yet persistent discomfort like grippe that lingered, never loosening its hold, a desperation tugging at him, forcing him to focus every idle moment on one topic: the vast distance between him and her.

In the dark, he got up and went to the window to gaze out at the stars. He had never felt like this about anyone before. Could she possibly feel the same? Why must she go away? Damn the war.

Through the night he tossed, as if drugged, vacillating between semi-consciousness and dream-plagued sleep. Reveille was a relief; he could focus on dressing, tea, briefing, the ride to dispersal. Then the waiting started again.

Pilots loitered on the grass in the sunshine around the dispersal hut. The wait was long, and as the sun climbed into the sky, men perspired in their heavy clothing. Cub tried to ignore the familiar, vague nausea that always plagued him when he waited to go.

Peter Duke sat on the grass under the wing of his plane, gazing across the field. Even from a distance, he looked depressed, and he'd been that way for so long. But the bastard was surely stubborn. He wanted no help from anyone. Cub considered talking to him, but that always met with the same result. Duke got angry, and the two would argue to a standstill.

Yet, Duke had saved his life. And he'd learned one hell of a lot from Duke and survived on what he'd learned. No matter how he looked at it, he owed Duke a big debt. And if Duke kept going like this, something inside him would break. He might kill himself. And others too. Cub couldn't sit by and let the man fall apart; whatever the cost, he had to try to help.

He rubbed his chin and searched for an alternative; when none turned up, he began to walk toward Duke's plane. As he approached, Duke dropped his head to stare at the ground.

"Morning, Duke."

The man looked up. His lids drooped, and his bloodshot eyes, dancing nervously, peered from dark recesses.

"What's fucking good about it?"

Damn! Cub thought. The man always put you on the defensive. "We're alive."

"You call this living?"

"It's better than the alternative. And we had a good day yesterday. Jerry never even made it to London. Also, I heard the Biggin Hill boys jumped a flock of Heinkels who'd lost their escorts and turned them all back before they even reached the coast. Something tells me Jerry's hurting."

"Rubbish! We've hurt him before, and he hasn't quit. He'll be back."

God, but Duke looked awful. "How do you feel?"

"How the hell am I supposed to feel? So many of us dying, then I shoot one to add to their score."

"Look, you did the very best thing possible."

"And for my good deed, I get a court-martial."

"But, Duke, they acquitted you."

"No thanks to you."

Did it make any sense to be nice to this man? "I only want to help."

"You nosey bastard, you're always trying to help. Well, lad, you glue your arse to my wing and follow orders and stay the hell out of my business. That'll help."

Cub's anger was getting the better of him. "For better or worse, you and I have to fly and fight together. We can't harbor big secrets, and it does me no good for you to be in pain. Unquote!"

"Piss off, lad."

"For Christ's sake, Duke, stop feeling sorry for yourself. You're carrying too big a load. Have you seen the Doc lately?"

Duke waved his arm toward the dispersal hut. "Fug off, will you."

To hell with him, Cub thought. "Is it Cecily this time too?"

"You little sonofabitch, what does she have to do with anything?" Duke struggled to his feet. His face was flushed, and he clenched his fists. "Now get out of here before I --.

Cub's sympathy evaporated in a rush of anger, and he interrupted, "You know, I used to admire you."

"What for?"

"You were my ideal. A real fighter pilot. A real man."

"Now you know the truth, eh?"

"I wanted to be like you. Talk like you. Move like you. Have girls falling all over me like they did you."

"What a load of balls."

"It didn't used to be."

"Naive little lad, getting your first glimpse of the real world, eh?"

"My world will never be yours. You're bitter. And sorry for yourself. And you take it out on anyone around. Cecily. Doreen. Me. All the people who tried in their own way to help. You don't want help. You want martyrdom."

"Listen," Duke said, "I was your coach, and I thought of you as a protege. Now you're like all the rest. Fuck old Peter Duke. He's an old fart who can't hit the broad side of a barn in the air and can't get it up in bed. Well, I can still take care of myself. And I don't need you."

Cub spoke calmly. "Peter, you need help. And you're too proud to ask for it. Too proud to show anyone what's eating you. You've got it buried where maybe even God can't find it. Well, I think Cecily's your problem. She dumped you for the guy in Hollywood, didn't she? Now she knows she made a mistake, I'd guess, and you're afraid you can't satisfy her."

For an instant, Duke's eyes rounded in amazement, then without missing a beat, he said, "Who the hell do you think you are, a fucking trickcyclist? Stick your bloody theory up your arse! Anyway, you won't have to put up with me for long. From one of these missions soon, I won't return."

"Peter, turn yourself into the Doc."

"Fugoff, boy!"

Cub turned away. Nothing was worth this hassle.

Just then, the dispersal telephone clicked softly, and everyone stopped breathing. The phone orderly held a brief conversation, then hung up. "Tea wagon'll be fifteen minutes late this morning."

Pilots slumped again into chairs or dropped onto the ground.

As Cub walked away, Duke spoke as if nothing had happened between them. "What time is it?"

"Ten o'clock," Cub said brusquely.

"Jerry's late. Not like the bastards. Wonder what's up."

In the late the afternoon, the Germans still hadn't come, and Arrow Squadron still wondered.

* * *

Squadron Leader Parsons looked over his half-glasses at Cub. "Sorry to hear about the girl leaving. I'm sure she'll be back."

Cub nodded absently. "The real reason I came to see you is that I want to transfer out of Peter Duke's flight. Don't want to fly with him anymore." He recounted his arguments with Duke, then concluded, "Other pilots who came in with me have made section leader already. Why not me? And why not somewhere else?"

"Hmm," Parsons said, nodding. "I wanted to talk to you about that. Skipper's noticed Duke's having difficulty too, and he's worried about him. Is he flying okay?"

"So far. But he could fall apart in a heartbeat. He's tired and depressed. And he's sure as hell got it in for me."

"Any idea what the problem is?"

"Who knows? Might be a girl. Maybe Ian and the trial. He's had a lot of combat time too."

"Yes, he has. Soon we'll be able to rotate people with many combat hours to easier billets. But right now we need him."

"Well, I want out."

Parsons hesitated, seeming to struggle with how to say what was on his mind. "Look, the Skipper wants to make you a section leader, but Duke won't give you up as his wingman."

Cub was dumbstruck. Why the hell not? he thought.

Parsons continued, "I accept what you tell me, but the Skipper and I need your help. You'll get your section, all right. But just now we're trying to keep Duke together and alive, and we want you to stay on his wing."

"Oh geezus. Can't you get someone else?"

"Skipper especially wants you there. Has faith in you. Will you do it?"

Cub had put up with Duke's hassle for so long without complaining; now he got no help. He seethed. But the expression on Parsons's face made it clear that this was not just a request. "Yes, sir."

"Good. And thanks."

Cub eyed him coldly.

Parsons ignored it and shuffled through the papers on his desk them until he selected one and waved it in the air.

"Did you know that before Ian Craigwell died, he wrote a citation for you?"

Cub was stunned. "What in God's name for?"

"Seems you rescued two children from a burning building in London one night. Is that right?"

Cub sat dumfounded, awed, as if Ian's ghost had entered the room. He stammered, "It wasn't burning until we got away."

Parsons gazed down his nose at the paper and nodded. "Craigwell and Stark signed it, and Lieutenant Duke approved it and sent it on to the Skipper." He handed the paper to Cub. "Read it and tell me if it's accurate?"

Cub handed it back when he finished. Poor old Ian. He'd gone to all the trouble to write this up. When had he found the time? And why, for God's sake, had Duke approved it? "Yeah, that's pretty much how it happened."

"Hair-raising stuff, son. Well done. I'm going to recommend the skipper approve it."

"Thank you, sir," Cub said blankly, and he didn't smile.

They stood up, and Parsons offered his hand. "Thanks for coming by." He waved at the citation. "We're proud of you. Now keep Peter Duke out of trouble."

Chapter 32

It had been six days since the last German daylight raid. Duke and Cub had settled into a truce; they didn't speak to each other.

In the early afternoon, Operations picked up a small target off the coast, and Arrow Squadron scrambled two fighters, Duke and Cub, to investigate. It was windy and overcast on the ground, and the cloud layer was thick. A long series of vectors from Shakespeare carried them well out over the North Sea barely above cloud tops at twenty thousand feet. They made contact with two Dorniers, who turned east and ran; Duke and Cub went after them. In a brief skirmish, a few shots were traded, but the fight ended quickly when the Germans plunged into the clouds. The Spitfires turned for home.

They had cruised for several minutes when Duke called, "Think I took a hit back there, lad. Look me over."

Cub slipped his plane underneath and focused on the white underside of Duke's machine, now almost close enough to touch. Without thinking about control motion or throttle adjustment, he maneuvered his plane where he wanted, fore and aft and side to side, while he scanned every square inch of the other ship's belly.

There was no apparent damage. On a hunch, he pulled astern into the propeller wash, and suddenly his windshield streaked with liquid. He eased forward and searched again.

Finally, he pressed the radio button. "Duke, it's a leak in your cooling system. Can't find it. But I got glycol all over my windscreen to prove it."

"Shit. Guessed as much. I'm heating up. Going to high boost before the stuff's gone."

Cub kept position as the other plane accelerated.

Duke called, "Shakespeare, this is Arrow Blue One. Do you hear me?"

No answer. He tried again. Nothing. "See if you can you raise him, lad."

Cub called. No luck. "We must be out of range."

"Temperature's gone off the scale," Duke said. "I'm going to fine up the airscrew pitch while I can."

"Turn on your running lights so I can stay with you in the cloud."

The green wingtip light winked on as Duke's plane dropped astern. Cub throttled back to idle and S-turned to move back into escort position.

"Lad, if you stick with me, you'll run out of fuel. Beetle for the barn now."

"And leave you?"

"Yes."

"Why?"

"So we don't lose two of us."

"But I can't just abandon you."

"Go!"

After all Duke had put him through, why the hell shouldn't he leave? Let the bastard fend for himself. But he couldn't do that; he still owed the man a debt. Besides he'd promised Parsons. He held his position and was silent.

"Are you disobeying me?" Duke said.

"I have to make sure they find you."

"You fart around here and you'll buy it too."

"I'll take the chance."

"It's not your aircraft."

"But it's my ass."

"That's not worth much, lad, but the kite is."

"You're garbled."

"I'm telling you, take that ship home."

"I can't hear you."

"It's an order."

"Then court-martial me."

They plunged into the cloud in tight formation.

"Shakespeare, this is Arrow Blue Two," Cub called. "Do you hear me?"

The reply was buried in static.

Cub concentrated on holding formation.

Passing through five thousand feet, he finally made contact with Shakespeare and explained the situation. He concluded, "Can you give us a radar fix?"

"We have many aircraft in the area. Can't tell which is you. Can you fly a pattern for us?"

"No. Got a dead Spitfire here. We're better off to continue toward the coast."

"Right. When he's in the water, circle him to the left and climb until we identify you."

Cub acknowledged.

"Damn it, lad, you'll end up in the drink too. Break it off and go home."

"Save your battery."

"Have you gone daft? We can't afford to lose two airplanes here."

"Your radio's intermittent."

"This is no joke, laddie."

"Stow it, will you. You're cluttering the radio channel." And Cub called Shakespeare to ask for the sea conditions.

"Wet and windy. Gusts north to twenty-five knots and rain squalls. Ceiling variable, five hundred to a thousand feet."

Great! A man in the water is hard enough to find when it's dead calm. In weather like this, they could run over him in a rowboat and never see him.

They broke out of the clouds seven hundred feet over the roiling sea. Duke said, "I'm turning now." He wheeled into the wind and opened his canopy.

"Get out of that thing before it sinks. And good luck."

"Same to you, you disobedient sonofabitch."

Duke's plane caromed off the top of one big wave and plunged headlong into the next. The nose submerged to the cockpit, and the tail rose slowly into the air, looking like an absurd buoy.

As Cub passed over the sinking wreck, he banked steeply and craned to watch. Still no Duke. Where the hell was he? Come out of there, don't be bashful, go for that swim, you bastard.

The cockpit slipped beneath the surface. Now, Duke, now! For Christ's sake, get out . . . if you're ever going to.

All for one lousy pinhole in the cooling system. Dear God, don't let him go like that. The tail slid beneath the surface, and Cub gazed at the spot, willing the sea to give him back. It was empty.

In every direction, as far as Cub could look, there was only angry sea, like a vat of molten lead churned to a frenzy. Duke had been swallowed up.

At first he didn't spot the small dark shape on the surface. When he did, it seemed only a shadow on the water. Slowly it dawned on him that it was a helmet with a head in it. A wave swept over the head, and it disappeared. It seemed minutes before it surfaced, then another wave swamped it. An age passed before he saw it again, this time against the bright orange of an inflated Mae West. He flew low over the man and waggled his wings; Duke waved weakly as waves washed over him.

God, it looked cold. But the rascal was still alive!

Cub breathed more easily. He swung out and circled the floating figure and called Shakespeare.

They couldn't locate him on their radar; he'd have to climb higher. As he reentered the cloud, the outside visibility went to zero, and he focused on the instrument panel. Throttle and control movements steadied both the turn and climb rate indicators, and he bored upward through the cloud, holding a constant spiral.

A couple of months before, Duke had made him master instrument flying. "It's been like California around here this whole summer," Duke said, "but it won't last. I know you studied blind flying in school, lad, but if it isn't second nature, you and that machine will dig a big hole someday." So on the days they stood down because of weather, Duke made him put hours in a Link trainer. And he flew several times in the Spitfire under a cloth hood with Duke in trail. Now, thanks to the guy freezing down there, flying the gauges came as easy as riding a bicycle.

"Arrow Blue Two, Shakespeare here. Believe we have you spotted. Confirm that you are at the northernmost reach of your circle, headed west . . . now."

"Affirmative, Shakespeare."

A long silence, then: "Arrow Blue Two, we have a crash boat four miles south of you. We've given him your position. He'll reach you in ten minutes."

Twenty-five knots, Cub calculated, into a twenty-five-knot wind. That was no pleasure ride. He started his downward spiral.

"Can I talk to the boat directly?" Cub said.

"He's on Channel D. Call sign Gipper."

"Also, Shakespeare, I'm short of fuel. Give me a vector to the nearest field."

"Manston bears two four five. Seventeen miles."

"Thank you, Shakespeare. Switching to Channel D." Cub flicked the radio selector. "Gipper, hello Gipper, this is Arrow Blue Two. Do you hear me?"

The reply was unintelligible through the radio noise, but they had heard him.

"Roger, Gipper. I am a Spitfire circling the downed man. Keep an eye out for me."

Cub gave a start as he looked at the fuel gauge. It was a needle's width from the bottom. Eight gallons at the outside. Can't leave him now, though. Come on, Gipper.

As he dropped out of the cloud, he spotted Duke. But where was the boat? Cub swooped over the downed man and headed directly south for half a minute, looking for it. No luck. He reversed course and strained to pick out the man in the water. But Duke was gone.

Where? He had just been there! Where was he now?

Cub's eyes probed the spuming waves. He clenched his teeth and slammed his gloved fist against the access door. How bloody stupid he was to leave Duke! Gipper would get there when he damn well arrived, but if Cub lost sight of the man, they'd never find him.

He was sure he'd overflown the spot where Duke had been, so he began to circle, and his eyes searched wildly across the undulating, misty surface. Slowly a terror rose in him: He had lost Duke. Condemned him to a miserable death. How would this repay his debt? And he'd let Parsons down. Could he ever face himself?

Suddenly, where a moment before, nothing had been, he spotted Duke's head bobbing in the waves. Cub heaved a sigh and ran his clammy glove over his face, then he flew low over the man and waggled his wings. He couldn't distinguish Duke's gesture from the motion of a limp body in the seaway.

"Gipper, this is Arrow Blue Two. Where the hell are you?"

The reply was clear: "We should be within a half mile. But visibility's bloody awful. We don't see you yet."

Cub looked at the fuel gauge and wrote off the idea of making land. He'd see Duke picked up, then put down beside Gipper. His eyes were riveted on the figure in the water; he wouldn't lose him again, no matter what.

After several more orbits, he called Gipper. They still didn't see him. Where was that goddammed boat? He had to steal another look.

At the southern end of his circuit, he leveled the wings and peered southward. There, nearly invisible in the swirling mist, the Vosper crash boat plowed through the seas, caroming off one wave after another. Each plunge of the bow lofted spray high over the bridge, to be carried off horizontally by the wind. It had to be mind-numbing, back-wrenching punishment for the crew, but to Cub, seeing her was like watching the cavalry charge onto the scene in a cheap western. He smiled.

"Gipper, I have you in sight. Come left thirty degrees. He's less than a half mile in front of you."

A minute later, Gipper called, "We see him. Thanks, Blue Two."

Cub would make certain they got Duke. He flew another circuit.

Gipper slowed as he pulled alongside the man in the water.

"Blue Two, your friend is wet and cold, but he's conscious. Good luck."

Cub eyed the hopeless fuel level. But what the hell, the engine still ran. He turned for land. "Gipper, I'm going for Manston on course two four five. If I run out of petrol, come and pick me up."

The airspeed indicator read one hundred and twenty. Cub glanced at the clock and estimated he would cross the beach east of Margate in just over six minutes. To keep the water in sight, he flew below the varying cloud ceiling, at three hundred feet.

Through the mist, he strained to pick out the coastline, but ahead, the sea faded abruptly into the mist. Directly below, the surface twisted and writhed, and occasionally a great swell reached up as if to drag him down. On he went, certain the motor would die in the next instant; and though the second hand pulsed along, the clock seemed to have stopped. He tried to ignore the fuel gauge, but sheer fascination repeatedly drew his eye to it. It read empty.

Six and a half minutes came and went. Where the hell was the beach?

"Shakespeare, do you hear me?" he called.

There was no answer.

Nearly eight minutes into the ordeal, a change in the sea color alerted him. The lead-gray grew milky, and suddenly there was a line of breakers, then sand. A tower stood off to the right, dead ahead was an ancient castle, and beyond it lay a golf course - all familiar landmarks of the North Foreland. Manston was only a few miles further.

He switched to the local radio channel and called the station, but got no answer. On he went, crossing farmland and an occasional road, peering ahead to pick out the landing area, and praying the engine would keep running.

Another minute and a half passed, when suddenly he spotted the wide grass lane of runway. He was tempted to lower the wheels and steepen his descent, but thought better of it in case the engine died and he had to glide in.

The plane droned on until the field boundary slipped well beneath the nose, then Cub lowered the flaps and landing gear and pointed the aircraft downward steeply. As he brought the throttle back to idle, the engine stopped altogether. He controlled the speed by sideslipping with rudder and aileron, then landed the plane smoothly.

Clambering out of the cockpit, he left the plane in the middle of the landing area, and hiked through the wind and rain up the grass hill toward the hangars, whistling to himself.

Chapter 33

Later that afternoon, on the parking ramp in front of the hangar at Hornchurch, Cub cut the switches on the Spitfire, and the engine clanked to a stop. The rigger who unstrapped him said a special meeting of flying personnel was going on in the squadron briefing room.

Cub slid into a seat at the back. On the platform, Squadron Leader Parsons was in the middle of a presentation; he referred to a display of large aerial photographs. "So you can see," he said, pointing to several pictures in succession, "at these harbors east of Dunkirk, the boats and barges are gone." He took down those photographs to reveal new ones. "And these airfields on the Pas de Calais were full of aircraft a week ago. Now they've left."

He looked at the audience, and a grin spread on his face. "So, lads, that's why we haven't seen Jerry in daylight for a week. He's moved out. Taken his planes and equipment and gone home. As far as the invasion is concerned, he's packed it in."

A cheer went up from the crowd.

Cub shook his head slowly. It was hard to believe the battle was over. Right up to the last, the Germans never showed a sign of weakness. But Mueller, the prisoner, must have been right, and they were hurting all along.

Gunnar Christian stepped to the platform. "Well gents, there you have it. We won." The crowd cheered, and Gunnar let it run a moment before he called for quiet. "This war is far from over, but from now on it'll be different. Jerry may continue to hit us at night, but in daylight, we'll be taking the battle across the channel to him. The fight won't be any easier, but it'll be there instead of here. And soon we'll get our first crack at it."

The audience shouted their approval.

When it was quiet again, Christian continued, somberly at first. "The Nazi came at us with over four thousand aircraft. Came hardened and schooled by years of air fighting. Came flushed with victory on the continent and confident of winning here. And he threw everything in his arsenal at us.

"Fighter Command started the battle with about six hundred fighters. We in Eleven Group, who bore the brunt of it, began with only half that number. And in our darkest moment, we were down to ninety serviceable aircraft.

"And we paid a price. Jerry dropped over forty thousand tons of bombs on this island and killed over twenty thousand of our people. Nearly five hundred of our airmen comrades died flying, while an equal number were injured.

"Yet we shredded his formations and destroyed his planes until he could stand it no longer. He lost half his aircraft and most of their crews. Yes, the largest air force in the world has gone down to defeat at the hands of a few hundred brave men like you in this room. We beat him. And you should be proud of what you've done.

"Now the Battle of Britain is over, and our island is no longer at stake. We can never forget those who paid the supreme price. But we can celebrate our victory. Indeed, we should, for ourselves and our fallen comrades. So, there'll be Champagne in the mess tonight!"

The audience suddenly transformed into a cheering throng of youngsters. Gaunt, tired looks were gone. The haggard men who slumped there moments before were now lively on their feet, shouting, shaking hands, and clapping each other on the back, as if they'd won a football match. And Cub lost himself in the cheering, too.

An hour later, a happy, raucous crowd filled the mess lounge with song and laughter as they put away a cache of Moet et Chandon. Cub stood with Burt Stark, who along with other Sergeant-pilots had been invited to this special celebration in the officers' mess.

They were wondering about Duke, when suddenly Cub spotted him standing, disheveled but smiling, at the door. They got him a drink, and he told of his rescue.

After a second Champagne, he took Cub aside. "I'd like to talk to you," he said conspiratorially. "How about coming up to my place? Bring your drink."

Cub followed him upstairs. Thinking of the painful critiques he'd withstood in Duke's room made him edgy, but Duke seemed calm and relaxed, as if something else entirely were on his mind. They entered.

"Sit down," Duke said, indicating a chair.

Duke tossed his flight gear on top of the wardrobe, then sat on the bed, took a drink of Champagne, and gazed at Cub for a long moment. "I want to thank you for staying with me out there. More than that, I owe you an apology."

Cub was stunned.

"You see," Duke said, "I haven't felt well for some weeks now, and along the way you got me upset. You're a bit pushy on personal matters. Maybe it's an American trait. Anyway, it irritated me. Then when Ian died, you blamed me. And the trial was the last straw. I stopped being rational. Figured you had it in for me.

Cub shook his head.

"Well," Duke continued, "I understand that now. I also see that you were really trying to help all along. And you were right about Cecily. She troubled me a lot."

Was this the same Duke?

The man's shoulders drooped and he stared at the floor, lost in thought. Slowly he began to rock back and forth. "She went off with this American bloke. And because you were a Yank too, I couldn't help taking out on you some of my frustration over him.

"Anyway, Cecily left because she didn't like the way I treated her. She wanted friendship, true love, a deep and undivided relationship. Well, I wasn't ready for that. My priority was to avoid getting entangled. But Cecily got herself under my skin, and I didn't realize it at first. Just went on playing my cool, distant act until she couldn't stand it any longer.

"After she was gone, I'd think about her leaving me and get mad as hell. Then I'd miss her. And I couldn't get interested in other girls. Not interested? Hell, let's be honest. Without even being here, she made me impotent. And I resented her. At least I did until I took that swim today."

Cub watched Duke's eyes as he talked. For the first time in a long while, they were calm. The nervous agitation was gone.

Duke continued, "God, that water was cold! At first I shivered and tried to swim and keep warm. But the bloody waves kept washing over me, and my shivering got violent. For a while, I couldn't figure out what this funny clacking noise was. It turned out to be my teeth banging together.

"I knew I should struggle and swim to keep my circulation going. I saw you overhead several times, and at first, I was grateful. But soon I began not to care, about you or the struggle or anything else. And I didn't feel cold anymore. Just wanted to sleep. I knew I was dying, and

I didn't care. When they pulled me out, I was nearly gone. Another ten minutes and they needn't have bothered.

"On the way back, they put me in the engine room where it was warm and covered me with hot blankets. When I was alert enough to take it, they gave me soup. Then I began to think. And the thoughts came like a revelation.

"I remembered knowing I was going to die and not caring. That scared the hell out of me. Through the fear, came the idea that each of us gets only one chance on this earth, and I very nearly had mine. And what had I to show for it? Did anyone care?

Duke waved at the pictures on the wall. "I thought about all these pretty girls I'd cultivated. Would they care? Hell, they're all other people's wives and gone who-knows-where. They couldn't care less. And I thought of my prewar mates in the squadron. Did they care? Most are dead. The few who are left would give me a funeral with honors, but then they'd put me out of their minds, just like I try to avoid pining over my dead comrades.

"I asked myself, who would care enough to remember?

"It was a long time coming, but it finally dawned on me that Cecily would care. At least she would if I paid a little attention to her. And I knew from her letters the invitation was open.

"Then I asked the crew how they found me. From what they said, I figured you spent an unreasonable period cruising around over me on dry tanks, risking my fate. But they never would have located me without you. And I thought, yes, you would care too."

Cub was dumfounded.

"Piece by piece," Duke continued, "I put together the idea that only a handful of people would care. And I was still alive, getting a second chance. I swore this time, I wouldn't blow it with those few.

"So I want to thank you for risking your arse out there for me. And I apologize for the way I've behaved. I always felt secure with you flying my wing, and I'd like to have you stay there. But the skipper wants to promote you, and . . . I guess I'd better let him."

"I'm going to try to get Cecily back too, and maybe I'll marry her this time."

Was Duke serious? "Are you sure you're all right?"

"I feel great."

"Have you seen the Doc?"

"As a matter of fact, I spent over an hour with him before I came here. He was worried about hypothermia. But I wanted to talk about my gut ache and the fact that it was gone. Told him this whole story, too. He says it's often like this when a person comes back from near death. Pieces of their life fall into place, and all kinds of problems solve themselves."

"I'm stunned."

"No more than I." Duke stood up and smiled and offered his hand. "Thanks for everything."

Slowly Cub got to his feet. Duke seemed more relaxed and calm than he'd ever seen him. Cub smiled, tenuously at first. Then he shook off his last doubts about Duke. Grinning broadly, he grasped Duke's hand. "You're welcome, friend."

The two returned to the party.

They had refilled their glasses and stood talking when Gunnar Christian clapped Duke on the shoulder. "Welcome back, old man. You look none the worse for wear. How are you?"

Duke grinned. "Better than I've been in months." He looked it too.

*

The mess bar closed shortly after dinner, and Cub went with a small group to The Gannet. They had been there for nearly an hour when suddenly he spotted Doreen Phillips. She sat alone at a table. He expected her to scowl and turn away; instead, she smiled and waved him over. There seemed no polite way out. He excused himself from the group and crossed to her table.

"Hello stranger," she said.

"Good evening."

"Sit down for a minute, won't you?"

"Can't stay long."

"I need to talk to you."

He studied her warily, then sat down. Her dress had a high neck, revealing less than her sweaters. She wore no eye shadow, and her nails were unpainted.

He said, "After our last meeting, I didn't think we had much to talk about."

She smiled warmly. "I want to thank you."

"Really?"

"Yes. For what you told me then. First, through it all, you treated me like a human being. Then, oh Cub, I've made such a mess of things, so many mistakes. And you made me see the truth. I lay awake all one night thinking about it. I prayed and swore I'd be faithful to Colin if God would forgive me. And you know what? The next morning I got a cable that he was coming home. It was like a miracle. And I wanted to thank you."

"Glad I could help."

"So if you see me here one night with an Army bloke, you'll know it's him. Come and say hello."

Cub shook his head slowly. "Doreen, one more piece of advice. If I were you, I'd find myself another pub, one as far away from here as possible. I'd take him there, and I'd forget about ever coming back here."

The radiance vanished from her face and her eyes widened. "Oh. I suppose you're right."

He stood up, put his hand over hers, and nodded. "Trust me. Now I've got to go."

He turned and walked back to his party.

*

When Cub returned to the mess, the orderly at the front desk handed him a note, a message from Victoria. She would be in London for a couple of days and wanted to see him soon.

As he bounded up the stairs, his spirit soared like a lark at sunrise.

Chapter 34

The following evening, Cub arrived at Victoria's flat in Wetherby Gardens after the first air raid of the night was over. They went to dinner at a little Italian restaurant around the corner. The place was upstairs over a delicatessen, and the delicious aroma of sausage and smoked cheeses filled the air. The walls were a tawny stucco brindled in the flickering candlelight, and red and white checkered cloths covered the dozen or so tables. A smiling waiter led them to a corner spot. They ordered a bottle of wine.

Victoria had chosen her dress to accentuate her figure, and the neckline left just a hint of deep, soft cleavage. She had taken special care with her hair and makeup; she wanted to look her best.

Cub seemed more rested and handsome than she had ever seen him. "You're looking well tonight," she said.

"Feel better, too. The battle's over, and Peter Duke and I have made peace. But being here with you is most of it."

She smiled. "I'm glad."

They lingered over the wine, studying the fare. When she raised her eye from the menu, she caught him gazing at her.

"Is my makeup on straight?"

"Perfect."

"You don't like the short hair?"

He chuckled. "It's different."

"Then what are you looking at?"

"You. The candle light brings out the highlights in your hair, makes your skin look like a creamy peach. You're worth a long look. But you don't need me to tell you that."

A warmth flowed through her, and she smiled. "I like hearing it from you."

"You're beautiful. I'll bet you have lots of boy friends."

"There was a time. Going through the debutante whirl here. Parties, yacht races, country weekends, fast cars, champagne, the whole kit. There were men at every turn."

"Sounds like tough competition."

"Not to worry. I can't tell you how much I enjoy being with someone interested in the real me. And not just whether he'll get a kiss goodnight."

"I'd lie if I said that thought didn't cross my mind."

She felt a warm rush. "And I'd lie if I said that made me unhappy."

The waiter arrived, and they both ordered fettuccine.

When the man left, Cub asked, "What'll you do after the war?"

"Well, I don't want to go back to the world I came from."

"Really?"

"No. A woman there isn't supposed to do anything or get anywhere on her own. Feminine competence is measured by manners and demeanor and cooking and how many parties she's invited to. Girls pretend to be empty headed when they aren't. They babble on about men and how to catch them. And your man is who you are. I'm not going back to that. I'll do something useful. Does that sound too rebellious?"

"Not really. Will you marry?"

Something stirred deep inside her. "Of course. If I find the right man."

"What kind would that be?"

"Someone who loves me. Who'll let me work at what I choose and won't demand a full-time housewife. Who'll make living a partnership." This was deliciously dangerous ground, she thought. "What do you think of that?"

"The right man probably wouldn't object."

"Will you go back to California when this mess is over?"

"Guess so." He eyed her apprehensively. "But then . . . Where'll you be?"

"I suppose I'll stay here.

"Why not come to California?"

She felt it stir again. "Never thought of that. Is the weather as warm as they say?"

He nodded.

"Sounds nice. But I'm not sure if I want to go so far away. And yet . . . People must like it. Would you be unhappy away from there?"

"I'm happy now."

"How about living here permanently?"

"Might be okay."

They were dodging and dancing around the subject like a couple of schoolchildren. Yet, they didn't know each other that well, and she would be gone in a few days, which probably spelled the end of the whole affair. Under the circumstance, what else could they do? She tingled with exhilaration.

Then the fettuccine arrived.

After dinner, they returned to her flat and she invited him in for a nightcap. The overstuffed sofa and reading chairs were arranged around a small fireplace that guarded a mound of glowing coals. The cream-colored walls of the living room displayed prints of horses and hounds and fox hunting. A portrait of her father hung on one wall.

She stood with her back to the fireplace, warming her hands and shuffling her stockinged feet in the forest-green pile of the carpet. She gave the portrait a fleeting glance and then looked at Cub, who sat on the sofa. There wasn't much similarity in looks, she decided.

He eyed the room. "It's homey. You going to miss it?"

She chilled at the thought of leaving, and nodded slowly. "Among other things."

"You still want to go?"

"Have to."

"I wish you didn't."

She couldn't look at him. "I know. Sometimes I wish I didn't either."

"Victoria, you've always been honest with me. And I have to level with you. I've grown . . . really fond of you."

"I like you too, Cub." Her words poured out of their own accord. "You let me understand you. And you treat me as a whole person. I feel good when I'm with you."

"I missed you when you were away. No, it was worse than that."

"Did it ache here?" And she laid her hand on her lower chest.

He nodded. "I've never known anything like it. A desperate longing. It actually hurt."

"Like the flu?"

"How did you know?"

It was wrong to lead him on; she shouldn't have pursued the subject. She simply smiled.

His gaze swept over her like a tropical zephyr. "Victoria, I probably shouldn't say this. But time is so short. For a long time now, I've done little besides eat, sleep, and think about flying and fighting Germans. I had a date here and there, but they didn't amount to much. But then . . . you turn up."

"And?"

"I've been attracted before. Infatuated. Gentle little roller coasters. Fun, yet easy to walk away from. But since you and I were at Croton Abbey, you've been in every thought. I'm being drawn into a whirlpool. I think . . . I'm in love with you."

She thought, I will be so far away, so unreachable, for so long. To encourage him now would be utterly unfair. Yet, his flashing dark-eyed look pierced her deeply and set off delicious impulses.

"Victoria, if this is a one-sided affair, I need to know now. I can't stand to go on."

She began to speak before she'd collected her wits. "When I came back from France, I decided I couldn't afford to fall in love until after the war. I made up my mind, and that was that. But when I was away this time . . . I couldn't get you out of my mind, either. And the feeling is dragging away from everything I've worked for. But I have a mission. And I can't give it up."

"You volunteered?"

She nodded. "A long time ago."

"Could you decline now?"

She looked at him, nonplused. "You mean, renege?"

"I mean, tell them you don't want to go."

Resentment nipped at her. "Do you beg off whenever you don't want to fly a mission?"

"That's different. I wear a uniform."

"I may not, but I've taken the same oath of allegiance."

"And you're going to let that tear our lives apart?"

Her anger flared. "Just because I'm a woman, don't imagine my obligation to King and country isn't as strong as yours." She shot a glance at the portrait and raised her voice. "And furthermore, loyalty to them was bred into me since I was a baby. I wouldn't even consider declining."

Cub's eyes rounded in desperation. "Victoria, I didn't mean it that way. I . . . I don't know what I mean. I apologize." He stood up. "Maybe I'd better leave."

Her anger evaporated. "Oh, no, Cub. Please. I lost my head for a moment. I'm sorry."

"Victoria, I love you."

Suddenly, she was in his arms. Feeling the press of his body. Engulfed in his warmth. Breathing his aroma. The soft touch of his lips drained her mind.

Out of nowhere, an impulse prodded her. She'd known the urge before, but always her guard was up, and the urge was caged like an animal. Now the guard had been swept away by the gentle charm of this man. She wanted him.

His fingertips nuzzled at her breast, and the urge flowed through her in a warm torrent.

"Cub," she whispered. "Make love to me."

He eyed her with a look of surprise. "Are you sure?"

"I've never been more sure of anything."

He drew her to him, held her close, and kissed her ear.

"Victoria, I'm truly in love. How do you feel?"

"Oh my darling, I feel so awful leading you on when I'm going to be so far away."

"But I must know."

She pressed her fingers to his lips. "No more talk."

She slipped her arm around his waist and led him slowly down the hallway to her bedroom. "Just hold me close."

Time vanished, and she lay on her bed enwrapped in the delicious warmth of his naked body. He held her in a tight, nearly vicious hug, and they kissed with a passionate ferocity she had never known. She wanted it to go on forever, but novelty defeated any attempt to approach the act slowly.

Suddenly, lusciously, he was inside her, and a torrent of delight coursed through her. The strength of his thrusts startled her, but with each, the torrent grew in crescendo. The gorgeous surges of his body beckoned, and she arched herself to meet them. The ravishing deluge rose, warm and heady, carrying her ever higher; then, like a genie released, it crested and swept her away in exhilaration.

She cried out softly.

Laying beside him on her back, she nestled in his wonderful warmth, her eyes closed and her head resting in the curve of his arm. Nothing, she thought, absolutely nothing could improve on the exquisite splendor of what had just happened. And nothing would ever be the same again.

She opened her eyes and, pushing her hand into the wet mat of hair at the back of his head, drew him down to her. They kissed - a long, languid affair.

Holding out now was hopeless, she decided. "I drove myself to get this job. Yet, maybe all I really wanted was the right person. I don't want to leave you. Oh Cub, I'm caught in the whirlpool too. I love you."

With sudden fear, Cub realized that to have a chance of keeping her in the long run, he had to let her go now. There was a long silence before he said, "I don't want you to go either. But I can't carry the blame for your missing out on something important in your life. You must decide." It was the hardest thing he'd ever done.

She pushed her face into his neck. Her tears flowed down his chest. "I know. And it's tearing me apart."

Chapter 35

Late the following morning, Squadron Leader Parsons stood on the briefing room platform explaining their mission. At last, they were going on the offensive, and the atmosphere in the room was electric.

Bomber Command was to make a daylight strike against German battleships berthed at Brest. Intelligence expected heavy fighter opposition, and the Arrows would provide escort. They would first fly from Hornchurch to Plymouth and refuel, and other fighter squadrons were to assemble there to complete the escorting unit. The escorts would wait for the bombers to overfly Plymouth on their way from bases in the Midlands to the target, then take off and join up. The bombers were to fly at varying altitudes from fifteen to twenty thousand feet. Arrow squadron would provide top cover.

Gunnar Christian took the platform and said, "We'll cruise at twenty thousand until we approach the French coast. Then Red and Yellow Flights will climb to twenty-six and Blue on up to thirty for the run over the target. After the raid, we'll exit with the bombers until we're well clear of France. Then we'll come back to Plymouth to refuel before returning to Hornchurch. Any questions?"

A few points were raised about air-sea rescue procedures.

"All right then," Gunnar said, "the lorry will pick us up in ten minutes. Now I have an announcement." He read from a document. "Pilot Officers Bayer and Kirkpatrick are promoted to Flying Officer. And Sergeants Lovelace, Moore, and Stark are commissioned as Pilot Officers. Let's give them a cheer."

The group shouted in chorus, "Hip, hip, hooray!"

The meeting broke up, and Cub was surrounded by a throng of happy faces. He glowed as he shook their hands and felt them pound his back.

As the crowd thinned, Parsons hailed him from the front of the room, and Cub pushed his way forward. Parsons congratulated him, then took him aside and said, "Keep a special eye on Duke today, will you? This is his last mission. He'll be going to a noncombatant assignment afterward. See that he gets back in one piece."

"Of course, sir. Does he know he's leaving?"

"Yes. And he's unhappy about it."

"Right, sir. I'll keep an eye on him."

Then he walked outside, and as he stepped through the door, Burt Stark was waiting. They shook hands and clasped each other in a bear hug.

"Too bad Ian isn't here to be part of this," Burt said. "I'm sure he would have made it too."

Cub felt a knot in his throat; he clenched his jaw and nodded.

From behind came, "Congratulations, you two." And they turned to face a smiling Peter Duke.

"Thank you, sir," Burt said.

"You can forget the sir, Burt," Duke replied.

Cub said, "Thanks, Duke." They shook hands.

"Cub, you'll fly my wing today as usual. And Burt you still lead the second section."

They nodded.

Cub said, "I hear you're leaving us."

Duke shot him a surprised look. "That's right. I . . . I'm going to be an instructor in an Operational Training Unit up north."

"We'll miss you," Cub said.

*

Arrow Blue Flight was spread out line-abreast at just over thirty thousand feet, with the rest of the squadron four thousand feet lower. A mile further down, the Wellington bombers paraded in three-plane V's with the close-in escort swarming around them.

Peter Duke pulled heavily on the oxygen and glanced in both directions at his flight, spread out beside him. They were a good group. No, they were the best.

They had crossed the coast at Portsall and now approached Brest from the northwest. The Island of Ushant lay off Saint Matthew Point far to the right. Ahead, through mottled cloud cover, Duke made out the city, the navy yard, and the roadstead beyond. As they drew closer, he began to pick out the docks. In there somewhere, he knew, were the targets. But where the hell were the Jerry fighters?

"Fingers out everybody," he called. "They'll turn up any time now."

Duke looked to his left at Cub, whose plane weaved gently from side to side. On each swing, Cub's head turned automatically to check his stern quarter, and in between, his gaze darted about the sky, concentrating in the area around the sun. The lad had learned well.

Duke turned back to scan the horizon ahead, and there they were: a swarm of dots filling his windscreen. "Fifty plus bogies," he called. "Dead ahead. Ten miles. All altitudes from twenty to thirty."

The Arrows' orders were to stay over the bombers, break up attacks, and avoid getting drawn into fighter engagements, but the eight Messerschmitts at the top of the oncoming gaggle had other ideas. They came straight at Blue Flight.

"Blue Flight," Duke called, "Split go!"

The sections separated, and the Messerschmitts roared down between them. Duke glanced around to check his stern quarter and noted with satisfaction that Cub was with him, still weaving and craning.

Duke was estimating the precise moment to make the turn in, when the eight Messerschmitts broke into two flights of four, each of which turned toward one of the Spitfire sections.

"Turn, go!" he shouted. "And watch it, Burt. Half of them are coming at you."

"Right, One," Burt called.

The Germans had neutralized the split, but with luck, both Spitfire sections could follow the initial head-on charge by an attack from behind on the opposite German flight.

Four yellow-nosed Messerschmitts bored in from dead ahead. Duke drew a bead on one, pressed his thumb into the gun button, and watched smoke come off his target as it grew in his windscreen. The one beside it was smoking too, he noticed. The attack was over in an instant; the Germans flashed by; Duke banked steeply and wheeled hard to the right, toward the Germans going away from him. A glance told him that Cub had drifted to his right and slightly below in order to maintain his position in the turn. God, but it was a comfort having a wingman who knew the ropes.

Burt's Spitfires flicked by, in a hard turn onto the tails of the other German flight.

"Watch out to port, One," Burt called. "There's more where the first ones came from."

Duke rolled upright and looked left. A new pair of Messerschmitts threatened.

He rolled hard toward them and called, "Break left, Cub."

As he steepened the turn, he felt the Spitfire shudder on the edge of stall. They were really high today.

His quick roll away from Cub had put Duke ahead, and now Cub followed, trailing by a couple of hundred yards.

"Watch it, Duke!" Cub shouted. "Coming in at your four o'clock."

Duke leveled his wings and snapped around to look over his right shoulder. A lone Messerschmitt slanted in on him. Sonofabitch! The bastards had him bracketed. Four o'clock had a better shot and so was a bigger threat, and Duke pulled around into him. He couldn't bring his guns to bear, and they flashed past each other harmlessly.

But the pair of Germans, now to his left, followed through. The lead plane closed on Duke's tail, and a burst of twelve millimeter tore through his lower fuselage. He looked up in the mirror to see the German's winking nose cannon.

This is the end, he thought.

"Break left, Duke," Cub shouted. "I'll nail him."

Duke hauled the controls over, and the detonations under him ceased. He craned over his left shoulder to see Cub's Brownings shred the wing of the Messerschmitt. But in setting up that shot, Cub had taken a deliberate risk; the Messerschmitt's wingman was hard on Cub's tail.

Duke gaped in horror as the German fired point-blank into Cub's plane. Debris flew off the Spitfire and whirled away in the slipstream.

"Break right, Cub. For Christ's sake, break."

Cub's Spitfire snapped into a roll and pulled for the ground. The Messerschmitt hauled after it, missing the quick turn but closing again as they headed down. The German fired, and the Spitfire sprouted smoke, as if it were trailing a ribbon of black velvet. Another Messerschmitt joined the downward chase.

Duke was suddenly aware of a German fighter hauling around behind him. He rolled hard to the left and lost sight of Cub.

"Cub, you're burning," he called in desperation. "And they're all over you. Get out of that thing."

Duke and his attacker passed cockpit to cockpit. He rolled the Spitfire violently to look down and barely made out Cub's smoking plane disappearing into the haze below with two Germans hounding it. Then another Messerschmitt curved in behind him, and he racked into a hard defensive turn. It was half a minute before he got clear enough to take another look down. Except for an oily black trail left by Cub's Spitfire and smoke over the harbor, the sky was empty.

Duke weaved back and forth for some time, straining to pick out any sign of Cub. Slowly, it dawned on him that the search was in vain. A knot formed in Duke's throat and he had to blink to keep his eyes dry.

The lad had deliberately sacrificed himself.

*

Back at Plymouth, Duke and Burt huddled together on the field perimeter. The rest of the squadron had returned to Hornchurch, but Gunnar had given them permission to stay behind in case Cub turned up. They intended to hold off leaving until the last possible moment, so they would get to Hornchurch just as darkness fell.

For nearly three hours, they had sat together on the grass in silence, scanning the sky to the south. Both knew it was hopeless; Cub's plane would have run out of fuel hours earlier. Finally, with no more communication than furrowed brows, the two climbed into their planes and took off in close formation. As their undercarriages retracted in unison, they wheeled to the left and disappeared eastward.

The station duty officer at Plymouth watched them go. He nodded his approval at their flying precision and noted their departure in his log.

Chapter 36

The MG roadster parked at the curb and the engine stopped. Peter Duke sat alone in the dark, motionless as a stone, gripping the steering wheel. Across the street, whispers and the click of heels marked a couple passing down the Wetherby Gardens pavement.

Earlier at The Gannet, he had explained to Doreen about Cub. When he had finished, she sat in stunned silence for a long time, then said, "He was special to me. And not for the reason you think. He showed me the truth." Then she had put her face in her hands and wept.

Now, Duke thought of comrades who had given their lives. One after the other their faces swam through his mind until he got to Ian and Tony and finally Cub. Why did so many have to go?

He lifted his head from steering wheel, rubbed his wet eyes, and groped in his pocket for a handkerchief.

A slight rain was falling as he crossed the street in utter blackness, his footfalls echoing from the buildings like a scene from a movie thriller. He walked down the steps and rang the doorbell. It seemed an hour before bolts clicked, the latch turned, and the door opened on a chain lock.

"Miss Kendall?" he said.

"Yes."

"My name is Peter Duke."

"Who are you? What do you want?"

"I'm Cub Bayer's Flight Leader. I must talk to you."

"Oh my God!"

The door slammed, and in an instant, the chain was off and the door flew open wide. The entry light came on and she stepped out, wrapped in a bathrobe. "What's happened?" she gasped.

Even though she wore no makeup, Duke had no trouble seeing why the lad had been attracted. He took a deep breath. "Cub went down."

"Where?"

"Over France. Saw him go. Nothing I could do."

"Is he dead?"

"His plane disappeared chased by German fighters. After we got back, we waited several hours, hoping, but there was no word. He's down for sure, and the prognosis is not good."

"Oh, my poor baby."

She swayed on her feet. He grabbed her shoulders to keep her from falling. After a moment, she steadied herself, stepped back, and wiped her face on her sleeve. "Why, oh why did this have to happen?"

"I've been asking myself that."

"Cub was so smart. And he knew people so well, little people and big ones too."

"That he did."

"Was he a good pilot?"

"Once he caught on, he was one of the best. On his way to being great. Shot down his fifth German today too. Made him an ace."

For nearly a minute, she was racked by sobs. Duke gave her his handkerchief. Finally, she wiped her eyes and said, "I'm sorry to be like this. Won't you come in for a moment?"

The agony in her face was too painful, and he looked at the ground. "Thank you, but no. I have a lot to do. I've got to write his family. Then, there's the orphanage at Croton Abbey. I have to get word to them."

When he looked at her face again, the tears were still there but the pain was gone. Her jaw was set, and her eyes were steady, focused somewhere far away. She spoke with a mystic reverence. "That settles it. I'll pay the bastards back for this. I'm going."

"Going? Where?"

"Scotland."

Without asking, he knew there was more to it than that.

Chapter 37

Two days later, in the morning, Peter Duke sat in front of Gunnar Christian's desk. The two grim-faced men were alone. Gunnar toyed with what looked like a small jewel box.

He forced a smile. "Well that's good news, Peter."

Duke nodded and eyed the wall clock. "It's midnight in Los Angeles. She'll have been on the Chicago train for six hours now. Takes a couple of days. Then on to New York. We still have to work out how she gets here from there, but at least she's on her way."

"Well, I wish you two all the happiness in the world."

"Thanks," Duke said without smiling.

Gunnar eyed him obliquely. "I'm awfully sorry about Cub."

Duke shrugged. "That's the way the damned war goes. But what a bloody shame to go through the whole battle unscathed, then get the chop on our first strike operation. I was going to recommend that he take over as Flight Leader. He was a natural flier and had an instinct for tactics."

Gunnar nodded in agreement, then flicked open the cover on the box and showed Duke the contents. It was a medal. "Parsons had this ready to pin on him when he returned. It's for rescuing those kids. He was a courageous young man."

Duke gazed at Christian for a long moment. "I made a big mistake about him when we first met. I named him Cub. Should have called him Grizzly. He was the bravest man I ever knew."

The two men sat for a moment in reverent silence.

Finally, Christian snapped the box shut. "Well, Peter, I guess you better be on your way, eh?"

Duke nodded and cast his eye about the room. "I've been here almost five years now. Going to miss the place. And Lancashire seems like the end of the earth. I feel like a quitter."

"Nonsense. If you keep at this, they'll get you too. And we need pilots trained by people who know the score here in the trenches --."

Christian was interrupted by pounding on the door. Before he could respond, Parsons bolted into the room, his eyes wide and his voice excited. "Sorry, but I thought you'd want to see this right away." He laid a yellow telex sheet on the desk.

As Christian scanned the text, the frown on his face faded into a grin. He handed the sheet to Duke.

> TO OFFICER COMMANDING ARROW SQUADRON
> HORNCHURCH FROM COASTAL COMMAND AIR STAFF
> PLYMOUTH STOP DURING ROUTINE PATROL OF
> WESTERN APPROACHES OUR CATALINA PICKED
> YOUR PILOT BAYER FROM WATER OFF BRITTANY
> COAST THIS MORNING WET BUT WELL STOP WILL
> RETURN HIM TO FALMOUTH THIS EVENING ON
> COMPLETION OF THEIR PATROL
>   BELLOWS GC COS

Duke handed the message back, grinning. "Well I'll be damned!"

"Never mind damned. The taxi's waiting and you'd better be on your way."

Duke stood up and grasped Christian's hand warmly. Then he turned for the door.

Christian waved the message sheet in the air. "And send us a lot more pilots like him!"